T0278656

THE VOICE UPSTAIRS

Also by Laura E. Weymouth

The Light Between Worlds
A Treason of Thorns
A Rush of Wings
A Consuming Fire

THE VOICE UPSTAIRS

LAURA E. WEYMOUTH

MARGARET K. MCELDERRY BOOKS

NEW YORK LONDON TORONTO SYDNEY NEW DELHI

MARGARET K. McELDERRY BOOKS

An imprint of Simon & Schuster Children's Publishing Division

1230 Avenue of the Americas, New York, New York 10020

Text © 2023 by Laura E. Weymouth

Jacket illustration © 2023 by Marcela Bolívar

Jacket design by Debra Sfetsios-Conover © 2023 by Simon & Schuster, Inc.

MARGARET K. McELDERRY BOOKS is a trademark of Simon & Schuster, Inc.

For information about special discounts for bulk purchases, please contact Simon & Schuster Special Sales at 1-866-506-1949 or business@simonandschuster.com.

The Simon & Schuster Speakers Bureau can bring authors to your live event. For more information or to book an event, contact the Simon & Schuster Speakers Bureau at 1-866-248-3049 or visit our website at www.simonspeakers.com.

Interior design by Steve Scott

The text for this book was set in Adobe Garamond.

Manufactured in the United States of America

First Edition

2 4 6 8 10 9 7 5 3 1

CIP data for this book is available from the Library of Congress.

ISBN 9781665926836

ISBN 9781665926850 (ebook)

For Edison Stairs, whose name
I borrowed and who began this story

THE
VOICE UPSTAIRS

CHAPTER ONE

WIL

Dawn stained the eastern sky above Thrush's Green shell pink, dew spangled the village's clipped lawns and immaculate front gardens, and across the cobblestoned main road, Wilhelmina Price could see Jenny Bright's soul leaving her body.

The first thin, smokelike tendrils had just begun to drift from Jenny's eyes and mouth and nose, obscuring her features from a distance. She stood speaking with Mrs. Grey, the postmistress, entirely unaware of the process occurring within her, oblivious to the fate only Wilhelmina could detect. Within a day or two, Jenny Bright would be dead. Within hours, it would look, to Wil, as if she walked within a cloud of fog, blanketed in the shroud of her own departing soul.

How human spirits sensed when death was in the offing, Wil couldn't say. She only knew that they did.

Catching sight of Wil, Jenny pointedly turned aside. She was pretty in a faded, careworn fashion and had been a friend of Wil's mother. Wil tried not to let the snub sting and carried on down the road. Her deathsense had earned her no friends among the villagers—they viewed her at best as an unknown who ought to be kept at arm's length, and at worst as an object of suspicion and scorn. Wil knew better than to stop or speak to Jenny now, for if she did, the hollow guilt gnawing at her insides might get the better of her. She might try to offer a warning, and it never went well when she did. Three times now, she'd tried to say something, *anything*, that might ward off an impending death. It had never done any good, in every case casting a terrible shadow over the doomed party's last day and stirring up ill feelings and bitterness toward Wil in those they left behind. Wil half believed the deaths she foresaw were a matter of destiny—that once a soul began its departure, it could not be halted. She'd certainly never succeeded in arresting one as it drifted off to the haunted halfway place some spirits inhabited.

Even late spring in Thrush's Green was not enough to dissipate the gloom that foreseeing Jenny Bright's fate had cast over Wil. She walked onward, out of the village proper and down a quiet country lane, before slipping through a gap in the hedgerow. Beyond it lay a beech wood, where Wil waded through a sea of ferny undergrowth, the air a glory of shifting golden-green light. The woods that fringed the village's old millpond were redolent with birdsong and warm breezes, the ground soft beneath Wil's sensible galoshes, and she thought how unlikely it all seemed. How impossible, even, that within earshot of this lovely place, her own mother had met her end and Wil's uneasy bond with the dead and dying had begun, brought about in some inexplicable way by her mother's passing.

Letting out a slow breath, she squared her shoulders and tried to shake off her melancholy. Today, at least, was for the living.

As if to confirm the sentiment, the clarion song of a train whistle rang out, signaling the earliest stop at Thrush's Halt. Reaching the edge of a clearing carpeted with fading bluebells, Wil spread a blanket over the damp ground and settled herself to wait. She smoothed her handed-down, made-over skirt, ran careless fingers through her mop of sunny curls, and attempted to calm the nervous wings fluttering to life in her stomach. It was foolish to be anxious over this, and yet she was, every time. She always thought, deep down, that perhaps he wouldn't come. Perhaps he'd finally realized how very unlikely their long friendship was and decided to leave it behind, along with the rest of childhood's outgrown objects and pastimes.

"Hello," a surprised voice said from the edge of the clearing. "You've gone and cut off your hair. The new fashion rather suits you."

Relief flooded Wil, sweet as spring rain. Scrambling up, she hurried to meet the boy striding toward her, the pair of them stopping before each other at the clearing's heart. The new arrival looked entirely incongruous in the woods, dressed in a school jacket and tie, and he peered owlishly at Wil from behind a pair of thick spectacles. But his gray eyes were kind, and his earnest face more familiar than her own reflection.

"Welcome back," Wil said, unable to hide how pleased she was to see him. Not that it mattered—he knew her well enough to catch when she was biting back a smile, anyhow. "How was term?"

Edison Summerfield shrugged. "Oh, you know. Bit of this, bit of that. I'd say I'm happy to be home, but we both know I'm only ever particularly happy to see you."

For a moment they stood in silence, a little space between them, taking a measure of each other. Wil was struck by the thought that Ed seemed vaguely worried, an impression that only grew more acute as a slight frown crossed his face. But then it was gone, and he dropped his valise and went to her. Wil stepped unhesitatingly into Edison's arms, and they held each other tight, as if their closeness might erase the past months of separation.

"It's very lonely when you're gone," Wil confessed, her voice muffled against his jacket. "I miss you."

"Poor old thing. Have they been awful to you?"

3

"No," Wil said. "It's not that. Mostly no one speaks to me at all."

"I've got an entirely different problem," Ed said wryly. "I can't get people to stop speaking to me. *You're socially maladjusted, Summerfield. You ought to be making connections, public school is for friendships that last a lifetime.* Someday I shall shock them all and tell them no one at school's to my taste, and that the best friend I've got is our butler's granddaughter."

Wil pulled away and fixed him with a stern look. "You wouldn't."

"No." He offered her a rueful half smile by way of a peace offering. "I never would. It might make things difficult for you and your grandfather, and we can't have that."

"Well, come and show me what you've brought me," Wil demanded, retreating to her blanket beneath the spreading branches of a venerable beech.

Retrieving his valise, Edison joined her and handed over a stack of nearly a dozen books. "You've got last term's Latin and Greek, an Old Norse primer, all of Trollope's Barsetshire novels, and geometry, because it was a nightmare and if I had to learn it, then you do too."

"Perfection," Wil said with a happy sigh, beginning to leaf through Edison's dog-eared Latin text.

"There's lots of Horace in there," he told her. "You'll like it. And here—I've brought what you're owed."

Ed dropped a fat envelope onto the pages of the Latin text, which Wil opened at once. Inside were banknotes, which she counted shrewdly.

"You do know I count those for you before leaving school?" Edison said, sounding vaguely put out. "I'd make it my problem if anyone was trying to cheat you."

"I know you don't like cheating," Wil teased lightly. "But you have to admit, I've made a pretty penny off your schoolfellows—odious little rich boys passing off term papers I've written as their own."

For several years Wil had, much to Edison's chagrin, been running a tidy racket assisting Ed's peers in their less-than-aboveboard academic endeavors. Via letter, she posed as a Summerfield cousin at Cambridge looking to make some extra money. She took perverse pleasure in perfectly fulfilling the role of the cash-strapped Mortimer Summerfield, and though Ed had always made it clear that he disapproved of Wil's moonlighting, he also lacked the fortitude or determination to stop her once she'd truly set her mind on something.

Edison pulled a disgruntled face. "Firstly, none of the sort of people who hire you to do their work are my friends. Secondly, it's frightening how convinced you have everyone that you're some profligate but gifted toff reading classics at Trinity College. I don't know how you can keep the details straight—you don't even write these things down."

"It's all up here," Wil said knowingly, tapping her forehead.

"And thirdly," Edison went on, "I happen to be an *odious little rich boy*, so I'll thank you not to paint us with such a broad brush."

"Don't be ridiculous," Wil said, setting the envelope aside and returning to her Latin. "You know you're the exception that proves the rule."

"Well, if we're having a day of exceptions . . ."

Ed spread himself out across the blanket and gave Wil a hopeful look. Rolling her eyes, she lifted the book she had gone back to poring over, leaving space for him to rest his head on her lap.

"Honestly," she said, without glancing away from the page. "You ought to have outgrown this when we were seven."

"*Why?* You're comfortable." Edison sounded offended. "You're the only comfortable person I know. Everyone else is like . . . a thistle, wrapped in satin. You're just you, which is much better."

Wil chose to ignore him, as she always did when he bordered on becoming maudlin. It made her anxious, nearly as much as the thought that someday she might wait for Edison and find he'd decided not to come.

"Were you even paying attention when you translated this stanza?" she chided. "You've written 'field' when it ought to be 'fold.' They're opposite things entirely."

"They're both farm-related," Ed shot back. "How am I supposed to know about farm things? I haven't done an hour of honest labor in my life, though I shouldn't mind trying if I got the chance."

"We'll trade, shall we?" Wil said. "You can write papers for your peers by night, then darn my grandfather's socks and do the washing and pull turnips by day, and I'll enjoy a leisurely existence at the Grange."

Ed's good humor evaporated, his voice growing dark and preoccupied. "You wouldn't like Wither Grange. It suffocates you. Wil?"

Wilhelmina's heart sank. A small piece of her had been waiting for this moment all along. For the strangled hope behind her name, as Edison spoke it like a question.

"Yes?"

"I . . . could we try to talk to Peter?"

Ed sat up. His brown hair, which would have been slicked down respectably that morning, was mussed and untidy. It made him look younger, like an echo of the child Wil had befriended in the woods years ago. The uncertainty in his voice lit his eyes as well, and it cut at her. She wondered if he'd be as devoted to her memory as he was to his brother's, if anything were to happen to her. She hoped he would—hoped so hard, it stole her breath. But sometimes she wasn't sure. There'd been a new distance between them for the past year or so. Wil couldn't say just when it had begun or what had caused it, but it haunted her, sure as any ghost.

"We can try," she said softly. "But I don't see why things would be different this time. The truth is, Ed, some souls just don't linger, and even with those who do, most of them don't want to speak."

Edison looked down, suddenly absorbed in tugging at a loose thread on his jacket sleeve. "No, I know. But I want to try anyway."

Setting her books aside, Wil shifted until she was facing him, both of them cross-legged on the blanket.

"Hands," she told him, and Ed held them out to her. The motion had become like habit—for three years, Edison had been doggedly trying to reach his elder brother, Peter Summerfield, who'd died in the hellscape of France during the Great War. Wil found Ed's loyalty both touching and commendable—she'd never met Peter, who was eighteen years their senior, but there must have been something remarkable in him to inspire such staunch devotion from Edison. Their efforts to reach Peter had never succeeded, and the failure rankled, a sole thorn between Wil and her one cherished friend. It hurt Wil because she wanted to give Ed what he so badly desired. It hurt Ed, she suspected, because despite his easy nature, he was unused to being denied a thing he really wished for.

And so he kept on pushing at the thorn.

In concert, the two shut their eyes. Wil took a series of steadying breaths, turning inward and dropping like a stone, down into that place inside her that sensed dying souls and the dead.

When she opened her eyes, Edison was gone.

Or rather, he was still there. Still sitting opposite her body, but in another place. She herself was the one who'd left, stepping out of her own skin into a shadowy other realm. This piece of it *looked* like the mill wood clearing, but faded, drained of color, all grays and blacks and dead browns. The trees were leafless, the ground bare, and not a breath of wind stirred the naked branches above. At the edge of the clearing, pervading the entire wood, a sort of fog swirled. Wil was practiced enough at this undertaking to know that it was no true mist but a multitude of half-formed spirits, most of whom would care little about her incursion into their realm. Wordless whispers rose from them, and she called out.

"I'm looking for Peter Summerfield. He lived here once, before his death. Has anybody seen him?"

The whispers grew louder, sharper, as the restless spirits considered her question. It would come to nothing, Wil knew. After a few moments the voices would die down, the mist would fade, and she'd find herself inexorably slipping back into her own body, a disappointment to Edison yet again.

Only this time things were different.

A cloud of mist separated itself from the rest of the fog at the clearing's edge. As it drifted toward Wil, she had an impression of something that might once have been human at its heart, and yet not entirely human, either. The insubstantial limbs were too long, the face devoid of features save a gaping, misshapen mouth. It flickered in and out of being, taking form, then dissipating into mist, then swirling back together. Pulled to Wil as a moth to flame, the figure drew closer.

With her heart in her throat, she beckoned to it and let herself slip back into the province of the living, pulling the spirit with her like a lodestone.

In the mill wood clearing, Wil opened her eyes. The colors of the living world always seemed painfully bright to her after spending a brief time in the land of the dead. Ordinarily she couldn't stay more than a minute or two—it was as if a tide tugged at her, some relentless force that drew her back to her own world. But Wil was able to slip through the crack between places just long enough that she could, sometimes, if the spirit was ready, lead something back with her.

Today something had been ready. Anticipation blazed through Wil like fire. Finally she'd managed the one thing Ed had always wanted.

The column of mist stirred between Edison and Wil, caught within the circle of their joined hands. Here, away from its own place, the soul at the mist's heart seemed a many-jointed and grotesque thing, mouth gaping, long, spidery fingers reaching out for Ed and Wil, only to pass harmlessly through them. Edison had seen Wil summon souls before, yet he still went pale at the sight of this one.

"It's only a spirit," Wil reassured him quickly. "The dead can't hurt you."

Swallowing visibly, Ed nodded.

"Peter," he began, his voice shaking. "I wanted to—"

But whatever he'd meant to say remained unsaid. The mist convulsed, and the being within it turned to Wil.

"Wilhelmina," the soul called out, in a hollow and despairing woman's voice. "Little lamb. Take care."

Wil's anticipation became a sickening sense of failure. Not Peter, then. Only her mother, Mabel Price, the first and least helpful of Wil's ghosts, who'd served as a fretful and inconvenient guardian since the moment of her dying. Mabel spoke in cryptic warnings, forever afraid of things that did not come to pass, and though it felt like a betrayal to Wil, she could not help finding her mother's sorrow wearing. Now Mabel's presence and her anxious grief were doubly unwelcome.

"It's not him," Edison breathed, defeat underscoring his words.

In abject frustration, Wil tore her hands from Ed's and pushed herself to her feet, the soul winking out of existence the moment she broke the circle between them. Stalking to the edge of the woods, Wil stared off into the empty spaces between the trees, angry tears burning at the backs of her eyes.

For five years now, the dead had plagued her, and what was the use of any of it? The deathsense that had blossomed in her like a midnight flower never served a purpose—never did what she wanted, never warded off illness or accident or disaster. The day before her mother's death, Wil had watched Mabel's soul leaving her, and it had been the first time she'd witnessed such a thing. Mabel's departing spirit shrouded her in a veil of fog before the fatal moment had even arrived, and Wil said nothing, because she'd been young and afraid and had not yet understood. But when Mabel slipped into the millpond on a moonless night and drowned, only a handful of hours after Wil's haunted foresight, she'd known.

She'd seen death before it came. She still did.

An image of Jenny Bright, soul departing her body, flashed through Wilhelmina's mind.

"Wil," Edison said, from just behind her. "It isn't your fault."

"No, it is," she said bitterly. "I didn't mean to give you false hope. That was my mother. She's never come when there was someone else with me before, but I should have known she might, if we tried to speak with Peter here. It's so close to the millpond, you know, where she . . ."

Ed was silent as Wil's voice trailed off.

In her darkest moments, she felt as if everything since had been penance—a punishment for her failure to avert her mother's death, when she'd been granted a sign to warn that it was coming.

"Can you look at me?" Edison asked.

With some reluctance, Wil turned, looking dolefully up at him through her lashes.

"Here." Ed fished in his pocket and pulled out something wrapped in a clean handkerchief. "They had muffins for breakfast on the train. I brought you one."

Wil sniffed. "Is it squashed?"

"Oh, probably," Ed answered. "I'm sure I sat on it at some point. But it'll still taste nice, and I haven't got anything else to cheer you up with."

Though she didn't feel especially cheered, Wil took a bite of the muffin to please him, and after finding that it did taste nice, and was only somewhat squashed, proceeded to eat the rest of it. With the failure to summon Peter dampening their spirits, she and Edison packed up the books and blanket and wandered through the woods, until by and by, pieces of Wither Grange grew visible between the trees.

The Grange was a forbidding old place—all weathered gray stone, and halfway to a castle. Wil had been into the kitchen, and the butler's study reserved for her grandfather's use, but that was all. The rest was a mystery, though her grandfather, John Shepherd, told her it was an endless labyrinth of drafty, immaculately decorated rooms, stuffed with ancient family heirlooms and expensive *objets d'art*. It seemed entirely foreign to Wil, who had dim memories of a small tenant farm from when her father was still alive, and who'd lived in a snug rowhouse with her mother and grandfather, then with her grandfather alone, in the decade since.

Before the wood gave way to open country around the Grange, Wil and Ed stopped.

"I'm sorry about Peter," Wil offered. "I wish I could reach him for you."

Ed stuffed one hand into his pocket, the other gripping his valise. "I'm sorry too. Perhaps we'll have better luck next time."

Wil sighed, weary at the knowledge that he expected there to be a next time. She never asked why it meant so much to Edison to be able to speak with his brother, and he never offered an explanation. That, more than anything else, was the source of her hesitance—Ed was generally forthcoming, and both of them were honest with each other. She hated the idea of asking only to be lied to.

"Next time," Wil said, forcing a smile.

They stood side by side, looking out at the Grange, and at last Edison nodded.

"Well, here I go. Time to beard the lions in their den. *Surgite*, and all that."

The Summerfields' motto, "Press on," had always seemed made for him, and Wil waited, watching as he picked his way through the last of the trees.

"Oh, Wil." Ed stopped and turned just before reaching the edge of the wood. "I *do* like your hair."

In spite of herself Wil grinned, and Edison beamed back. They made it a habit to always part on good terms, even if they'd quarreled.

And yet, this time, Wil couldn't help feeling that the shadow cast between them by her uncanny gifts had grown longer than ever.

CHAPTER TWO

EDISON

ith his back to Wil, Ed carried resolutely on, crossing the parklike lawns and gardens that surrounded Wither Grange. He'd done well, he thought. He'd seemed careless and easy, and Wil had been her usual self, which meant, once again, she hadn't managed to see through him. He'd succeeded in misleading her, making it seem as if things were just as they'd always been. Never mind that his heart was still going like a steam engine, his knees weak as water, his head full of cobwebs and sparks. During term, he forgot what it was like to be near her—how devastatingly hard he had to work just to give the impression of his old frank, uncomplicated enjoyment of her company.

There were, Ed knew, worse things in life than having the misfortune to fall in love with your best friend, but that plight was currently the worst thing in his.

Running a hand through his disheveled hair, he let out a helpless sound, halfway to a groan. It was all impossible. It would have been difficult enough to find words for everything he wanted to say if they were on equal footing, but Wil's security and position in life came entirely by way of her grandfather's service to Ed's family. Edison was agonizingly aware of the disparity, and it meant he could never, *never* give voice to what he felt.

Not when he held all the cards, and Wil still waited for him the way she did, smiling and straightforward and empty-handed. He'd give up a limb before putting her in an unfair position, and so for over a year, Edison had kept the state of his unruly heart scrupulously hidden. It wasn't his only secret—not by a long shot—but it was the one he guarded most jealously, and the thought of inadvertently betraying it kept him in a state of constant, low-grade panic.

Ahead of him, the Grange loomed larger and larger, diaphanous borders of mixed flowers hiding its ancient foundations. Ed ducked his head, refusing to glance up. He supposed he ought to feel some loyalty to the old place—some sense of duty and responsibility, as it was all to be his one day, now that Peter was gone. But homecoming only ever stirred resignation in Edison, a wearying sense of *here we go again*. It was why he went in through the back every time he returned. The house was still enormous and awe-inspiring and frightfully well maintained, if you went in for that sort of thing, but at least the back aspect looked lived-in, with the croquet lawn and swimming pool and paddocks. Kitty had carelessly left a cardigan lying out, draped over a privet hedge beside a bench that bore a tray of half-finished lemonade. It didn't occur to Edison to gather up his sister's things and bring them in—someone else would look after it. There was always someone to tidy up your messes at Wither Grange. But he did stop upon noticing a wasp swimming desperate circles in the dregs of Kitty's abandoned glass, trying and failing to find purchase on the slippery sides.

Setting down his valise, Ed broke a twig from one of the privets and dropped it into the glass. He waited, gnawing at his lower lip, until the wasp finally laid hold of a leaf and hauled itself out into the sun. It stayed there for a few moments, shifting its wings to dry them, light warming its small, vicious body.

"Ed?" A bell-like voice rang out over the lawns. "Eddie, is that you? How absolutely perfect. I'm awfully pleased I found you before anyone else got their claws stuck in."

Turning, Edison found himself smothered in an easy embrace. A cloud of jasmine scent closed around him, its cloying sweetness grounded and undercut by the earthier aromas of horse and hay.

His sister, Kitty, let him go and held him at arm's length.

"Look at you, darling," she said, the words coming out like lines she'd rehearsed. "I think you've grown a foot."

Edison hadn't grown at all. He hadn't done for years. But Kitty always said so, and he never corrected her, because to be merry and opaque was her habit. Things had been different between them before Peter died— they'd been a joined force then, often miserable, but transparent with each other about that misery. Now they both feigned happiness, to what Edison strongly suspected was their detriment.

Kitty studied him for a moment as he returned the favor and took her in. She was impossibly glamorous, in a fresh, modern sort of way that Ed suspected no one else would quite manage to pull off. Some time ago, Kitty had taken to riding astride, setting her ever-willing maid, Jenny, the task of tailoring Peter's old jodhpurs to fit her. She wore them now with a pair of tall boots and a loose linen shirt, and in Edison's absence had cut off quite a lot of her hair. It had been long before—though not as long as Wil's, and not so short now. It fell just past her shoulders in a cloud of auburn waves, which caught the light and gleamed like copper. Ed rather liked the new mania among girls for cutting off their hair. He was jealous of it—of the capacity his female counterparts had for constant and ongoing metamorphosis, remaking themselves to reflect the times or the state of their own emotions. It made him feel drab and stodgy by comparison, an immovable thing trapped by expectation and tradition.

"Did Mother tell you about my party?" Kitty asked, her dazzle especially bright. "This is the last day of calm before the storm—there'll be a dozen families coming to stay in June. The next week will be madness while the house is got ready. It's going to be lovely, just like things were before the war."

"Not just like," Edison said automatically. Nothing was ever going to be entirely the same, and he was tired of the frantic rush everyone seemed to be in to forget what had gone before.

Kitty frowned, the expression a charming thing with no ill will behind it.

"*Don't* be a wet blanket," she warned him. "It's for my birthday, and I expect everyone to have a nice time, even you. I know a house party isn't your idea of fun, but you can at least try to like it. I'm going to be nineteen, which is positively ancient—before, I'd have had a whole marvelous season in London already, but we can't stretch to that now, so this is what I get. I'm making the best of things, so you'd better just fall in and do the same. Besides, Mama has plans to throw every boring but eligible peer at me she possibly can, and I'll need your help with that. My only romantic aspiration is to have as much fun as I can without being tied down, then become a spinster overnight, so I can keep on looking after all of you."

A faint, toneless sound caught Edison's attention, and he glanced down to find the wasp taking flight. It turned a sugar-drunken circle around the lemonade glass before gaining height and disappearing over the privet hedge.

"I'll be good, and I'll help however you like," he promised Kitty, though her scolding had not had solely the purpose she intended. What stood out to him most was the offhanded *we can't stretch to that now*— Ed was already on alert regarding the subject of money, and hearing the words struck him like a blow.

15

"Can I ask you something?" he said to Kitty, stuffing his hands into his pockets and hunching his shoulders. "Are we in some sort of trouble when it comes to expenses and things? I know I can make a mountain out of a molehill, but there was a mix-up over my books and meals being paid for at school. It all got squared away, but I can't remember anything like that happening before. And then one of the boys—Stapes, the head-master's nephew—said something snide to me about old families that are circling the drain. He's the sort who likes to prey on anyone who shows weakness, so I wouldn't have thought twice about it if it hadn't been for that problem with the school bills at start of term. And Mother wrote to me about your party—I thought it was what you wanted, but if it's not, and it's some sort of consolation prize . . ."

For a moment Kitty was silent. Just a moment, but it made Edison think. Then she laughed, a sweet, brilliant sound that rang out over the little stretch of garden like chimes.

"Oh, Ed, you do love to worry," she said, resting a consoling hand on his arm. "Of course you're seeing trouble where there isn't any—I only meant we can't stretch to anything more than this because of how we've all been since Peter. We're none of us quite up to what we were before. But I think this summer and this party might get us back on our feet. We've all been living under a cloud, and it's time to come out into the light again."

She looked, as she spoke, as if she believed every word. But there was an odd note to her voice—a hint of sternness, as if she was trying to convince herself of what she'd said as well as Edison.

"All right," Ed conceded. He'd been a fool to expect truth between himself and Kitty any longer. "If you say so."

"I do say so. And don't you dare mention money troubles to anyone outside the family. You know what people are like. Vultures, just waiting for us to fall."

"Are they?" Ed asked, but he didn't expect an answer, and Kitty didn't give one.

Instead, she pressed a kiss to his cheek, her lips petal soft, her scent enveloping him once more.

"I'm going in to change," she said. "I have to run up to Wynkirk to see about my frocks for the party. We've both missed luncheon already, and you look like you've been tramping through a field. Mother and Father are out of sorts with you—they went on and on again about how they can't think why you won't come home on the early train and let Bede pick you up in the car."

"I like to sleep later, and I like to walk," Ed said stolidly, as an unbidden recollection of Wil rose up: golden curls radiant around her earnest face, her nose scrunched slightly as he lay with his head on her lap while she tried to read. God help him, things were getting to the point where he'd do murder for her, if she only asked it.

With a dismissive wave, Kitty headed into the house. Ed waited a few minutes, wanting to go in alone. From somewhere nearby, the rhythmic snick of clippers opening and shutting began, signaling that the Summerfields' meticulous gardener, Henry Ellicott, was at work. Briefly, Ed thought of going to say hello. But it wasn't the sort of thing you were supposed to do, greeting the staff before your parents, and Ed knew that if he did, somehow his failure to follow protocol would come to light at the least opportune moment.

Instead, he stood patiently in the sun, listening to the sounds of the garden before finally following in his sister's footsteps. A set of French doors, installed along with the swimming pool when Edison was a boy, led into the house's cool and shadowy depths. Beyond them, a long corridor stretched out before him, tall and broad and not at all claustrophobic, with portraits and palm trees and little end tables bearing family artifacts lining the walls.

You could see straight through Wither Grange from its central hallway, which ended in the distant, much grander front entry. The way the corridor ran through the house had always unnerved Edison somehow. It gave him an impression of hollowness, as if the Grange was a place meant to be passed through rather than lived in. When he'd been a few years younger and a voracious reader of detective novels, the lurid thought had once struck him that it was as if Wither Grange had been subjected to a gunshot wound. The plush crimson carpet running down the center of the hall had done nothing to temper his morbid imaginings.

On either side of the corridor a series of closed doors stood like silent sentinels. No one ever left doors open at the Grange—it was one of the things that had been drilled into Edison as a child. To his right, upon entering from the back of the house, there was a sort of garden room. Not a true conservatory, but a large, lushly furnished parlor with vast windows, which housed a collection of orchids and ferns and potted lemon trees. It was where any of the Summerfields at home in midafternoon took their tea, and a favorite place of Edison's mother.

Ed himself preferred the room opposite. It was, he supposed, as close as Wither Grange got to having a junk room. Or, at least, as close as the parts of the house he frequented got to having one. Edison's grandfather had fancied himself a scientist and set up a sort of amateur laboratory for himself there, complete with dozens of esoteric instruments of inquiry and exploration. There were long tables cluttered with microscopes and telescopes, astrolabes and armillary spheres, barometers and Leyden jars, and even a Wimshurst machine. No one understood any of it now, but they'd gotten used to the room being the way it was, and so it stayed.

Though he wasn't of a scientific bent himself, Ed appreciated his grandfather's old laboratory for being both ugly and functional, in a house designed primarily to awe and impress. There was, too, the library nook hidden behind one of the bookshelves that flanked the laboratory fireplace—like something out of a Gothic novel, the miniature library could only be reached by operating a hidden lever on one of the shelves, at which point hinges groaned and a dusty secret room was revealed. The nook was a small, tomb-like space with only one high window that could not be gotten in or out of, and a single armchair and end table surrounded by legions of books. When Edison first came upon it as a child—for his grandfather had died before his time—the nook's shelves had been lined with outmoded scientific volumes. Little by little Ed replaced them, transforming the nook into a retreat filled with his outgrown detective stories, shelf after shelf of poetry, and a wealth of excellent novels. It was the only place he particularly liked at the Grange—he could spend hours in there with little chance of being found.

"I hope you aren't thinking of vanishing already," a dry, humorless voice said, as Lady Summerfield stepped out into the hall. "Not when you've only just gotten home."

She'd come from the music room a little farther down the corridor, and Ed went to her dutifully, kissing his mother's cheek. When he was a very small boy, Lady Summerfield had smelled of rose water and talcum powder, but those scents were barely detectable now, overpowered by the sickly sweet aroma of sherry. His mother nursed a glass in one hand, and Ed knew that by this time of day, it must have been refilled numerous times. Lady Summerfield never showed it, though, beyond an occasional vacancy of expression or understanding. It was simply as if she lived at a slower, less immediate pace, while all the world around her was burdened with urgency and strong emotion.

"Mother," Edison said. "You're looking well."

He fought back an urge to frown, or wince, because there was as much truth and real feeling to his words as there had been in Kitty's greeting to him. He knew what was expected and fulfilled the expectation, even though for as long as he could recall, his mother's face had always been vaguely flushed, her eyes distant and clouded.

"You've tracked mud all over the carpet," Lady Summerfield said, a hint of disapproval creeping into her tone. "The last thing we need is extra work for the housemaids at the moment—they're in over their heads just trying to get all the bedrooms freshened and ready. Why can't you be sensible and take the car?"

"And just when will the horde we're preparing for descend?" Edison asked, knowing the easiest way to avoid his mother's chiding was to steer the conversation into safer waters.

"Thursday next," Lady Summerfield said, taking a languorous sip of her sherry. "It'll be just like old times, won't it?"

Ed tamped down the annoyance that had risen within him when Kitty had implied the same. Why any of them wanted to feel as if nothing had changed since the war was beyond him—life had altered irrevocably, in some ways for the better, in others for the worse. But there was no point trying to move backward and behave as if none of it had happened.

"Your father's in his study," Lady Summerfield said when Edison stayed silent. "I'm sure he'd like to see you. And I'm terribly busy, so run along."

Edison stood where he was, watching as his mother wandered back into the music room and seated herself at the piano, where she proceeded to pick out idle notes with her free hand—the opening refrain to "Green Grow the Rushes, O," which had been a nursery favorite of the family. She'd be in there for another hour or so, he expected, until it was time to rally herself for tea. After that she'd drift around the house until dinner, appearing at the table ten minutes late and impeccably dressed, as remote and serene as a Fra Angelico Madonna. Lady Summerfield's days then invariably finished with an aimless moonlit wander through the garden, followed by laudanum and bed.

The pattern never changed. Sometimes all Edison wanted was to find a way to shatter it.

But if the rest of the Summerfields were small cogs, grinding along repetitive tracks to maintain the smooth operation of their family and estate, Ed himself was no different. Taking up his valise yet again, he soldiered on, through the impressive front entry with its soaring ceilings and black-and-white marble floors. His father's study led off the main atrium itself, the better for Lord Summerfield to keep a hawklike watch over anyone coming to and going from the house.

"Good afternoon, Father," Edison said quietly, leaning against the doorway because he always found himself in want of support when facing Lord Summerfield. "I've just gotten in."

The study spread out before him had once been a reception room— Lord Summerfield had found the office his forebears used too small for his liking and too removed from the house's main thoroughfares. As a result, the space was incongruously large given its purpose, though Lord Summerfield had no trouble filling it. He'd had a desk made to order—a great wooden edifice of a thing that reminded Edison of a pipe organ more than anything else, though it certainly produced no music. The hundred drawers and slots were stuffed with documents that contained the minutiae of life on the estate—contracts for household help, for tenant farmers, for solicitors. The desk sat in a sort of cabinet created by a pair of bookshelves on either side. Doors could be shut in front of the desk and locked so that it and its contents were no longer visible, the room transforming into a gentleman's lounge instead. When Lord Summerfield wished to make a commanding impression, he kept the alcove doors open so that the ponderous desk dominated the room, an inescapable reminder of the toil and responsibility inherent in the family title and the maintenance of the estate. When he wished to seem genial—a man of leisure and means—he shut up the alcove so that the fireplace and armchairs and ornately carved drinks cabinet became the focus instead.

Ed had never been invited into the study when the alcove doors were shut, though before the war, his father and Peter had retreated there every evening for a glass of something and a long conversation. They'd been cut from the same cloth, while Ed considered himself a sport in the botanic and genetic sense—an offshoot that did not grow true to the whole.

Lord Summerfield raised a massive hand to command silence, continuing to write for a moment before pushing his chair back and turning to look at Ed. Even seated, he projected a sense of power and energy. Peter had been the same—tall, thickset, and broad-shouldered like their father, whereas Edison was slight and no taller than Kitty.

"Let me look at you," Lord Summerfield said, his voice a low and bearish rumble.

With some reluctance Edison moved forward, walking to the center of the room and standing with his chin raised a defiant inch or two.

"I don't pay for you to look like a farmhand," was all Lord Summerfield said, taking in the state of Edison's shoes and the mud staining the legs of his trousers. "Go make yourself decent."

But Ed couldn't shake the recollection of what had happened at school, or the way Kitty had paused before assuring him the family was still on solid financial ground. With a wretched party in the offing, he might not have another chance to speak with his father in private for ages, and the longer he waited, the more daunting the task would become.

"Father," he ventured. "I wanted to say something."

Lord Summerfield had already half turned back to his desk, and he shot Ed a look of transparent irritation. "Can't it wait?"

"No," Edison said staunchly. "No, it can't. I wanted to tell you that if we're ever in any sort of difficulty—anything, you know—you can confide in me, like you did with Peter. I know he was the eldest and everyone expected him to inherit and that we're two very different people, but if there's ever a way for me to help, even if it's only just to listen, well, I'm . . . I'm here."

The speech he'd planned out with great care ended on a faltering note, for Lord Summerfield's expression of annoyance shifted to one of patronizing condescension as he spoke.

"Do I strike you as being so incapable of carrying out my duty that I'm in want of assistance from a schoolboy?"

Ed's heart sank. "Of course not. I only thought—"

"Yes, well," Lord Summerfield said, dismissive now, "*thinking* is about all you've ever had a talent for, isn't it? Best leave the business of life to those of us with a bent for action, rather than philosophizing."

"Yes, sir," Ed answered without emotion, refusing to let even a hint of defeat enter the words, for if there was one thing Lord Summerfield hated, it was any sort of weakness or self-pity.

"Oh, and Edison," Lord Summerfield said, already with his back to his son, "we'll have a houseful next week. I've had the staff move your things out of your room and into the old nursery wing for the summer. Your mother objected at first, but I assured her you wouldn't mind, and it wouldn't cause any trouble. You won't make a liar out of me on that score, will you?"

Edison swallowed. One more family member to greet, then.

"No, sir," he said. "Whatever you think is best."

"Good. You're far too old now to play the fool over childish imaginings. Go get yourself settled, and *don't* be late for dinner—it's bad enough you insist on getting home halfway through the day."

Ed knew better than to linger once his father had dismissed him. He trudged up the soaring main stairs, which rose in a pair of graceful arcs from the sides of the front atrium. And at the top, instead of going left as he was used to doing, he went right, past a number of guest rooms and then down a windowless length of uninhabited, unaccountably shabby hallway. The passageway ended in a single firmly shut door.

Gathering his courage, Edison opened the door and stepped through it, ensuring it closed fast behind him.

For a moment nothing happened. He saw the old nursery, just as it had always been—one light-soaked main room with an expansive hearth, hobby horses and dollhouses still pushed up against the walls, several doors leading off into small bedrooms and one to a bathroom. Two little desks still bore neat stacks of copywork he and Kitty had done what felt like a lifetime ago. Before he'd gone off to school. Before the war. Before—

Without warning, the heavy velvet drapes whipped across the windows, cutting out all daylight and plunging the room into darkness. The temperature dropped precipitously, sending a brutal chill through Ed, as somewhere in the gloom a senseless, wordless whispering began, all sound and no meaning. Though no fire had been laid, a hellish glow rose up on the hearth, and Ed could make out his own face in a mirror across the room, pale and weary and ancient-looking in the ghost-light.

"Hello, Peter," he said dully. "I see you're still here."

CHAPTER THREE

WIL

The mantel clock in the tidy rowhouse where Wil lived with her grandfather, John, had struck midnight nearly an hour ago. Wil sat, curled in a wingback chair she'd pulled over to the front window, and waited. The glow of a kerosene lamp made a pool of light all about her so that in the window glass, her reflection shone back—the sole thing in color, superimposed upon a dark world. Nearby, hanging on the wall beside the front door, a blurred photograph of Wil's parents kept vigil with her, though they did not look out from the frame that hemmed them in. Instead they regarded each other, seated side by side, their eyes locked in a moment of eternal communion. Wil remembered them just so: as being always in accord, never out of tune with each other. The few memories of both parents that she possessed were golden-hued and idyllic—she recalled the time before her father died as the one bright, unmarred span of her existence—and every time she left the house, she stopped to kiss their fading portrait.

At last a piece of the night drew toward the front garden, slipped in at the gate, and turned a key in the lock.

"You ought to be in bed," John Shepherd said flatly at the sight of his waiting granddaughter.

John was a tall, spare man, elegant in his appearance and movements. Wil could not recall a time before his hair had gone snow-white, but his sharp blue eyes were still clear, and the lines written across his face added distinction to it more than anything else. He was arresting, though in the way of a mountain peak or a troubled sea, and in looking at him, Wil did not find it difficult to understand how her mother had come to be reckoned the beauty of the county. But Mabel had been soft and warm and welcoming, while John was a hard and exacting man. He kept his own counsel and rarely spoke from a place of kindness, though he was unimpeachably thorough in carrying out his duty, whether it was toward Wither Grange or Wil herself.

"Jenny Bright is dying," Wil said, matching his dispassionate tone note for note. "I thought you should be told, as she works at the Grange. I know it's Mrs. Forster who oversees the housemaids, but I can't tell her."

"You've no idea how it will happen, or when?" The question was put to her blandly, emotionlessly—when her own mother had died, Wil had seen little in the way of outward grief from John. It did not surprise her to find him unmoved by news of Jenny's fate. But she'd thought her grandfather might have realized by now that while Wil could see a death before its coming, she could not predict the manner of it, or the exact hour in which it would arrive.

"It'll be soon," was all she could offer. "They never have long once I see it. I don't expect she'll make it through tomorrow."

It sounded so awfully bleak when Wil said it out loud. It made her feel low and empty and hopeless, and instinctively she reached for the book of Latin poetry sitting on her lap, drawing it close.

John frowned, catching sight of the volume.

"They were cross with Master Edison when he arrived home," he said. "After luncheon, and with his shoes and the bottom of his valise all over mud. They press him, at the end of every term, to take the early train and let the chauffeur meet him at the station. He says he prefers to take the ten o'clock train and cut through the fields on his way home. But he's never taken the ten o'clock, has he? He goes to you first."

Wil said nothing. John was the only one who knew of her clandestine friendship with Edison Summerfield—even her mother hadn't known. It was a bone of contention between the two of them, for John strenuously disapproved. But though Wil tried to keep the peace with her grandfather whenever she was able, she refused to give way over this.

How could she, when the words *he goes to you first* set something strange and warm and pleasantly uncomfortable stirring inside her? Wil wasn't used to someone else putting her first. She had all she needed, yes—John Shepherd looked after her requirements with the exactitude he applied to everything he undertook—but that was all. He did his duty and no more, and Wil never asked for anything beyond what he offered. But Ed was a lamp after midnight to her—as in that golden era when both her parents had lived, he made the world brighter, and they'd belonged to each other in some perfect and indefinable way since their very first meeting in the woods.

"Bed," John ordered, when Wil's stubborn silence stretched on.

Taking her book and trying not to think of Jenny Bright, Wil went.

*　　*　　*

Despite the fact that he was required to preside over the servants' table at Wither Grange, John Shepherd preferred to eat at home whenever possible. Wil wondered sometimes if it was because it bestowed him with an added measure of power, to be seen by his underlings as someone without the usual human requirements. Certainly he slept little, and for the most part, he ate only what Wil herself made. She'd become a reasonable plain cook out of necessity, though she had no real talent for it.

After John's departure at dawn, Wil cleared away the breakfast things.

Her grandfather ran his own household with the same efficiency and thoroughness as he did the Summerfields'—as always, a list of tasks was waiting for Wil, pinned to a corkboard beside the kitchen sink. John didn't believe in idleness for his staff or his granddaughter. Every item on his list was in its proper order, and Wil was expected to complete her chores just as they'd been laid out. Life had been so ever since she had outstripped the village schoolmaster and been asked to stop attending classes four years back—a tedious round of domestic endeavors shot through with the occasional interest of receiving new books from Edison or turning out clandestine term papers for hire.

Today Wil's books would have to wait. She'd dust, though goodness knew the house didn't need it, then run to the market and post office and weed the kitchen garden. After that, there were a few items of her grandfather's uniform that needed mending—at any other great house, one of the maids would see to the task, but John preferred to be seen as untouchable. If he lost a button or tore a cuff, that was for him and Wil to manage, not the staff at Wither Grange.

With the dusting done, a basket of eggs and vegetables on one arm and a package to send off beneath the other, Wil slipped in through the door of the Thrush's Green post office. The bell overhead rang out cheerfully, and Mrs. Grey, the postmistress, glanced over from where she stood behind the counter, deep in a murmured conversation with Jack Hoult, who served as footman at the Grange. It was still early enough in the day that Jack had not gone up for work, but at the sight of Wil, he gathered his letters and left, brushing past her with a scowl as he went. Wil had foreseen the death of his grandmother, old Mrs. Hoult, during the first disorienting year of coming to terms with her deathsense. She'd warned the family, but it had come to nothing besides a day of fear and panic before Mrs. Hoult had succumbed to a sudden and fatal stroke.

Setting her package down on the post office counter, Wil smiled hopefully at Mrs. Grey, who only tucked in the corners of her mouth and looked disapproving.

"Suppose I don't need to tell *you* what's happened," Mrs. Grey said sanctimoniously. "I suppose you know already."

"It's Jenny Bright, isn't it?" Wil answered, a helpless sorrow resting inside her. "I did know, yes. I'd have done anything to be able to help."

Mrs. Grey let out a disparaging noise. "You're taking it very well. I'd have thought you'd be a little more stirred up, given how she went. But then you've always been uncommonly comfortable with death. Why let a thing like that bother you?"

Wil frowned. "A thing like what?"

"Like how she died." Mrs. Grey leaned forward, her eyes alight, forever eager to impart a piece of gossip or ill news. "Jenny Bright drowned in the millpond, in the woods behind Wither Grange. It's your mother all over again. Passing strange, too—I never heard of anyone drowning there until your mum, and now a friend from back when she was alive has met her end in just the same way. Though Jenny hadn't seemed herself lately, if you know what I'm getting at—downcast she was, so much so that I wonder if there'll be a church burial for her at all."

"*What?*" Wil breathed. A shocked numbness ran through her veins, starting at her heart and turning her limbs to lead.

Mrs. Grey gave her a small, malicious smile. "So there is a limit to what you can foretell. I always thought you might be putting it on, pretending to know less than you really did. Everyone in your family's been the sly, secretive type, and what's bred in the bone will come out in the flesh."

"I have to go," Wil stammered, because the air in the post office seemed far too hot and stuffy. Something was happening to her breath as well—she couldn't quite catch it, as if she'd been running. Her mother's death had always carried an air of uncanniness and uncertainty for Wil—she'd never seen Mabel's body, only watched a plain pine box being lowered into her churchyard grave. One day Mabel had been there and the next she was gone, leaving a hole at the center of Wil's life, with ghosts and premonitions of death embroidered around its frayed edges.

Leaving the package behind, Wil stepped back out onto the pavement along the village's winding main road. She felt suddenly like a shadow herself, made insubstantial and colorless by what she'd learned from Mrs. Grey. *Passing strange,* she'd called the whole matter, and on this one point, Wil couldn't help but agree. It had always struck her as improbable that the millpond, fed by a laughing brook, with its gently sloping green banks, should have served as the site of her mother's end.

And now it seemed that tragic, unlikely piece of history was repeating itself.

Wil had no specific intention of visiting the millpond, and yet her feet led her there, through the woods by way of a little bridle path that meandered along the forest's fringe. The miller's cottage stood empty and abandoned just as it had done all Wilhelmina's life, the windows boarded up, the mill wheel still and silent. The pond banks were grassy and unmarred, dipping easily down to the dimpled brown water. Nothing about the spot seemed to whisper of tragedy besides the constable standing on the opposite bank, writing in a small notebook as he consulted with an elderly couple who had their arms around each other. Wil knew Walter and Ada Bright well enough to recognize them, as she knew most people in Thrush's Green, but they'd never spoken. She hadn't known anyone would still be there and tried to recede back into the forest, but Mrs. Bright had already caught sight of her and broken away, moving toward Wil with a pained but determined gait.

Biting at her lower lip, Wil stood where she was. As Mrs. Bright drew closer, she could see tear tracks on the old woman's lined face, her eyes still dim and anguished.

30

"Wilhelmina Price," Mrs. Bright said. "Is it true you can speak with the dead?"

Wil's anxiety grew to a fever pitch, and she twined her hands together in front of her. "In a way? They don't always linger, and with the ones who do, I can speak to them, but there's no guarantee they'll answer. I know that makes it sound like I'm shamming, but . . . it's just the truth."

"We're all full of contradictions and confusion in life," Mrs. Bright told her with a trembling sigh. "Why shouldn't we be in death? I was wondering if you could try to reach Jenny for me."

Wil winced. "No one ever likes the outcome when I do that sort of thing. It's probably best if we don't."

"Please," Mrs. Bright pressed. "It's important. We're not far from here—our Jenny would cut past the millpond on her way to the Grange. Come home with Walter and me, and try for us."

Shifting the weight of her basket from one arm to the other in an agony of indecision, Wil looked past Mrs. Bright to the millpond beyond. Two deaths, and she'd never seen the way of them. She could imagine how they might have looked, though—her mother, floating in the shallows with duckweed clinging to her hair. Death would have drained all her loveliness, turning her to pallid gray. And Jenny, who'd been sharp-tongued and shrewd—perhaps she'd washed up by the old mill wheel, pushed there by the pond's gently swirling eddies. Perhaps her lifeless fingers had brushed the wheel, which might have been her salvation if she'd laid hold of it sooner.

"They've been asking if she was in low spirits about something," Mrs. Bright said softly, almost as if Wil was not there and the words weren't intended for her. "The constable pressed us very hard to come up with some reason our Jenny might be in a difficult frame of mind. They mentioned three times how she had her boots on, and they grow heavy in water.

31

"It's true she'd been fretting lately, but she hadn't put rocks in her pockets, and when she was just a little thing, we took her to the seaside every summer. She could swim like she was born to it. So I don't know . . . but they said it's clear-cut. That either she slipped in, like your mum did, or maybe walked in. We've seen the rector already, and he's been very kind. Told us she'll get the benefit of the doubt and have a churchyard burial so long as nothing's definite."

"I'll try to reach her," Wil said suddenly. An uneasy feeling was expanding in the pit of her stomach, set there by Mrs. Grey's *passing strange* and Mrs. Bright's *could swim like she was born to it.* "But we must do it now, to have the best chance. Some souls pass out of reach at once. Others only linger a day or two."

Mrs. Bright nodded resolutely.

"Walter?" she called to her husband. "Nearly finished?"

Mr. Bright and the constable spoke for another moment, after which Jenny's elderly father joined them. Wil followed the Brights along yet another tangled and twisting path through the mill wood, the pond serving as a blighted heart at the forest's center, from which a hundred veins ran out.

They left the woods at their western edge, emerging in a bee-loud meadow of wildflowers. Several hives stood near the shelter of the trees, and farther into the meadow a thatched cottage sat in the sun, chickens scratching about and rustling the grasses that grew right up to the small house's foundations.

"It's very pretty," Wil murmured politely. She hadn't thought of Jenny Bright living in such a sweet place. She hadn't thought of Jenny living anywhere at all—like Wil's mother, her life had revolved around the Grange, home forced to take an uneasy second place at best.

The Brights ushered Wil into a dim, low-ceilinged kitchen, where herbs and saucepans hung from the beams above. Wil sat down in the chair she was offered and took a steadying breath.

32

"I think it would be best if I bring her back alone," she said uncertainly. "Sometimes I'll reach out with the help of someone else— someone the spirit knew in life. But if she'd always lived here, and with the two of you being so close to her, that might be overwhelming. If there's not enough of the familiar, they won't come back, but if there's too much, all they do is weep."

Wil did not say that experience had taught her this—that she sometimes inadvertently slipped into the halfway realm while dreaming and woke to her mother's disembodied and unnerving spirit, sobbing at the foot of her bed.

At a nod from Mrs. Bright, Wil shut her eyes, felt for the seam between places, and slipped into the shadowland of the restless dead.

It was an undertaking she chose to manage without fanfare. The year the gift or curse had first come to her, Edison had found it unspeakably fascinating. He'd brought her books and newspaper clippings portraying famous mediums from the last century's end and told her they'd been famous and lauded for their talents. That they made a show of it and charged for their services, calling themselves spiritualists. The whole thing turned Wil's stomach. She couldn't imagine anyone in Thrush's Green paying for her morbid skill—the only thing it had ever brought her was grief, not coin. And so she learned to exercise every aspect of it as quickly and surreptitiously as possible.

She found herself now in a ghostly version of the Bright cottage. The kitchen was empty, stripped of furniture and life, the window glass shattered into jagged teeth, the thatch roof rotted and collapsed in places, showing glimpses of sere gray sky.

Through the broken windows and open door, Wil could see the ever-present swirl of unhappy souls.

"I'm looking for Jenny Bright," she called. It helped to use the same words whenever she visited, to fall back on the rote and the familiar. "She lived here once, before her death. Someone wishes to speak with her, and so I've come to lend her my voice."

For the second time in as many days, a piece of the mist broke away. But this time it was followed by another that trailed along behind it partway across the parched meadow, before hovering uncertainly among the dead grasses. Even from a distance, Wil recognized the second spirit, not by sight or sound but by its mannerisms and essence. Her mother. Her attentive and ineffectual keeper. If she'd been paying even the slightest attention when she tried to summon Peter for Ed, she'd have realized it wasn't him. But she'd been hoping too hard to see clearly.

The first column continued through the door and over to Wil, who balled her hands into fists and steeled her nerves. This was her least favorite way to carry a spirit back to the world of the living—it upset and unsettled her, but there was no denying it helped a soul find clarity sometimes.

Holding out her hands as if in welcome, she presented herself to the spirit. It rushed forward eagerly, giving Wil a confused impression of preternaturally long limbs and staring, pupil-less eyes before she was hit by a wall of intolerable cold, and they tumbled back together, returning to the living world.

Wil had tried explaining to Edison once what it felt like to have a spirit held within her, as if she was an empty vessel and they were the cargo she carried. It turned her into a husk of herself, a pallid, half-alive thing who could do no more than watch and wait as her own body was given over in service to something else, her own feelings subsumed beneath those of a dead soul.

And as this dead soul took hold, Wil realized she'd made a grave error, because the spirit she housed was consumed with wrath. It shot through her, electric and furious, as she opened her eyes and saw the

Bright kitchen once more, still unfamiliar to Wil but given a veneer of timeworn familiarity by the thing that was not her.

Dimly, she felt her jaw unhinge, move in a tense, unnatural way. Her head tilted to one side, fingers scrabbled at the table, and the spirit that had been Jenny Bright forced her to her feet.

"*Surgite*," it hissed fiercely, leaning toward Ada and Walter. "Rise up, we rise, arise. *Surgite*. We rise."

The voice was at once recognizable as Jenny's and twisted into an unbridled malevolence that had been beyond her in life. Frantically, Wil struggled against it. Though she'd given over temporary control of her body and voice, she could still always move in one direction—toward the fissure between worlds, that kept the dead in one place, the living in another, and Wil herself caught between the two.

With every scrap of willpower, every ounce of determination she possessed, she hauled both herself and the spirit back over the divide.

It was obviously unhappy to return. Life-sappingly cold mist engulfed Wil, setting her at the center of a spinning fog-devil through which insubstantial limbs reached and grasped. But they could not lay hold of her unless she offered. Standing rooted to the spot, she set her jaw and fought the riptide pulling her back toward the living world, unwilling to chance dragging the spirit with her again. After a few moments, it seemed to grow confused, then weary, and finally surrendered, wandering to a distant corner of the abandoned kitchen. The dead never seemed especially resolute to Wil—they were forgetful, muddled things for the most part, who required her to serve as an amplifier and a reminder of a time when they'd had purpose and emotion.

Seizing the opportunity, Wil let herself go, returning to full possession of her own body with a wild, dizzy rush. At first, she could hardly focus; everything seemed so bright, so loud, so overwhelmingly *living*. Pain brought her back to center. It radiated up from her fingertips, sharp and immediate, honing her awareness to a single point.

When she glanced down to find its source, she saw deep grooves scratched into the surface of the Brights' kitchen table, her fingers raw and torn from the splinters, her nails chipped and cracking. Blood welled up to her skin, and she stuffed her hands into her skirt pockets immediately, wanting to hide at least one symptom of her brief possession from the Brights.

"That," Walter Bright said, with venom to match the dead soul Wil had channeled, "was never our Jenny. That was something wicked. Get out."

With a nod, Wil rose. She'd expected this—no one ever *really* wanted to know how their loved ones were faring in the places that lay beyond life. They thought they did but were never happy when granted a glimpse.

Outside, her brush with death had rendered the bees jarringly loud and bright, the wildflowers oversaturated and garish. Wil had made it halfway across the meadow when Mrs. Bright caught her up.

"What did it mean?" Mrs. Bright asked. "The thing she said? I've never heard that word before."

"I—" Wil hesitated, her mind racing, her heart pounding. "I'm not entirely sure what it meant."

Which was both true and untrue.

Mrs. Bright glanced back over one shoulder to the thatched cottage and her husband, who stood waiting in the doorway with a scowl written across his face.

"I'm going to tell you something that stays between us," she said. "My Jenny only ever breathed a word of it to me and made me swear I'd never tell. She said she couldn't prove it, and that no one would believe her, but she didn't think your mother's death was an accident. Well, now she's gone too, and I can't prove it, and perhaps no one will believe me, but I don't think hers was either. They say you're clever—that besides

36

that deathsense, you've got a head for books and numbers and problems. Well, I'm making *this* your problem. It's not one I can solve."

Turning, Mrs. Bright walked back to the cottage, where her husband shut the door firmly behind them. Wil stayed as she was, motionless and silent in a sea of daisies and red campion, while bees droned idly about her, and the taste of despair and brackish water rose in the back of her throat.

CHAPTER FOUR

EDISON

Edison was meant to be reading with Wil, the two of them once again lying alongside each other on her checked blanket in the beech wood. She, at least, had a book dutifully propped up against the roots of an obliging tree. But Ed couldn't help dozing, his head pillowed on his arms. It was warm and quiet, and being with Wil felt like shedding a century of worry and nervous tension in exchange for another, lighter concern. Sleeping in the nursery wing with its violent additional resident was proving near impossible.

The night before, Ed had finally managed to doze off, only to be wakened by a sound of rending fabric as the curtains were torn to shreds. When he'd gone to investigate, one of the heavy cords meant to bind the curtains back had snaked around his left arm, tightening like a snare. He'd only been able to get free by reaching for a penknife still sitting out on one of the old desks and cutting through the cord with the dull blade. There was a vicious black-and-blue bruise just below his elbow, but he'd carefully hidden it beneath his shirtsleeve and, come morning, had bundled up the curtains and surreptitiously taken them down to the housekeeper, Mrs. Forster, to dispose of. He'd invented an excuse—that he didn't care for them and wanted a change if he was to stay in the nursery wing. Neither of them said anything about the disastrous state of the fabric, and Edison prayed Mrs. Forster wouldn't mention it to his mother, or worse yet, his father.

The last thing he needed was to revive the massive, ugly row they'd all descended into in the weeks after Peter's death.

"Did you hear Jenny Bright is dead?" Wil asked quietly from beside Edison.

With an effort, he shook off the fog of exhaustion still hanging over him and sat up. "Jenny Bright, our housemaid? The one who looks after my sister? It must have happened quite recently; Kitty never said anything."

"They only found her body this morning," Wil said, still subdued. Her quietness pricked at Ed—he knew what it meant.

"You saw it coming, didn't you?" he asked, striving for gentleness, because Wil always blamed herself after seeing a death she couldn't prevent.

With a decisive movement, Wil sat up too and faced him.

"Jenny drowned in the millpond," she said. "Just like my mother. Isn't that a strange coincidence? History's repeating itself."

"Oh, Wil," Ed breathed. "I'm so sorry."

She stared down at her hands, resting in her lap, and for the first time Edison noticed that the skin on her fingertips had been cruelly scraped, leaving them red and raw, while several of her nails were cracked or broken. Wil had, until two years back, bitten her nails to the bloody quick, but she'd mastered the habit, and this was different. It was true damage, not just the byproduct of anxious inattention.

"Wil?" Ed asked carefully. "What happened to your hands?"

For an instant Wil remained motionless. Then she looked up and met his eyes. "Please don't ask. I don't want to have to lie to you."

Sickening worry pooled in Ed's stomach—as far as he knew, Wil had never withheld anything from him before. He hated that she felt some need to now. Hated that he couldn't solve any problem plaguing her with a nod of his head, or a word to the right person, or a stack of banknotes, as his father easily managed any trouble facing the family.

"Just promise me it wasn't someone else that hurt you," Edison said, still with great care. "I have to know that much."

"It . . ." Wil faltered. "It wasn't someone living."

"You told me spirits can't hurt anyone."

Ed had thought—had hoped—that perhaps it was true spirits couldn't harm *her*, given her strange and unprecedented connection to them. For his part, he'd known full well they could do damage. Peter had hurt him in a thousand small ways during life—death had not changed that, only slightly altered the pattern. Peter alive had left bruises— injuries of the body. Peter dead did more than just that. Worse than the bruises was the fear and uncertainty and mental anguish his presence at the Grange caused—wounds of the heart and soul.

"It seems I was wrong," Wil conceded, something sad and anxious in her face. "I don't know everything about the dead, after all, nor would I ever want to. Ed, would they give me a job at the Grange, since there's so much going on with your sister's party and they've lost Jenny? I could do a housemaid's work easily enough."

The question took Edison by surprise. Never, not once, had Wil expressed an interest in following her mother and grandfather into service. He'd always received the impression that John Shepherd discouraged her from doing so and that Wil was content to take her grandfather's advice on the matter.

The prospect of Wil at the Grange filled him with a maelstrom of conflicting feelings. To him, she existed entirely outside the troubles of his life there. It was an unfair perspective, and one he knew to be

40

false—given Shepherd's role as butler, difficulties at the Grange couldn't help but come to bear on Wil as well—and yet the idea of her in close proximity to his family set Edison's skin crawling. The Summerfields' world was one of artifice and excess and superficiality. Wil, by contrast, was straightforward and honest and good down to her core. He'd be ashamed, he realized, for her to see the rest of his life.

And if trying to hide the way he felt for her was an effort when their meetings were prearranged, how much more difficult might it prove when he could come across her around any corner?

"I don't think that's a good idea," Ed said dismissively. "You wouldn't like it, I'm sure. As far as I can tell, a housemaid's job is long, back-breaking, and dull. Why waste your mind on something like that? You're worlds sharper than I am; you ought to be doing something with it."

The sadness and discomfort he could see in Wil only grew.

"That's just the thing," she said. "I want to. I've been thinking about university—that when I'm ready, I might try for a degree. More and more women are doing that sort of thing; it's not as uncommon as it once was. And I've had an education of sorts, thanks to you. But it's a terrible expense, even with what I've earned writing and selling papers to your wretched schoolmates. I couldn't possibly ask Grandfather to pay for something like that alone. So I think I'd better start earning what I can and put it away until it's needed."

It had never occurred to Ed that Wil might not be able to unlock any door she wished to walk through. And he felt like an absolute fool being confronted by that fact, because of course he should have realized. Wasn't his father forever saying that money made the world turn?

"Please, Ed," she added, a wanting in her voice he'd never heard there before. "I need this."

With a sigh, Edison cast about himself, searching for some sign that might indicate what he ought to do. Across from them, still leaning against the beech roots, sat Wil's hand-me-down volume of Horace. In the space between each line of Latin, she'd carefully printed her inspired translations. But in the broader expanse of the margins, she'd written a single word, over and over, in a sloping, uncharacteristic script.

Surgite.

Rise up.

Getting to his feet, Edison held out a hand to Wil. If she needed his help, he'd give it—he hardly had a choice in the matter any longer.

"Come on. We'll go have a word with Mrs. Forster."

* * *

"There's a girl outside," Edison said from the threshold of the housekeeper's open pantry door. "She says she's here to see if we're in want of an extra housemaid, so I thought you'd like to know."

Mrs. Forster got to her feet at once, a solid, ruddy-faced woman in her late middle age.

"Master Edison," she said in dismay. "I'm so sorry you've had to play errand boy. The silly thing should have known to come to the servants' entrance."

"No, no," Ed hurried to reassure her. "She's exactly where she ought to be. I'm the one who's out of place—I was walking, and I came in through the kitchen because I can never seem to avoid getting my feet muddy. Mother and Father were already cross at me for that yesterday, so I thought I'd go up the back stairs to my rooms and change. Could you send Shepherd up for me before you go out and fetch your new hire? I want a word with him."

Mrs. Forster shook her head. She'd never have taken the liberty of disagreeing with Peter, or even Kitty, but Edison didn't mind. "She's not a new hire yet, and mightn't be, if she doesn't prove suitable. But I don't deny we could use the help. You've heard about Jenny? God rest her soul."

"I have," Edison said. "And I'm sure because of that, and . . . another reason you'll discover, you'll consider the new girl an excellent addition to the household."

Since childhood, Ed had been aware of a pointed and unvoiced dislike that existed between Mrs. Forster and Shepherd, and he had prepared Wil for it. All she needed to do was imply that her grandfather would disapprove of her employment at the Grange—which Wil said he certainly would—and Mrs. Forster would hire her on the spot. It felt strange and uncomfortable to Ed, to be scheming about the staff in such a way. He knew they often played the Summerfields against one another, asking for things from whomever would be most likely to assent, but somehow for Edison to do the same felt sordid and inappropriate. Shepherd would have no recourse, after all, to complain about Ed's intervention in his affairs, whereas any member of the Summerfield family who felt they'd been dealt with unfairly by the staff had only to speak a word, and the offending party would be gone.

Never again, Ed promised himself to assuage a little of his guilt. *Just this once, and just for Wil.*

Meanwhile he needed to keep Shepherd out of the way.

Trudging up the back stairs to the nursery wing, Edison braced himself for the inevitable welcome. Peter was in fine form—no sooner had Ed pushed open the door leading into the wing's spacious main room than it slammed violently shut again, narrowly missing his fingers. Shoving his way through, Ed ignored the electric lights flickering wildly overhead and the hobby horse rocking violently in one corner. Whispers began too, rising to a fever pitch until one of the bulbs overhead shattered with a pop, sending down a glittering rain of glass.

Ignoring it all, Edison kicked off his muddy shoes and put on a new pair, leaving the old ones where they lay, as a knock sounded at the nursery wing's main door. Immediately the clamor around him ceased. If not for the broken glass on the floor, Ed would have doubted it had ever happened.

"Master Edison?" Shepherd's voice said from outside, cool and businesslike. "You wished to see me?"

"Um. Just a minute," Edison said, hastily sweeping the fragments of glass under the rug with an old page of copywork. Casting about himself, he saw no other sign of the ghostly inhabitant's furious activity. Good. Ed knew he must take great pains not to complain or to mention the things that happened there. He'd learned his lesson on that score in the weeks after Peter's death.

Hurrying to the door, he opened it with what he hoped was a breezy, debonair smile.

"Hello, Shepherd. I wanted a word with you."

John Shepherd stood in the hallway, several inches taller than Edison and ten times more self-possessed. He waited patiently, the silence between them stretching into something agonizing, as Ed realized he'd failed to come up with a task that might occupy Wil's grandfather until her interview was at an end.

"I wanted to . . . that is, I was hoping . . . perhaps we could . . ." Edison fumbled before an idea struck him. "I'd like to clear out the old nursery things. Perhaps take up residence at this end of the house for good. Do you think you could help?"

Shepherd fixed Ed with an inscrutable stare. "Surely a footman would be more suited to the task, Master Edison."

"Perhaps," Ed answered, thinking fast. "But I . . . I thought I'd bring up some things from my grandfather's laboratory as well. A telescope, a microscope. Anything else that might prove interesting. I took a liking to natural science this term, and you were here during Grandfather's time, so I thought you'd be the best man for the job. You'd know the most about the instruments—how to transport them, how to lay them out."

"A correct assumption," Shepherd conceded. "I'll get Jack to clear away the old things up here and meet you in the laboratory, shall I?"

"No," Edison said hurriedly. "I'll get the footman. You start looking over the laboratory and decide what might be most suitable to move."

"Consider it done."

With a nod, Shepherd was off. He never seemed to walk so much as to glide through the halls. Between Shepherd's gliding, Lady Summerfield's drifting, Lord Summerfield's masterful stride, and Kitty's lightsome tread, it was no wonder they were always haranguing Ed about the way he tended to stumble on the stairs or track mud into the house. He was always out of step with the rest of them and unable to find a way to fall back in.

Downstairs he found Mrs. Forster and Wil just finishing up, Mrs. Forster already buttoning Wil into a maid's uniform. It was deeply disorienting to see Wil so—as if she'd somehow managed to climb out of her own skin and into someone else's.

"Well, you two have made quick work of all this," Edison said. Wil kept her eyes fixed on the floor, as if they'd never met and she was somewhat overawed by his presence, but he caught a hint of a smile playing about her lips.

"And you have started what's likely to be a tempest in a teapot, Master Edison," Mrs. Forster said. "Don't try to tell me you didn't know who the young lady is. You had her name out of her and knew she's John Shepherd's girl, which was why you were so keen to bring her in."

Edison shrugged. "Don't let on that I'm on your side, Mrs. Forster. I'm not supposed to be paying enough attention to know that there *are* sides. When you've finished with her, can you send the new girl to the nursery wing? I've been horribly clumsy and broken some glass up there."

He knew better than to try to speak to Wil with Mrs. Forster watching. It would be too easy to give some hint that their acquaintance went far deeper than an ostensible first meeting outside the servants' entrance that afternoon. Instead he brushed past her and into the kitchen, where Jack Hoult was shamelessly flirting with Abigail, a girl only a few years older than Ed and Wil, but who Ed supposed must be head housemaid now that Jenny Bright was gone.

"Jack," Edison said flatly. "I need you upstairs."

The older man shot him a look of thinly veiled annoyance. For the most part, the Summerfields kept themselves out of the servants' domain, which was a policy Ed approved of and generally tried to abide by. But today had turned a number of his habits on their heads.

Leading the way, Edison bit his tongue. It was none of his business that Jack Hoult was a married man with two small children and another on the way. His parents had warned him time and again that outside the performance of duties, the lives of the servants were none of their concern. And Ed could hardly quibble about morality, given his feelings for Wil and the underhanded way he'd spent the afternoon securing her a position at the Grange.

Just outside the laboratory, he stopped and turned to Jack.

"Look, I'm sorry if I intruded," he said. "At school we're more independent, and I forget that isn't the way here. Next time I'll ring for you instead of coming downstairs."

"That's all right, Master Edison," Jack said with an easy smile. "I know you're a good sort and that you mean well."

The last came out somewhat pointed, but Ed chose to ignore it.

Inside the laboratory, Shepherd was methodically inspecting the old Lord Summerfield's instruments. He had a few labeled already with a clean, legible script, and glanced up as Edison and Jack entered the room.

"Is this what you had in mind, Master Edison?" Shepherd asked with perfect deference, causing a fresh twinge of guilt to start up in Ed's stomach. "I've nearly finished looking everything over and marked out whatever might be of interest to you. I can instruct Jack on how to pack up the instruments that are to be brought upstairs, and if you don't mind waiting an hour or two, I'll unpack them myself and instruct you in their use. At the moment, though, I'm wanted to oversee some deliveries that are being brought in for next week, when your sister's guests arrive."

"That's marvelous—thank you, Shepherd," Edison said. "You always seem to know just what's needed. I'm sorry to be a bother when there's so much going on."

"I'm happy to be of service," Shepherd replied, light from the back garden streaming across him and glimmering on the polished brass and copper of the antique instruments. "I'm pleased you're settling into your new quarters so well."

It was an innocent-sounding comment, but an entire era of unspoken history lent the words a dozen possible meanings. Ed's rooms were still in the nursery wing when Peter had died and the spirit there had first begun to plague him. It had all gone so very, very badly and led to some terrible fights within the family, culminating with one ill-fated night in which Ed was unceremoniously packed up and moved elsewhere and the nursery wing was locked up for years. That bought peace for a time, and Ed was determined that whatever the cost, he would not be the one who shattered the Summerfields' fragile veneer of serenity again.

"Yes, thank you," Edison said, aware that he sounded insincere and full of bluster. "Time heals all wounds, I suppose. I'll leave the two of you to your work."

A few languid notes sang out from the music room as Ed passed by. He glimpsed his mother inside, her chin resting on one hand, the other picking away at the piano's black and white keys. Her glass of sherry sat half-finished and within easy reach beside the music rack. Experience had taught Ed that she wouldn't welcome interruption, so he carried on and up the main flight of stairs, his nerves like a live wire as he did so.

Wil was in the corridor already making her way to his rooms, her lips parted and her eyes wide as she took in the house, the furnishings, the endless doors and paintings and precious things. But when Ed came up alongside her, the wondering expression she wore immediately shifted to something softer and more vulnerable.

"Mrs. Forster gave me my mother's old uniform," she said, the words low and uncertain. "She told me it seemed right and that we're the same size. Her name's still embroidered on the collar. I didn't expect that."

The uniform seemed to have flattened Wil somehow—to have stolen some of the color and life from her. Ed hated it. He wished he'd told her no from the first, when she asked about the position. Surely there must be other places in the village that would have hired her, or some shop in Wynkirk.

Glancing down the corridor to ensure no one was watching, he reached out and took her hand.

"You don't have to do this," Ed told her earnestly. "We can find you work somewhere else. Or if it's money you need, I have an allowance—"

Wil pulled her hand away as if he'd burned her. "I won't take your money, Ed. Not unless I've earned it."

"You're my friend," he ventured. "The best one I've got. Isn't that worth something? Can't I give you something for that?"

"Not money," Wil said with a shake of her head. "You know as well as I do; it would be the end of us if you paid for my company. We've always been able to forget that we're not really on equal footing. There'd be no overlooking it if money came into things."

Frustration joined Ed's nerves, the two of them starting up a jangling counterpoint within him.

"You're happy enough to be paid so that others can cheat their way through school by taking advantage of your intelligence. And now this?" He gestured to Wil's uniform and to the broom and dustpan she carried.

"Why can't you just let me help you? It'd be a vast deal easier for me to forget I handed you a banknote now and then, than to overlook you sweeping the ashes out of my fireplace every morning like the Grimms' Cinderella."

Wil gave him a forlorn look. "Things were so much simpler when we were children, weren't they?"

"I just don't understand why *this* is something you want."

"It's not, really," Wil said. "I can't explain; it's just . . . something I have to do."

"I think," Ed told her, and felt like a brute even as the words were leaving his mouth, "that perhaps things were simpler before because we didn't keep secrets."

In answer, Wil gathered herself up, erasing every trace of emotion from her face. "You had some sweeping that wants doing, sir?"

"Don't," he begged. "You'll be the death of me."

But Wil refused to relent. She only stood waiting, as patient and docile as her grandfather could be, until Ed turned and led her to the nursery wing door.

With his hand on the knob, Ed sent up a silent plea.

Please, Peter. Please. Do your worst.

But the door swung open easily at his touch. The sunny main room lay before them, silent and peaceful, made all the brighter for being in want of curtains. Nothing moved. No spirit stirred.

"Where's the glass?" Wil asked after a moment, when Edison didn't speak.

"Under the carpet," he said, trying to hide the wretched disappointment and discouragement churning through his veins.

He hardly saw Wil as she knelt and tidied up the mess his ghost had left behind.

"Is that all?" she said, when the job was done.

49

"You don't—" Ed cleared his throat, finding it unaccountably dry, the words difficult to get out. "You don't notice anything peculiar about this room, do you?"

Wil turned a slow circle, taking it all in.

"I'm not sure?" she said with a frown. "You need curtains, I think. And you'll want a new bulb for your light fixture, to replace this one that broke. What am I meant to be looking for?"

"That's all?" Edison pressed. "You're certain? There's nothing else?"

"Yes, I'm sure. Ed, what's wrong? You look rather pale."

He rallied, giving her a smile. "Nothing. Nothing's wrong. You'd better get back to Mrs. Forster; I'm sure she has a list of things for you to do as long as my arm."

Wil went, with a worried backward glance over one shoulder.

"Always close the doors," Ed offered, and shut his own firmly in her wake.

No sooner had she gone than a howling resounded from the chimney, despite the fair, late spring day outside. The children's storybooks still lining the room's low bookshelves shook and juddered, several falling to the floor. And from the corner of his eye, Ed could see mist filling the looking glass as a shadowy, indistinct figure peered out from its heart.

In abject despair, he turned his back to it all and rested his forehead against the door he'd closed between himself and Wil. Since Peter's death, no one else had ever witnessed the wrathful, furious haunting Ed was subjected to. He'd explained it all to his parents, who'd dismissed it at first and then grown angry when he insisted there was truth to the story. Finally, when living in the nursery wing had taken an obvious toll and he'd refused to back down from his explanation as to what it was that robbed him of sleep, leaving bruises on his arms and wreaking havoc every night, there had been doctors. Doctors and doses and inconclusive diagnoses.

Ed had kept every bit of it secret from Wil. His brilliant friend, who could see and summon the dead and even predict a death before it came. Because if she could not see what he saw, could not witness what he witnessed, then it could not be the dead at fault.

It could only be Edison himself—the defect not one of the spirit world, but of his mind.

And she had not seen.

She had not seen.

CHAPTER FIVE

WIL

"He never looks at you," Abigail Phelps said to Wil as they went through the arduous process of dusting, airing out, and turning over yet another of Wither Grange's seemingly unending guest rooms.

For three days, Wil had done a housemaid's work at the Grange. It was at once familiar and jarring—as if she'd assumed her mother's life along with her uniform. Abigail had made the transition easier. She'd slipped into Jenny's position as head housemaid as if she'd been born to it, and if she felt any grief over Jenny's death, she hid it beneath a veneer of good-natured efficiency. Abigail was on excellent terms with the kitchen staff, was spoken highly of by Mrs. Forster, and flirted often enough with Jack Hoult and the groom that they'd pay her favors when asked, but not so often that they lost their heads over her. She was, in short, a paragon among housemaids, none of which seemed to favorably impress Wil's grandfather. John Shepherd, Wil had learned, treated all the female staff below a certain age with a coldness bordering on disdain.

"He's angry with me," Wil said in reply to Abigail's comment as she tried and failed to tuck in the bed linens on her side as tidily as Abigail had done. "He never wanted me to take work here. After my mother died, he said it was the one stipulation he had for me—that I could do whatever I liked and make myself into whatever I wanted, but that I must stay away from the Grange. And I don't usually cross him. He's a hard person to disobey."

Abigail had been arranging pillows at the head of the bed, and she straightened as Wil spoke, a bemused look crossing her pleasant face.

"I didn't mean your grandfather," she said, in a tone Wil found hard to parse. "I meant Master Edison. It's stood out to me because he's the only one of the family who usually *does* look at the staff—meets your eye when he speaks to you, acts like you're a real person. Always has done. But not with you. Three times now we've served tea for the family, and each time he'll look anywhere else but in your direction. It's funny. I've never seen him so, and I've been here since we were both small, though he was a child in the nursery then, and I was a child serving as a scullery maid."

Wil focused very intently on the bedsheet she was attempting to tuck smoothly, though it *would* keep pulling back out.

"I suppose he finds it awkward," she said. "Me being Shepherd's granddaughter. Or perhaps I remind him of the deaths they've had in the household—of my mother and Jenny."

Coming around the bed, Abigail dismissed Wil with a wave of her hand and immediately set the linens to rights.

"Perhaps," she said, though the word came out doubtful. "But I'm not sure the family thinks on us enough to be bothered by that sort of thing."

You don't know Edison, Wil thought staunchly, but all she did was shrug.

"Then I don't know," she said. "Maybe I just remind him of someone he doesn't care for."

"Could be," Abigail conceded, though she did not seem convinced. Thumbing through a notebook she carried in her apron pocket, Abigail frowned. "We need the lotus vase from downstairs. Lady Summerfield says it's to go in here, but your grandfather wanted it cleaned first. Can you run and get it from his pantry?"

"Of course," Wil said quickly.

In the corridor outside the guest room, she took a moment to get her bearings. The Grange was bewilderingly large, and twice already Wil had lost her way when sent on some errand or other. The ground floor was all right—there, if she could only find the crimson-carpeted central hallway that ran the length of the house, she could reorient herself. The two floors above were harder and more of a warren.

Setting off in the direction from which she and Abigail had come, Wil realized after a minute or two that she must have taken a wrong turn. Surely she ought to have reached the house's south end and the servants' stairs by now. Stopping short, she let out a frustrated sigh.

It had seemed so clear to her, when she'd first asked Edison about a position at the Grange, that this was what she should do. Her mother and Jenny Bright's deaths were millstones around her neck, made all the heavier by old Ada Bright's implication that there had been something untoward about their passings, and that Wil herself ought to be responsible for ferreting out the truth. She'd thought that if she put herself in a position to look and listen and ask questions, it might prove possible to unlock what had previously been kept secret.

But all she'd done so far was work from dawn to midnight: repetitive, dull, wearying tasks that left her feeling worn out and used up, as if a fog had settled and was sapping her of the wit she'd hope would serve her well at Wither Grange.

"It hasn't always been like this," Abigail had told her cheerfully midway through her first full day, as they worked through a dizzying list of things that must be done. "But they let two other housemaids go earlier this spring. It was just me and Jenny for a bit, and we managed—she'd been here longer than me, even, and we both knew the job like the backs of our hands. But then she . . ."

Abigail's voice trailed off.

"I'm sorry," Wil said softly. "I wish I'd come earlier; it would be easier for you now."

"No." Abigail shook her head. "Don't be silly. We can't change the past, and you deciding to go against your grandfather when you did is my saving grace. Otherwise it'd just be me, and I'd be drowning."

It was only a figure of speech, but Wil had gone cold at the words.

Now, as she glanced up and down the unfamiliar corridor with its plush carpeting and expensive wallpaper, its elegant electric sconces and occasional tasteful painting or sculpture, Wil felt entirely out of her depth.

In her mind she'd always known that she and Edison were on a different footing in life. But it had been a nebulous idea—something that never seemed truly real. Her grandfather spoke little of his work at the Grange, and the building itself was so vast and awe-inspiring that Wil hadn't really been able to believe it was a place where someone like Ed—her kind, self-effacing friend—could live. For all their years together, it was as if he only existed within her once they parted company, and the life she knew he led was only a fairy tale or a dream.

"Wil?"

As though Wil's thoughts had summoned him, Ed stepped out from a door at the end of the hall, shutting it carefully in his wake. It was only then that Wil realized her bewildered wandering had brought her to the old nursery wing, where Abigail said he'd taken up residence for the duration of Kitty Summerfield's party.

Seeing him here, in the larger context of his life, cut at Wil. And not because it highlighted the disparity between them, or because he carried an air of familiarity with a world and surroundings that were alien to her. Just the opposite—standing before her now, Ed held himself as if something had splintered inside him. He seemed skittish and anxious, as if at any moment something unseen and unpleasant might come through the door at his back or surge up the grand main staircase Wil had passed by along her way. He never seemed so in the woods—though he'd mentioned feeling ill at ease at home, he'd always been settled in himself when he and Wil were together.

And it was not just discomfort afflicting him, Wil realized with a twist of her stomach. She knew Ed better than anyone, and what she could feel from him was fear—deep-seated, unconquered, gnawing away at him like some cancer of the soul. She could not for the life of her divine the root of it, but she wanted, more than anything, to drive it out. To find some way of comforting and reassuring him beyond the means that existed between them now.

"What are you doing down here?" Ed asked with a frown. He was pale and drawn, haunted shadows etched beneath his eyes, and Wil thought she could see a wide bruise marking his forearm, just before he self-consciously tugged at his shirtsleeves.

"I'm lost," Wil confessed, and Edison's frown melted into a tired smile.

"I know," he said. "It's easy to get that way here, isn't it? Where do you need to go?"

"Down to the butler's pantry, but I don't want to be a bother. I could just use the back stairs from the nursery, if you like."

"No." Edison spoke the word so quickly that it came out adamant and sharp-edged. "Not through there. I . . . don't want you going in there."

And for the first time, an unbidden and horrific thought struck Wil.

He never looks at you, Abigail had said.

What if the depth of unease and fear she felt from Edison had not existed until now? What if it was *her* putting him on edge? For over a year, she'd been aware of some new and unaccountable distance between them, and he'd been against her taking a position at the Grange. He'd only given in because she insisted.

Involuntarily she took a step back.

"I'm sorry," Wil said with perfect calm. "I'll find another way."

It could be anything bothering him, the logical part of her mind insisted. *Don't assume the worst, not unless you know for certain.*

But the softer parts of Wil, the ones that counted Edison's friendship the dearest treasure she possessed, were already in tatters. She'd ruined things, she was sure. They'd always kept their lives separate, save for secret meetings on neutral ground. Wil had disrespected and bypassed their unspoken boundaries, perhaps shattering her one great joy and solace as a result.

And for what? The furious words of a barely coherent dead soul, and the veiled hints of an old woman.

A pained look crossed Ed's face. "Wil, no. I didn't mean to snap. I'm just used to a certain degree of privacy, is all. And you're all right to use the main stairs. There's no company yet; no one will mind."

"I'm sorry," Wil repeated. "I know you didn't want me here, and I promise you, I won't overstep again."

Though Wil was a master of hiding her true feelings, Ed must have realized how miserable he'd made her, because he stepped forward and, after a surreptitious glance down the corridor, put his arms around her. Wil stood stiffly for a moment before relenting and returning the gesture, burying her face in Edison's shoulder and taking in a breath of his particular scent—books and ink and peppermint. Dimly she thought she felt him brush the barest hint of a kiss to the top of her head, but it might have been no more than wishful thinking—the aching desire to put a seal on their closeness, to reassure herself that he truly did not wish her elsewhere.

"It isn't not wanting you," Edison said with an intensity Wil had never heard from him before. "Don't think that. And look, if you want to use the nursery stairs, you can. I'm being an ass for no reason."

Pulling away from her, he opened the door and stood patiently waiting. Wil followed him as he shut them in and the rest of the Grange out. But worry bit at her as she took in covert glimpses of her surroundings. Every bulb in the hanging light fixture overhead had shattered, and the shards of glass still glinted, sharp and dangerous, on the carpet. The rug itself was damp and discolored, smelling vaguely of something unpleasant and vegetative. All the books had fallen from the low bookshelf, and they lay in a splayed and jumbled heap before it, spines cracked, some of the pages torn free. Before the great, curtainless window, a long table had been laid out with scientific instruments, but several of them had toppled over, and one lay on the floor in pieces.

"Ed?" Wil asked hesitantly. "Do you want me to tidy up in here?"

"Don't trouble yourself," he blustered. "It's my mess; I'll get to it."

"Well, it's my job to do that sort of thing now," Wil said, in an attempt at dispelling the tension she could feel singing through Edison. "So you might as well get your money's worth."

He only stared at her blankly. "It is never your job to look after me or try to solve my problems."

No, Wil thought. *No one would have to pay me for that. I'd volunteer for it if you'd let me.*

"All right," was all she said. "Suit yourself. And I know—shut the door to the steps behind me."

Belowstairs was another world, and one where Wil felt far more at home. It was still a maze, but this time one of narrow and twisting whitewashed passages that led from the dairy to the cold store to the wine cellar, from the staff dining room to the kitchen to the butler's pantry. The corridors echoed with a clamor of voices emanating from the direction of the servants' entrance—every day, more deliveries of foodstuffs and outdoor furniture and flowers came in, all in preparation for Kitty's extended party. Only that morning, an enormous marquee tent had arrived, causing a great deal of commotion among the male staff, who'd have the task of erecting and furnishing it. Mrs. Forster and Abigail would be responsible for the decorating, under Kitty's watchful instruction. Wil, having only just arrived, would continue with the less exciting tasks—ensuring the house shone and glittered by the time guests began to appear.

Outside her grandfather's study, Wil stopped. Striding past her on his way down the corridor, Jack Hoult offered a half-pitying nod, which was quite a concession, coming from him. It was impossible for anyone on staff to miss that things between Wil and her grandfather had been fraught since her intrusion into the well-ordered world of the Grange. John had hardly spoken to her over the past few days, choosing to make his disapproval known through icy silence.

With a hand on the study doorknob, Wil sought to gather her courage. She let out a slow breath and shut her eyes.

The moment she did so, an icy jolt hit her, followed by an awful, relentless pull—a wild and urgent need to leave the world of the living and enter the halfway realm of the dead. Wil had never felt such a thing before. For her, the slip from one plane into the next had always been purposeful, something she'd chosen. But this was no matter of choice—it was force, an alien power of will exerting itself against her own. Briefly Wil struggled, forcing her breath to stay even, her eyes to remain shut, the ordinary and tangible sensation of the doorknob beneath her palm to remain.

It was not enough. The rip current dragging her away from life and beyond its bounds became an irresistible compulsion, thrusting her through the gap and into that shadowed hinterland.

All was as it had been. Nothing was as it should be. The corridor and the entrance to her grandfather's study looked the same, yet the air had grown dim and murky, the edges of the hall haunted by half-formed spirits. One of them had been waiting, all mist and elongated limbs and anger. The moment Wil stumbled into their realm it rushed at her, and in the confusion of being pulled into the spirit world rather than choosing it, Wil did not have the presence of mind to shut the dead soul out. With a sudden shock of cold, it inhabited her, flooding her veins with lead as they tumbled back into life and warmth and reality.

Relegated to the corners of herself, Wil watched, everything in her poised to seize control as the spirit took governance of her body. But it only stood silent, with its hand—her hand—on the knob to John Shepherd's study. Not a word spoken, nor a twitch of the limbs, indicated its intent.

Wil knew it to be whatever was left of Jenny Bright. She could recognize the quality of the soul, the outrage and fierceness and strength. But as the spirit held her there, waiting on the threshold of her grandfather's study, Wil felt something else from it.

Familiarity. An overpowering sense of déjà vu, as if it had stood just so before. And mingled with that, resignation and a stifling sense of fear. A fear so great, it threatened to choke her.

I mean to say something, Wil heard, echoing out from behind her grandfather's door. It was Jenny's voice, long ago and far away, remembered by the soul that held her. *Something about Mabel. I don't know what, yet, but I won't keep quiet anymore. I won't keep swallowing it back.*

As suddenly as it had gripped Wil, the spirit let go. It left in a shocking rush, the world growing intolerably bright and loud and hot as Wil's body became her own once more, the soul slipping back into the halfway realm.

Shaken, Wil lowered her hand, but as she did, the door in front of her opened abruptly. John Shepherd loomed over her, a stern expression on his face.

"Don't just linger on my doorstep," he said coldly. "If you're to fill a position here, I require you to at least be a credit to the job."

Wil swallowed, her throat gone dry. "Yes, of course. Abigail sent me down for the lotus vase."

Receding, John fetched it, setting it carefully in her hands.

"It's older than this house," he warned her. "Handle it with care."

Wil could not shake the fear that the spirit had set in her bones, and that only intensified at the sight of her grandfather's closed-off, unwelcoming face, but she nodded.

"You're dismissed," John said curtly, and shut the door between them. In the wake of Wil's unwanted foray into the halfway realm, the small click of the latch sounded as loud as a gunshot, and she flinched.

"All right, Wil?" a curious voice said from the end of the corridor.

Daphne Ellicott, the kitchen maid, stood on the threshold between the hallway and the kitchen, a frown etched across her pretty, ebony-skinned face.

Wil opened and shut her mouth, and was mortified to find she couldn't speak. The weight of John's displeasure, the tension between herself and Edison, the burden of her own unwanted powers, and the pervasive guilt she felt over her mother and Jenny Bright were all churning bitterly in her stomach. She felt herself near tears, shaken by her loss of control over her own body and spirit and by the shift between realms.

"Come and have a cup of tea," Daphne offered. "Abigail can wait a minute."

Mutely Wil nodded. She wanted a moment to collect herself before returning to the perfectly curated, immaculate world of the Grange abovestairs. She needed something warm and fortifying to ground her among the living and drive back Jenny Bright's lingering fury and fear.

Only Mrs. Ellicott, the Grange's cook and Daphne's mother, was in the kitchen. Several pots and pans simmered on the massive range, dinner preparations already underway, though luncheon hadn't yet been served. Setting a teapot and cup and saucer down on the wide worktable at the kitchen's center, Daphne gave Wil a nod before returning to what she'd been doing—slicing cucumbers and finely baked white bread for sandwiches.

Gingerly Wil settled the lotus vase on a sideboard before pouring herself a cup of fragrant tea. The smell itself was a small oasis of calm, as was the little tendril of steam that drifted from the cup, a symbol of comfort rather than an indicator of death.

"You know, you shouldn't mind your grandfather," Mrs. Ellicott said from where she stood at the stove, her back still toward Daphne and Wil. Her tightly curled black hair was pulled back, and her hands—moving perpetually from one pot to another, testing the contents, stirring here, adding a pinch of salt there—were practiced and capable. "He's always been hard on the housemaids. Even your mother, when she was alive. He's good enough to the rest of us and a fair manager, but there's something about your job that seems to bring out the worst in him. Don't know what or why, but it's always been so, at least as far back as I can remember."

Wil took a sip of her tea, scalding and bitter, and her borrowed fear began to recede. The urgency behind Jenny's temporary possession gnawed at the corners of her mind. *Surgite.* Rise up. Two housemaids gone from the world of the living, and neither of them resting peacefully.

There was a language at play here—a dead language, a tongue spoken only by those who'd already gone down to the grave. They'd left words to be deciphered, some message to be translated—if only Wil could find the trick of it, as she did so deftly with Latin and Greek.

"Was my grandfather like that with Jenny?" Wil asked, choosing her words with care as she blew on the swirling surface of her tea.

"Mm," Mrs. Ellicott said, a sound of assent and pity. "He was almost cruel with them both. More so in the week or two before they passed. Had terrible fights with your mother and Jenny behind closed doors. Shouting and berating them, when I've never seen him lose his composure with anyone else. He was all right with Abigail for years, but now that Jenny's gone, I've heard him starting in on her. Took her to task last night while you were tidying up the dining room. It wasn't over anything that mattered, either—she'd polished a candlestick that morning, and he decided it wasn't up to standard. Well, I've seen Abigail's work—it's always better than good. She could do any job in this household if asked, and she knows the Grange inside out and upside down. We're lucky to have her, though heaven knows if she'll stay now that your grandfather . . ."

Mrs. Ellicott stopped and turned for the first time, a sympathetic expression etching itself across her earnest face.

"I'm sorry, lamb," she said. "I ought not to speak ill of your own family when you can hear it. Perhaps being our Mr. Shepherd's blood will keep him from coming down so hard on you."

"I expect not, if it didn't protect my mother," Wil said quietly. "He always seemed gentle with her at home, or as gentle as he ever is—I had no idea they were at odds here."

"*At odds* is one way of putting it." Daphne cut through a sandwich with fierce efficiency. "I heard him the night before—"

"Enough, Daph," Mrs. Ellicott said, her voice stern. "That's her kin. We're all better off not knowing the worst parts of those we love best."

Daphne subsided, but across the worktable, her eyes caught Wil's.

"And is there anyone else," Wil asked, "either on the staff or in the family, who had any sort of difficulty with my mother and Jenny? Or who was on bad terms with them before they died?"

Mrs. Ellicott shrugged. "Not that I can think of. Most of the staff get on well enough. And Peter would bother the housemaids sometimes, but he's dead and buried."

Letting out a sigh, Wil placed her cup in the sink and murmured a thank-you to Mrs. Ellicott for the tea. She took the lotus vase and drifted from the kitchen, purposely setting a slow pace, and after a moment Daphne caught her up.

"I don't know what it is," Daphne said under her breath, "but Mum's right about Mr. Shepherd. Your grandfather and the housemaids— they're always like oil and water. If you want to keep the peace, I think you'd best not stay at the Grange. That night before your mother passed, I was clearing up the kitchen and could hear them with each other. He was shouting, and she was crying her heart out. They were vicious things he said too, about her being a senseless fool and no good to anyone, and how he'd drive her off the staff if she didn't leave herself. The next day, they found her washed up on the bank of the millpond."

Wil felt cold, as if the halfway realm or some restless spirit gripped her, though there was no tug toward the gap. She'd known her grandfather to be reserved and exacting. She hadn't realized he could be brutal as well.

Daphne placed a hand on Wil's arm. "I'm not telling you because I want you hurt. Just the opposite. If you stay on, you ought to do it with your eyes open. You ought to know."

Wil nodded. "Yes. You were right to tell me. I'm glad you did."

Glad wasn't exactly the word for it. A sick sense of dread had pooled in Wil's stomach, dredging up the last of Jenny Bright's cast-off fear. As

Daphne retreated to the kitchen, Wil glanced at John Shepherd's firmly shut door.

A whole household of staff to manage, and her grandfather and guardian had been vicious to the only two who'd died. It wasn't a language, perhaps, but an eerie conjunction. The sort of thing that could have meaning or not, depending on your perspective. A coincidence or a pattern, determined by your frame of mind.

And whatever Wil's ties to John, however it hurt her to think he might in some way have been connected to her mother and Jenny's deaths, Wil did not believe in coincidences. She believed in patterns and hidden significance—that every action meant more than it seemed to at first glance.

CHAPTER SIX

EDISON

Being home had a way of making Ed feel like a ghost himself. At school, he knew what was expected, even if in some regards, he chose not to live up to those expectations. With Wil, he felt like he belonged and could, in all respects save one, let down his guard.

Home, by contrast, was a place where he had no sense of purpose or belonging, no clear idea of what was wanted from him. He drifted through the halls, at a loss as to how to occupy himself in a way his parents—his father—would find fitting. Reading and studying were considered foolish and wasteful pastimes by Lord Summerfield. One summer, Ed had attempted to throw himself into the sort of pursuits Kitty favored instead—riding and frenetic outdoor activity. It had not been to his taste, but he'd tried, only to eventually overhear his father refer to him as selfish—bent on his own pleasure and no one else's. There was no way of satisfying him, Ed realized then, and yet the desire to do so remained.

"What did *you* do that was so different?" Edison asked the air around him as he lay on his back in the nursery wing, brooding over his troubles.

The whispers coming from the wing's far corners grew louder but did not resolve into words. With a frustrated sigh, Ed rolled over, burying his face in his pillow. No sooner had he done so than there came the sharp retort of a slamming door.

Springing to his feet, Ed wrenched the door to the bedroom back open. Except for the doorway leading into the nursery wing from the outside corridor, they were all open—if he was going to be relegated to the one corner of the house that tormented him, he'd at least follow his own rules there. But the doorknob beneath his palm began to rattle angrily, then judder, as one by one the doors to the nursery wing's sun-soaked central room slammed shut as well. The moment Ed lifted his hand, he found himself shut into the bedroom again, a *bang* still echoing through the confined space.

Unreasoning fury woke in him.

"I've had enough of this, Peter," he snapped. "I don't care what anyone else wants—if I'm going to stay up here, I'll damn well keep the doors open."

At the foot of the bed sat a neat kit of tools Shepherd had procured for Edison to use in reassembling and tinkering with his grandfather's scientific collection. Rifling through it, Ed dug out a chisel and a mallet and strode over to the door. Though it was cumbersome and unwieldy, it took no more than a few minutes for him to slip the pins from the hinges and triumphantly heave the door into the center of the wing's main room, where it landed on the rug with a dull thump and a crunch of broken glass. Ed hadn't bothered cleaning up the shattered bulbs—what use was there in sweeping up and changing them, when Peter's senseless anger would only break them again?

Methodically Edison went through the nursery wing, taking every door down from its hinges and leaving them in a pile at the central room's heart. Already his gaze glossed over the chaos there—the books

67

that didn't seem worth picking up, the jagged teeth of glass jutting from light fixtures, the glint of further shards strewn across the carpet, the gaping eyes and mouths of bare windows and doorways.

His attention did catch on the back lawn outside and below him, though. As he set down the last door and straightened, sweat beading on his temples, he could see the magnificent marquee tent that had been placed beyond the gardens. People trailed in and out of it like ants fussing over their nest, and it all seemed so far away and foolish to Edison. What was the point, really, of any of it? Of Kitty's party, of the Grange, of the lives they led like little mechanical pieces, moving back and forth along prescribed tracks? Eventually they'd all end up like Peter or the wistful remnants of Wil's mother.

Dead and witless. Shapeless, repellent things, capable only of sound and fury, signifying nothing.

"Ed," Kitty said sharply from the entrance to the nursery wing. "What on earth are you doing?"

Edison felt as if he'd been wandering in a fog and only just stepped out of it. He blinked at his sister before running a hand over his face. "Oh. Um, a bit of rethinking the space? No one's done anything with it since we were small."

Kitty's frown stayed firmly in place, her eyes fixed on Edison. "Is this you falling apart again? Are we going to have a problem? Because I really *can't* deal with that right now, on top of everything else."

She did not clarify what constituted *everything else.* Certainly she might have meant nothing more than the organized chaos of preparing for entertaining. But Edison wondered. If he was haunted, Kitty had begun to look vaguely so herself, and he could never remember his sister seeming that way before.

"There's no problem," he hurried to reassure her. "A job like this always makes a mess before it gets better. Kitty, is there anything I can help you with?"

He made the offer impulsively, wanting some way to restore her usual unflappable composure. For a moment Kitty wavered. It seemed to Ed as if she was on a knife's edge, trying to choose between her habitual forced levity and something truer. Something darker.

"I don't . . . I don't know," she said at last, and the haunted look was stronger now, like a shadow behind her bright eyes. "I'm not sure it's the sort of thing you *could* help with."

"Try me," he answered. He crossed the room as he spoke and stood in the doorway, blocking out the view of Peter's chaos. Ed took both of Kitty's hands in his, and she looked down at them, unable to meet his gaze as she spoke.

"I can't say yet," she told him, her voice heavy, as if the words cost her. "But if it came down to it, could I count on you? No matter what—even if it meant trouble for the household and the family, and some really ghastly unpleasantness?"

"Always," Edison said without hesitation, and he meant it. When they were children, he'd been closer to Kitty than anyone else in the house, and though they'd drifted apart as they grew older, she was still his first and best ally at the Grange. Ed didn't cast an allegiance like that aside lightly. "And I don't care what it's about. If you ever need me, Kitty, I'll stand by you."

She drew in a quavering breath. "You're a darling, do you know that? But at least for now, there's nothing. Just . . . take care of yourself, for the time being." Her eyes drifted uncertainly to the nursery room door. "And if I need you, be ready."

Clearly believing herself to have said everything necessary on the matter, Kitty turned, shutting the door in her wake. At once, the distant muttering that insisted on emanating from the corners of the room rose up again.

"You shut up," Ed said fiercely to the disembodied voice. "You never could make us turn on each other while you were alive. You certainly won't be able to now that you're dead."

69

*　　*　　*

That night, he dreamt of Wil.

She and Abigail had been serving at dinner—Jack and Shepherd, apparently, were too preoccupied with converting the grounds into some lavish fairyland of Kitty's imagining. It made Edison feel guilty and robbed him of his appetite, to be sitting at a table laid with crisp linens and sparkling crystal and gleaming silver while Wil stood silently against the wall, only stepping forward to hold out serving trays or to clear dishes at the beginning and end of courses. He wanted to give her everything he himself had, or to give up anything he possessed that she did not. Each day she spent at the Grange seemed to be one in which the barrier between them widened. Ed hated it, as he hated to see his family wordlessly accepting her service, not one of them aware of the full person behind the uniform she wore.

Wil was on Edison's mind as he went to bed in his wing full of whispers, and sleep was powerless to drive her out. He dreamt of the warren of corridors belowstairs—of himself wandering through them, searching for her, and unable to find her. Then, in the way of dreams, he was on the ground floor in a moment, standing at the head of the long, crimson-carpeted corridor that ran the length of the house. He could see Wil at the far end, not in her maid's uniform, but one of the checked skirts and white blouses she favored when given a choice. He called out to her, but she turned away, leaving the Grange behind. Drawn after her, Ed found himself emerging not onto the back lawns and gardens, but into the mill wood. There was a sound of running water from where the stream emptied into the millpond, and he could make out a glimpse of swaying reeds between the trees.

A sense of unfounded horror swept over Edison as his feet rooted to the spot. He stood where he was, unable to move or call out as Wil appeared on the green bank before the reeds. A cloud of fog-shrouded, gruesome spirits rose up around her, and she held out her hands to them, then followed as they led her through the reeds and into the water, which engulfed them all.

He woke to gray daylight and the sound of rain against the bare windows. Soft noises emanated from the nursery sitting room, and Ed pulled on his dressing gown with a muttered curse. Whatever Peter was up to now, he wasn't in the mood for it.

"Enough of that," Edison said sharply, leaning against his bedroom doorway and stifling a jaw-splitting yawn. "Whatever it is you're doing, I don't want you here if you're going to be like this. I wish you'd just tell me what you're really after and move on."

For a moment nothing happened. A vague sense of discomfort was still clinging to Ed in the wake of his unnerving dream, but it grew into unbearable, stomach-turning anxiety as Wil straightened up from where she'd been clearing out the hearth and laying a fire. The haphazard pile of doors had hidden her from view. Edison would have given his right hand to take back the words he'd just spoken, and to erase the look of disbelief and hurt and anger that wrote itself across Wil's face.

"At least you've said it now," she told him, standing straight-backed and proud, though he thought he could see a sheen of tears in her eyes. "But I can't leave, not even for you. Not unless you have me dismissed outright. Truth be told, I'd rather I was anywhere but here, as well. But there are more important things in this world than our comfort, Edison Summerfield. And until I set them to rights, here I'll stay."

"Wil," Ed began miserably. "I—"

But with a clatter of broom and dustpan, she gathered up her things and left. Wil had never failed to listen to him when he spoke before, Ed realized with a dull shock. Sometimes it seemed she was the only person in the world who really heard him. He knew he'd broken some thread between them that had already begun to fray, and mending it would require confessing something he'd never put into words before and tried to think of as seldom as possible: that Edison was as plagued by death as Wil herself, but his ghost seemed a denizen of his own mind, rather than any spirit realm.

It had been the very day of Peter's death that his troubles began, though Edison hadn't known it at the time. He sometimes thought that might be proof he was haunted rather than half-mad—that he couldn't have known about Peter's dying, far away in France. But his family and the doctors never thought it signified. He misremembered, they said. He'd learned the date when that fatal telegram came and manufactured prior disturbances to fit in with what he knew.

Ed could recall it all so clearly, though. The second of February—a cold night with hard frost, which had feathered the panes of the nursery wing windows. There'd been a catastrophic problem with the boilers at school, resulting in all the boys being sent home for a week, much to most of their delight and Edison's resigned disinterest. It was only he who still kept rooms at that end of the house back then. Kitty had moved out years ago, wanting something more grown-up. But Edison liked the familiar. He hated the bother of making a change. So he'd remained, long after outgrowing the remnants of childhood still scattered throughout the wing.

He woke with a jolt in the small hours of that night, filled with a sickening sense of aloneness. He'd always liked the isolation of the nursery wing before, but it struck him suddenly that no one could hear him there, no matter how loud he called. At first he could not make out what it was that had wakened him. Then he realized that the bedcovers, so carefully and smoothly tucked in by the housemaids every day, were being pulled inch by slow inch off the end of the bed.

It was precisely the sort of thing Peter might have done, crouching below the bedframe to stay out of sight. He'd been fond of the sort of jokes and comments and barbs that provoked fear or shock. But Peter was in France, and though moonlight shone through the half-drawn curtains, Edison could see no one in the room. He shut his eyes tight, breath coming hard and fast as the bedclothes slithered down past his knees and then off the bed entirely. But when ice-cold hands gripped his ankles, his eyes flew open of their own accord, and he sat up with a jolt.

The room was still empty, bathed in serene silver light. Until morning, Ed sat on the floor beneath the window with the poker clutched in his hands.

Nothing else had happened that night. It all began gradually, a few disturbances occurring over the course of that week. But when summer came and Ed was sent home for the holidays, the incidents grew in intensity and frequency until Ed couldn't keep quiet any longer. He mentioned it first to his mother, then his father.

Talking about it at all had been a grievous error, a mistake it seemed he'd never live down.

And so, though it wrenched at him to think of damaging what lay between himself and Wil, he resolved not to explain his words or the slow rot eating away at their connection now that she'd come to the Grange. He knew what the result of keeping silent would be—a growing distance between them and a hurt on her part that would eventually heal. She would not stay at Wither Grange forever—she was too bright and good for that. She'd go, when the time was right, and leave him behind.

He knew the consequences of silence and believed he could live with them. Speaking up would mean a step into uncharted territory, and if there was one thing Ed had learned in life, it was to fear the unknown.

Stepping across the nursery sitting room, he began to pick up books and stack them back on the shelf methodically. Perhaps it was an exercise in futility, but he must attempt to live as he was and where he was.

He lacked the courage to try for better.

CHAPTER SEVEN

WIL

Wither Grange fairly shone.

By virtue of a week of little sleep and a great deal of backbreaking labor, Wil and Abigail had prevailed and rendered the place resplendent. Guests were due to arrive the following day, and the Grange was a cascade of fresh flowers, the floors and wood gleaming with polish, the myriad bedrooms fresh and airy. On her way to fill a final vase upstairs, Wil stopped in the soaring foyer, her footsteps inaudible as she crossed the black-and-white patterned floor in soft-soled shoes. She drew in a deep breath of the scent of the place—florals and citrus cleaning scrubs and money—and a twist of jealousy niggled in her stomach. Wouldn't it be nice, she thought with a hint of bitterness, to be the sort of person who enjoyed all this, and who took it for granted, rather than the sort whose labor made that leisure possible?

Wouldn't it be nice to be the sort of person who had no compunctions about casting off a friendship so old and familiar and well-worn that it had served as the foundation of Wil's small world?

And yet, however harshly Edison had spoken to her, Wil was worried about him. She, at least, could not set aside the affection and sense of responsibility she felt so quickly. The state of his rooms had unsettled her—while he could be absentminded in his personal habits, she'd never known Ed to tolerate true disorder. It seemed a sign of some larger disturbance, but how could she help if her very presence had become burdensome to him?

You can't, she told herself sternly. *You can't do anything for someone who'd rather you were elsewhere. Work for those who wish for your help. Focus on your ghosts.*

But Wil couldn't help it. It was habit and second nature by now for her to care for Ed, and her feet led her to the side of the sweeping double staircase that ran closest to his wing. She lingered in the gallery above for a moment, looking down at the terminus of the corridor and its shut door, and wondering.

"So you're Shepherd's girl," a cool, businesslike voice said from a nearby doorway. "The one Edison thinks so highly of—yes, I know about that. Neither of you are quite as sly or underhanded as you seem to think. I've seen you from a distance in the village before, and out in the woods with Ed when I was riding, but never at close quarters. Come over here and let me get a proper look at you."

Kitty Summerfield stood on the threshold of her bedroom, fresh and composed in a filmy, drop-waisted gown, which was a mist of translucent white fabric overlaying a silken layer of sunshine yellow. A waft of jasmine reached Wil, who felt drab and washed-out and vaguely dirty compared to Ed's immaculately presented sister. Reluctantly she drew closer to Kitty, who fixed Wil with a long, calculating stare.

"You know, it's rare for anything good to come of the family consorting with the help," Kitty said at last.

Wil's pride stung her, causing her to forget her shabbiness and position in a wash of self-righteous anger.

"I *wasn't* the help when Edison and I became friends," she answered hotly. "Neither do I intend to be for a moment longer than is necessary. I

75

was only myself, then and now and forever. And nothing ill could come from what's between Ed and I—I want the best for him, no matter his opinion of me. That's how I am when I care for someone. He could throw me over tomorrow, and if I was certain it was what he really wanted, I'd go without a murmur."

She was surprised by her own forwardness, but then she'd never felt herself to be less than the Summerfields or deserving of mistreatment. Her mother had been fond of saying that God's rain fell on the rich and poor alike, and that He saw everyone for who they were, not for what they could afford.

Better a bent for justice and mercy, my darling, Mabel had told her, *than all the money in the world.*

"And what if you weren't sure of someone you cared for?" Kitty pressed, moving forward and shutting the door to her bedroom behind her, so that Wil could not see into her private space. "What if you couldn't read them well enough to know what they really wanted, or thought they might be acting under some wrong influence? What would you do then?"

Wil could feel her chin jutting out stubbornly, which she supposed was rather bad behavior for a housemaid. "I'd stand by them. Through anything. But I trust Edison, at least, to be honest with me and to tell me what he wants or needs."

"What if doing what was right for someone you loved came at a cost?" Kitty went on. "What if it meant going against your family, say? Or what if what was best for them wasn't what was best for you? What then?"

Kitty's prodigious attention rested on Wil like a weight. She seemed to want an answer to her questions badly—not just to want one but to need it. Wil had sense enough to realize that the way Kitty focused on her, and the way she twisted her hands in the delicate fabric of her skirts as she spoke, could only mean that any answers she gave would be as much about Kitty Summerfield as they were about Wil Price.

"I don't turn my back on someone important to me," Wil said. "Even if it proves difficult."

Kitty pounced on that, seeming to take it up and mull it over, worrying over it as a cat might trouble a mouse. A frown creased the smooth skin between her brows. "Loyalty comes very dear sometimes. Is there any price too high to pay, to maintain loyalty you feel is owed?"

Wil thought over her answer carefully. She wanted to be truthful and to answer rightly, but it was difficult to give Kitty what she needed without knowing what trouble lay behind her questions.

"Yes," she answered after a moment. "I'd never pursue loyalty past the dictates of my conscience. But then I hope I'd never find myself in a position where I feel a great deal of loyalty to someone who'd ask me to go against my conscience in the first place. It's everyone's responsibility to choose their friends wisely and ensure they won't be put in a false position by their companions."

"And what of family?" Kitty asked. Her gaze shifted away from Wil until she stared unseeingly into the middle distance. "We don't choose our family. Yet they say blood is thicker than water—would you honor a blood tie past conscience's bounds?"

Wil shifted, uncomfortable and unsure. "Is it a requirement of my position to be subjected to interrogation?"

Kitty fell silent, though she remained where she was, once again pinning Wil to the spot with her gaze.

"I'd like to ask you a question now," Wil ventured. "As I've answered a number myself. Mine's about Jenny Bright, your maid. I'd like to know more about her frame of mind before she died."

"That's a matter of loyalty too," Kitty said sharply. "Whatever happened to Jenny, she was my maid and my responsibility. All that nonsense they've spouted about her having walked into the millpond is baseless gossip. Jenny could be . . . mercurial at times, but I considered her a friend as well as a servant. She'd looked after me from the day I outgrew my nursemaid. And she was a friend of your mother's—a fact you ought to remember and take into account when you speak of her. There was no cloud over Jenny, I'm certain of it. I make it my business to know the staff, even if they don't trouble themselves to know me."

"Does it bother you, not being known by us?" Wil asked, a little taken aback by the hollowness behind Kitty's words.

Kitty let out an empty, chiming laugh. "Why should it? I don't think anyone's ever really known me, not since I was a child. I wouldn't know how to go about being known, even if I decided to try."

"I'm sorry," Wil said impulsively. "How sad for you."

Kitty's laugh died and became a scowl with startling swiftness.

"I don't want your pity," she ground out. "If anything, I should be the one pitying you. The poor, fatherless daughter of a dead housemaid."

Wil was struck suddenly by all the varying degrees of connection between herself and the Summerfields. But for the few years between her and Kitty, it could just as easily have been the two of them who met in the woods and forged an iron-fast friendship. During her childhood, it had seemed as if she and Ed moved in different worlds, but they weren't separate spheres, not really. It was more a tangled web that they inhabited, and somewhere in that chaos of adjoining threads lay a myriad of connections between her and Kitty, both seen and unseen.

"What is it *you* believe happened to Jenny?" Wil pushed. As Kitty seemed inclined to force truthfulness from Wil, she felt no compunction over reversing their positions.

"An *accident*," Kitty shot back in a resolute tone. "Same as your mother. These things happen. They're dreadfully sad. But that's all there is to it. Those who don't wish for trouble ought not to go seeking it out."

"I don't wish for trouble," Wil said. "What I wish for is the truth. My mother used to say it has the power to set us all free."

"Then ask your grandfather for the truth," Kitty snapped, her patience finally spent. "He's been here longer than anyone else. But he won't like it—he never does like a prying housemaid."

Wil's heart sank. An echo of what Mrs. Ellicott and Daphne had said. But she would not show Kitty that the words had found their mark.

"Very well," she answered. "I will. Thank you for your assistance."

Kitty gave her a narrow look. "Stay here. I have something for you to do."

She disappeared into her room, and Wil heard a drawer being opened and shut. When Kitty returned, she held an ornate silver frame in one hand, containing a photograph of an infant in an elaborate christening gown. The child was solemn and round-faced, just old enough to sit alone, and had been placed in front of a shadowy, artificial backdrop painted to look like a forest.

"Here," Kitty said, holding the frame out to Wil. "They've set up a table in the marquee with mementos from my childhood. I didn't want it, but Mama insisted, and it's not often she sets her mind on something, so I'm humoring her. Put that at its center."

"I'll see to it," Wil said.

For a moment Kitty looked as if she might say something more. Then, with a vague shake of her head, she stepped back into her elegant bedroom and shut the door between herself and Wil.

*   *   *

Wil had not been out to the marquee at the center of the lawn yet, and as she stepped beneath the shelter of its tall, arching canvas roof, her lips parted involuntarily, wonder and irritation rising within her. Wonder because the place had been turned into a fairy glade, greenery and potted trees hemming the borders of the marquee and hiding its prosaic canvas. A glory of flowers bloomed everywhere you looked—there were tables throughout the marquee, where dainty, individual arrangements of bud roses and lavender sparkled in crystal vases at every place setting. The tent posts were hidden beneath garlands of ivy and jasmine, and the flower's potent scent hung in the air until the whole place seemed suffused with the presence of Kitty Summerfield. Clear glass lamps and paper lanterns in pastel shades sat waiting, ready to be lit and to suffuse the whole place with a magic glow.

That accounted for Wil's wonder. Her irritation stemmed from the fact that the marquee stood not a quarter mile from an actual woodland—what was the use of creating something false when the genuine article was only a stone's throw away? The purposefully whimsical nature of the marquee seemed at odds, too, with the tragic history of the forest that bordered Wither Grange. Here was a place built for frivolity and amusement, modeled after a wood that had seen too much of tragedy and death.

Pushing her conflicted feelings aside, Wil crossed the broad carpet of lawn to reach the far end of the marquee, where a tiled dance floor had been set down. Near it stood the table Kitty had mentioned, covered with souvenirs of her childhood—a lock of hair set behind glass, paintings made by a childish hand, a set of baby shoes. Placing the frame she'd been given in a likely-looking place, Wil turned to go.

And found Edison sitting alone at a linen-swathed table.

A monumental arrangement of blue hydrangeas and delphiniums had obscured him before, and at the sight of Wil, he got abruptly to his feet.

"I'll go," he said, his face flushed and unhappy.

"No," Wil said, summoning the impervious air of self-containment that was her birthright by way of John Shepherd, and which she'd never needed to employ with Ed before coming to the Grange, "I will. It's your house."

"I don't want to lie to you," Ed blurted out. She could see him struggling, warring with himself over some secret he wouldn't share with her.

It made Wil angry, because he wouldn't bare his soul. It made her weak, because she wanted to help him anyhow. Stupid boy. Stupid, wealthy, bewildering boy. She wanted to step forward and push back that one lock of hair that *would* fall over his forehead when he was meant to keep himself tidy. She wanted to straighten his collar and erase the agonized expression from his face, whether she did it with a word or her fingertips or her lips.

Wil froze. She'd never thought such a thing about Edison before, and it sent a frisson of prickling, electric nerves running from the crown of her head to the soles of her feet. They were always easy together—a thing she took for granted, like breathing or gravity. She mustn't think of him so. It would ruin what lay between them, if that hadn't been ruined already.

Ruthlessly Wil discarded the idle thought and met Ed's eyes, nothing betraying her inner turmoil.

"Then don't," she told him.

"I won't," he said, taking a step forward. "I swear it. Wil, when I spoke to you so harshly, I . . . I thought you were someone else. It's true I don't want you at the Grange, but not for my own sake—for yours. I want better for you than to wait on my family. But if this is what you've chosen, I won't try to push you out."

"Other people wait on your family." Wil could feel herself growing more austere by the moment. "I don't think myself any more deserving of life's benefits than them, or of them as a fraction beneath me because they make their living in service. So there's no call to speak of better or worse."

Edison scuffed a foot against the immaculately kept grass, his obvious misery growing acute. "That's not what I meant at all, Wil, and you know it. Don't purposefully misunderstand me. *Please.*"

"I don't know what to do with you," Wil admitted, letting her reserve slip a little. "Something is eating away at you, Ed. You're being incomprehensible. And you ought to know by now that I hate anything I can't get my head around, whether it's a line to be translated or a geometry problem or a friend who won't tell me his troubles."

Ed ran a hand through his hair in frustration, rendering it more disheveled than ever. The light gleamed on his spectacles, and Wil was struck all over again by how fiercely she liked him. She had since the first day she laid eyes on him in the mill wood, when they were two lonely children in search of a kindred spirit.

"It isn't that I don't trust you," Edison said. "I'd trust you with my life. It's just . . . it's not trusting myself that's the problem. There are some things about me—about who I've been and who I am—that I don't even like to *think* of, let alone share. It takes courage to be entirely honest, and I've never been very brave."

He looked so anxious and unhappy that Wil couldn't bear it anymore. She went to him, picking her way between immaculately set tables until they stood just inches from each other. Reaching up, Wil fitted one hand to the line of his jaw and brushed her thumb across his cheek.

"Foolish boy," she said. "You don't have to be brave with me. I've always taken you just as you are. Nothing's ever going to change that, unless you set out to do it on purpose."

Ed covered her hand with his own, and she could feel a slight tremor running through his fingers. His gaze, locked on Wil's, was unreadable, and something warm and wanting and unfamiliar pooled within her. It caught her, once again, by surprise, and she couldn't be sure what she might have done had Edison not pulled away. He returned to the table he'd been sitting at, and Wil heard him let out a short, sharp breath as he went.

"What are you doing out here, anyhow?" she asked, to cover her discomfort and to attempt a return to normalcy between them.

Ed sat once more and gestured to a plate in front of him. "Eating cheese biscuits and feeling sorry for myself. Would you care to join me? I've heard there's some lord's son or other who's been a boor to you recently—surely that's grounds enough for self-pity and a biscuit."

His voice, as he spoke, was light and mocking—Wil could feel in the air how desperately hard they were both trying to restore things to rights. To pretend they were still as they had been, before Jenny Bright's demise had brought Wil to the Grange.

"Unfortunately," Wil said, matching his flippancy, "I have *actual* work that needs doing. We can't all sit about idle in the middle of an afternoon."

With a wave, she began to make her way back to the house, but she couldn't resist a surreptitious glance over one shoulder.

Edison was still sitting alone, watching her go, and she couldn't be sure if the worry in his eyes was on account of her or Wither Grange, its imposing bulk looming skyward as she stepped into its shadow.

CHAPTER EIGHT

EDISON

E dison's ghost was out of sorts.

People had been arriving at the Grange all day, driving out in their own motorcars or being run up from the station by Bede in one of the Summerfields'. There had been glad voices ringing through the corridors, doors opening and shutting, lilting and irrepressible ragtime standards filtering from the music room, wafts of strange perfume in the air. The whole thing felt to Ed like a very congenial and well-heeled invasion. But then he'd never been especially fond of company, and he found himself actually sympathizing with the nursery wing's chaotic spirit.

At present the thing that haunted him was murmuring eerily in the vicinity of the fireplace, which was surrounded by a hovering cloud of soot. Ed didn't mind, so long as it kept clear of his evening clothes—there'd be the devil to pay if he went downstairs with them all over ashes.

The dinner gong had only just sounded, but he was already dressed. As he wasn't much use welcoming company and had received an impression from both his mother and Kitty that they were afraid of him causing some sort of scene, Ed had thought it wisest to stay in his rooms rather than join the fray downstairs. Peter, by contrast, would never have kept out of sight at the beginning of a party—he'd loved the game of social favors and had made it his business to ensure everyone who mattered thought well of him.

Perhaps that was why the ghost seemed so disgruntled now, Ed thought as he straightened his tie before the bathroom mirror. Perpetual fog clouded the glass, as if someone had been filling the bath with very hot water. Ed could hardly make himself out but assumed he was presentable, which was about all anyone expected of him anyhow.

At the moment the halls were quiet. The guests had retired to their designated rooms to gossip and dress and compare this visit with their last. Ed was struck by the sudden thought that he'd been presented with a golden opportunity to slip downstairs and into his grandfather's secret library, where he could pocket a book to hide beneath the table at dinner. Certainly Lord Summerfield would be livid if he knew his son was scheming to be antisocial, but Edison had coaxed the seating arrangement out of Mrs. Forster that afternoon. He knew he'd be between the Baroness de Vouche and Mrs. Carlisle, both of whom were nearly ninety and apt to keep up a loud and interminably dull conversation about their physical ailments while ignoring Ed completely.

It would not be his first dinner seated between the two of them— either his mother and Kitty influenced every table arrangement in the county, or the worthies of the surrounding countryside *all* agreed that this was the setting in which Ed had the least potential to cause embarrassment.

So. A book.

A little cheered by the prospect, and a great deal more cheered by the tentative peace he'd arrived at with Wil, Ed emerged from the nursery wing. Cautiously he scanned the halls, but the way was clear.

With a lighter step than usual, Edison hurried down the stairs and the crimson-carpeted central hallway. At the Grange's far end, the laboratory stood waiting for him, half the tables sporting gaps where Ed had pilfered scientific instruments in order to cover for Wil. The change did the room no favors—with its odd collection intact, it had seemed like a place caught in time. But with instruments missing, it seemed more like a forgotten collection of rubbish than ever. A room with no purpose and no function.

Beyond the tables, a bank of long windows looked out to the back lawn. The light was low and golden, the sun nearly eaten up by the mill wood that it sank behind. Smaller lights glimmered from the marquee, though dinner would be indoors tonight. Afterward, according to a schedule Kitty had pressed upon Ed, the party would move out to her fairy wood for dessert and dancing.

A prospect which he did not relish.

Pressing the latch that revealed the secret library, Ed stepped inside and pulled the paneled wall shut. In a few places, knotholes had been bored out of the shelf that hid the nook from the rest of the house, and Ed could catch glimpses of the laboratory through them, though they remained effectively hidden, flanked by dusty books on the exterior shelf. It occurred to him sometimes that his grandfather might not have been the nicest sort of man, to keep a secret room from which he could spy on others. But Edison had never known him, and Lord Summerfield rarely spoke of the dead.

In the last light that barely sifted down from the library nook's high window, Ed squinted at the collection of books he'd amassed. All of Conan Doyle and Poe. Shelf after shelf of old and tattered penny dreadfuls, discovered in boxes in the Grange's attic. Shakespeare. Austen. Dante. Sophocles. Ovid. After lengthy consideration, he pulled a much-read copy of *Gulliver's Travels* from the shelf and pocketed it.

But with his hand on the latch to exit the hidden library, Edison stopped and listened. A small, muffled sound from beyond had caught his attention, and he shifted his weight until he could see through one of the library's spyholes.

Lord Summerfield and Abigail, the Grange's head housemaid, had just stepped into the laboratory. The noise Edison had heard was that of the door shutting behind them. Had they moved toward the window, he wouldn't have been able to catch sight of them, but they stayed near the door, rendered invisible to anyone passing through the garden by the shadows along the wall. Ed, however, could both see and hear them well enough.

Lord Summerfield cast a disparaging look around the room, taking in the cluttered tables and scattered instruments.

"What is it about this room that always gives me the creeping horrors?" Edison's father said in his dry, commanding voice. "Somehow it looks worse than usual tonight. Particularly when the house is full of company. Abigail, we've had enough of this claptrap—see to it that it's all cleared out by tomorrow."

"Yes, sir," Abigail answered obediently.

"And about that other errand," Lord Summerfield added. "I wanted to tell you that there's no point going out tonight. It can just as well wait till tomorrow. If there are any complaints, say you were following my direct instructions. I'll give you what you need now, though."

"Yes, sir," Abigail repeated.

Striding over to the nearest table, Lord Summerfield took a checkbook and pen from the inner pocket of his dinner jacket. After scrawling out a check, he tore it loose, then handed it to Abigail along with a separate handful of banknotes, which he withdrew from a pocket as well.

"You know, when I first offered payment for this, I expected you to refuse." Lord Summerfield's words were an icy reproach. "I expected you'd be happy enough to undertake an additional service to the family,

87

given how we had sheltered you as a girl. But I suppose I shouldn't have thought to find loyalty when I stooped so low."

Abigail made no reply, only held out her hand for the check and the money, which she tucked into her apron as Lord Summerfield left the room. An air of satisfaction suffused her, and Ed watched until she'd left too.

Only once they had gone did he drop down into the single moth-eaten armchair that fit within the hidden library. Around him the low light faded into gloom.

Try though Edison might, he could think of no good reason for his father to be handing money to Abigail. Mrs. Forster oversaw everything to do with the maids, from their hiring to their duties to their pay. There had only ever been one other occasion on which Lord Summerfield paid off a maid directly, as far as Ed knew. For the most part, he tried not to think of it—Ed himself had been a child of seven at the time and had come across his brother Peter and a housemaid at the end of a corridor, locked in what Lady Summerfield would have languidly called a *compromising position*. Not knowing what to think of it, Ed had mentioned what he'd seen to both Shepherd and his nursemaid, then finally his mother.

The last proved both his undoing *and* that of the unfortunate maid, who had come to the Grange only three months back. After supper in the nursery, Ed had been called down to Lord Summerfield's office—an unprecedented turn of events. There he'd found his father and Peter, as well as the housemaid. Lord Summerfield provided the maid with a check, just as he'd done for Abigail, and informed her that her services were no longer required.

Edison could still remember the look on the girl's face. A potent combination of shame and shock, regret and relief, all with an under-current of despairing pride. Peter, by contrast, smirked throughout the entire interview, seeming to find the situation entertaining rather than a cause for consternation.

After the girl was dismissed, Lord Summerfield had pulled Edison aside. He lectured his youngest child sternly about differences in status— how the Summerfields were meant for a certain station in life and could not stoop below it, no matter who attempted to seize their attention and use their wealth and position to elevate themselves.

Peter received no such lecture. He sat near the hearth, nursing a glass of whiskey and grinning into the fire. Only Ed had found it impossible to keep his gaze from wandering to the drive, where the dismissed housemaid was retreating—a shadowy figure in a world newly touched by frost. When she'd finally disappeared into the darkness, it had hurt Ed in a way he couldn't quantify then. But even as a child, he'd known something he disagreed with had happened. That the Summerfields had damaged the girl in some way while remaining unscathed themselves. Perhaps that was the difference in station his father spoke of, Ed realized at the time—that there were those who could inflict harm with a wave of the hand while never suffering it themselves, and others who were rendered vulnerable.

A day later, he met a girl called Wilhelmina Price. She had seemed entirely beyond the new tensions he was only dimly becoming aware of—so bright and eager that surely she must exist outside the capacity to harm or be harmed. She'd been playing in the mill wood alone, not digging for treasure but burying it herself.

"In case something awful ever happens and we need it," she'd said solemnly, as she handed Ed a leather pouch stuffed with small coins from her money jar at home. She'd welcomed Edison so wholly and warmheartedly when he stumbled upon her play that he opened to her like a plant to sunlight. Whatever he'd said of his frustrations as he dug, and of the interminable nature of life at the Grange, she'd taken in stride. When he mentioned the last, Wil, in her torn and ruined pinafore, with dirt smeared across her face and a trowel in one hand, reached out to him with the other.

"Come and see me again," she'd told him staunchly. "It'll give you something to look forward to, and I'd like it very much. I think you're nice, Edison Summerfield. I think you're the nicest boy I've ever met."

He didn't think she was right. Since the nameless housemaid's dismissal, he'd felt horribly guilty over his part in it, losing both sleep and appetite over what he'd unwittingly done. But when Wil glanced over at him with her knowing gray eyes and spoke those words, his guilt gave way to a sense of possibility. If she said he was nice, it must mean he at least had the potential to be. Because Ed was sure from the very beginning that when Wil looked at him like that, she was speaking the truth.

It was nearly dark in the library nook now, and Ed's thoughts of the housemaid he'd seen dismissed and his own Wil were all tangled up together. He'd sworn to himself as a child that he'd never use his station to damage her, but rather to help and shelter her if she ever needed it.

Yet here she was at the Grange while his father repeated history.

When Ed emerged from the hidden library, the light in the laboratory came as a surprise. Sun still filtered through the mill wood, gilding every surface in the room, while the library itself had been cast into shadow. Outside the laboratory, in the crimson-carpeted hall, a dim echo of voices was beginning to drift from upstairs and from the music room and sitting room down the corridor. Ed's stomach twisted as a figure appeared at the head of the hallway, carrying a stack of wooden crates and casting a furtive glance over her shoulder as she went.

"Here, let me help," he called out as he hurried to meet Wil.

She shot him a grateful look as he took most of the crates from her. "Ed, you're a lifesaver. Abigail said your father wants the laboratory cleaned out and that he wants it done now, but that I'd better hurry because he wouldn't like it if anyone saw me wandering the halls like this either."

Ed let out a sound of annoyance and confirmation. Lord Summerfield liked to give the impression that his household ran smoothly at all times, and a maid out of place minutes before dinner was not in keeping with his idea of a perfectly run estate. Securing the crates between one hand and his chin, Ed managed to get the door to the laboratory open once more, and he ushered Wil inside before shutting them in together.

The two of them set down their crates and straightened up, and the pang within Ed intensified at the sight of Wil, flushed and breathless in her demure uniform. She looked tired, and a sudden image rushed into his mind unbidden.

Lord Summerfield, his father, paying Wil off before dismissing her, because she was the one who'd become collateral damage to his family's reputation and lifestyle.

A rush of unreasoning, reckless anger surged through Ed, and he balled his hands into fists at his sides, counting back from ten as he let out a slow breath. Wil herself was already looking over the tables laden with instruments, as the pointed interest he knew so well rekindled in her eyes.

"I haven't been in here yet," she confessed. "Ed, these are *fascinating*. Is this where you got the ones upstairs? Are you going in for natural science now? I thought it was all books and languages and history for you."

She turned to him, her face warm and trusting—every inch the Wil he'd learned by heart. He'd given her so many reasons to hold back over the course of their friendship, particularly since she'd come to the Grange. Yet here she stood, and she wanted to hear from him. Wanted to know him.

It was more, Ed thought, than he'd ever deserved.

"Wil," he said with infinite care. "If I took you up to Wynkirk tomorrow on my bicycle, and stood reference for you at some of the shops, would you consider giving all this up and taking a job there? I swear to you—swear it on anything: the Bible, my own name, Peter's grave, even—that it's not because I want to see less of you."

She stood silently for a moment, a slight frown creasing her forehead. The deadening, flattening effect of the maid's uniform had been erased by the glory of dying light spilling through the windows, the richness of it rendering Wil once again as Ed always saw her—golden, surrounded by a glow that emanated outward from her peerless mind and soul.

"I can't," Wil said at last, and there was a finality to the words Ed recognized. He knew it meant she'd hear no more arguments on the subject and that he would respect her wishes. He'd lost this particular battle, which for her sake he'd so badly wanted to win.

"I know you think you have my best interests at heart," Wil went on—*More than you know*, Edison thought—"but I'm not here just for me. I haven't been entirely honest with you about my reasons for coming to the Grange, but if I was, you'd understand."

"Then tell me," Ed answered, fighting to keep from giving away how desperately he hated having her hide things from him. "Tell me your whole truth."

Wil fixed her eyes on his, and with that golden aura about her, he could hardly meet her gaze. "Like you tell me yours?"

Shame flooded Ed, and he looked away. But Wil was better than him and braver, and despite the barb she'd fired, she hadn't finished speaking.

"I didn't want to hurt you, or worry you in any way," she said quietly. "But I heard from someone who believes my mother's death and Jenny Bright's weren't accidents or coincidence. She thinks they were killed. And I spoke with Jenny, or she spoke through me—it doesn't really matter how. She had only one word to say, and she was furious about it. It was '*Surgite*,' Ed. She might as well have pointed at the Grange.

92

"So I'm not here for me. I'm here for Mabel Price and Jenny Bright, and I don't mean to leave until I find out who killed them and see justice done. I can't turn aside, not even for you."

Edison went hot and cold. The idea of the Grange being connected to the death of Wil's mother and Jenny beyond the matter of their employment there appalled him. And the thought of Wil in the house with the express intent of unearthing any secrets kept by the family and staff—it might not have been so unsettling if Ed knew her less. But he did know her—knew full well that she was methodical and brilliant and relentless in her own unassuming way. If Wil had set her mind upon learning the Grange's hidden truths, then a reckoning would come as old sins were dragged to light.

Ed could hardly bear how much he loved her. No one else would set themselves such a task, or even consider that they might succeed at it. But Wil, he was sure, was about to shake the Grange to its ancient foundations.

Let her, he thought fiercely as he stood looking at her—an ordinary girl in a faded uniform, but to him, touched by the sublime. *Let her drag us all to hell if she wishes. Perhaps it's what we deserve.*

A small whine of hinges kept him from making any reply.

"Master Edison," Abigail said from the doorway. "They've sent me to find you and to say you're late for dinner."

93

CHAPTER NINE

WIL

Wil sat up at the kitchen table in the rowhouse where she lived with her grandfather, studying by lamplight and trying not to fall asleep.

Every time she drifted off, she could feel herself being pulled toward the halfway realm, and Wil didn't want the mental disturbance of another encounter with her sorrowful mother or wrathful Jenny Bright. In spite of everything, she meant to keep up with her books—doing so had started as a game with Edison when they were younger, him bringing home a term's worth of work and her outpacing him within a matter of weeks. Then it had become something more serious for Wil.

When Ed had been twelve, Lady Summerfield had prevailed upon several of his school acquaintances to visit the Grange for a week over summer holidays. At a loss as to what to do with them, Edison had introduced his schoolfellows to Wil. Wil had made Ed promise to lie about who she was, knowing the truth of the matter would only cause trouble for them both, so they'd claimed she was a distant Summerfield cousin and had an astonishingly miserable picnic in the woods with Edison's peers. Ed's dislike of them was palpable and Wil's disdain immediate—the boys were snobbish and mean-spirited, needling Wil for her sex at one moment and making inappropriate advances the next. When Ed snapped at them, they jeered. When Wil met their ill manners with frigid politeness, they attempted to break her reserve.

She was unbreakable.

But the afternoon yielded unexpected fruit—none of Ed's classmates had questioned the story Wil had concocted of herself as a Summerfield scion. And they'd spent a great deal of time bemoaning the rigors of their education and the unnecessary nature of it.

It had been all too easy for Wil to contrive a way to capitalize on their insipid credulity, as well as their desire to get out of the work set before them. Though Edison swore to Wil his schoolfellows would never be invited back to Thrush's Green, he'd been reluctant to take advantage of them at first. Wil, as always, wore him down in the end—for four years, she'd been exacting a slow and lucrative revenge on Ed's fellows by impersonating yet another Summerfield cousin and hiring out her intellect. She'd amassed a tidy nest egg, meant to aid in her plans to attend some manner of college herself, and had every intention of pulling the rug out from under Edison's classmates at the last moment—during their final year at school, she'd refuse to work on their behalf, instead writing to the headmaster and revealing that they'd cheated and lied for years.

It was, Wil thought, only justice. A boy who would cheat and lie and take advantage of others became a man who would do the same, and to far more devastating effect. Better that they learn a hard lesson at her hands and be given an opportunity to reform.

But the vengeance she'd chosen required a great deal of study, and now, try as she might, the figures on the page of the geometry book propped up before her swam and blurred, and her head nodded.

A wave of borrowed fear and anger. The sensation of beginning to fall backward through the gap between realms while eager hands reached for her from the other side.

With a jolt, Wil came fully awake. John Shepherd stood in the kitchen doorway, looking as patrician and composed as ever, though Wil thought she could see a slight hint of disapproval or concern in the set of his mouth.

"You ought to be in bed," John said evenly. "If you mean to stay at the Grange, you won't be able to keep studying in addition to minding the house. You'll have to choose between them."

He nodded toward her books and the uncharacteristically untidy kitchen as he spoke. Wil had meant to get to the dishes after she finished with her studying, but even the idea of them seemed impossibly daunting now. Still, she had her pride.

Wil squinted up at John as the lamplight cast strange shadows across his face.

"Oh, I don't know," she said. "I think I'm strong enough to burn the wick at both ends for a little while."

"And how long is *a little while?*" John asked, seating himself across from Wil and reaching for a plate of bread and butter she'd set out. "I should like to know how long my granddaughter intends to keep this foolishness up and exactly what she thinks she's doing. You know, I've always admired your resolution to learn and make something better of yourself. It's why I've never pushed you to be in society more or to make the sort of connections that might lead to a husband and family in time. If I'd known you were only going to throw yourself away in service, I'd have married you off at fifteen."

Perhaps fatigue had shortened her temper, but Wil, often subjected to her grandfather's lofty disdain, found she could no longer abide it.

"You've never considered your own position to be a waste," she said, keeping her own voice flat. "And you've certainly never bothered to say that you think well of my studying before. Besides, my mother was a housemaid. Why shouldn't I follow in her footsteps?"

John's patrician face darkened. "I will lie dead before I see you end up like your mother."

"She was afraid of you," Wil went on. "They were both afraid of you, and you were cruel to them. My mother and Jenny Bright, I mean. I've been told you were on bad terms with them both just before they died. And now you've begun to work on Abigail, too."

"Nothing spreads faster than gossip and lies," John answered acerbically.

"Is it gossip and lies?" Wil pressed. "Or is there some bone of contention between you and the housemaids at Wither Grange? As I'm one myself, I feel I ought to know."

John took a meditative bite of bread and butter, chewed with his usual care and efficiency, and wiped his mouth on a napkin. Only once he had done so did he speak again, his words filled with calm assurance.

"You won't last at the Grange. Your mother and Jenny Bright knew of no way to support themselves besides the uniform, but they were grossly unsuited to the position, as is Abigail. You're equally unfit for it, in your own way. Before long it will bore you like all the rest of Thrush's Green does, and you'll search for opportunities elsewhere. Rightly so—you've made too much of yourself for service, and for a place like this."

Wil hated the way he made her sound. Prideful and bent on nothing besides her own ambitions. She didn't see herself that way at all, but hearing John describe her so made her wonder. Was she simply unaware of her own conceit? Was she as he said?

"What is it that rendered Mama and Jenny and Abigail so unsuitable to you?" she shot back. It seemed to Wil that she was pushing into potentially dangerous and uncharted territory—she and John had never truly fought before, as she'd given way over everything but

Edison, and in that one regard he had not insisted on mastery. "Was it their sex? Their inferior position in the household? I would have thought your own daughter, at least, might have gained your approval and support. But perhaps if I've made too much of myself for service, you've made yourself too much *because* of it. Perhaps you enjoy being able to order and direct those beneath you, and if they aren't sufficiently subservient, you view it as an insurmountable shortcoming."

With the first flash of unchecked anger Wil could ever recall seeing from him, John pushed back his chair with a clatter and got to his feet.

"When it comes to the Grange," he said fiercely, "I expect to be obeyed. Particularly by you, Wilhelmina Price. I have clothed and fed and sheltered you—a scrap of loyalty seems a small price to pay in exchange for such care. If I give you an order in regard to that house, you will do as you're told. If I tell you the time has come for you to leave, then you will walk out the door and never look back."

Wil could feel stubbornness transfiguring her, even as a hint of Jenny Bright's secondhand fear sparked in the pit of her stomach.

"And if I don't?" she asked, equally indomitable. "What then, Grandfather? What do you do with a housemaid who won't obey?"

A muscle worked in John's jaw, and his gaze was flint.

"If you wish to avoid coming to harm, you will do as you're told."

Every word came out crystalline and sharp, and the moment he'd finished speaking John left the room. Wil sat in her place and listened to his measured tread on the stairs, now crossing the floor above her.

Her grandfather was the sort of person who did not waste words and who disapproved of frivolity or deception. When he said a thing, Wil believed him implicitly. And the slow, dull fear that churned through her veins was no longer a castoff from some fretful ghost.

It was entirely her own.

* * *

98

"Gently!" Lady Summerfield snapped.

Wil's attention jerked back to the task at hand. She and Abigail were serving tea in the garden. The mixed borders were a riot of blooms, all pinks and blues and purples, with silvery-green foliage as a backdrop. Wil had heard Lady Summerfield mildly accepting praise for the gardens with a look of satisfaction, which struck her as absurd. Edison's mother was not the sort to get her hands dirty. Or, Wil thought now she'd seen more of the woman, the sort to have any part in the planning at all. It was entirely left to the capable head gardener, Henry Ellicott, and if anyone ought to be praised, it was him. Lady Summerfield had made no mention of the man, though, receiving the compliments as her due.

But Wil deserved the reprimand. She'd been preoccupied all morning, muddled by too little sleep and the dreadful, sinking feeling John's threat had set within her. It had made her clumsy and distant, and she'd set a tea tray down too forcefully, sloshing a little from the pot and onto a stack of folded linen napkins.

"My apologies, ma'am," Wil murmured politely, removing the soiled napkins and drying the teapot so that it gleamed pristine and silver once more. "It won't happen again."

Moving away, Wil kept her attention on the task at hand—on weaving among the round tables dotting the garden, the elegant figures seated around them like flowers themselves, dressed in bright silks and crepe fabrics or crisp white suits. It felt disorientingly like being in another version of the halfway realm—as if she'd come to yet another place whose inhabitants were different creatures from her entirely, and who she could never truly meet with on friendly or comfortable terms.

A riot of laughter rose from one of the tables, and Wil glanced over involuntarily. Kitty sat there, ringed by half a dozen terribly fashionable girls, their hair all cut short, their teeth gleaming, their eyes bright. A small, milling crowd of young men in linen suits and straw Panama hats played court, vying to fetch Kitty and her companions anything they needed, or to be the one whose jokes elicited a peal of good humor.

At least they were making life easier, Wil thought grimly, by doing a little of the serving work in their attempts to be noticed.

As Wil thought it, Kitty glanced up. Her gaze locked on Wil's, and for a moment the two girls fell motionless. Something dark and brooding flashed across Kitty's face, at odds with the levity of her surroundings. But quick as it came, it was gone. Kitty tossed her head and laughed merrily, turning back to her attendants as if Wil did not exist, or was no more than a biting insect that irritated her with its passing.

Letting out a sigh, Wil carried on.

Near the house, a smaller serving tent had been erected. Abigail stood beneath its shade, carefully organizing trays for each table.

"Wil, you've been a miracle, arriving and pitching in when you did," Abigail said without looking up. "But you've got to be more careful when we serve—I've seen the Summerfields let someone go for less than clumsiness. And I'd be at my wit's end if they got rid of you now; truly I would."

Wil frowned. If she herself was tired after a week of unrelenting preparations, Abigail looked exhausted. There were dark shadows beneath the housemaid's eyes, and perpetual worried lines at the corners of her mouth. But when she took up two serving trays and headed out to the garden revelers, her tread was light, her smile reserved but genuine. She practically floated among the tables—an elegant servant for an elegant setting. Wil knew she could never match that studied poise. The best she could hope for in her present role was adequacy, which irked her. She was used to finding herself competent and seldom had to struggle.

Taking up another tray, she turned impatiently, only to clip something solid with her elbow and upset the platter of sandwiches onto the lawn. Dropping to her knees with a breathless curse and a hot wave of anger directed only toward herself, Wil began clearing away the mess. But everything in her went tense as she glanced up and found Lord Summerfield scowling down at her. It was him she'd bumped into, and Wil thanked her stars that his suit was still spotless, rather than a mess of egg salad and parsley.

"That's twice you've embarrassed yourself now," Lord Summerfield said, not bothering to lower his voice. "And when you embarrass yourself in that uniform, it reflects badly on me as well. If you can't find a way of doing your job with more grace, you'll find yourself no longer employed, no matter whose granddaughter you are."

Wil clenched her jaw, the anger she'd felt swiftly redirecting toward the towering man standing over her.

"Get up." Lord Summerfield's voice dripped with disdain. "Abigail will deal with this. I want you indoors and out of sight for the rest of the day."

Materializing as if by magic, Abigail held out a hand and helped Wil to her feet.

"Don't worry about it," she said reassuringly. Lord Summerfield had already strode off, but a few of the guests were stealing covert looks at Wil and hiding mocking smiles. "Most of the work's done out here already; Jack and I will manage the rest. There's still the laboratory to be dealt with too, and we can only touch it while everyone's otherwise occupied. Try your hand at that, and maybe being out from under watching eyes for a while will help you collect yourself a bit."

Wil nodded. "Abigail, I'm sorry. I'm not trying to make life harder for you."

Abigail smiled, an open, confiding expression entirely different than the one she wore while serving. "I've already said—you just being here makes my life easier, so do your best to stay, won't you?"

The sunlit laboratory and a task that required more of diligence and less of docility and proper bearing *did* calm Wil. It seemed strange that someone new could grasp an essential part of her nature after only a few days' acquaintance. She'd spent so much of her life cut off from the society of Thrush's Green by virtue of her uncanny abilities that she looked for understanding in no one but Edison. Finding it in Abigail was odd and a little discomfiting—Wil had grown used to being an island unto herself while Ed was away at school, her year shot through by incandescent bright patches when he came home and she was granted the brief sweetness of sympathetic companionship.

The methodical rhythm of dusting and carefully packing up instruments, and the interest of being able to look them over and guess at their function, pushed Wil into a place of peace. But she realized she'd grown too content, and let her guard down too much, when the sensation of falling backward gripped her without warning and the laboratory lost its color.

Not now, she thought grimly, but it was too late.

Around her everything faded, ornate paper peeling from the walls, the laboratory's cobweb-strewn instruments vanishing. The room was empty save for a foggy cluster of spirits gathered around the wide windows that overlooked the lawn. The windows themselves had shattered, leaving a windy gap edged with thorns of glass. Wil's lips parted as she looked past the cloud of dead souls, though, because beyond them lay the garden party, still carrying on in blazing color, so bright it hurt her eyes to look straight at it.

She'd never seen such a thing before—never known a place where something occurring in the land of the living had any sort of foothold in the realm of the dead. The searing realness of it drew her forward into the cold, damp ranks of the spirits themselves. The swirl of half-formed limbs and staring eyes enveloped her, but she could still see that tantalizing prospect in the garden beyond them, still feel herself being drawn toward the semblance of life it offered.

Ice bit at Wil's arms as one of the spirits gripped her. Inexorably it pushed and chivvied her backward, away from the window. Another soul trailed mournfully in its wake, and Wil knew from the quality of the anger radiating from the spirit who held her and the sorrow from its follower that Jenny Bright and her mother were still very much present in this hinterland.

"Let me go," Wil said petulantly. "I want to look."

In answer, Jenny Bright shoved her hard, a ripple of frigid cold running through Wil at the contact. Behind her, she could feel the magnetic gap between realms—a fissure that Jenny was pushing her toward, adamant on crossing to the world of the living. Unwilling to risk an involuntary possession or a new fear to distract her, Wil spun and darted through the gap before Jenny could lay hold of her and follow.

Back in the laboratory, all was as it had been. But Wil frowned as she walked to the window and looked out at the lawn with its butterfly-like crowd of revelers. Most of life was heightened when she returned to it from the halfway realm. Not so the Grange's glittering guests. Though the world around them shone with added brilliance, they'd lost a bit of their color. It hadn't drained away entirely, but they were muted somehow, less giddy and careless than they'd seemed in the halfway realm. As if, in some way, death already had a finger upon each of them.

That night, Wil was needed to serve at dinner. Several more guests had arrived during the afternoon—a few debonair stragglers from Kitty's set, as well as the Osbournes, old friends of the family who came with a nursemaid and three children in tow. The Grange was well and truly full now, and the kitchen seemed in utter chaos. Mrs. Ellicott called out orders, and Daphne stood at the center of it all, an island of serenity as she carefully assembled individual trifles in cut glass bowls.

There were smells of glazed duck and lobster croquettes and delicately roasted vegetables and strawberries drowning in sweet cream.

"Just keep your head down and your elbows in, and no one will pay you any mind," Abigail told Wil as they stood on the landing, in yet another gap between two realms. "They help themselves, so all you've got to do is lay out and clear places and hold platters. Oh, and keep your feet under you. Be sure you stand to the left of whomever you're serving, and don't speak unless spoken to. You're to look after ten seats, from Master Edison to the foot of the table. Watch me, and you'll do fine."

Abigail seemed anxious, and Wil realized any mishaps on her part would reflect not on Lord Summerfield, as he'd claimed, but on Abigail herself as Wil's direct superior.

"I'll be perfect, I promise," she said staunchly. And surely she could be, if she really applied herself to it—it couldn't be possible that she was able to tear through Edison's schoolbooks, yet fail at this.

Ahead of them, Jack Hoult nodded, then drifted through the door. Beyond it lay a sparkling world of candlelight and conversation, the table laden with flowers and fine china and glinting silver, each thing in its proper place, not a napkin or a dessert spoon out of order. John Shepherd already stood to one side of the room, prepared to be called upon, directing every movement with a nod or a gesture. Silently Jack, Abigail, and Wil took their places before him as he dished out soup from a vast tureen. The first course was bouillon, and they'd be setting out bowls one at a time. Wil didn't envy Jack, who had the job of serving the entire upper half of the table while she and Abigail divided the lower half between them. But he seemed unbothered at the prospect, taking the first serving of clear soup to Lord Summerfield with aplomb.

Abigail went next, and then Wil stood before her grandfather, who neither spoke nor met her eyes. It was as if they'd never fought, nor even been introduced before this moment. Taking the warm bowl, Wil did her best to glide as she brought it over to Edison. At the sight of the book discreetly tucked away on his lap, she fought back a smile, though her heart twisted as she made out the title—*The Swiss Family Robinson.* Ed only went back to his old childhood adventure stories when he felt entirely off-balance and wanted the reassurance of something familiar.

All went well for a short while. Wil managed to serve her places without incident and was nearly back to the rest of the servants waiting behind the head of the table when Lord Summerfield's voice rose above the polite chatter.

"Am I . . . no longer master of my own household?" he asked, sounding bemused. He had an effortless capacity to make himself heard without evidencing any sort of strain, and around the table, silence fell. "I believe, Shepherd, that I ordered your granddaughter to stay of sight for the rest of the day, after she made a spectacle of herself this afternoon. Are my orders no longer to be followed?"

Wil had wondered at Lord Summerfield's willingness to speak to her so forcefully before his guests earlier. It seemed a direct contradiction to what Edison had said—that his father liked to give the impression of a perfectly run household. But as she raised her eyes and looked at the dinner guests around the table, Wil realized that she herself had already undermined that impression of perfection through her mishaps, and that in response, Lord Summerfield was proving himself the unquestionable master of Wither Grange. Besides which, she could see from the amused smiles hidden behind gloved hands or napkins that he was providing an entertainment of sorts for those present.

An entertainment at her expense.

Wil's face flamed with humiliation and anger.

"I'm terribly sorry, sir," John began, perfect sincerity behind the words. "I shall—"

A voice from near the foot of the table cut him off.

"Would you prefer that I wait on our guests myself, Father?" Edison was on his feet, the book he'd kept hidden held, forgotten, in one hand. "We're obviously short-staffed, and the girl's doing a credible job. I see no reason to dismiss her, unless you wish to punish the rest of the staff and ensure we all have a cold meal. I, for one, would prefer to eat Mrs. Ellicott's excellent duck à l'orange as it's meant to be eaten, even if it comes at the cost of setting aside one of your less reasonable orders."

He spoke sardonically, leveraging the wicked dry wit Wil had only ever heard him use once before, on that momentous picnic with Ed's odious schoolfellows. It was brazen and foolish of him to behave so now, and Wil dared not meet Edison's eyes, because she could *feel* the frustration sparking off him, electric and intoxicating.

"Sit down," Lord Summerfield barked. "I will not be spoken to in such a fashion."

"No," Edison said, a mocking note in his voice as he started around the table. "As I've said, I'll serve the next course myself if you send the girl out of the room. I've watched the staff be run ragged over the past week, and I won't see them inconvenienced still more simply to satisfy one of your whims. Shepherd, it's lobster croquettes and perch stewed with wine, yes? I'll go fetch it from Mrs. Ellicott—I wanted to tell her the bouillon was especially good anyhow."

Lord Summerfield graced the guests around the table with a dangerous smile. "I'd ask you to proceed with your meal. My son and I need a word."

A low, acutely uncomfortable murmuring rose up around the table as Edison stalked to Lord Summerfield's place.

"Yes, Father?" he said, every syllable rife with rebellion.

Wil was near enough that she could overhear every word they spoke, her feet rooted to the spot. She could not be certain if it would make things worse or better for her to retreat.

"You will go to your rooms," Lord Summerfield said with menacing calm, "and you will not come down until I send for you."

"I won't," Edison answered evenly. "You may find it easy to dismiss others, and I might once have allowed you to do it to me, but I assure you, it will never happen again. If you wish me to leave this room, you'll have to order Shepherd and Jack to drag me out or prevail upon some of our fine guests to do it for you. But I don't think you're willing to take our little disagreement that far. So what I will do is go back to my place, and the staff will continue to serve our dinner just as they've been doing, and we will all pretend that this never happened. Because isn't that what our family does best?"

Without another word, Ed returned to his seat. Lord Summerfield waved a hand to Wil, and she too resumed her station. Only when she laid out the next course did Edison look up, catching her with the full force of his gaze.

"Thank you, Wil," he said quietly.

"You're welcome," she murmured back, but her heart was a caged bird sorrowing within her. She'd thought all this time that Ed's resistance to having her in the house was based on embarrassment or shame or frustration, but she'd seen something entirely different in his eyes.

It hurt him for her to be there. She cut him to the quick with her presence, and for all the years she'd known him, Wil had only ever sought to make things gentler and easier for Edison. *Why* her being at the Grange hurt him so, she couldn't comprehend, and she'd have given anything to leave and mend that wound.

But she couldn't. Not if it meant turning away from the mournful dead, who had no voice in the world but her own.

Little lamb, Mabel Price still called her. Still came to her in the night, still dogged her steps in the halfway realm, a disembodied guardian who remembered nothing beyond the fact that Wil meant *something.* And then there was Jenny Bright, desperate to infuse Wil with the fury she felt—so bent on it that she kept reaching out through the void.

It wasn't in Wil to turn her back on them, no matter the cost.

*　*　*

The sun-soaked laboratory was moonlit now, the gardens below spangled with torches and crystal lanterns and gauzy dancers spinning through the night like fey creatures. Kitty had hired a string quartet for the week, and strains of Strauss's waltz "Tales from the Vienna Woods" drifted in through the windows. Wil had pushed them open, the better to hear the music, and it came in softly with the cool night air.

She knelt in a puddle of dim lamplight, instruments and crates spread out around her, the last of them finally ready to be catalogued and packed. The room echoed now, wide and empty—before dinner, Jack Hoult had taken the tables away. Though Wil's hands moved, carrying on the work she'd been given, her mind was with the music, her gaze straying often to the lovely spectacle beyond the windows.

As she watched, a figure broke off from the others. It ventured across the lawns, up the terraces around the house, and onto the veranda. From the hallway, Wil heard a familiar tread. She let her hands fall still on her lap, her face turning expectantly toward the laboratory door.

"I saw the lamplight," Edison said as he stepped inside. "And I'd ever so much rather be in here with you. Douse it, won't you, though? Or someone will see."

Obediently Wil blew out the lamp, leaving them surrounded by shadows and silver. Silence fell too, as if she'd temporarily snuffed out their ability to speak. There was only the waltz and the gaiety beyond—a thing they were witnesses to but not part of.

"It's all so lovely," Wil said at last, a wistful sigh escaping her. "What a beautiful thing."

108

"Only from a distance," Ed answered. He stood leaning against the doorframe, and Wil couldn't be sure if his eyes were fixed on her or the party beyond. "When you're in it, none of it means anything. It's lifeless at the core—a distraction from everything real."

"Still." Wil could feel a sad smile playing across her face. "I wouldn't mind a distraction of that sort every now and then."

"Then you should have it." Ed came toward her and held out a hand. There was something in his face Wil didn't quite recognize—a bit of the fey atmosphere that surrounded the partygoers, perhaps. "Wilhelmina Price, may I have this dance?"

Wil flushed. "Oh, Ed, don't be silly."

"I'm not." He shrugged. "You said you want a distraction of that sort, and I may not be able to take you down to the gardens, but we can certainly hear the music, and you can have a dance with the lord's son."

She bit back a smile. "I *do* like the lord's son."

Putting her hand into Edison's, Wil let him pull her to her feet and lead her out into the open space, beyond the little clutter of leftover instruments.

"You know how to do this, yes?" Ed murmured as he put his free hand on Wil's waist and she lifted hers to his shoulder.

Wil nodded. She didn't trust herself to speak or to look up at him. Everything in her felt buoyant and hollow, filled with light and wings. Together they began to move, Ed assured as he led, Wil unfaltering as she followed. Dancing was, after all, just another puzzle or problem— one that required not only the mind but the body to create an elegant outcome. And Wil could not escape the realization that she and Edison, so close that she could feel his breath stir her hair and hear the way he hummed the music under his breath, were more than just a problem solved. They were a perfect verse, a flawless proof, a moment of epiphany.

"You were rather a knight in shining armor at dinner," Wil said as they moved through the moonlight. "But I could have managed. That was very brave and very foolish."

She allowed herself to look up, just enough that she saw a muscle work in his jaw.

"*Brave and foolish* would be something else entirely," Ed answered. "That was just instinct. I'm a coward at heart."

"I think facing up to your father like that was brave," Wil insisted. "More than that. Noble, even, to risk what people thought of you."

Edison stopped dancing but stayed as he was, one hand on Wil's waist, one holding her own. "I don't *care* what those people think. They lost any sort of respect for me years ago—even my family. You're the only one whose opinion still matters. And that's what I'm a coward about. If I was brave, I'd—"

"You'd what?" Wil's breath caught in her throat, and she couldn't bear to be circumspect anymore. She met Edison's gaze and found something untranslatable there. A world of piercing fear and hope and longing.

Until coming to the Grange, she hadn't realized what she wanted from him. An admission. A confession. A baring of the soul.

Wilhelmina Price, I want more from you than what we've had.

"Wil," Edison said. "I want you to try to reach Peter for me, one more time. And if you can't, I'll never ask again."

Her heart sank.

"Of course," she answered dully. "But it needn't be the last time. There's nothing you could ask for that I wouldn't give."

CHAPTER TEN

EDISON

Already Ed was regretting his words in the laboratory. But Wil had called him brave, and if she saw him so, he wanted to be as she said.

A wash of cold fear took over as he stood before the door to the nursery wing. For so long he'd avoided this moment. Kept himself away from the truth of what lay beyond this particular threshold—either a chaotic spirit or a disorder of his own mind. If the truth could set you free, then Wil was the key to his shackles— the one person who could prove the source of the disturbances he'd weathered for years.

He only needed the courage to let her in.

I've changed my mind, he thought at her. *I can't do this. I don't want you to see.*

But when he turned, she was standing behind him with nothing on her face but gentle encouragement. She always found the best in him, even when he couldn't see it in himself, and it was time. If any brightness could illuminate this darkest aspect of his life, it was hers.

And he'd begun to realize there was no future for them, not as friends or anything else, if he couldn't bring himself to expose the shut-up corners of his own soul.

"After you," Edison said quietly, pushing the door open and stepping out of Wil's way.

"Oh, Ed." The words came out with a soft, involuntary gasp as she took in the extent of the nursery wing. Since Kitty's party began, the thing Ed kept company with had grown increasingly restless—and vicious in that restlessness. The children's picture books did not just lie in a heap now but had all been torn to shreds, tattered paper drifting about the room. The doors Edison had pulled down were riven with splintering gashes, as if someone had taken a point chisel to them in a fit of rage. The wallpaper itself had been ripped from the walls in places, and Edison's bed sat askew in the center of his doorless room, the mattress dragged half off it. He'd wakened an hour before dawn to the force in those rooms pulling him out of bed, and had not bothered to set it to rights.

Beyond the sitting area the bathroom could be seen, molding towels piled in the corners and the bathtub and sink filled with fetid, slimy water. Ed had tried to unclog them with the tools Shepherd had left, but as with any attempt to restore order in the nursery wing, it proved an exercise in futility.

Wil took it all in with her clear, brilliant gray eyes, and when she looked at Ed, he could read nothing of fear or disgust in her face. When she spoke, it was not to chide or blame or harass him, as his family had done in the early days, intent on forcing him into normality.

"Tell me what's gone wrong," was all Wil said as she reached out to take his hand.

For a moment Edison struggled to maintain his composure. He could feel his throat tightening, heat at the back of his eyes. He'd put this off for so long—dreaded it more than all confessions save one—and here it was. He had his feet at the edge of the precipice, and there was no turning back, not with Wil looking at him so.

"Do you remember the summer I left home halfway through the holidays?" Ed asked. "It was the year Peter died—he was killed in February, and I came home for a little over a month, then went elsewhere."

"Yes," Wil said. "You wrote to me. Told me it was too hard being at home after what had happened to Peter, and that you'd gone to your great-aunt in London."

Edison shook his head. He looked down at Wil's hand, small and worn in his own, the faint impression of a blister showing on one of her fingers. "I didn't go to Aunt Porter. I went somewhere else entirely. Was *sent* somewhere else entirely. A cottage hospital, run by someone called Dr. Winstead."

"I didn't know you were ill." The worry in Wil's voice was at once a thorn and a balm. "You never said. Why wouldn't you tell me if you were ailing?"

Ed found, somewhere within himself, the strength and fortitude to raise his eyes. He met Wil's own and truly began the story he'd always dreaded to tell her.

"I never said because it was an asylum, Wil. Or rather, the sort of place wealthy people send their shameful relations to instead of an asylum."

"What?"

"Look around you." Ed took his hand from Wil's to gesture at the nursery wing, every corner and aspect indicating something gone terribly wrong. "Is this the way a sane person lives?"

Wil's chin jutted out stubbornly. "You never did this. I know you. You can be a little untidy, but this is more than that."

"Yes," Edison said, his voice growing urgent as he tried to make her understand. "This is more than untidiness. It's more than carelessness.

It's madness. And I'm the only one who's been in here. So if it's not me, then what is it?"

Wil said nothing.

"I thought it was Peter at first," Edison said, raking a hand through his hair. "I still try to tell myself it is. He was unkind to me, and sometimes to Kitty, in a thousand little ways. The sorts of things that I see and feel now are exactly what he'd have done. He liked to make people afraid and to have them in his power, and he found any anger directed toward himself amusing. Besides which, everything began falling to pieces in this part of the house the night he was killed—I was home then, you know; they'd had to replace the boilers at school and sent us all back for a week that February. But no one else has ever seen the things I see in here, Wil. Things that seem like a haunting—furniture moving on its own, chaos coming into being. All they see is me. Even you've said you can't sense anything unusual about the rooms."

"That's why you've wanted to reach Peter so badly," Wil said in a despairing whisper. "And I've never managed it."

"No." Ed's voice cracked on the word. "You never have."

"Were they cruel to you at the hospital?" If Wil had sounded urgent before, the force with which she spoke all but scorched Ed now.

"Not in the ways you'd think. But they dosed me like a horse—I could hardly keep a thought in my head for all the medicines I had to take. I wasn't ill before I arrived, only panicked and worn down, but everything I took *made* me ill before very long. It was like being in a fog or watching yourself from outside your own body. And I couldn't leave until I owned up to being unwell. That was my father's condition for my being let go. I had to admit that I was off my head, because he said I'd never get past it until I did. By the end I wanted to get away from there so badly, I just said it. I'd have said anything. But saying it—well, it felt like giving in. I've half believed everyone else was right ever since."

He'd expected Wil to look fearful or embarrassed. But all he saw in her face was that intent, piercing look she wore when thinking her way through a problem.

"Did your room at the hospital end up like this?" she asked, pointing to the disaster around them.

"No."

"And your room at school, has it ever looked so?"

"No."

"Have you always stayed in the nursery wing when you're home?"

Edison put his hands in his pockets, feeling terribly low. "No. After I got out of hospital, Mother put me in a new set of rooms on the third floor. That was the end of all the trouble, unless I came in here to try to speak to Peter. But with Kitty's party, Father said I'd have to move back in here for the summer, and that I'd better be over whatever lapse I'd gone through before. As you can see, I'm not. I don't dare let anyone in. Or anyone but you."

Wil walked to the bank of windows that overlooked the back lawn. "Doesn't it seem odd that this is the only place you're ever troubled? Come here, please, there's no need for us to stand staring at all this mess."

He joined her, moving to her side and looking out at the sweeping, moonlit gardens surrounding Wither Grange. People still spangled the lawns, their clothes and champagne flutes glittering like fool's gold, the sounds of their voices and laughter swallowed up by the distance.

"I don't care what you've been told or what they've done to you," Wil said. "If you're mad, you're mad everywhere, not just in one room."

Hope flared to life in him, agonizing in its unfamiliarity. "Yes, but—"

"If it isn't Peter, that doesn't mean it's you," Wil told him, her stubbornness grown into steely determination. "Something is doing this, and it's *not* my Edison."

Even in the midst of his mental turmoil, Ed's knees nearly buckled at the sound of the words *my Edison* coming from Wil. He shot her an agonized look, but she was staring straight ahead, her eyes fixed on the view before them.

When at last Wil turned, the determination he'd heard in her voice was radiating from her face.

"Well then, let's raise the dead," Wil said to him. "You're being haunted, and I don't mean to leave this room until I find your ghost."

"You're sure it's a ghost?" Ed balled his hands into fists at his sides to hide that they'd begun to tremble. "Because I've always hoped, but—"

"What I'm sure of is that you're not mad," Wil answered firmly. "So what else could it be?"

She sat down just where she was, in the midst of everything that had haunted Edison for years. Dim light spilled over her from the window, turning her to a creature of silver and gold, and for a moment all that mattered was that Wil was here and she believed him. Never mind that a sibilant, wordless whisper was rising from one of the corners, and she seemed unable to hear it.

Wil was here.

Wil believed him.

Ed settled himself in the posture he'd been taught, the two of them cross-legged with their knees touching, and put his hands into hers. He hoped against hope that she could not feel the sick fear singing through him and that his grip would stay steady.

If Wil sensed any of his anxiety, she gave no sign of it. She shut her eyes and sank into herself, as he'd seen her do a dozen times before. *The halfway realm,* she called it. The place where dead souls lingered. She'd never made it sound frightening or eerie when she spoke of it, only sad and lifeless. Yet Edison wondered sometimes. Wil had begun her forays into the world between during childhood, and she was exactly the sort of person who might be able to accept something as a matter of course that others would find terrifying.

Across from him she let out a faint sigh, her eyes moving behind her eyelids as they might in a dream. Ed knew better than to interrupt, but his tightly wound nerves were burning with tension by the time she looked at him again.

And there was no spirit materializing between them. No ghastly emanation from some place beyond that she'd dragged back into the living realm through sheer force of will and the brightness of her being.

Everything in Ed shattered. He should've known, should've been able to realize that it was him and not some ghost. He'd seen Wil's facility for the dead and imprinted on it, using it as a way to avoid his own troubles. It had been foolishness—no, madness; he'd best get used to thinking the word. . . .

With a small shock, Ed realized Wil's eyes were still fixed on him. She had not blinked. She had not moved. Slowly her hands around his were tightening to the point where her grasp grew painful. And as they did, Wil's eyes glassed over and brightened unnaturally, glowing with a cold and baleful blue fire.

"Wil?" Edison murmured, attempting to draw his hands away.

When she smiled, he knew without a shadow of a doubt that it was no longer Wil Price looking out at him. It was something other, and fierce, and brutal.

"Surgite," a strangled and vicious voice said, rising from her throat.

Ed did not have a chance to break free from her grasp or recoil before the creature within Wil launched itself at him. They went over backward in a tangle of limbs, hitting the floor with a bone-jarring jolt. Preternaturally strong hands gripped Edison by the throat, and he couldn't breathe, or feel, or think, beyond a single desperate resolution rattling in his brain.

He could not fight back, for fear of hurting Wil.

The world went red around the edges, and black spots crowded out his vision. It was all so beyond anything he'd ever feared, even in his worst nightmares, that Ed was sure it couldn't be real, that something had finally tipped him over the edge and proven his family's point. He'd lost his grip and would soon wake in a fog, alone on the nursery wing floor. He'd confess to what had been going on and be discreetly shuttled back to hospital, perhaps to stay forever.

But just before the point of no return, the slide into unconsciousness, he felt the implacable grip on his throat let go and his body reflexively draw in a gasp of life-giving air. A panicked voice called to him as if from a very long way away.

"Ed," the voice said, growing closer by painfully slow degrees. "Edison Summerfield. Say something to me. Wake up."

There was saltwater on his face, and then something so unfamiliar it took Ed a moment to place it.

Wil's lips on his forehead, his cheeks, his hair. He'd truly lost hold of himself. He was in a place beyond reality now, and God only knew what his body was doing in the absence of his mind. Wandering the mill wood in a stupor, most likely, where he'd stumble into that ill-fated pond and drown as the others had done.

At least in the end, his madness had taken a turn from the horrifying to the sublime.

Reaching up, he drew Wil closer, and when her mouth met his, it was everything Ed had never dared to hope for, not even in his dreams. He kissed her as if she was all that tied him to the world of the living and rational, not bothering to open his eyes, because even if it meant he'd finally frayed and fallen apart, he *wanted* this. Wanted the plush softness of a kiss from Wil Price, her sweet breath worth drowning for as her lips parted, welcoming him as she'd always done, proving herself the spark that set him aflame.

A small, yearning, distinctly human sound rose, no longer from a distance but very much present. There was nothing of the dreamworld about it—it was real and raw and sent sudden horror searing through Edison as his eyes flew open.

He'd been kissing Wil. *His* Wil, in the flesh, in the nursery wing, surrounded by all the trappings of his own disastrous life.

Without stopping to think, Ed scrambled away, chest heaving, panic flooding his veins.

"Wil, I'm sorry, that was all wrong. I won't ever do it again."

The words came out in a rasping jumble, and he was sure he'd ruined everything. This was the end of him and Wil, the one good thing in his blighted existence of constraint and expectation and false impressions.

A single flash of abject confusion crossed her face, only to be replaced by that borrowed semblance of Shepherd's calm. He knew what was happening—she couldn't sort out the problem of what had taken place between them and would simply set it aside until a solution came to her.

"Are you all right?" Wil said, ignoring what she could not parse and moving on. He might have thought she had steel in place of a heart were it not for the fact that she was so very good to him. "I've been having a difficult time with Jenny Bright lately—she's been trying to take over. But I didn't think she'd do that."

"Is it her?" Ed asked. "I mean her that's been . . ."

He waved feebly about himself. Ed often felt that he bordered on disaster, but now he was well and truly over the border, filled with razor-sharp anxiety and a longing for Wil so powerful it hurt.

"No," Wil said, refusing to meet his gaze. A worried frown creased the place between her fair brows. "There's something here, but it's not her. It's . . . it's older than that. Been in the halfway realm longer, I mean. I couldn't get a good look at it, but it felt like all of this. Like something gone badly wrong. Like chaos."

Wil shivered, a haunted light in her eyes, which would not meet his own. Ed wanted to go to her, but he didn't dare move from the spot he'd retreated to, his back to the empty bookshelf, his hands knotted firmly together on his lap.

"But it's definitely not me?" he pressed, just to be sure.

Wil finally gave him a look. The *really, Ed, how can you be so thick* look she'd been employing with him for years, and he clung to the fact that it still existed, that they were still, in some way, what they'd always been.

"Of course it's not you. And I can't believe you just lived with thinking it might be, instead of asking for my help sooner."

The smile Ed managed felt like a paltry, half-broken thing. "I keep trying to tell you I'm a coward."

Wil got to her feet. Ed glanced up as she drew nearer and set her hand atop his head briefly, like a benediction.

"Well, you've finally got it out in the open. And I don't know how I'm going to fix this, but I will."

Just as she'd promised to draw out the truth behind Mabel and Jenny's deaths. That was three ghosts now that Wil had promised to lay to rest. When he considered the Grange, with all its tight-shut doors, and the violent spirit that plagued him, Ed couldn't help wondering if for once, Wil had set herself a task that might prove beyond her capabilities.

But he pushed back that doubt immediately, replacing it with determined assurance. This was Wilhelmina Price pitting herself against the Grange, and Ed had always believed her capable of luring the moon out of the sky if she chose.

CHAPTER ELEVEN

WIL

T hough her body was abysmally tired, Wil's mind would not let her sleep. She felt herself to be drowning, caught up in a morass of conflicting feelings and obligations. At the forefront of her mind was Edison, because Edison had become a problem.

Try as she might, Wil could not escape the way he'd looked after kissing her. As if he hated himself for it. As if it had been an ugly and reprehensible thing.

That was all wrong, he'd said. *I won't ever do it again.*

Wil buried her face in her pillow and let out a muffled groan. Because contrariwise, all she wanted was for Ed to kiss her again. She'd been aware, vaguely, that how she felt toward him was changing in some way. Not lessening but experiencing a phase shift. A metamorphosis of sorts. He'd always had her heart, and she knew herself to have his, but there'd been an additional pull growing in her of late, like the tide that inevitably bore her back to the land of the living.

She wanted the rest of him now too. She'd grown greedy when it came to Edison. She had his heart and wanted his body. Had him as the friend of her soul and wanted him as a lover as well. She wanted to kiss him again and do more than that—she wanted her hands in his unruly hair, his on the row of demure buttons that kept her small and confined, turned into an accessory of the Summerfield household rather than the force she knew herself to be. She wanted to free him from his own maddening life and have him do the same for her, both of them shedding the layers of inhibition and constraint that bound them until they stood guiltless before each other, with no way to hide and no wish to do so.

With frustration burning in her every part, Wil rolled over, fixing her eyes on the water-stained ceiling. There was no *point* to this line of thinking. Ed had made it clear that their brief foray beyond the bounds of friendship had been distasteful for him, even as it had lit a fire in her. Better to put it aside, as she did any problem that seemed past her capabilities.

Better to focus on the dead, if the living were proving impossible.

There had been something in the nursery wing, just as Wil knew there would be. But it was old and twisted, worn down to a malevolent shadow. How long it had clung to the edges of the living world, she couldn't imagine, but she'd felt little of sense in it. Mabel's ghost was still guided by a doleful and singular devotion to Wil, Jenny's by anger over her untimely end. And Jenny was so newly dead that she still held full memories of life.

The thing in the nursery, by contrast, was death incarnate. In the shadow realm, Wil had seen it—a dark soul crouched in the bathtub full of pond water and duckweed, only its hollow eyes visible above the surface. She'd tried to draw closer, wanting to gain a better sense of the soul's nature and intent, but Mabel and Jenny had materialized from the halfway realm's perpetual fog and pulled her away.

As they'd done so, Wil had heard a scrap of maddeningly familiar song, drifting from the bathtub and its gruesome denizen. She hadn't been able to place it, and she screwed her eyes shut now, digging her fists into them as she turned that bit of melody over and over in her head.

There. Words to the tune. She had it.

I'll sing you one, O
Green grow the rushes, O
What is your one, O?
One is one and all alone
And evermore shall be so.

Nothing but a foolish nursery rhyme, and what it could mean, Wil did not yet know. But she trusted the dead not to speak idly and tucked it away beside Jenny's adamant repetitions of *"Surgite"* and her furious attempt to do violence to Edison.

Wil hadn't expected that. She ought to have redirected her attention to escaping Jenny's clutches, rather than trying to struggle back toward the dark soul in the bath. She hadn't noticed Jenny's ghost pushing them to the fold between worlds until too late, and she'd been forced to draw the dead woman back with her.

Ed had nearly paid the price for Wil's distraction. For a moment she thought she'd killed him—he'd have bruises on his throat for days. But then he'd kissed her and—

With a single decisive motion, Wil threw the covers aside and got out of bed. Back where she started, and there was no use going down that rabbit hole again. No more thinking of the way Ed had reached for her and pulled her mouth down to his, as if they were made for each other.

Gray dawn stained the eastern horizon. If Wil could not sleep, she would work.

A quarter of an hour later she was out of doors, ignoring the disarray of the kitchen in favor of slipping through the silent streets and out toward the mill wood. Surely there would be something to keep her idle hands and fretful mind busy at the Grange. Back at home her grandfather was not yet awake, his bedroom door shut soundly as if he couldn't shake the habits of his employers. But Mrs. Forster began her days much earlier, as did Mrs. Ellicott and Daphne and Abigail. They'd be glad enough to see Wil. And she wanted conversation, not silence—anything to keep her mind off what had transpired between her and Edison.

Though faint golden light was beginning to filter into the wood, shadows still pooled in the hollows and beneath the thickest-branching trees. From a distance, Wil could hear the chattering of the mill stream as it rushed along its course and down into the still, reed-fringed pond. A glimpse of mellow stone wall and wooden waterwheel through the trees was as close as she planned to get to the pool itself—a dull, superstitious aversion to the place had risen within Wil, and though she knew it to be foolishness, she obeyed her instinct to give the millpond a wide berth.

The path she charted through the woods brought her to the edge of the clearing where she met Edison after each school term. Stopping for a moment, she couldn't help but envision all their assignations there, stretching back for over half her lifetime. There'd been an air of fate to their first encounter—Wil's mother had said that she met William Price in a forest glade, and that from the very first, the two of them had known they were meant to be together. Wil had never tired of hearing the story of her parents' meeting, of how they'd fallen head over heels for one another at first sight and been married only a month later. It was her best and brightest fairy story, in which the princess and gallant prince were her very own parents.

So when Edison had stumbled across her in the woods and some sense of kinship and sympathy had sparked between them, Wil had known. They were meant for each other, just as her mother and father had been. Oh, maybe it wouldn't take the same shape as things had for Mabel and William, but fate was undeniable.

Wil was Ed's, and Ed was hers, from that moment on.

They'd been knights and merry men and castaways in their clearing together as children, and then bypassed any awkwardness that might have come with adolescence by turning to a new sort of play, devised of words and numbers and the testing of one another's wit. They'd made each other better—not just cleverer, but kinder and more understanding. Without Edison, Wil knew she'd long ago have succumbed to the temptation to live entirely within a world of the mind, at an arm's length from everyone and everything around her. Without her, it would have been all too easy for him to fall prey to the prejudices and vagaries of his own class. They were who they'd become because of each other.

A muffled sound brought Wil's attention back to the present with a snap. The clearing, which she'd thought empty, wasn't so at all. At its far side, hidden in the dappled shadows beneath a spreading oak, were two people. They were so wholly absorbed in each other that Wil hadn't noticed them at first, and they did not seem to have noticed her. It took only a moment for her to recognize Abigail, back pressed against the tree, face upturned and eyes shut in an expression of bittersweet rapture. There was a man with her—broad-shouldered and roughly clad, his mouth tracing the line of Abigail's neck, one of his hands beneath her skirt.

Only an instant, and everything in Wil flamed with shock and embarrassment and desire, because *this* was what she wanted with Ed. She turned aside at once, not wishing to intrude, but the image had seared itself across her mind. And as she backed away, her foot fell upon a bone-dry branch, splitting it in two with a crack like a pistol shot.

Instantly Abigail and her companion separated, wariness in every line of their postures. Wil stood rooted to the spot, not sure what to do—to step forward and declare herself or vanish into the trees.

"It's all right," Abigail said, sparing her the decision and sounding acutely relieved. "I can see. It's only Wil, and she won't tell."

Wil moved into the clearing, desperately trying to force the heat from her face.

"Morning," she offered with an attempt at cheerfulness and normalcy.

"I couldn't sleep, so I'm on my way back to the Grange. I'd say we can walk the rest of the way together, Abigail, but it seems you've already got company."

Now it was Abigail who flushed, reaching for the stranger's hand with a sudden, uneasy gesture. "Yes. And you won't say anything about this, will you? I'd lose my position if anyone found out; they're awfully strict at the Grange about not allowing staff to have followers."

"Of course not," Wil promised. Now that she stood before the two of them, she could see Abigail's sweetheart was a fair bit older than her fellow housemaid—perhaps fifteen years Abigail's senior. The disparity unnerved her, but Abigail's companion smiled frankly as she searched his face, and he offered a hand to shake.

"Nathaniel Halliday," he said. "You're the Wil Price that Abby tells me has been her saving grace."

"I don't know about that," Wil answered with caution. "I've never seen you in Thrush's Green before—are you from these parts?"

Nathaniel shook his head. "My family's from the Midlands. But I've come down for farm labor over the summer—I've got a cousin with a holding north of Wynkirk who needs a hand. Abby and I met each other in town on one of her half days."

Wil could feel herself relaxing. She had vague memories of a pair of men her father would employ during harvest when she'd been a very small child. And the way Abigail fixed her eyes on the ground, a small smile playing about her mouth as Nathaniel spoke, was charming. She'd only ever seen the other girl as a model of efficiency and propriety—it made Abigail seem more real to Wil, that she was the sort to keep a sweetheart on the side.

"I'm happy for the both of you." Wil smiled, and she meant what she said. "And I'm sure you don't want my company when you've got each other, so I'll leave you be. Good morning."

But she'd only just left the clearing when Abigail caught up with her, slipping her arm through Wil's own.

"I'll walk with you after all," she said. "Goodness knows there's plenty to do at the Grange, and we might as well get a head start."

For a moment they went on in silence, though Wil could sense Abigail fretting and see worry in her face.

"Wil," the other girl ventured at last. "You *swear* you won't say anything about this? Not to anyone? Not Daph or Mrs. Forster or your grandfather or Master Edison?"

Wil blinked. "Why should I say anything to Master Edison? You told me yourself; he doesn't so much as look at me."

Abigail stopped in her tracks, forcing Wil to do the same. Her face was deadly earnest, her hand on Wil's arm no longer a gesture of affection but a restraint.

"We all have our secrets, Wil," she said. "What I'm saying is, this one could be the end of me, so don't tell mine and I won't tell yours."

Something cold and unpleasant slithered down Wil's spine. She'd never once been threatened before coming to the Grange, and now both her grandfather and Abigail had brought something to bear against her. What was it about the place that drew out the worst in people?

Taking in a steadying breath, Wil chose the high road.

"As far as I'm concerned, we're two dutiful housemaids with no thought beyond ensuring the Summerfield household runs smoothly and the family reputation stays unimpeachable," she answered. "And I promise I won't tell a soul about your sweetheart."

With a small, relieved sigh, Abigail squeezed Wil's arm fondly. "Good. I knew I could count on you. I was right when I said you're my saving grace."

"Don't be foolish; it's only common decency. But I swear to you, I haven't got any secrets of my own. At least not of the same sort as yours."

Abigail shot Wil a look of disbelief. "I've been at Wither Grange twelve years. And not once in those twelve years has Edison Summerfield ever stood up to his father. He's kind enough on his own, but when it comes to family, he does as he's told and as they want, because he's the sort who hates trouble. So for him to suddenly pick a fight on account of Lord Summerfield chiding you . . ."

"Means there must be more going on than we know. I was just a convenient excuse," Wil finished for her without hesitating.

"I saw you dancing together," Abigail said bluntly. "And I saw the two of you going into his rooms. He's told all the rest of the staff to keep out."

Wil fought for calm. She'd never truly counted the costs of maintaining her connection with Ed while working at the Grange before. But if the Summerfields learned of it, it wouldn't just mean the end of her own employment there. It would undoubtedly lead to her grandfather being turned away without a reference as well. He'd never find work again at his age, with a cloud over his departure from a household he'd been employed in all his adult life.

And that would mean very hard times, for both him *and* Wil.

"As you said," Wil offered, unease stirring in the pit of her stomach. "You keep my secret, I'll keep yours."

Abigail patted her arm. "That's all I'm asking for. No more, no less."

A fraught silence fell between them, stretching on until they reached Wither Grange and the cobbled courtyard that lay before the servants' entrance. Abigail went in at once, but Wil lingered on the threshold, needing the cool morning air to steady her.

"Do you smoke?" a voice asked presently.

Kitty stepped out from the gloom near the corner of the house, where dawn light did not reach, and held a gold and mother-of-pearl cigarette case out to Wil. There were blue shadows beneath her eyes—if she'd gone to bed at all, it couldn't have been for more than a few hours. Rather than the gossamer party dresses she'd draped herself in all week, Kitty wore her jodhpurs and a jumper, and mud stained her tall boots. When Wil shook her head to decline the offer, Kitty shrugged and took a long drag off her own half-finished cigarette.

"Did you . . . have a pleasant ride?" Wil asked, dismayed to be shifting from one uncomfortable confrontation to another.

"No," Kitty said flatly. None of the usual music or laughter were in her voice, and she stared across the courtyard at a stack of crates, brooding. "No, I did not."

"I'm sorry."

Kitty raised an eyebrow. "Yes, I almost believe you are. Wil Price, do you consider yourself to have been happy in life?"

Wil stifled a sigh. It was becoming a pattern, it seemed, for Kitty to ask her odd, invasive questions, which seemed to have little to do with Wil and everything to do with Kitty. "Yes, I think so."

"You do understand you're an orphan? But you'd call yourself happy nonetheless?"

"I was lucky in the family I had, when I had them," Wil said. "My mother and father were very kind to each other, and to me. They'd been in love from the first glance, and I don't think that ever stopped, not even when my father died. I'd catch Mama sitting quietly with a look on her face like heartbreak. I know she was thinking of him. But after he died, she kept on being as kind to me as she was able. I never doubted that my parents cared for one another and for me. Not everyone has that. And by the time Mama passed, I already knew your brother."

Exhaling a curling tendril of smoke, Kitty gave Wil a critical look. "A happy girl. What a rarity. You truly have no regrets?"

"One," Wil answered, feeling herself flush as she remembered Mabel, wreathed in the fog of her own departing soul. "I don't care to speak about it."

Kitty fell silent for a while, and Wil began to think of asking if she could be dismissed. But Kitty hadn't finished yet.

"What about strength? Do you consider yourself to be a strong person?" she asked presently, stubbing out her cigarette on the stone wall, tossing the end aside, and lighting another. "Someone who can weather change, no matter how far-reaching? If your family—your grandfather, perhaps—turned out be nothing like what you thought, and everything fell apart, could you bear it?"

Wil's heart dropped. All she could think of was Daphne and Mrs. Ellicott, and their revelation that John had been at odds with both of the maids who'd died—even his own daughter.

"I don't know," Wil murmured. "I don't think anyone can know that sort of thing until they're faced with it. But most people, even in dire circumstances, carry on, don't they? They do their best and keep going."

Kitty laughed, a note of dark humor ringing through the sound. It was nothing at all like her company laugh—the bright peal of hollow mirth that she adorned herself with like a piece of jewelry. "Do your best and keep going. Would that be your advice to anyone in trouble? Me, for instance?"

"I don't think you can go far wrong with it," Wil said. "Kitty, do you need help with anything?"

When Kitty smiled, it was like nothing Wil had seen from her before. It was knowing and weary and confiding, and for all Wil could not make heads or tails of Kitty Summerfield, and generally hated problems she couldn't untangle, she found herself liking the older girl in spite of herself.

"You're already helping," Kitty said. "Not as a housemaid, of course— you're a disaster at that. But I can see why Edison values you."

Wil was about to answer when a young man came striding around the corner, his suit very fresh, his hat pulled low over his eyes.

"Oh, Nick!" Kitty exclaimed in delight, her gleaming and merry façade falling back into place seemingly without effort. "What are you doing up so early? I've just been out for the most bracing ride. Do you think Geordie will mind I went without him? I did promise to show him the grounds from horseback, but I'm sure he's still asleep, and his head will be splitting once he's up. Have you seen the rockery? Let me show you—you could take Moira out there later; it's just the place for a pair of lovebirds to get away for a bit."

The look Nick gave Kitty clearly showed that he would prefer the rockery in Kitty's company to that of the unfortunate Moira, but if Kitty noticed his lovelorn air, she gave no indication—only slid her arm through his in a comfortable, entirely platonic gesture. As she led him away, back around the corner of the house he'd appeared from, Kitty glanced back once at Wil. For the briefest moment, her beaming smile turned mocking, as if she was having a laugh at the expense of Nick, the Grange, her guests, and her own life.

Then Wil was alone. Moving into the shadows Kitty had inhabited, she leaned her forehead against the solid wall of the Grange and drew in a few slow breaths. But she couldn't idle for long. Straightening, she smoothed her apron and skirt with a meticulous gesture reminiscent of John Shepherd and turned for the servants' door.

Whatever ghosts and secrets she had to manage, a day of service was waiting.

CHAPTER TWELVE

EDISON

I realize this may be a fraught question given that you're never espe-cially happy at home, but are you and your sister close?"

Wil stood in Edison's doorway, and when he glanced up, he couldn't help the fierce and involuntary flush that crept across his face at the memory of her lips on his. Letting herself in, Wil picked her way across the nursery wing's rubbish-strewn central room, moving to sit beside Edison on his unmade bed. It didn't escape his notice that where before, she'd have come right to his side, the two of them shoul-der to shoulder, bolstering each other with their closeness, now she sat a careful foot away.

Ed let out a stifled sigh.

"Kitty? I . . . well, she's complicated. We were very close as children—closer than anyone else in the family, except perhaps Father and Peter. Peter had a tendency toward unkindness and a habit of toying with any-one weaker than him. The staff, his younger siblings. He was so much older than us, and Kitty and I became allies by default. But after he died, she started to grow distant. The way she is now, I mean. Unreadable and bright and always moving. You can't see any deeper than the surface with her anymore. We've stayed on good terms, though, and I'd stand by her through anything if she only asked—if she'd only let me in."

Wil chewed at her lower lip for a moment, a frown creasing the space between her gray eyes. "She's been asking me very odd questions. Ever since I came to the Grange, it's been as if she's trying to sort something out about herself, or is in some manner of trouble, but I can't make sense of what it is she's driving at."

"You might never," Ed answered with a helpless shrug. "That's who she is now. I don't think anyone really knows her anymore."

"I hate that," Wil said, sudden passion lending strength to the words. "She ought to have *someone*."

"She does. She has me. But I can't force her confidence, can I?"

Wil's eyes shot to Edison's as if he'd said something that cut too close to home. In response, Ed attempted to do what Wil herself managed so effortlessly—to rearrange his features into a bland semblance of disinterest, a mask behind which he could hide his last, most damning secret.

Don't let her see.

I wish she would see.

"I think we ought to find out who your ghost is," Wil said after a moment, once the question Ed had posed had withered and died without an answer. "It's got to be here for a reason—the dead don't just linger without cause. And given what's happened with my mother and Jenny, it could be connected in some way. That's what I've come up for—are you all right if we do some digging?"

Ed shifted anxiously in place, thinking of how their last encounter with the nursery wing's resident had gone. Wil's hands on his throat, the world fading, and what came after. If he only had to run the risk of being throttled by Wilhelmina Price, he'd say yes without hesitation. But he couldn't risk another kiss. The lack of sleep and general discomfort of living with his own personal ghost had him on edge, perilously close to the edge of his ability to keep any aspect of himself in check—his temper, his tongue, his heart. At some point, his self-control was going to shatter, and he wouldn't let Wil be on the receiving end of that failing.

"Just what would that entail?" Ed asked with a hint of panic.

"Nothing like last time," she hurried to reassure him. "It's impossible to get anything sensible out of the dead—God knows I've tried. You can't just go up to them and say, 'Hello, I'm Wil, pleasure to meet you, what was your name when you were alive?' I thought we could just . . . think back together. See if maybe there's someone or something we haven't considered."

"All right." Ed moved back a little so he could sit against the wall. Wil joined him, and from downstairs, piano music and laughter drifted as if from another world.

"They'll miss me in a few minutes, so we can't be long," Wil said. "But your spirit's tied to the nursery wing, so we'd best focus on children, nursemaids—anyone who'd have a connection to this place."

"My mother lost two babies between Peter and Kitty," Edison told her. "One stillborn, the other at six weeks old. Could it be one of them?"

Wil squinted into the middle distance, thinking it over. "I don't think so. The thing I saw in the halfway realm—I could feel some sort of intention from it. Some sort of awareness. I wouldn't expect that from a child so young. They'd have to be a little older, at least."

Ed raked a hand through his hair, though he knew he'd have to be downstairs and presentable for tea before long. "Kitty and I had the same nursemaid until I went off to school. A Nurse Finch. She and Kitty still write to each other, though I was never much of a favorite with her. But there was another nurse before her who left when I was very small—I don't remember her, but Kitty mentioned her occasionally. Kit might know what's happened to her."

"Good. It's a start. What about other children?" Wil asked, casting

134

a wider net. "Any born at the Grange or connected to it in some way? The Ellicotts live on the grounds—did they lose any children young? Or maybe . . ." She faltered. "Maybe one of the housemaids at some point was sent away in disgrace? Something of that sort?"

Ed fought back the urge to flinch. The memory of seeing his father dismiss a girl while Peter watched in amusement flashed back, stronger than ever.

"I can't recall the Ellicotts ever losing a child," he said. "Though of course you'd have to ask Mrs. E., if you can be careful enough about it—it's not the sort of thing you just put to a person out of the blue. As for housemaids, Peter was always more interested in them than he ought to have been. Like I said, he enjoyed reminding anyone he considered beneath him of his own power. Enjoyed making a game of other people. I know of at least one maid who was dismissed over her connection to him."

"What was her name?" Wil asked. "I'd prefer not to leave any loose threads—we ought to find out what's become of her."

Ed's reluctance grew. "I can't imagine she'll want to hear from anybody connected to the Grange. It was shameful what they did—just sent her off with no reference because of Peter. It wasn't her fault she caught his eye. And anyway, I can't recall what her name was. Mrs. Forster or your grandfather would know, though again, they'll find it odd if you ask."

"Would Kitty remember?" Wil said.

"I should think so—she's always made an effort to keep track of the staff. Even when we were children, she'd want to know where everyone was, what they were up to. Not much gets past her, though she doesn't like to let on. I can ask her about it and about the nursemaid; you needn't bother."

"Excellent." Wil scrambled to her feet. "I've already been gone too

135

long—they'll be setting up for tea on the lawn. I'll do my best not to spill anything onto your lap, but I can't make any promises."

Ed thought the last sounded a little too grim to be strictly humorous, but all he did was nod. Wil left by way of the servants' entrance, rather than through the hallway door she'd come in from. The moment she'd gone, his ghost took up muttering again, its voice echoing eerily down the chimney while dim reflections moved in the window glass. Wiping his spectacles on one sleeve, Ed put them back on and wandered into the nursery's central room, squinting at the windows as if he could make the haunted shadows showing in them come clear. But by and by they faded instead. Below him he could see Wil and Abigail moving about on the lawn, following directions from Mrs. Forster. Kitty appeared, spoke briefly to the staff, and breezed past them toward the rockery, which was out of view of the house itself.

Well, it would be a private place for Ed to ask her about maids who'd left service. With a decisive movement, he pulled his jacket from the back of a chair and left the nursery wing. Where his own desolate little stretch of corridor joined the main hall, several of Kitty's guests were loitering. The elderly and perpetually disapproving Baroness de Vouche was on her way out of her rooms, busily taking snuff and glaring at the young people, and Ed was half inclined to agree with her scowl, for one callow and especially enterprising gentleman was lounging halfway up the stairs, the better to regale anyone of interest who passed by either above or below.

"If you'll excuse me," Edison said, suppressing the urge to roll his eyes as he stepped past the staircase lounger. "But you're making a fire hazard of yourself, and it is my house."

"Oh, you're the *brother*," the lounger said lazily, glancing up at Ed and giving an impertinent wink. He had a thin mustache and a way about him that instantly irritated Edison, who'd have been happy enough to brush past and carry on his way. "Not the dead one, the

136

younger one. What was it they said about you? That's right. When you were a boy, you went off your head for a bit. I don't suppose you'll do it again? Would make for some entertainment—there's been nothing going on for hours."

"If you weren't here at my sister's invitation," Edison said with a warning smile, "I'd have you thrown out of the house. But if you can't get yourself out from underfoot, I *will* have you thrown off the stairs. Jack?"

Jack Hoult stepped forward immediately from where he stood by the front doors, and from the look he gave Edison, it was easy enough to see that the footman would relish any chance to put some of the Grange's more insolent guests in their place.

"See to it the stairs are kept clear," Ed told him, in a voice pitched to carry. "If anyone argues, you can feel free to remove them. And if they make a fuss after that, you can tell His Lordship that I gave the order."

With a sullen scowl, the young man on the steps got to his feet and slunk off. Jack nodded to Edison, repressed humor glinting in his eyes, before returning to his post.

Ed carried on down the Grange's gunshot corridor and through the French doors onto the terrace. He was surprised by his own boldness—while Wil coming to Wither Grange had initially seemed a terrible idea, he couldn't deny that her advent at the house had infused him with a new and unexpected confidence. It was as if, with all his secrets constantly so close at hand, he couldn't help daring fate to do its worst. To dredge up everything he kept hidden and draw it into the light.

With equally formal nods to Abigail, Wil, and Mrs. Forster, Ed followed in Kitty's wake. He hurried along the walk, hands in his pockets as the air grew cool in the shade of the lime trees, then across a wildflower meadow where the sun bore down on the top of his head and his shoulders. At the edge of the meadow, a woodland sprang up—not the mill wood yet, but a contrived, artificial little forest, made of acers and birch and copper beech, underplanted with tree ferns. As if to echo the mill wood with its troubled pond, at the heart of the Summerfields' forest lay a sunken grotto. It had no history—though it looked like the foundations of something ancient and crumbled, the stones had been placed there by Edison's grandfather, made to look as if they'd weathered centuries when, by the Grange's standards, they were brand-new. Mosses clung to the rocks, water dripped from the false tumbledown walls, and a gazing pool that gleamed golden with fish sat like a jewel at the grotto's center.

Kitty stood near the pool wearing a frock the color of pearls. Ed went down to her at once, his eyes on the damp steps as he spoke.

"Kit, I had a few questions, I don't suppose you could—"

The words died in his throat as he reached the floor of the grotto and felt unspent tension singing through the air. Kitty's hands were clenched into fists, her face blanched and drawn, and Ed cast about himself at once, searching for the source of her distress. Some partygoer, he supposed, a cad like the lounger on the stairs.

But what he found was John Shepherd, immaculate and unflappable as ever, waiting near the mock ruins. Shepherd all but blended into the shadows, the crisp black and white of his uniform mimicking the variegated shade.

"It needs to come out," Kitty said furiously, looking past Edison to Shepherd, whose expression never changed. "All of it. And it's going to—I don't care what it costs, and I won't let you stand in my way."

"It will be a danger to you if you speak," Shepherd said, a warning note in his usually even tone. "Don't think for a moment that being part of the family will keep you safe if you go this far. You'll be every bit as vulnerable as Mabel was, or Jenny."

"Stop," Kitty snapped. "I won't hear another word. This has gone far enough, and I don't intend to keep quiet any longer. Come with me, Ed—we're quite finished here."

Seizing Edison's hand, Kitty led him out of the grotto and away—not back toward the Grange, but to the in-between space where the Summerfields' false forest began to give way to the mill wood itself. Stopping at last, she drew in a great, trembling breath.

And all at once it was gone. Her fury with Shepherd. Her passionate refusal to back down from whatever it was he'd attempted to deter her from. All Edison found in its place was a glittering smile.

"Well," Kitty said lightly. "That was some awful unpleasantness, and I'm sorry you had to hear it. But it's nothing for you to trouble yourself over, so promise me you won't."

"Kitty," Edison said, frowning. "If you're in difficulty, you can tell me about it."

"I know. And I mean to ask for your help very soon, but . . . not yet. I want to keep you just as you are for a little longer. Clear of all this. Unspoiled by it."

"Unspoiled by what?" Ed asked in frustration. "You know something about Mabel and Jenny, don't you? Whatever it is, I wish you'd say. If you won't tell me, at least go to the police."

"You mean the village constable?" Kitty laughed, bitterness in the bell-like peal of her voice. "I might as well confide in my horse. Honestly, Ed, I promise that when I really need something, I'll come to you. But for now I prefer to manage on my own."

"I don't like that," Ed grumbled. "I want to stand with you."

"I know." Kitty leaned forward and kissed him. "You're a darling, of course you do. Were you out here looking for me?"

"Yes," he said. "There were a few things I wanted to ask you about."

"Ask away."

"Do you remember when I was quite a small boy, there was a house-maid sent away in disgrace because of Peter?"

"Which one?" Kitty asked darkly. "There were several."

"I would have been involved with this one," Edison said. "I caught Peter with her and mentioned it, not knowing what would happen."

"That was Elinor Howard."

"And the others?"

"Nellie Burke and Mary Seldon. There may have been more—those are the ones I can recall."

"And what about our old nursemaid? I know there was one from when I was little more than a baby who left, and then Miss Finch came."

Kitty's eyes cut to Edison for a brief moment and then drifted to the woodland floor. "Don't trouble yourself over her. Whatever it is you want with all these women, they're fine; I've made sure of it."

"What was the nursemaid's name?" Ed pressed.

Kitty set her jaw and stayed silent.

"*Katherine.*" Ed was pleading now, but Kitty shook her head.

"No. I won't say. Nothing good can come of it."

"I will find out. One way or another, whether you tell me or not. Shepherd will know, and Mrs. Forster and Mrs. Ellicott."

"None of them will tell you either. They're under orders not to."

"*What?*"

"I'm begging you to trust me," Kitty said. "Just leave this be for . . . another day. That's all I ask. Until tomorrow night, after my wretched birthday party quiets down. Then we can talk things through, and I won't have to be so damned mysterious. Perhaps we can even set some old wrongs right."

"I'll say it again, Kitty—I thought you wanted this," Edison told her bluntly. "Why subject yourself to all this bother if you aren't even enjoying yourself?"

"I did want it," Kitty said, shifting her weight in annoyance. "I planned it all out myself, and then something else came up for which the timing couldn't be any worse. It's taken all the fun out of everything—I'd rather be anywhere but here."

"I know the feeling."

Ed's own dissatisfaction with life at the Grange must have been written across his face, because Kitty squeezed his shoulder comfortingly with one hand. "Don't fret. It'll all come out right. I'm going to make sure of it. *We're* going to make sure of it; I promise."

"I'll hold you to that," Ed warned. "The moment you can get clear of all that fuss tomorrow night, I want an airing out between us. We haven't been on the same page since Peter died. Enough's enough. Let's stand back-to-back again, like we did when we were small. Turn over a new leaf for your first full day at nineteen."

For a moment Kitty's mouth worked, and Edison had a terrible, sinking feeling that she was on the verge of tears. He couldn't remember ever seeing Kitty cry, not even in the nursery when they were children.

"I'd like that," she said after a moment, and her voice was firm. "Ed, I would like that so very much."

With a swirl of pearlescent silks, she turned toward the Grange and its revelers. The last Edison saw of Kitty as she went was her looking back to wave at him, a small silver ring glinting on one of her fingers like a star.

CHAPTER THIRTEEN

WIL

Where's Abigail?" Mrs. Forster asked sharply, shattering Wil's fierce concentration.

Kitty's birthday—the centerpiece of the house party—had finally arrived. The day had passed in a blur of activity. There were lawn games and music, riding and cards, walks in the mill wood or tours through the Grange's less frequented rooms. Something was on offer for everyone, and the staff had been kept on the run since sunup, from the moment they had served a first hot meal to early risers in the breakfast room, or to the more indolent in bed. Every corner of the house had required an occasional inspection to ensure that anyone present was liberally supplied with tea, champagne, or whichever of the kitchen's exquisitely crafted delicacies they desired. It had been Kitty's idea to have anything available at will throughout the day rather than a formal luncheon or tea, so that when the time came to gather for her birthday supper, the anticipation would have been building since breakfast. Afterward the company would have a day of indolence to recover, followed by a Wednesday departure.

Now twilight cloaked the back lawn of Wither Grange. Fairy lights sparkled against the dusky air, the string quartet was sending up a lively melody, and in the marquee the festivities had reached their height. A towering birthday cake, crafted by the artful Mrs. Ellicott and Daphne, blazed with candles on the marquee's main table, surrounded by the trappings and mementos of Kitty Summerfield's childhood.

Every guest was in attendance, and the air within the tent was close and stuffy, the atmosphere heady and ebullient. All hands had been called on deck—Daphne and Mrs. Forster were serving along with Wil and her grandfather and Jack Hoult. Even the five of them were in difficulty, attempting to meet every request with an impression of ease. Wil was additionally hampered by sleeplessness, which had plagued her ever since she and Edison had contacted the nursery wing ghost—for two nights she'd been unable to shake the memory of their kiss. And yet it was her own fault, for she dredged it up willfully, wanting to sink into the recollection of how being with Ed in a new and electric way had felt. As a result, it was taking all her willpower and mental effort to avoid the sort of clumsiness that would draw Lord Summerfield's ire.

She could have used Abigail's help. They all could use Abigail, and the girl was nowhere to be found.

Though part of Wil wondered if her fellow housemaid had gone off to meet her sweetheart once more, she'd never known Abigail to shirk her duty. Nor did she wish to see Abigail in difficulty, so as Mrs. Forster asked after the other maid, Wil glanced up with a shake of her head.

"She's poorly," Wil lied. "Something she ate, I think. But she was in no condition to serve tonight."

Mrs. Forster frowned. "Of all the nights. Your grandfather will take it out of her, that's for certain, and he won't care what the reason for her absence is. Lord Summerfield will do the same to Master Edison— hiding himself away on his own sister's birthday. Mark my words, Wil— you and I had better keep our heads down and our eyes on the job once the company take their leave. There'll be some unpleasant days at the Grange to come."

Distracted, Wil scanned the confines of the marquee. She let her gaze move methodically from one glittering, linen-draped table to another.

No Edison.

She'd grown increasingly loath to face him, plagued by how her feelings were shifting, and by design her path hadn't crossed Edison's once that day. It was putting off the inevitable, she knew—she'd have to manage herself long enough to hear whether he'd learned the names of the housemaids and nursemaid from Kitty. His absence troubled her, for it was as out of character as Abigail's disappearance. While Ed had done nothing to hide his lack of enthusiasm about the endless succession of cards and teas and croquet matches and dances he'd been subjected to since the week began, he'd attended everything dutifully, if somewhat dolefully.

Only to vanish at the pivotal moment.

There was nothing that could be done just now. Wil forced herself to focus once more, falling into the exhausting rhythm of clearing places without fumbling a single fork or glass, all while a polite smile stayed pasted to her face. At some point Kitty stood up and made a speech—a pretty, artificial thing, thanking the partygoers for their attendance and saying what a delightful time she'd had. She certainly looked happy. She smiled so brightly, it dazzled. And yet Wil hadn't failed to notice that Kitty Summerfield, who never drank anything but water with her dinner, had downed three glasses of champagne that evening and spoken not one word to her parents.

The quartet struck up the opening notes of "For She's a Jolly Good Fellow," and Kitty moved to the long dessert table that held her birthday cake, all but dancing her way over on slipper-clad feet. Wil watched as her own grandfather solemnly handed Kitty a knife, and with a show of concentration, Kitty cut the first slice of cake. Applause broke out, followed by little explosions of confetti from party crackers, as the partygoers—no, the audience—rose up to sing along with the strings.

Standing at the front of the marquee, not far from the dessert table, with the rest of the staff, Wil halfheartedly joined the singing. She watched as Kitty stood for a moment with her back to the tentful of well-heeled guests. In that instant there was nothing of life or light or joy behind her eyes. There was only darkness, brackish and fathomless as the depths of the Grange's cursed millpond.

But it passed in a flash as Kitty spun and dropped a mocking curtsy, her silvery laughter ringing out above the swelling chorus.

For another half hour, Wil was kept busy serving slices of cake, in addition to setting out stands of macarons and tarts and other dainties created by the kitchen staff. When a lull finally arrived, she rejoined Mrs. Forster by the serving table.

The housekeeper let out a sigh. "Well, that should hold them for a while. We're mostly through it now. Thank you, Wil—I know you did your own work and Abigail's tonight. Once the house is empty again, I'll see to it you get a half day."

"Could I take a few minutes before dessert needs clearing?" Wil asked. "I only want to run into the house and check on Abigail."

"Of course." Mrs. Forster nodded. "Don't be long, though."

Wil hurried across the shadowed lawns and into the house, which stood silent and empty in contrast to the lively marquee. She did not, however, go up to the servants' quarters—she'd checked Abigail's room earlier after first noticing her absence and found it empty.

Instead, Wil went to the nursery wing.

"Ed?" she called softly as she knocked on the door. "Ed, I only want to make sure you're all right. Are you in there?"

Nothing.

After another knock, Wil pushed the door open.

The nursery wing was as silent as the rest of the house, with no sign of Edison inside. Wil pressed a hand to her forehead, trying to think where else he might be. The laboratory was the only other room he seemed to have any affinity for—it couldn't hurt to look.

But when she went back downstairs and peered in, the wide room was emptier than all the others even, devoid of furnishings and life. Wil was just turning to leave when something caught her eye.

A faint glimmer of light, drifting out from between one of the bookshelves and the wall.

Lips parting in fascination, she crossed the room, only to find the bookshelf to be not just a shelf but also a door, and one left ajar.

Pulling it open, she found herself looking into a secret library, lined floor to ceiling with books. A single small window let in moonlight, and a lamp burned warmly on an end table beside a wingback chair, which was turned away from the door and hid its occupant from view.

"Now you know very nearly all my secrets," Edison's voice said from the armchair. "You've seen the nursery wing and this place. I've only got one other."

"How did you know it was me?" Wil asked, lingering on the threshold. She was worried that if she stood face-to-face with him, he'd see *her* secret. That she wanted to repeat what had happened between them several nights before, when he clearly never wished to again.

"I've been waiting for Kitty, but I could tell the two of you apart in the dark. We're supposed to clear the air between us tonight, but I couldn't watch Kitty being the person she makes herself into for company in the meantime, not when I know there's something eating away at her. I caught her arguing with *Shepherd* the other morning, of all people. And when I asked her about staff who've been dismissed, she wouldn't give me a straight answer. I'm worried about her, Wil."

Ed sounded weary and out of sorts, and Wil couldn't help herself. He was so often a comfort to her that she always wanted to put things right when he descended into a bleak mood. It only took five steps to get from the doorway to the other side of the hidden library, where his chair faced her rather than away.

But once she was there, Wil froze with her back pressed against the shelves. Everything in her ran to ice.

Seated in the chair with an open copy of *Grimms' Fairy Tales* on his lap was Edison. But a thick layer of fog clung to him, obscuring his features and rendering his form indistinct.

His soul had begun its departure.

The fog that swathed Ed like a shroud hung thickly enough that Wil could barely make out his features. He was so far gone; it must have begun that morning while Wil had been busy—had been using her busyness as a reason to avoid him, if she was honest, and she had no doubt now that death would come before dawn.

"Wil?" Edison said, a note of worry in his voice. She couldn't see his expression through the mist of his own retreating soul. "Is something wrong? I'd say you look like you've seen a ghost, but I've watched you do that without batting an eyelash."

"No," Wil answered numbly. "Nothing's wrong, I'm just . . . I have to get back to the marquee. I only wanted to be sure you're all right."

He wasn't. He was leaving her, and she was powerless to change his fate.

"Always better when you're here," Ed quipped, though the words seemed to require effort from him, when once they would have come easily.

Wil couldn't bear to look at him, half gone as he was already.

"I can't keep Mrs. Forster waiting." She kept her voice entirely flat, relying on the unbreakable composure she'd learned from her grandfather. "I'm off."

"Stay just a minute?" Ed was wistful now, but when he reached out and touched Wil's arm, his fingers were cold as death and damp with fog.

"No," Wil snapped. She felt she might be sick—everything in her was falling to pieces, but she would not, could not, let Ed spend his last hours in this same desperate fear. "No, I can't stay."

Spinning on her heel, she swept out of the hidden library and pushed the shelf closed behind her. She could see, upon closer inspection, where a latch pivoted, open and shut, to work the catch and operate the door. Wil stared at it until it blurred, hot tears filling her eyes.

Not him, too, she thought at nothing and everything at once. At Wither Grange, the halfway realm's restless souls, God himself. *My mother was bad enough. Don't take my last good thing as well. If he dies, there will be no color or light left for me. Even the living world will be no better than a blighted purgatory between here and death.*

A flicker of movement beyond the laboratory's bank of windows caught Wil's eye. Dashing away her tears, she watched as Kitty Summerfield slipped out of the marquee and into the night air, her silver-sequined party dress glistening like a downed star. Kitty started toward the house and then halted suddenly, as if in indecision, before beginning to pace the length of the middle terrace between the house and the lawn.

A wild idea took shape within Wil. For all her insight into the realm of the dead, she'd never been able to avert crisis. But there was power unlike her own, and perhaps it could be brought to bear against fate when her own talents could not. Perhaps Kitty, who seemed to know far more about the Grange and its inhabitants than she would say outright, might have some perspective on Ed's doom that could alter what was coming.

Without pausing long enough to let doubt creep in, Wil pulled books from the laboratory side of the hidden library door and jammed them beneath the latch until it stuck fast, imprisoning Edison in the little space beyond. Then she hurried out of doors, winging her way to Kitty like an arrow from a string.

"Kitty, I need your help," Wil said without preamble, panic forcing aside any thought of politeness or propriety. "I'm in awful trouble, and so's your brother. I don't know who else to turn to with this."

Kitty's face in the moonlight was drawn with frustration, and a little breeze stirred the tendrils of auburn hair that rested on her graceful neck.

"We're all in trouble," she answered. "You and Ed are hardly an exception to the rule. I haven't been able to help anyone else—what makes you think I can help either of you?"

"What do you know about me?" Wil said. "I mean, when you hear 'Wilhelmina Price, John Shepherd's granddaughter,' what's the first thing that comes to mind?"

When Wil glanced down, she saw that the older girl's hands clutched folds of her sparkling party frock and were white-knuckled with some unspoken stress. "I can't say the first thing that comes to mind. Not with every secret this house holds sitting like a noose around my neck."

Wil chose to ignore Kitty's cryptic hints. If she wished to be enigmatic, let her. Wil had no time for trying to puzzle out Kitty's riddles at present.

"They say in Thrush's Green that I'm some sort of medium, or have the second sight," Wil blurted out, the words caustic against her throat and stinging on her tongue. "They say I can see and hear the dead, and predict a death before it comes. It's true, every word. Your brother Edison is dying. I've seen it. He won't live till daybreak."

Before Wil's eyes, Kitty underwent a sort of metamorphosis. Her already pale face grew whiter still, her cornflower-blue eyes shifting to gray as some shock of purpose moved through her body, draining it of its perpetual lightness and leaving straight-backed resolve in its place.

"There'll be no help for me, then," she murmured under her breath, before fixing her gaze on Wil.

"What do you know about my brother?" Kitty asked, turning Wil's question back at her, though there was steel behind the words now. "I mean, when you hear 'Edison Summerfield, heir to Wither Grange,' what's the first thing that comes to mind?"

"He's the best of you," Wil answered without hesitation. "No one else in this family can hold a candle to him. He's good down to his core."

Kitty nodded. "I know. Have you ever tried to forestall death itself, Wil Price?"

"Yes. It never works."

Standing beneath the stars, before the backdrop of her own fey party, Kitty looked more than elfin. She could have passed for a great lady of the fairy realm, a queen of the *daoine sídhe*, a denizen of some older and more complicated realm that had long fallen out of step with the mortal world.

"Then perhaps," Kitty said, her eyes not on Wil but on the silent and towering bulk of the Grange beyond her, "it's time for me to try my hand."

"Do you think you can manage?" Wil said in agony. "Nothing I've done has ever been enough."

The bleakness Wil had seen in Kitty before rose up in full force, and for a moment they stood without moving.

"I'll be enough." Kitty's confidence was half defiant. "I'm a Summerfield, and we always rise to the occasion. *Surgite*, you know."

"Whatever it is you're going to do, wherever it is you're going to go, do you want me to come?" Wil offered. "I know I'm not family. I know I'm nobody to you, really. But I'd help if you'd let me."

For a moment Kitty looked as if the offer might sway her. Then sorrow and regret joined the darkness behind her eyes.

"No. I can't do that to you. You don't deserve it. You don't deserve any of this. Better you be free of it all for as long as you can."

Stepping closer to Wil, Kitty did the last thing she'd ever expected. With a waft of jasmine scent, she pressed a kiss to Wil's cheek.

"That's for you, and also for Ed," Kitty told her solemnly. "Tell him . . . tell him I knew about the nursery wing and Peter and all of it all along, only I never said anything because I'm a coward. I've done a great many foolish and hurtful things, but that's my worst fault by far."

"Tell him yourself, if you manage to save him where I fail," Wil said.

Kitty shot her a rueful smile. "No. I never confess my own sins like that, and I think he'll hear it better coming from you."

Squaring her shoulders, she set off toward the Grange's darkened southern side and the low-lying shape of the stables.

"Kitty, *please*, won't you let me—" Wil began to call softly, but Kitty raised a hand.

"No, darling," she said. "Don't ask again."

Wil retreated to the shadows fringing the house and leaned against the stone wall, which had gone cold in the night air. She stood that way for some time, fighting back despair over Edison, over her mother, over the helpless half knowing her deathsense brought with it, rather than any sort of actionable answer.

After several minutes, the barely audible sound of hurrying hooves on gravel drifted to her. Wil shut her eyes and felt a sudden jerk—not just a pull, but a forcible drag back toward the halfway realm. This time she didn't bother fighting it. What was the point, with Ed's life already hanging in the balance? Instead, she let herself be drawn to the gap between places, where Jenny Bright's hands reached through the fissure and sank themselves into Wil's living flesh.

She could tell the moment Jenny's spirit took control of her body. Wil began walking forward with a stiff and unfamiliar gait, following after Kitty. She rounded the corner of the Grange and watched dispassionately as her body conveyed her across the graveled stable yard and into the dark and dusty confines of the stable. There was no sign of Sam Jenkins, the groom. A few sleepy horse sighs sounded around her, and borrowed frustration surged through Wil as Jenny walked her into the just-emptied stall that must have held Kitty's horse.

Frustration mounted to rage as Jenny led Wil back out of the stall and into the stable's center aisle. The spirit kicked viciously at a can of paint, overturning it so that the poorly tightened lid snapped off and a viscous pool of green spread across the aisle. Still unsatisfied, Jenny reached for the nearest stall door and began to claw at it, all the while muttering *"Surgite"* over and over again in a husky whisper.

Enough, Wil thought. *Enough. I won't have you damage me again.*

Something near the stable door seized the attention of Jenny's vengeful spirit, and Wil used the opportunity to wrest control of her body back, drawing the spirit through the gap into the halfway realm. It was the work of a moment to shake Jenny off once there, but as Wil returned to herself, she realized it had still been too long. Her head snapped back with a jerk as someone seized her from behind, having crept up while she was occupied with the internal work of ridding herself of the dead. This time she was being controlled not from within, but from without. An iron grip held her by the back of the neck, her arms twisted behind her and pinioned fast by the wrists, so that she could not turn to catch a glimpse of her assailant. Though Wil cursed and fought and struggled, panic searing through her, she could not shake her attacker off. She was marched roughly down the stable's aisle and out a door at its farthest side, across a little graveled space to where a shed stood. The grip on her neck loosened just long enough for her attacker to push open the shed door and shove Wil inside.

She leapt to her feet at once but wasn't fast enough. Wil heard the bolt to the shed door slide home and the snap of a padlock shutting. When she threw herself against the door, the choking anger she felt was all her own, rather than a borrowed sentiment from Jenny.

But though she shouted until her throat was raw, the door stayed shut fast, the darkness around her complete.

A sickening thought struck Wil, and she began to beat at the door with her fists and shout all over again, never minding the state of her voice.

Unless Kitty managed to alter the course of fate, by the time anyone found her—*if* anyone found her—it would all be over for Edison. She'd have missed her chance to do anything else that might help, or to say goodbye, or just to see him once more. He'd be dead.

Another of Wil's useless, inhuman ghosts.

CHAPTER FOURTEEN

EDISON

At his core, Edison had a pragmatic streak and a tendency toward inertia when faced with any obstacle that seemed insurmountable. Accordingly, when the door to the hidden library failed to give way after a few determined pushes, he settled back into his armchair. He meant to read and to wait for Wil to come looking for him. She'd discover the jammed door and set him free, and that would be the end of his dull misadventure.

But in the absence of the nursery wing's disruptive inhabitant, he soon fell into an exhausted dead sleep, only to wake with early morning light streaming through the high window. There was the sound of someone rummaging about on the other side of the hidden library's door, and then it was pulled open, revealing Abigail on the other side.

"Master Edison," she said in surprise. "Whatever are you doing in here? Mr. Shepherd told me to come straighten the books on the shelf, and I found a latch behind them and—has this room always been back here?"

"As far as I know," Edison answered. "I use this place as a bolt-hole of sorts. Stupid of me to leave books where they could jam the catch, though. I didn't think anyone but my grandfather and Kitty and I knew about this spot, but of course Shepherd knows the house like the back of his hand. Are you feeling better today?"

"I beg your pardon?" Abigail asked with a frown.

"I heard you were ill yesterday. All's well again?"

"Oh." Abigail flushed. "Yes, of course. Thank you for asking."

Ed was already halfway across the laboratory, thinking of nothing but cleaning his teeth and splashing some cold water on his face, when Abigail stopped him.

"Master Edison." There was a note of anxiety in her voice, and he turned at once.

"Yes, Abigail?"

"You haven't seen Wil Price, have you? She didn't turn up this morning, and when I asked Mr. Shepherd about it, he said she never came home last night. Not that he seemed bothered, but you know what he's like. I don't think Armageddon itself could get more than a frown out of him."

"Wil's *missing*?" It felt as if the floor had dropped out from under Ed. The conversation he'd overheard between Kitty and Shepherd rattled around his sleep-heavy brain. It had seemed as if Shepherd was threatening Kitty with some unknown ill fate. And now instead Wil had vanished.

"Yes. I . . . I hoped she was with you."

Edison blinked and pushed his spectacles farther up with one finger as worry began to churn slowly in the pit of his stomach. "That would be wildly inappropriate, Abigail. When's the last time anyone saw her?"

"Mrs. Forster says she was serving in the marquee last night and asked to take a short break around ten. She never came back."

Ed couldn't help thinking of the millpond. He could hear Wil confiding in him that it felt as if history was repeating itself, and a fear like

155

he'd never known swept over him. The sharp-tempered ghost upstairs sometimes caused spikes of panic, but this was different. It was a low, bone-deep dread, a twisting and bitter root, and Ed wasn't sure he could bear up if it grew to full flower.

"She came in here around a quarter past," he said numbly. "Unless anyone else met her, I'm the last person she spoke to."

"How did she seem?" Abigail pressed.

"She looked afraid of something." Ed hated himself as he spoke the words. She'd been afraid, and he hadn't pressed to find out what it was. "I'm not sure what, though—she wouldn't stay."

"Did she say where she was going?"

"She said she needed to get back to the marquee."

"But she never did."

Ed and Abigail stood staring at each other, united by concern.

"I'm going to start a search," Edison said decisively. "We've got to do something. You take the house; I'll manage the grounds."

Abigail shifted her weight from one foot to the other, an agony of regret written across her face. "I can't. I already asked Shepherd if I could look, and he forbade me. So I went above him and asked your father. He said the same. Told me the staff have enough work to keep twice our number busy, and that I'd better tend to my duties. Then he said that if Wil misses a whole day's work, he'll sack her for negligence."

Edison let out a disapproving sound that was halfway to a growl.

"That's why I came to you," Abigail said. "I can't lose my post, Master Edison. But you could—"

He was already out the door, stalking down the crimson wound that ran through the Grange's heart.

"Wil!" Ed shouted, throwing open door after shut door and not bothering to close any. "Wil Price, where are you?"

He went over the entire ground floor that way, only to be met by his

156

father as he shoved open the study door near the house's front entrance. Lord Summerfield's face was furious as thunder, and he seized Edison by the arm.

"Just what do you think you're doing, making this racket when we have guests in the house?"

Ed pulled away sharply, scowling up at his father. "I'm seeing to it that our family takes responsibility for the people we're meant to look after, rather than tending solely to our reputation."

"That is *enough*," Lord Summerfield ordered. "You will stop all this and return to your rooms at once."

But Ed had already glanced past him and seen no sign of Wil in the expansive office beyond.

"Or what, Father?" he shot back over one shoulder, already on his way up the stairs. "You'll have me thrown out of the house and consigned to a hospital for people who are off their head again? I went quietly last time, but I wouldn't now. I'd raise hell on my way out the door."

On the next floor, he did just as he'd done below. Went the length and breadth of the house, shoving open doors and calling for Wil, ignoring the shocked faces of vaguely familiar guests as he roused them from sleep.

"Sorry," he repeated, over and over. "Sorry, I'm looking for someone."

"You're a rude, disrespectful boy," the Baroness de Vouche said shrilly when Ed came to the Green Room. She was sitting up in bed with curling papers in her thinning hair. "Your brother Peter never would have behaved so."

No Wil. "I'm sure you're right. And I'm sorry."

Then it was the attics, with the servants' quarters that sat mostly empty now. Nothing. Next the kitchen and scullery and larder and dairy on the Grange's lower level.

Nothing. Nothing. Nothing.

At last Edison headed outside. By then he could see people clustering in the breakfast room, ready to be fed on toast and muffins and soft-boiled eggs and to gossip furiously about that unhinged Summerfield boy.

Let them.

He'd lost the heart to keep calling out, but he carried on searching, looking through the marquee, which was disorderly and lifeless after the merriment of the night before. A few chairs lay overturned, and a silver-framed photograph of an infant in a christening gown had fallen over onto some of the other mementos of Kitty's childhood. Ed set it upright while the dread he felt grew to an all-consuming ache.

He searched the meadows, the rockery, the kitchen garden, the stable. Finally he sat down at the stable's far side, out of view of the rest of the house, and tried to summon the last of his failing courage.

He ought to check the millpond. He knew he should, but he couldn't find the strength to do it. So long as he didn't, he could sit here forever, with Wil alive and just missing. She'd still be somewhere in the world with him. But if he went out there and found—

No. He couldn't even think of it.

Through the grimy, cracked window of a nearby shed, Ed caught sight of something naggingly familiar. A flicker of faded, blue-white light. It shifted like sun on water and was so out of place that he squinted at it, then stood and drew closer.

Ed wiped dirt and cobwebs from the window with one sleeve and peered through the clear space he'd made.

It was a spirit. One of the alarming souls Wil drew back with her from the halfway realm, composed of limbs with too many joints and staring gas-lamp eyes and swirling fog. It hovered over a slumped form on the shed floor, and Ed knew beyond the shadow of a doubt that if there was a spirit within that place, it must be Wil on the floor.

He only hoped to God that the drifting thing was one of the hapless souls he'd seen her summon before, and not her own.

It was the work of a moment for him to dash back into the stable and rifle through the groom's locker in the tack room, where he found a bolt cutter. Hurrying back out, Edison had to try twice to get the padlock lined up between the bolt cutter's jaws, for his hands were shaking and his palms had gone slick. It took everlasting minutes and more effort than he'd thought possible to shear through the metal arm of the lock, but at last with a soft *snick*, the cutters sliced through, and Ed tossed them aside. He fumbled with the lock, and then the door was opening and Wil was sitting up, her face wary and bewildered, streaked with dirt and tears, but she was *alive*, and the look she gave Edison broke him clean in two.

"Edison," she said, her voice a choking rasp. She threw herself into his arms, and Ed held her tight, his cheek pressed to the top of her head. Wil was shivering and sobbing silently, and he'd never seen her so distraught before. She was always enough for whatever life brought to her, but this— this was Wil undone, and it filled Ed with a great surge of longing and helpless anger.

He said nothing, though, only stood and held her till she'd calmed a little, and then fished a crumpled handkerchief from his pocket and offered it. Wil took it and sat down abruptly, as if her knees wouldn't bear her up any longer. She wiped her face and fixed her eyes on him, as if she could not tear them away. Ed settled himself opposite her, and she held out both hands, a desperate, wanting gesture.

He took them at once and held her gaze.

"What is it, Wil?"

"I . . . ," she began, and drew in a deep, shuddering breath. "Last night, when we spoke, I saw your soul leaving. I knew you were going to die. I've never seen that without it meaning a death only hours later. I've tried to stop it happening and never managed. So I didn't say anything, because I didn't want you to be afraid."

"Good Lord, Wil." It felt as if the wind had been knocked out of him. To know he'd come that close to death and been spared for some unknown reason.

"I know. And then someone locked me up in here, and I knew you'd be dead before I could get out. That I'd never see you again. But now here you are, and everything about you has been put right. You're whole, and alive, and I—"

Her eyes filled with tears again, and she hid her face in her hands. Ed couldn't stand it, seeing her so small and heartsore in her soiled and wrinkled uniform. He reached out and drew her to him until they were side by side with their backs to the shed wall, Wil safe within his arms.

"I'm not going anywhere," he said, with everything he felt for her reverberating in the words. He knew himself to be perilously close to the sort of confession he so carefully avoided, but it couldn't be helped. She needed him right now—needed all of him, and this was part of who he was. "Do you think I could die if you still wanted me, Wil? I'd never dare to."

Wil looked up at him, and there was something in her beloved, upturned face—something soft and delicate and yearning.

"Ed, I love you," she murmured.

He swallowed and forced a smile. "I know. I love you too."

Wil shifted to look at him more easily and grew suddenly urgent.

"No, you *don't* know," she said, "and I hate for there to be anything unspoken between us. So I'm going to tell you, and if you find what I have to say distasteful or unwanted, then you're free to ignore it. Pretend I never said a thing. But it does need to be said, because I can't keep secrets from you.

"I don't love you the way I used to anymore. Things have changed.

160

Maybe if I tried hard enough, for long enough, I could get back to that old way of being, if it's what you want, but for now it isn't how I feel. I don't look at you any longer and think, 'My friend, Edison Summerfield.' I look at you and I want. I want you soul and body, like I've never wanted anyone before."

Ed shut his eyes. He could hear his own heartbeat going like the tide or a steam engine—powerful and desperate, striving toward a longed-for but unattainable end.

Don't speak, he ordered himself. *Don't say a word. This can only bring trouble to her.*

"I know you think that kissing me was a mistake and you're not eager to repeat it, but it was everything to me. And I don't want to pretend otherwise, because I never hid things from you before coming to the Grange. That's not the way with us. So I won't deceive you now, not even if it means you need time apart from me for a while."

Brave. She was so brave, his Wil, always able to own up to what he couldn't bring himself to face. Willing to walk through any outcome, so long as she did what she believed was right.

Don't, he repeated, eyes still shut as he heard her get to her feet in the face of his silence. *You don't deserve her. Hold fast for her sake.*

"I'm sorry," Wil said, her voice low and defeated. "I'm sure I've ruined things, at least for now. But I couldn't see my way around telling you. I'll keep out of your sight until we can both get past this."

Don't, Ed prayed as her steps retreated across the gravel.

Don't.

Don't.

Hang it all.

He was on his feet in an instant and after her, drawing her up short and turning her to him with a hand on her arm. And it wasn't him or Wil who began what came next; it was both of them—her rising on her toes and him stooping, his hands on her waist and hers at the back of his neck. They were hungry for one another, and when Edison kissed Wil, the intensity with which her mouth met his hit him like a fiery shock.

They found their way to the shadow of the stable, Wil against the wall and Ed between her and the world, where he'd always wanted to be. She was singular in her focus, and he'd expected no less, though he had not guessed that his Wil held such depths of heat and passion. It was more than he'd hoped for, more than he'd dreamed, but he pulled away from her at last.

"Wil," Ed said breathlessly as she carried on kissing him. Her warm mouth traced the line of his jaw and trailed down his neck, and God help him, he wanted to do things to her he'd never even let himself *think* of before. "Wil, stop a moment."

She stopped at once, looking up at him expectantly, her face flushed and her lips parted. Ed had thought himself lost before when he loved her with no hope of return. But it had been nothing compared to this.

"I've never said anything," he told her. "I couldn't. It wouldn't have been fair, because of my family and your grandfather and, oh, everything. But I have wanted this for what seems like an eternity. I only said the other night was a mistake because I didn't know you felt this way too. I couldn't be the first one to speak. I couldn't put you in that position."

"Poor boy," Wil murmured, cupping his face in her hands. "Poor honorable, tormented boy. I'm sorry you've had a hard time."

Ed lowered his head and kissed her again, slower this time and softer.

"All in all," he said against her mouth, "I think it's been worth it."

Wil laughed at that, her unselfconscious, unstudied, golden laughter, and when she slipped her arms around Edison's neck and held him close, he couldn't help but marvel. They were still what they'd always been, but also something else entirely. The old camaraderie and comfort he'd had with her was still there, coupled with this new, delicious pleasure. He couldn't have wished for more.

Ed felt the moment Wil stiffened in his arms. At once she pulled back, smoothing her dirt-stained apron with an odd, furtive air. When he turned, he found Abigail standing at the corner of the stable, her eyes red and a handkerchief twisted in her hands.

"They sent me out to look for Master Edison," Abigail said, her voice shaking. "Your family says you're to come at once."

"Abigail, what is it?" Ed asked. "What's wrong?"

Tears spilled from the girl's eyes. "I hate to say. I oughtn't to be the one who tells you."

"I'd rather hear bad news from you than from my father or mother," Ed told her with complete honesty.

"It's your sister. Kitty's dead."

CHAPTER FIFTEEN

EDISON

"Goodbye. Thank you for coming. We're sorry about all this."

Edison stood near the Grange's wide front doors, shaking hands and bidding farewell to a sporadic stream of guests. Kitty's would-be suitors; her sharp, glad friends; the class-bound worthies of the county—everyone was leaving. Lady Summerfield had insisted they all be turned out of the house before retiring to her own rooms with a bottle of laudanum. Lord Summerfield, who generally served as the family's bulwark in times of trouble, was nowhere to be found.

Which left only Ed.

Once there would have been Peter to take the reins during a crisis like this one. Though Edison was too innately different from his brother to have ever gotten on especially well with him, there was no denying Peter had performed the role of lord of the manor well. He managed upheaval proficiently, always knowing just the right thing to do and the right thing to say. Peter had been an expert in understanding and fulfilling the requirements of his class.

And Kitty—she'd seemed all foolishness and gaiety, but there was steel at her core. After Peter had been killed, Ed knew she was the one who'd held the family together, forcing them gradually back into some semblance of life and lightness through sheer force of will. She'd written to Edison every day that he was entombed in that wretched hospital, assuring him it was temporary, coaxing him to do as Lord Summerfield asked and own up to his shortcomings, even if it was a lie. What did it matter, Kitty had told him, so long as he regained his freedom? So long as there were two of them at the Grange again? She needed an ally, she said. She couldn't stand being left to manage the Grange and their parents alone.

Those letters had been the most truth Ed had ever had from his sister, at least since she'd put childhood aside. They'd stripped away her veneer of levity, revealing an underlying loneliness and desperation. He'd given in at the hospital more for her than for himself, and come home to find everything all at once the same and horribly changed.

The Grange ticked on like a well-oiled machine. Lord Summerfield was as masterly and absorbed in matters of business as ever. Lady Summerfield as distant and reserved. Kitty as laughing and seemingly carefree. Nothing different, and yet beneath it all they were in pieces.

Now Ed stood in further ruins. It was just him left to step into the place his brother and sister had filled, and which he'd always felt himself entirely unfit for. And while Peter's death had not been such a blow, Kitty's hit so hard that it had barely begun to hurt. Instead Edison was left numb, knowing that when the lack of feeling wore off, he'd find a gaping hole had been carved straight through his center. An irreparable wound, like the crimson track that ran straight through the Grange itself. It wasn't the sort of thing that would ever really heal, but something you had to learn to live with.

"Goodbye."

"Thank you for coming."

"A terrible thing, I know."

And then the last of them were gone. Ed hadn't wanted the party in the first place, but somehow when the final guests were packed into their motorcars and sent spinning off down the driveway, he wished they were back. The Grange had always seemed too big to him, but now it felt lifeless as a tomb.

He was spared by the sight of Lord Summerfield coming across the lawns, leading Kitty's horse Captain by the reins. Putting his hands in his pockets, Ed went out to his father.

"Everyone's off," he said. "Mother wanted the house emptied, and I thought she was right, under the circumstances. She's upstairs, asleep. What *happened*?"

Lord Summerfield's broad shoulders slumped, and it hurt Edison to see his indomitable father made vulnerable. "A stupid accident. Your sister went out on Captain. She is—was—a hell of a horsewoman, but she'd been drinking champagne last night, which you know she never does. A farmer found Captain in the church lane early this morning, and Kitty in the graveyard. She'd fallen and hit her head on one of the gravestones. It would have been quick—that's something, at least. That she didn't suffer."

"When did it happen?" Ed asked. "Was it last night or this morning?"

Lord Summerfield frowned. "Does it matter?"

"I suppose not." Edison ran a hand across his face. "Not really."

But it bothered him. It felt like teeth gnawing away at the back of his mind, knowing that Wil and Kitty had both come to harm when no one had known where they'd gone. A sudden wave of razor-sharp anxiety came over him—he needed to know where everyone was. If he could only keep track of them, they'd be safe.

"You did well, getting the house back to rights," Lord Summerfield said, setting a hand on Edison's shoulder. Ed couldn't remember the last

166

time his father had touched him or said something to him that bordered on approval. "Your mother and I may need to lean on you for a bit. Can you cope?"

"Of course," Edison said. It was all he'd ever wanted from them—to feel as if he was less the odd man out and more a part of the Summerfield whole. "Whatever you want me to do, I'll manage it."

"Good," Lord Summerfield said, and absentmindedly mussed Edison's hair, which Ed could never remember him doing before. "You're a good boy. Go check on your mother, won't you? And if she's awake, ask her about a day for the funeral."

Lord Summerfield walked away, heading toward the stable with Captain, and for the first time Ed thought his father looked small.

Upstairs the house seemed emptier than ever. The doors to every guest room had been left open, which gave the normally closed-off Grange an air of abandonment. Ed could see unmade beds, half-full glasses on dressing tables, a few trinkets that had been left behind in their owners' haste to leave their ill-fated surroundings. He caught a glimpse of Abigail and Wil, already at work stripping one of the beds and clearing wilted flowers. In a day or two it would be as if none of this had ever happened, except for the fact that Kitty was gone.

Kitty, gone. Ed nearly stumbled and reached for a side table to steady himself. But he settled in a moment and carried on to his mother's rooms.

Lady Summerfield lived in a perpetual shadowy gloom. The windows in her bedroom and dressing room were swathed in heavy velvet curtains that were never drawn back, the only illumination coming from a small electric lamp on her nightstand. She lay in bed now, motionless and white-faced against the pillow, with something clutched in her hand. But her eyes glittered in the dim light, and they fixed on Ed as he quietly shut the door behind him.

"You're meant to be sleeping," Edison said, crossing the room to

167

his mother's bedside. He could see now that the thing she held was the silver-framed picture he'd noticed in the marquee—an infant in a christening gown staring out of the photograph.

Lady Summerfield made no reply, only glanced up at him with a look that barely bordered on recognition. Ed let out a sigh and retrieved a chair from her dressing table, which he pulled over to the bedside.

"She was a pretty baby," Edison ventured, gesturing to the picture. "But of course how could she have been otherwise?"

"That isn't Kitty," Lady Summerfield said flatly. "It's no one you know."

Chastened, Ed subsided for a moment before trying again.

"Father says we've got to set a date for the funeral," he said. "He wanted me to ask you what you prefer."

The light in Lady Summerfield's eyes grew hectic.

"I have no intention of burying another child," she said, each word pronounced with some effort. "You can tell your father that."

"Mother," Ed told her, trying to sound encouraging and reasonable. "No one wants it, but it has to be done."

"No." Lady Summerfield sat bolt upright, and her face in the lamplight looked skeletal. "Tell him I refuse, and that if he takes her away, I shall . . ."

She faltered, as if she wasn't sure what threat or plea might be sufficient to sway Lord Summerfield on that point. But Edison understood. He knew what it was to want something so badly that you'd risk impropriety and transgress expectations to gain it.

"We won't do a thing until you're ready," he said soothingly, and Lady Summerfield took his hand.

"Good boy, Edison," she slurred, and he could see that sleep was finally coming. "You're a good boy. We've been too hard on you."

Her eyelids drooped and shut.

Ed did not go back to the nursery wing. Instead he went to the room that had been his before that summer. It smelled of strangers; the bed was in disarray, and one of the bureau drawers yawned open. Ed felt no desire to take up residence there again—it seemed entirely unwelcoming, as if he'd never slept in that bed or touched the furnishings before. Even the nursery wing with its sharp-tempered inhabitant was preferable, and he knew he'd stay there for as long as he could. Until his father or mother discovered the state of the rooms, and everything grew worse yet again.

Taking a blank notebook and a sharpened pencil from the desk, Ed went back out into the hall. He glanced at his wristwatch and jotted down the time, writing neatly below it, *Mother—bed. Father—stable.* Walking the length of the first floor, he caught sight of Abigail and Wil yet again, adding their names and locations to the list. Then he went down to the ground floor, scanning the uninhabited rooms. No one.

Down once more.

John Shepherd—butler's study.

Mrs. Forster, Mrs. Ellicott, Daphne—kitchen.

Jack Hoult—butler's pantry.

The grounds.

Henry Ellicott—rockery.

Bede—garage.

Sam Jenkins—stable.

And as Lord Summerfield was no longer in the stable, Ed carried on back indoors to begin again. He scribbled a new time into his notebook and, beneath it, *Father—study.* The meticulous action of wandering the house and grounds and reassuring himself of everyone's whereabouts soothed him. It set some anxious, nagging piece of his mind at rest and gave him a sense of purpose. Though he had misgivings about it—a suspicion that it might become a practice that was easier for him to begin than to stop—he surrendered himself. He refused to think about his mother's habitual wandering through the house in the years since Peter's death and instead let himself fall into the reassurance of routine.

There was no dinner that night. Lord Summerfield ate a cold supper in his study. Lady Summerfield slept. Edison walked, and no one seemed willing to interrupt. The moon rose high overhead, and he'd logged most of the staff as having gone to their rooms or departed for their own homes in the village.

"Ed," Wil's voice said softly from behind him. "I've brought you a cup of chamomile with honey. Come drink it, won't you?"

Edison found he couldn't speak. Not properly. He let Wil take him by the hand and lead him to the nursery wing, where she'd done a bit of tidying up. It hadn't made much of a difference, but even through his numbness he appreciated the effort. His bed had been set to rights and made neatly, and the thing that inhabited his rooms had not torn it apart yet.

Edison sat, and Wil wrapped his fingers around the warm mug. He made a show of sipping the tea, but in the back of his mind, a clock was going.

Ten in the evening, and where were his parents? Where were Mrs. Forster and Shepherd and Abigail and Daphne and—

"There's something I have to tell you," Wil said. "I thought about keeping it to myself, but that didn't seem fair. It's about Kitty."

For the first time, Ed turned and looked at her, seated on the bed beside him. She was pale and worried, the halo of golden curls around her face dimmed, the habitual black-and-white uniform making her small. That morning—when Ed had kissed Wil—seemed a thousand years distant. As if it had happened to someone else entirely.

Wil bit her lip and shot him a sidelong glance. Everything about her posture spoke of nervous energy, and muscle memory took over for Edison. He reached out a hand and twined his fingers through hers.

"I told you this morning I'd seen you dying," Wil said, her voice very low. "I've seen death coming, oh, dozens of times before. And I always try to do what I can, but nothing ever stops it. Nothing until you. Ed, I told Kitty what I'd seen. I asked for her help, and she said she meant to give it. She'd been on her way to speak with you, but she changed her mind and rode off on some other business, and I think you're alive because of her. She knew something about what's happening here, and whatever she did and wherever she went last night saved you. She wanted me to tell you something too—that she'd known about the nursery wing and Peter all along, but hadn't said anything because she was a coward, and that she was sorry for it."

Abruptly Edison got to his feet. He set the mug of chamomile down on his nightstand and took up the notebook and pencil he'd put aside.

"I have to go," he said. "I need to go make sure everyone's where they're supposed to be."

Wil frowned. "Is that what you've been doing all day?"

"Yes, I—"

Getting to her feet as well, Wil put her hands on Ed's shoulders and gave him a long, searching look.

"Edison Summerfield, do you trust me?" she asked at last.

"Always," he swore.

"Then let this go. I don't think it'll do you any favors. And you can't really change what's meant to be—not by knowing where the living are, nor by seeing the dead. God knows I've tried."

"But Kitty—" Ed began to protest.

"Kitty changed the pattern *somehow*," Wil said, her frown turning into that expression of fixed concentration she wore when pondering an intractable problem. "I don't know how yet, but if you could have heard her—she knew what she was doing. She chose it. You and I are just blundering in the dark. But I mean to find us more light, by and by."

171

As she spoke those last words, every one of the nursery's electric sconces lit, though their shattered bulbs ought to have been incapable of it. Ed said nothing—he was too accustomed to the chaos there. But Wil put her head to one side, as if she were listening.

"It's getting bolder, your ghost," she said. "Do you hear that?"

He did. Faintly, as if from a great distance, there came an echo of a voice filling the nursery wing corners.

One is one and all alone, and evermore shall be so, it sang, the words hollow and eerie.

Ed shivered. It felt too much like a reflection of his own feelings now that Kitty was gone.

"What did Kitty tell you when the two of you spoke about staff who might've had some connection to the nursery wing?" Wil asked.

"She remembered the housemaids—they were called Elinor Howard, Nellie Burke, and Mary Seldon," Edison said. "But she wouldn't tell me the nursemaid's name."

Wil frowned. "I'll have to ask Mrs. Forster or Abigail, then."

"There's something else," Ed told her reluctantly. "A few days ago I interrupted Kitty and your grandfather arguing about something. If she knew something about the deaths tied to the Grange, Wil, I think Shepherd knows it too."

Wil fell motionless for a moment.

"Yes," she said woodenly. "I . . . I've heard elsewhere that he might have information about my mother and Jenny. That he might have been involved in some way."

Wil spoke the last words so dispassionately that at first Ed couldn't fully grasp what she meant. But the absolute stillness of her face in profile was as good as a translation.

"You don't think—" he began, horrified. "It did seem awfully tense, the talk between them I walked in on. He was *threatening* her, it seemed."

"She wouldn't be the first he's made threats against."

"Wil, you can't go home with him," Edison said in agony. "I need you to be safe."

Wil only stared down at her hands and said nothing. For a long while they sat together, the only sound in the nursery the faraway singing of its ghostly inhabitant.

"Can I ask you something?" Ed ventured. "Whether she chose it or not, if I'm alive because of Kitty, that means she's dead because of me, doesn't it? How do I live with that?"

There was something raw and wounded in Wil's gaze as she looked back at him. "I'd tell you if I could. But since I watched my mother's soul leaving, I've wondered every day if the people I see going aren't dead on my account. Surely it's *for* something, being able to see death before it comes. If I were cleverer, or braver, or . . . more, in some way . . . I could stop their dying. I never manage it, though. And Kitty did. She was enough where I always failed, which means it isn't that death can't be turned around—it's that I'm too stupid and witless to sort out how to do it. That puts every soul I've ever seen dying on my conscience. So don't ask me how to live with guilt, because I don't know how to beyond this—you get up every morning, and you try again."

"Will you remind me of that tomorrow?" Edison asked, and Wil smiled halfheartedly up at him, though her eyes were weary.

"I can do better than that," she said, rising on her toes, the kiss she gave him soft as shared secrets. "If you don't want me going home, I can *stay* with you until tomorrow."

CHAPTER SIXTEEN

WIL

Edison's ghost was quiet that night. Wil had silenced it with her own voice—as she'd done when they were small and trouble came, she lay beside Ed, her fingers in his hair, and sang until his gaze blurred and his eyelids drifted shut.

She woke before dawn, with thin gray light drifting through the wide windows across the nursery wing. Edison's arm was around her, and Wil pressed a kiss to the back of his hand. Her uniform was more a disaster than ever—still dirt-smeared from her night of captivity in the garden shed, and now with a network of new wrinkles. But it didn't matter.

Slipping away without waking Ed, Wil smoothed his notebook open to a blank page and wrote carefully across it with pencil—

Wake up. Try again.

And that was all she had time for. The first songbirds were beginning their chorus outdoors. Downstairs the kitchen would be coming alive too. Wil meant to get herself unseen to the housemaid's closet, where she and Abigail each kept a spare uniform, and to make herself presentable before the day truly began.

Even the lowest level of the Grange seemed uncharacteristically subdued and devoid of life. Wil met no one until she slipped into the housemaid's closet—a whitewashed space stuffed full of cleaning supplies, with a single window, a washbasin, and a battered old wardrobe pushed up against one wall, where Abigail stored linens in need of mending and spare uniforms.

But Abigail was already within the close confines of the closet, standing at its single small worktable and laboring over a pair of shoes.

"Good morning," Wil said evenly, feeling no desire to explain herself or her appearance to the other maid. At the sound of her voice, though, Abigail glanced up as if stung, a penitent expression on her face.

"Oh, Wil. I've been meaning to get you on your own and apologize for what happened the last night of the party, before all this awfulness with Kitty. I didn't mean to just vanish, but something came up."

Wil blinked. The last two days were a blur already—a fog of shock and horror at seeing Edison on the threshold of death, of fear and helplessness at being forced into the stable shed and made temporary prisoner there, of exquisite joy upon realizing she and Ed were in accord. That their hearts beat as one.

And then the crash. The terrible news about Kitty, and the knowing that she and Edison had, in some inadvertent way, been a part of it.

"I left you on your own," Abigail went on, "and I know from what Mrs. Forster's said that you covered for me. That was very decent of you."

"No." Wil pressed a hand to her forehead. "It was nothing."

She looked down at the table and at Abigail's hands, busy with the work of cleaning and blacking a pair of shoes. There was something familiar about them—letters had been marked onto the soft lining at the back of the heel of each shoe.

J. S. John Shepherd. He had a habit of labeling anything that was his, and Wil's own mother had picked it up, following suit with the embroidered initials stitched into each of the uniforms Wil herself now wore.

"I only came in to change before starting morning rounds," Wil said. "I forgot to bring home my spare uniform last night with everything that's been going on, and this one's a mess."

Abigail nodded, untroubled and accepting of Wil's lie.

With a twinge of guilt, Wil turned to the wardrobe and skinned out of her filthy uniform. She'd do murder for a bath, but that would have to wait. Instead she pulled a clean uniform over her underthings and turned back to Abigail.

The girl had finished brushing the pair of shoes she was at work on and had turned them over to clean the treads on their undersides. An unpleasant jolt ran through Wil at the sight of them, for the soles of each of her grandfather's shoes were streaked and stained in places with green paint.

Wil knew that color. It was the shade of the lettering spelling out every horse's name on the box stalls in the stable, and the precise tint of the paint that had spilled while she was being forced out of the stable and into the shed behind it.

Wil's stomach dropped out from inside her. She had hoped against hope to find something that proved John Shepherd had not been involved in the deaths at Wither Grange—that his abrasive conduct toward the maids and finally to Kitty was simply the result of his unbending personality, and not of something more sinister.

But here lay further cause for suspicion—not laid out in black and white but in arsenic green.

"Are those my grandfather's shoes?" Wil asked with forced lightness. "Why don't you let me finish with them while you go have a cup of tea with Mrs. Ellicott? I don't mind at all."

Abigail hesitated. "Are you certain? Not that I wouldn't mind—I'm always happy to avoid a run-in with Mr. Shepherd, but he did ask *me* to clean them."

Wil held out a hand. "I wouldn't have offered if I didn't mean it. And I can manage Grandfather. You go have your tea—you must have been out late the night before last."

"And last night." Abigail smiled. "I know I ought not to be sneaking about and making a fool of myself. It's my position on the line if I'm caught, but—I think Nat really cares for me. I think we could be something, Wil. And he doesn't seem to mind at all that I'm common and kinless and have nothing. None of that matters to him."

For a moment Wil was silent. How simple it would be, she thought, if she and Edison were on equal footing. If one of them rose or fell to the other's sphere.

"I'm happy for you," she told Abigail, and meant it. "You deserve someone like that. Everyone does."

Wil waited until Abigail had disappeared down the corridor and into the kitchen. Then she drew in a trembling breath, took her grandfather's shoes in hand, and rapped on the door to the butler's study.

No answer.

Glancing over one shoulder, Wil tried the knob and slipped inside upon finding the room unlocked. Everything within was in perfect order. John's desk was kept immaculately tidy, and there were few personal touches in the room beyond a single badly embroidered sampler on the wall, which Wil herself had made as a much smaller girl.

And yet John couldn't have gone far if he'd handed over his shoes to Abigail not long ago, and she believed him to be on the property still.

Sitting down at her grandfather's desk, Wil dropped his shoes and put her head in her hands. If she was John Shepherd, flawlessly dutiful to a fault, what would she be doing now?

Wil's eyes fixed on the shoes, the only thing untidy or out of place in the room.

Of course. He'd asked Abigail to take care of them. He was systematically cleaning up the mess he'd made by interfering with Wil, because John Shepherd could not abide chaos or disorder.

Rising abruptly, Wil cut through the kitchen on her way out to the servants' courtyard. She set the shoes down beside Abigail, who'd settled in with a cup of tea.

"I'm sorry," she said, hoping the other girl would accept the apology. "But I've just remembered something I left undone yesterday, and it has to be seen to. It can't wait another minute. So I couldn't do these after all."

Abigail gave Wil a searching look over her teacup.

"It doesn't matter," was all she said. "I can take care of them, like I meant to."

Wil could feel Abigail's eyes on her as she hurried up the steps to the servants' entrance. Once outside, she gathered her skirts and sprinted across the courtyard, coming up short before rounding the corner of the stable. Taking a moment to catch her breath, she peered around the stable wall toward the shed.

And there he was. Her grandfather, removing the shorn padlock from the shed door and pocketing it before striding away into the mill wood.

For the briefest moment Wil thought about turning back. She considered forgetting everything she'd seen and heard when it came to John Shepherd. She would give her notice at the Grange and go back to life as it had been. Clandestine meetings with Edison. Security, if not love, when at home. Study undertaken independently to occupy her mind. And an ongoing attempt to ignore her nagging facility for communicating with the dead.

John had nearly vanished into the trees. An invisible threshold loomed before Wil. But she knew that, unlike the Summerfields, she could not live life surrounded by closed doors. She wanted openness and clarity, the assurance that she had known the truth, and that in some way, it had set her free.

Without allowing herself to hesitate again, Wil started out after John.

She trailed him through the mill wood, always far enough back that he would not notice her lingering presence in his wake. John's path never faltered—he led her straight through the woods and to the banks of the millpond. Wil suppressed a shiver and skirted the pond from within the trees, watching as John moved along the shore and to the boarded-up mill cottage, which adjoined the silent, defunct waterwheel. From his pocket he took a key and let himself into the house.

Wil flitted across the small open space between the cottage and the woods, and she peered through the nearest window, squinting through the gap between a pair of boards. Inside there were signs of habitation, though Wil had expected that. The Summerfields held the mill's title, and when they were younger, Wil and Ed had sometimes used the cottage as a playhouse. There were still leftover belongings strewn about and signs of a recent fire in the grate. It wasn't surprising to Wil in the least that Ed might have returned to their old bolt-hole to escape the shallow busyness of the house party. He had, she was beginning to realize, a penchant for hidden, out-of-the-way places.

What Wil did not expect was to move to the next grimy window, which looked into an inner room, and find it full of people.

Not just John, but Mrs. Forster, Jack Hoult, and Sam Jenkins, the groom, all stood inside. It could have been a meeting of the Grange staff had the Ellicotts and Bede the chauffeur not been missing, along with the housemaids. And there was one incongruous addition—Nat Halliday, Abigail's sweetheart, stood among the staff, all five of them involved in some manner of serious-looking conversation.

With an anxious, sinking feeling at her center, Wil retreated to the cover of the trees. Ahead of her the water glimmered darkly, the stream murmuring voiceless threats as it ran over the rocks and into the pond's still depths. Whatever was happening at Wither Grange, she no longer trusted any of the staff to answer her questions honestly. Her only truly straightforward witnesses were the dead, though their cryptic warnings and communications made them difficult allies at best.

It was high time she uncovered the identity of her one nameless ghost—or rather, Edison's nameless ghost. And if answers could not be found at the Grange, Wil knew who to turn to next.

*　　*　　*

When, at midafternoon in the lull between luncheon and tea, Wil murmured a word to Abigail about ducking away for an hour, the older girl agreed to cover for her without hesitation. It might be wiser to hang on to the fact that Abigail felt as if she owed Wil a favor, but what Wil had seen in the mill cottage was gnawing away at the back of her mind. If she didn't begin turning up some sort of useful information soon or gaining some sort of forward momentum, Wil worried her growing frustration would boil over.

So she slipped away from the Grange and into the busier, pretty environs of Thrush's Green. It felt like a parallel world already—once the village school had been the center of Wil's life, and even after she'd left, she'd been a fixture there, studying on the commons and running whatever errands John required. Now, though, she spent precious little time in the village, for the Grange was all-consuming.

Above Wil, the post office bell jangled as she stepped inside. Mrs. Grey was alone, seated behind the counter with a women's magazine and a cup of tea.

"Wil Price," the acid-tongued postmistress said with a tilt of one eyebrow. "Here I thought you'd outgrown us all, now that you're working up at the Grange."

"Mrs. Grey," Wil answered evenly. She couldn't recall how she'd ever allowed the postmistress to worry or cow her, now that she'd been subjected to Kitty's interrogations and Lord Summerfield's scathing critiques. "I need information, and you're the person in Thrush's Green who knows everyone and everything."

"Well, I do like to keep my ear to the wall, as it were," Mrs. Grey said, visibly pleased by what she took as a compliment. "Not much happens in these parts that gets by me. It comes with the job, though."

"Naturally. I was wondering if you still had the forwarding addresses for several housemaids who used to work at the Grange—Elinor Howard, Nellie Burke, and Mary Seldon."

The information came readily to Wil's mind. In the quiet, small hours of the night before, she and Edison had discussed the information he'd gained from Kitty and the argument he'd overheard between his sister and John. Wil had no need of jotting the details down—once she heard a thing, it would be kept safe within, ready to be called upon as needed.

"I should," Mrs. Grey said. "Let me just take a look in my ledger and copy them out for you."

She moved busily down the long counter to where an enormous leatherbound book waited. It took several minutes for Mrs. Grey to locate the information and a great deal of paging through the ledger. At last she returned with three addresses on a card.

"There they are. As far as I know, all three of them are happily settled now—Elinor on her family's farm in Wiltshire, Nellie with a cook she met at her next posting in York, and Mary's gone on to get secretarial work in London. Why exactly do you want their addresses?"

Mrs. Grey's eyes glittered as she asked, and Wil knew the gossips of Thrush's Green would hear of her visit and her inquiries within the hour.

"I wanted to ask their advice on cleaning solutions," she said blandly.

"Apparently there was some sort of citrus wood polish one of them had a recipe for, and they took it with them. No one's been able to buy or brew anything that worked better since, so I'm trying to hunt it down to please Mrs. Forster."

Mrs. Grey looked vastly disappointed.

"One more thing," Wil said. "The nursemaids have always done the tidying up in the nursery, so it might have been one of them who came up with the polish. I have the information for Nurse Finch, but I haven't been able to find a name or address for the nursemaid who came before her."

The glitter in Mrs. Grey's eyes lit once more. "Well now, that was Margaret Willis—Maggie, we all called her. She was a nice girl but not happy at the Grange. Didn't like the position, for some reason or other, though they paid her well enough for two nursemaids. Funny about her leaving—she just packed up one night and vanished. Was gone in the morning without having given notice or even hinted that she planned to go. I asked anyone I could think of but never did sort out what happened, nor could I find where she'd gone."

Questions crowded Wil's mind, but she knew better than to ask anything else of Mrs. Grey. Let her cover stand—that she was interested in no more than a recipe for citrus polish and would not be especially crestfallen if her search came to nothing.

"Pity," Wil said. "I hope it was one of the other maids who has what I'm looking for, then."

"Yes," Mrs. Grey answered, giving Wil a narrow *I know you're up to more than you let on* sort of look. "A pity indeed. Shouldn't you be getting back to the Grange? They'll miss you if you're gone too long."

"Will they miss me?" Wil asked, and for the first time she could ever recall, a moment of shared understanding passed between her and the acerbic postmistress. The look Mrs. Grey gave her was near sympathetic.

"No," Mrs. Grey said. "I suppose they'd go on just as they always have. It's not for the likes of you or me to get in the way of a house and a family like that. Nothing we do much matters to them."

"Thank you for the information." Wil took the card and gave Mrs. Grey a grateful nod. "I appreciate your help."

"Hm," Mrs. Grey clucked. "You just be careful out there, Wil Price, and remember what I've said to you. Nothing we do matters to folk like that. Not our living, nor our dying. You land yourself in some sort of trouble, like your mother or Jenny Bright, and that place will close in around you as if you never lived."

*　　*　　*

Mrs. Grey's parting words were still ringing in Wil's ears when she returned to the Grange, where she found what seemed like a living manifestation of the postmistress's warning.

At the heart of the house, an exquisitely ornate coffin sat in state. It rested on a stand in the center of the soaring front foyer, so that whoever entered or exited the house by way of the main doors could not avoid it and anyone who used the central corridor would be forced to acknowledge its presence. A drift of flowers obscured most of the stand, and the air in the foyer was heavy with the scent of jasmine.

Wither Grange, as Wil passed by the coffin, seemed preternaturally still. Even the sound of the landing clock was muffled, as if it did not dare to chime. There were still bedrooms to be cleared out, stripped of leftover signs of life and rendered as empty and sterile as the rest of the Grange, but as Wil rounded the coffin and came within sight of the staircase, she stopped.

Edison sat on the lowest stair, notebook and pencil in hand, scratching away at it with an intent look on his face. At the sight of Wil, he set the notebook aside with a furtive, guilty gesture.

183

"Is she in there?" Wil asked. There was no need to clarify what she meant—the coffin drew all attention to itself, demanding acknowledgment. Kitty, at least, warranted remembering for now. Aside from the initials stitched in the collar of Wil's own uniforms, Mabel Price did not. Jenny Bright was gone without a trace. Whoever the ghost in the nursery wing was, they'd been forgotten. Their only voice left in the living world—their only intercessor—was Wil herself, by virtue of her uneasy connection to the realm of the dead.

Ed nodded, and with a sigh, Wil went to sit on the stair beside him, lacing her arm through his and resting her head on his shoulder. It was a risk, but she didn't care. Couldn't care, in light of what had happened.

"Mother won't set a date for the funeral," Ed told her, staring straight ahead at the coffin, though there was no look of recognition in his eyes. "This was all she'd agree to. She said we'll keep Kitty here with us until something changes. Until things get better. But I don't see how they can."

Wil twined her fingers through Edison's, clasping his hand in both of her own. "What can I do? Is there any way I can help?"

A long silence fell between them, during which the Grange seemed to consume all sound and thought.

"My father says it was a riding accident," Ed ventured at last. "But we all know Kitty sat a horse like she'd been born in the saddle. If you could ask her what happened—"

Wil winced. "Ed, I wish I could just walk into the halfway realm and find out what's been going on. But I have tried and tried and never been able to make any sense of all this. The spirits there—they aren't who they were in life anymore. They're not *whole*. You've seen them. Their minds are as tormented and twisted as their bodies. All they have to offer is fragments, and I've never been able to sort those pieces out."

"I want you to keep trying," Ed told her, his voice adamant, though she could not see his face. "You're better at finding the meaning of a thing

184

than anyone I know, and if anybody can untangle all of this, it's you."

Wil's throat tightened, and she swallowed hard. The reliance of the dead was already an impossible weight to bear—Ed's expectations added to those seemed enough to crush her. But she fell back on the reserve Shepherd had passed on to her, refusing to show how her heart quailed within her or how wretchedly tired she already felt.

"I'll do my best," Wil said. "But there's a great deal of difference between this and making a stanza of poetry come out right in translation, or doing the same with an equation. I may not be enough for it."

"You're always enough," Ed answered with unshakable certainty. "You're the only thing I'm sure of in the world anymore. And I know something will come to you sooner or later. You don't fail, Wil."

She ducked her head so that he could not see and bit viciously at her lower lip. Because as far as Wil could tell, she'd been a failure since the day her mother Mabel had died.

"There is one thing," she said, dredging the truth up from within her because she did not want to speak of it, but the honesty she'd cultivated with Edison compelled her to do so. "I have . . . concerns . . . about some of the staff. More than one of them, actually. There's nothing conclusive yet, but I've heard and seen enough to worry. And I'm all but certain I know who was responsible for shutting me up in the stable shed the night Kitty died."

"Who is it?"

Ed pulled away to look at her, but Wil couldn't meet his eyes. She couldn't bring herself to say the name. To acknowledge that perhaps she'd spent the years since Mabel's death living with someone who'd brought about her mother's end. But Edison knew Wil better than anyone. She didn't need to speak—all she had to do was let him read it in her face.

So she dragged her gaze up to his and heard the moment he divined the truth. Ed took in a short, sharp breath, and his jaw tensed.

185

"Wil, no."

"I can't be sure yet," she said, voice flat, her expression a mask, only her eyes speaking of what it would mean to her. "But I have serious concerns. And I saw something unnerving. It wasn't just my grandfather, it was . . ."

Wil faltered, and to her shame, she could not go on. She prided herself on her strength—with the exception of her lapse upon finding Ed still alive after seeing his soul departing, she kept herself upright. Weathered the storms life brought with the same reservoir of calm her unshakable grandfather possessed. He had been, in so many ways she'd barely acknowledged, a bulwark and an inspiration to her. He'd set the tone after Mabel's death and taught Wil by example what it meant to carry on.

To think all of that might be false and rotten at its core turned Wil's stomach and set her blood to running cold. To think the Grange might harbor more than one tainted soul felt like the walls of a cage closing in around her.

"Are you safe?" Ed asked, taking both of her hands in his. "Whatever comes next, that's what I have to know."

Hesitantly Wil nodded, then with more certainty. "Yes. Yes, I think so. Grandfather might have done anything that night he locked me away. But he didn't. He didn't harm me at all. And in his own way, he's always been kind."

John Shepherd had fed and clothed her. Seen to it that she was looked after when she was still too small to look after herself. Sent her to school and never mentioned service or employment or marriage, even when she grew older and took an interest in nothing but books and her assignations with Edison.

But it was the uniform he seemed to stand against. The drab black and white her mother had worn, and Jenny Bright, and that she and Abigail now wore in their place.

And then there was Kitty. Wil could not for the life of her sort out how Kitty fit into it all. The coffin at the heart of the Grange, the incongruous nature of Kitty's death—not a servant, but the precious heart of the Summerfield family; not drowned in the millpond, but killed in the churchyard—ate away at Wil. Kitty was a piece out of place, a missing page, a crack in the mold, as was the bizarre assignation Wil had witnessed in the mill cottage that morning.

"I would feel better," Ed said carefully, "if I knew where you were. Especially if your grandfather's had some hand in all of this. I don't suppose you'd consider moving into the servants' quarters upstairs?"

It was all at once unbearably tempting and an appalling notion. The idea of being away from John as her suspicions bore fruit or withered was a relief, yet to allow herself to be wholly absorbed by the Grange—something deep and instinctive in Wil rejected the arrangement out of hand.

"I can't," she said. "Look what happened the last time I tried to alter the way of things. I've learned my lesson. I mean to watch and wait. I expect you can help me with that."

Ed shifted uncomfortably, one of his hands straying to the notebook by his side with an automatic motion.

"Yes. We'll both be on our guard."

Wil got to her feet, retrieving her broom and bundle of linens. Once she had them in hand, she stopped and looked at Ed, still sitting pale and terse on the bottom step.

"Everything's just awful," she said to him on impulse. "It's all right to feel that it is. Reasonable, even."

Some of the tension drained from Ed, and he shot her a look of gratitude. "It's a nightmare. What the *hell* are we going to do?"

"I don't know," Wil answered as she started up the stairs. She was glad to be past him, so he couldn't see the bleak expression on her face. "But I'm sure I'll sort something out. And there is one bit of good news—I've put a name to the nursemaid who served here before your Miss Finch. She was called Margaret Willis, but she left without a word of warning and seems to have fallen off the face of the earth."

"You'll find out what's happened to her." Ed's voice followed her like yet another ghost. Another haunting thing to hang on to her heels, tripping her up and insisting on attention. "You always manage."

"Yes. I always do."

CHAPTER SEVENTEEN

EDISON

U pstairs.
　　Downstairs.
　　Servants' quarters.
　　Kitchen.
Stable.
Garage.
Gardens.
Again.

It was the only thing that kept Ed together—the constant repetition of assuring himself of everyone's whereabouts. After Wil and Shepherd and the rest of the day staff left, their absence gnawed at his insides. Anxious restlessness, a burning need to know that the Grange's people were safe and well, drove him out of bed several times over the course of the night to carry out his rounds. Once, in the small dark hours when late blended into terribly early, he peered in at his mother's door and found her awake. She lay in bed still, her eyes glittering in the gloom, lamplight glinting off the silver-framed portrait on her nightstand. Though she looked at Edison, she said nothing, and he couldn't find words for her either. Without speaking, he shut the door and carried on.

During the in-between times when Ed lay in the nursery wing, trying to quiet the compulsion to get up, to walk, to determine everyone's location yet again, the spirit there sang endlessly. Its more destructive tendencies had, for the present, come to a halt, but it droned on and on.

Two, two, the lily-white pair,
Clothed all in green, O.
Green grow the rushes.
Green grow the rushes.
Green grow the rushes, O.

The night passed in a fever dream of half-awake activity and ghostly song, until finally dawn broke, and Edison caught sight of both his father and Abigail out on the lawn in the lee of the house. Though it sat like a splinter inside him, seeing them together, it was no longer the shock it had been at first. He watched from the nursery-wing windows as the two of them spoke together for several minutes, and then as Lord Summerfield placed an envelope into Abigail's hand.

Yet another payoff, Edison assumed, though he'd seen nothing untoward between his father and the housemaid beyond the exchange of checks and banknotes. Below him Abigail and Lord Summerfield parted ways, the maid heading toward the mill wood and his father toward the stable. After several minutes Lord Summerfield reappeared, leading Captain. He swung into the saddle and rode off down the Grange's drive.

Something sparked within Edison at the sight of his father leaving. Meticulous and prideful Lord Summerfield, who managed half the county from his study just within the Grange's grand front doors. The study was his sanctum, which he'd welcomed Peter into but from which Edison was perpetually barred. He kept both his business and his secrets there, secure in the knowledge that no one would invade his personal sanctuary.

Stuffing his notebook and pencil into his trouser pocket, Ed hurried out of the nursery wing and down the front stairs. As always, the door to the study was firmly shut, and through the foyer windows he could see Lord Summerfield riding off through the gate. Pointedly refusing to look at the coffin resting in state only feet away from him, Ed went to the study and tried the door.

Locked. But of course at the Grange, almost every room had more than one way to enter.

Taking the nearest stairway down to the warren of servants' rooms, Ed nosed about the whitewashed halls. With the exception of a few main areas—the kitchen, the staff dining room, the butler's study—he was unfamiliar with the layout of the Grange's lowest environs. But there must be a way up to Lord Summerfield's office. Ed's father was not one to let staff come and go through the doorway he himself used.

"Master Summerfield," a mild voice said from behind Ed. "Can I be of assistance?"

Turning, Edison found Shepherd staring down at him. Wil's suspicions swirled around in his troubled mind—he'd known Shepherd all his life. The man had been a serene and unruffled presence as far back as Ed could remember. It seemed impossible that he might be capable of anything involving violence or passion.

"Oh, I, um. I wanted to fetch something from Father's study, but he's gone out and left it locked. I had a letter come with the mail, and he has it in there."

"I have the keys," Shepherd said. "I'll fetch the letter for you. Where shall I bring it?"

"No, no." Ed hurried to throw him off. "I don't want to trouble you; I can do it myself. Just tell me how to get up there from down here."

"I'll show you," Wil cut in, stepping out from the housemaid's closet while still in the act of tying on her apron. "Don't worry about it, Grandfather—I need to clear up anything His Lordship left out last night anyhow. Abigail warned me he always has a nightcap in the study and gets out of sorts if the glass isn't taken away."

Though Shepherd's mouth tucked in at the corners in a vague gesture of disapproval, he turned toward the kitchen and vanished around a bend in the corridor.

"You're here," Edison said, relief surging through him at the sight of Wil. "And you're in one piece."

"Yes," she said, her lips pursing faintly in an unconscious echo of Shepherd's gesture. "Why wouldn't I be? You told me yourself—I'm always enough and I always manage, no matter what life brings."

Something niggled at Ed. Wil seemed displeased, though he couldn't imagine why. But he couldn't waste time, not when his father might be back at any moment.

"Father's study?" Ed prompted, and Wil swept past him.

She led the way to a narrow back staircase he'd never seen before, at the head of which was a still-narrower door. Wil pushed through it and Ed followed, finding himself disoriented by the odd view of his father's office. He'd come out at the wrong end, near the enormous desk. An ancient, slightly moth-eaten tapestry hung near it and neatly hid the servants' door.

Without a word to Edison, Wil walked through the room methodically. She bent and pulled a crumpled piece of paper from beneath his father's armchair and set it into the wastebasket, then straightened the hearthrug and the antimacassars draped over the armchairs' backs. Last she picked up the glass from the sideboard that still had the amber dregs of a whiskey-and-soda at its bottom, then stood waiting for Ed, blank-faced and dutiful.

A twinge of irritation shot through him. She was clearly out of sorts, and it irked Edison how she'd begun to wield her new position as a weapon. For anyone else, the uniform and the duties and degree of invisibility it brought might be a shield—something to hide behind. But Wil, damn her, could brandish them like a knife, and the way she stood now was a twist of the blade.

Impatiently Ed turned to his father's desk. He opened and shut drawers and shifted papers, taking care to return everything to its precise place. At last, in the bottom righthand drawer, he found a massive, clothbound ledger.

Setting it on the desktop, Ed scanned the entries for the last few months. Everything seemed in order. A lot of outlandish party expenses. Household purchases. Notes set down for the staff payroll. Nothing unusual, unless Lord Summerfield had hidden Abigail's clandestine windfalls by padding another payment.

Frustrated, Ed rifled through the pages, starting at the beginning and letting them drop like a fan. As he did, a loose paper slipped from the ledger and fell to the floor.

"Here," Wil said evenly.

He turned and found her holding the page out to him. Taking it, Ed was about to return it to the ledger, and the ledger to its place. But something stopped him.

A rill of eerie music.

Come and I will sing you.
I will sing you two, O.
Two, two, the lily-white pair,
Clothed all in green, O.

Ed had never heard the nursery-wing spirit outside of its specific realm before. Its voice emanated from everywhere and nowhere at once and sent a chill down his spine. On instinct, because he needed something to occupy and calm himself, he unfolded and smoothed the paper Wil had handed him.

In neat rows across it marched a record of payments. Each recipient was designated by number, not by name, and while most had received payments regularly for some eight years, a few stretched back further, thirteen years into the past. Edison would have thought it significant—Mabel had died eight years back—but for those aberrations. Something else bothered him too—there was no payment listed as first.

Turning the page over, Ed found what had been missing. A numeral 1, along with a name and address, a date thirteen years past, and a single sum twenty times that of the others.

Margaret Willis. And an address in London, along with something that had been jotted down later.

Three digits.

A telephone number.

Mutely Edison held the paper out to Wil, who took it and scanned the contents.

"Is this what you were looking for?" Wil asked.

"Yes. No. I wasn't sure what I was looking for, really. Only I've seen Father paying Abigail for something more than once now, and that's not the way things ought to be. Your father and Mrs. Forster pay the staff. I didn't expect to find anything about the nursemaid."

Wil was silent for a moment before speaking.

"It's not—there's nothing *between* them, is there? Your father and Abigail, I mean."

Ed shrugged. "Not that I've seen."

"Well, you've still found something useful. Ring that number up," Wil urged. "We might never have a better chance. The only telephone's in here, and who knows when your father will be gone next?"

A great reluctance crept over Edison. For some reason he hated the idea of doing it. So long as he didn't, they could go on believing that the ghost in the nursery wing might be Margaret Willis—that they'd made progress of some

194

sort. But if he rang, and the woman who'd been a nursemaid at the Grange proved to be alive and well, they'd be no better off than at the beginning—worse off, even, for at least once Wil had divined that the ghost upstairs *was* a ghost, they'd had an idea of how to begin searching for its identity. If this proved a dead end, Edison was at a loss as to how they'd continue.

Slowly, he moved to the telephone as Wil took up a position beside the front window, where she could see if Lord Summerfield returned. Ed dialed for the operator and gave the number listed. The tinny ring that followed felt as if it would jar his bones.

"Glendon House, this is Graham speaking," a distant male voice said after what felt like a terribly long time. "How may I help you?"

"I'm looking for Margaret Willis," Edison said. "Is she there?"

Silence fell. Then, "Who may I tell her is calling?"

Damn. The truth, perhaps, would be best. "Tell her it's Edison Summerfield from Wither Grange."

"You'll wait, please."

If the time it took for the telephone to be answered seemed long, what passed next was a small eternity. Wil stood motionless by the window, a silent and inscrutable sentinel.

Finally a tense voice on the other line.

"This is Margaret Willis. Who's speaking?"

"Miss Willis. I'm so pleased you're there. This is Edison Summerfield, and I—"

"Have they enlisted you, of all people, to badger me now?" Margaret Willis asked, the words crackling with emotion. "You're far better off leaving me alone. If I haven't said anything about the Grange yet, I'm hardly going to now."

"I don't mean any offense," Edison said in bewilderment. "You were the nursemaid at Wither Grange for myself and my sister Kitty when we were both very small. I'm afraid Kitty's been in an accident, and—"

"Dear God. *Another* accident?"

"Yes. She had a bad fall while riding. Nothing could be done. It'll be a private funeral, just family, but I thought perhaps you'd want to know, as you helped raise her."

All things considered, Edison thought he was doing very well, covering for the fact that all he'd wanted was to ascertain if Margaret Willis *did* still exist somewhere in the living world. It certainly didn't seem to be an imposter on the other end of the line. The depth of feeling seemed genuine, the responses too baffling, for someone attempting to perpetuate fraud.

"Little Edison on the line, and Kitty dead," Margaret said, as if to herself. "I can't think what . . . Are you at the Grange now, young man?"

"Yes," Ed answered. "In my father's study."

"If you are Edison Summerfield, you ought to leave," Margaret said abruptly. "Now. Take whatever you need and go stay with relations or friends. It doesn't matter much who, only that you get yourself out of that house."

"If it's really her, ask about the ghost. Ask her about it outright," Wil said from the window. "What have we got to lose? Maybe she saw or heard something while she was here."

Edison nodded dutifully. "Miss Willis, there have been disturbances in our nursery wing for some time now. Events that seem inhuman in origin. Did you ever experience anything of that sort when you were here?"

"I *knew* this must be some ne'er-do-well looking to dredge up old troubles," Margaret said furiously. "Whoever you are, don't ever reach out to me again."

The line went dead.

Edison frowned, moving to join Wil at the window.

"Well?" she asked expectantly.

"I think it was her," Edison said. "She seemed agitated. Told me that if I am who I say I am, I ought to leave the house. But then when I asked about the ghost, she got angry. Seemed to think the whole conversation must be some sort of vicious prank. I don't know what to make of it."

"Neither do I," Wil answered softly.

"But you will."

Edison spoke for his own reassurance more than anything else. He needed to believe that when everything felt as if it was crumbling around him, *someone* could put the pieces back together. Wil had always been that someone. His faith in her was implicit. Since the very first time she'd sorted out his discomfort and anxiety over being a Summerfield through the simple act of letting him be with her—of letting him be just Edison, Wil Price's less brilliant friend—he'd known she was the solution to any problem he might face.

He needed that faith now more than ever. But the look Wil gave him as he spoke of his confidence was so devoid of the hope he felt, it cut him to the core.

*　　*　　*

That night, in the scant hours between making his compulsive rounds of the house, Edison dreamed.

He dreamed of the nursery wing. Not as he knew it now, torn apart and obviously inhabited by some force of chaos. Not as he'd known it in childhood, when it had been a sunny and well-managed haven. He dreamed of a shadow version of that familiar space. There was no roof, just walls open to a high and unforgiving gray sky. The windows were long broken, fringed with thorns of glass. A thick layer of dust lay over everything, and nothing within that dead space moved.

Ed stood at the center of the silent, motionless nursery wing for a long time, until he began to feel lifeless and overshadowed himself. He could not find the will to move, or think, or feel.

And then the faintest whisper stirred before him. A little hiss, the sound of something small and granular falling. It broke Edison's reverie, and he cast about himself, searching for the source of the sound. After a moment he found it—a thin stream of mortar was falling from the back of the brick fireplace. Frowning, Edison drew closer.

The mortar stream grew heavier, then died away, but in its place, one of the bricks began to judder and shake as if animated by some unseen force. It continued to rattle, making a grinding, grating sound of stone against stone. With a dull, floor-shaking thud, something struck against the back of the fireplace from behind it, sending spiderweb cracks running through the brickwork.

A vague horror had begun to stir in Edison, but now that he'd reached the hearth, he found it impossible to turn away. The cracks grew and widened, gaping into fissures from which mortar and shards of brick fell. At last, with a terrible scraping noise, an entire brick dropped to the floor.

With the lightning-fast, jerking motions of an insect, a human hand shot through the gap. But it was hardly recognizable—the flesh was mottled and bloated, the fingers swollen and rotting away in some places, all the pale skin gone to decaying shades of gray and blue and black.

Everything in Ed screamed at him to turn, to run, but he could not move. Another brick fell, and the hand was joined by its mate. Those rotting fingers made quick work of the fireplace backing, prying it all away with inhuman strength, and then someone—some*thing*—crawled from the recess behind the hearth.

Wil's spirits were always definitely that—spirit. There was nothing truly bodily or enfleshed about them. It was as if they clung to a semblance of the human form through force of habit, despite being made of an entirely different substance. But this creature—it was all body in a way that sickened Ed. It crawled out from between the teeth of leftover brick and crouched before him on its haunches, with its fingers splayed against the ground. A foul, nauseating smell emanated from it, and it looked up at Edison with its ruined face, its eyes a sightless milky white.

"Don't," he breathed as the creature sidled forward. But the word had no effect on it.

"Please don't," Ed tried again, but the thing was already at his feet. It whimpered, like a small child or a dog, though the sound came out all wrong, emanating from torn vocal cords. The creature reached for Edison and wrapped its arms around his knees, burying its face in the fabric of his trousers and carrying on with its whimpering. A shudder jolted through him, running from head to foot.

In the dark of the nursery wing, Ed came awake, the aftershock of that shudder still coursing through him. He sat up at once and threw back the bedclothes, padding through the nursery's central parlor to the bathroom, where he splashed cold water onto his face.

But when he straightened, the shattered and cracked glass of the bathroom mirror was obscured by fog. Within the largest glass pieces, written out in a sloppy, painstaking hand, was a single word, spelled out letter by letter.

Surgite.

"Rise up," Ed whispered.

As the words left his mouth, the bathtub faucet began to pour at full strength. Water rushed into the bath, pooling and swirling at its bottom as the stopper shifted into place of its own accord. In the gloom, Ed hurried to shut off the faucet and remove the stopper, fishing through several inches of water to do so. But once he'd drained the bath, his hands came away not just wet but streaming with pond weed and smelling of decayed vegetation.

When he turned to dry them on a towel, the mirror's cracked glass was clear once more, the ghostly inscription on it gone. An expectant calm settled over the nursery wing, broken only by faint singing.

> *Five for the ferryman in the boat.*
> *Four are the truth speakers.*
> *Three of them are strangers.*
> *Two of them the lily-white pair*
> *Clothed all in green, O.*
> *But one is one and all alone, and evermore shall be so.*

CHAPTER EIGHTEEN

WIL

Raised on her mother's stories of the whirlwind romance between Mabel and William Price, Wil had always believed that she and Edison were just as fated for each other as her parents had been. But recently her idyllic view of the bond between herself and Ed had begun to crack at the center and chip at the edges. She loved him—that was never in question; she'd loved the boy in some way or other since the moment she first clapped eyes on him—but his steadfast belief in her was a heavy burden to bear. Now, in the midst of all their troubles, Edison seemed more convinced than ever that Wil was capable of anything—an unstoppable and undamageable force.

Wil, meanwhile, knew herself to be frail and fallible and afraid. Between Ed's dependence and that of her ghosts, she'd begun to fall back on old habits that had formed in the wake of Mabel's death. Foregoing entire nights of sleep to study because she wanted both the numbness of exhaustion and the comfort of an undertaking she could excel at, where all the answers were right or wrong. Worrying at her nails till they bled and smarted.

She was at the desk in her bedroom at home, head pillowed on her arms and nearing the verge of true sleep, when something jerked her awake. A glance at the traveling clock on the nightstand showed the time as half past four—still the small hours then, between night and morning. The world's own halfway realm.

Casting about herself, Wil was unsurprised to find the source of her abrupt awakening. Mabel's ghost hovered behind her, a drift of fog punctuated by unnaturally long and insubstantial limbs.

"Oh, Mama," Wil said, running a hand across her face. "I've got so much to look after already. Can't you rest easy, just for now?"

In answer, the spirit's staring, will-o'-the-wisp eyes widened, condensation from the fog pooling in them like tears. Drops of moisture pattered to the floor, and Wil's heart sank.

"I'm sorry," she hurried to apologize. "I didn't mean to hurt you. Don't mind a word I say."

Little lamb, the spirit's gusty voice murmured. *Little lamb, take care.*

Eagerly the ghost surged forward a few inches, then stopped, hesitant. With a sigh, Wil got up from her seat and knelt in the middle of the open floor. Fog enveloped her, and the essential parts of the spirit shrank down, folding inward and collapsing until it became something featherlight but substantial, the radiant essence of a lost soul that rested in the cradle of Wil's outstretched arms.

"I'm sorry," Wil said again. "How can I help?"

But Mabel's ghost could not answer. Death had left her a creature of thoughtless sorrow, and Wil knew from long experience that she was powerless to cheer or comfort her mother's trapped soul, just as she could not temper the force of Jenny Bright's unreasoning anger. Instead she sat within the fog of Mabel's spirit, the heart of it held in her arms, and after a moment Mabel's windy, graveyard voice began to hum. Wil joined in, and it took her some time to realize, with a cold shiver, that the tune was a borrowed one.

"'I'll sing you one, O,'" Wil whispered. "'One is one and all alone, and evermore shall be so.' Mama, where did you hear this? Who have you been speaking to?"

With a blast of air and a rush of wind, the fog tore itself away from Wil, dragging Mabel's essence with it. The ghost hovered before her, rising in a forbidding column from the floor nearly to the ceiling, and its enormous eyes grew hectically bright.

Surgite, Mabel commanded with more force than Wil had ever heard from her before. *Rise up, press on, arise.*

Another current of air whipped at Wil, making her eyes smart. When the room calmed and she stopped blinking, Mabel was gone.

Outside the window, a lark had begun to sing. Another day was dawning in beautiful Thrush's Green, and Wil, her vision blurry for want of sleep and her head aching fiercely, wished that for once the sun would stay down and the light would fail to come. Night was when she felt clearest—its quietness and its softness brought her thoughts together in a way nothing else did. If she could only have the dark for longer, perhaps all her problems would untangle themselves. Edison, the Grange, the ghosts that haunted Thrush's Green. She just needed to be left alone, with only the moon and her own self for company.

Sighing, Wil got to her feet and pulled on her uniform.

Only to find John Shepherd sitting in the little rowhouse's front room, nursing a half-drunk cup of tea.

"Grandfather," Wil said cautiously.

"Granddaughter," John replied.

Wil glanced at the open windows, flung wide to catch the soft summer breeze. She thought of Thrush's Green, with its busy little streets and byways, its ever-present neighbors. The village was nothing like the silent, out-of-the-way millpond, nor yet the churchyard. There was always someone listening. Always someone taking note of your business.

She decided to be bold.

"How do you know Nat Halliday?" Wil asked.

Shepherd gave her a blank look. "Who?"

"Nat Halliday. Abigail's sweetheart. I saw you with him, as well as Mrs. Forster and Jack Hoult and Sam Jenkins, in the mill cottage. What were you doing?"

"I'm familiar with the man in question," Shepherd said slowly. "Though I had no idea he was involved with Abigail beyond a passing acquaintance."

Wil's stomach dropped. Foolish and careless. She ought not to have let that piece of information slip.

"Well, you didn't hear about it from me," she warned, and Shepherd nodded, sipping his tea.

"Why did you lock me in the stable shed the night Kitty died?" Wil pressed on, determined to get some sort of straight answer from her grandfather. "Yes, I know it was you. Don't bother denying it. Why would you do something so underhanded and cruel?"

"Because you persist in asking questions you shouldn't. In involving yourself with things that are unsafe. It is my job to keep you whole and well. If I must harm you a little in service of your greater good, so be it."

"You can't just tell me what I ought to do?" Wil asked desperately. "Haven't I done enough to earn even a little of your trust or your love? I've tried to be a good granddaughter to you—a replacement for Mama, even. Besides giving up Edison and going to the Grange, I've never fought you on a single point."

Shepherd sat forward, and for the first time a cloud crossed his face. "What do the smaller obediences matter, if you go against me on the only things that count? Had I warned you to keep clear of Kitty and

Edison that night, you'd only have rebelled. So I did what was necessary to look after you, as I have always done."

"If that's your idea of looking after me, I don't want it." Wil could not help the bitterness that crept into her voice. "I wish instead that you'd leave me alone."

"That's the one thing I can't do," Shepherd said, and Wil refused to acknowledge the regret behind his words.

Rising to her feet, she moved to the door.

"Where are you going?" Shepherd asked.

"To the Grange," Wil shot back. "Sooner or later I *will* find someone who'll answer the questions I have about that place, and about Mama and Jenny Bright and now Kitty. You won't be able to stop it. You can't keep me locked up forever."

"More's the pity," Shepherd said drily.

Hunching her shoulders, Wil stepped out into the gray morning. She could not escape her family, though—her mother was waiting in the front garden, a foggy and indistinct presence. Mabel met Wil at every turn, repeating her doleful whisper.

Little lamb. Take care.

When Wil reached the mill wood, Mabel trailed in her wake, repeating the words like a litany. *Little lamb. Little lamb. Take care. Take care.*

No wonder Ed had questioned his own soundness of mind, Wil thought grimly as she pressed on through the forest. Mabel's constant murmuring had her feeling scattered and on edge, and she'd only been subjected to it for a quarter of an hour, not day after day. It was an acute relief when the sound of muffled hoofbeats drifted through the trees, growing stronger and closer until a rider came out onto the path alongside Wil. She hadn't realized how it wore on her sometimes, carrying the dead with her always when she wanted to be among the living.

Nat Halliday smiled down at Wil from where he sat astride a shaggy cob.

"Morning," he said expansively as, with a last doleful look at Wil, Mabel's ghost vanished. "Miss Price, wasn't it?"

"Yes," Wil said. "Kind of you to remember."

"Not at all," Nat answered. "You're a friend of Abby's, which makes you a friend of mine."

Unsure of how she ought to reply, Wil nodded politely and carried on. Nat fell in alongside her, and even if what Nat had been doing with half of the Grange's staff remained a mystery, Wil found the solid, warm bulk of the cob and the sound of its heavy breathing unaccountably comforting.

"Going to the Grange?" Nat asked after a moment.

"Mm." Wil nodded. "I'll be a bit early, but I don't mind. Gives me a chance to settle in for the day."

Nat smiled again. "I know how you feel. I'm an early bird myself. I'm headed past the big house—don't suppose you'd like to ride the rest of the way? It'd be rude of me not to offer."

Wil considered. Truth was, she was tired. Everything in her ached with the taxing monotony of the work she did from sunup till well past sundown. And in spite of what she'd seen, Nat had a way of putting one at ease. It was as if he could see what you wanted from him and become that person. Wil wanted someone easy and straightforward and honest, and here he was. She also wanted to do something her grand-father would disapprove of—the conversation she'd just had with John Shepherd rankled, along with his inability to provide the closeness and camaraderie she so badly needed.

"All right," Wil said defiantly, and taking Nat's hand, let him help her up so that she sat before him on the saddle.

Once there, however, doubt about the wisdom in agreeing to his offer immediately set in. They were so close together that she could feel his breath on the back of her neck, and the image of him and Abigail in the mill wood burned itself across her mind. Wil was glad she had her back to Nat and that he couldn't see her flush. But he did nothing to further her discomfort—only chirruped to the cob, which began to walk with a little more purpose.

"You said you're here for summer farm work?" Wil asked Nat, tamping down her worry and striving for lightness. "Will you go back to the Midlands after harvest?"

"That depends," Nat answered, with a shrug Wil felt rather than saw. "I'd prefer to stay. I've been looking for a reason to. And I think I've just about cleared the way for me to do it."

"We'll miss Abigail at the Grange if you stay. She's very good at what she does."

"Yes," Nat said good-naturedly. "I'm sure she is."

Ahead of them, the shadowy bulk of the house showed through the trees.

"Better let me off here," Wil said. "They're particular about who the housemaids keep company with."

"Don't fret so," Nat said, dismissing her concern. "There won't be anyone about yet. Let me take you to the servants' courtyard, at least."

"Well, all right." Wil relented because the morning air was still cool and damp, while the cob beneath her and Nat behind her radiated warmth. None of her worries had come to fruition either, and she felt a twinge of vicious pride at having done something small and measurable to spite her grandfather.

The woods gave way to lawn, which silenced the sounds of the cob's hoof-falls, leaving nothing but its heavy breath and the occasional jangle of the bit. Then lawn became gravel, and the servants' courtyard was all around them. Wil was just about to dismount when the door to the servants' entrance swung open and she stiffened instinctively.

It was only Edison, notebook in hand, looking disheveled and owl-eyed as if he hadn't slept in weeks.

"Don't worry," Wil murmured to Nat behind her. "Ed doesn't make trouble."

"No," Nat said, his voice warm with amusement. "I'm sure he doesn't."

It struck Wil as an odd thing to say. She glanced back at Edison in confusion, only to find him gripping the doorframe with one white-knuckled hand and holding the other out to her.

"Wil," Ed said hoarsely. "Wil, come here."

But she was still caught in the circle of Nat's arms as he held the reins. For a moment, just a moment, she felt him grip her hard by the waist. A flood of panic surged through Wil, and then subsided into a hot rush of bewilderment, because it had been nothing. He'd only been helping her off the cob, and she slid to the ground, hurrying to where Edison stood. Ed put an arm around her at once and pulled her close, and Wil could feel him shaking.

Nat swung out of the cob's saddle, speaking easily as he did, though the timbre of his voice sounded different, and his mannerisms had changed.

"So you finally found someone who caught your fancy, eh, Ed? Never thought I'd see the day."

Wil's confusion trebled as Nat left the cob where it was, striding past them and into the bowels of the servants' floor. Edison did nothing to stop him, only ensured that he and Wil were well out of Nat's way.

"Ed, what is it?" Wil asked the moment Nat was out of sight and out of earshot. Any lingering resentment she'd felt over his reliance on her had vanished at his stricken look. "What's going on?"

"That's Peter," Ed said, staring after Nat in disbelief. "That's my *brother*. He's come home. I—I have to go."

And Edison vanished, pulled into the house in Peter's wake like a scrap of metal after a lodestone, or a meteor drawn in by an inexorable star.

CHAPTER NINETEEN

WIL

Wil waited for a moment until her pulse slowed, the shock faded, and she felt the veneer of calm that was her birthright settle over her. Then she strode purposefully into the Grange, not stopping for a friendly word in the kitchens with Mrs. Ellicott and Daphne, who were already at work. She went straight to the long, narrow staircase that climbed four floors up to the attics and began the ascent.

By the time Wil reached the attic, she was breathless and damp with sweat. But she did not pause on the landing, nor in the empty corridor lined with unoccupied bedrooms. All the doors stood open, showing their uninhabited interiors, save for one room at the end of the hall, to which the door was resolutely shut. Wil went to it and knocked, gently at first, then louder as the moments ran on and no one answered.

"Abigail!" she called out finally, an involuntary sharpness in her voice. "Abigail, it's Wil. Let me in."

A tired groan sounded from the other side of the door. "Ugh, Wil. I don't need to be up yet, and neither do you. What on earth are you thinking?"

"Peter Summerfield just came home," Wil said, tension lacing the words.

Footsteps sounded immediately, and the door swung open. Abigail stood before Wil, still in her nightgown, her tumble of mousy hair pulled into a disheveled braid and her eyes wide.

"His Lordship let him back?" she blurted out.

Wil felt a frown write itself across her face. "What do you mean, 'let him'? And what do you know about all this? I think it's time we had a word."

For the briefest instant Abigail only looked at Wil stubbornly, and Wil thought the girl might shut her out again. But then, with a sigh, Abigail stepped aside and gestured to Wil to come in.

The girl's room was sparsely furnished. There was a bed, covered with a drab, threadbare quilt. A bureau. An old wicker chair in one corner. A fraying and faded rag rug. And that was all. There were none of the personal touches that Wil would have expected in the place where Abigail had lived most of her life. No pictures or postcards or books or trinkets. If the girl walked out of her own existence, the Grange would close seamlessly around the space she'd inhabited, just as the postmistress had warned.

Wil shivered as she settled into the wicker chair, Abigail seating herself on the unmade bed.

"How long have you known Nat Halliday is Peter Summerfield?" Wil asked.

Abigail raised her chin in a small gesture of defiance. "Always. Since the beginning. I've been here every day of my life since I was eight years old and Mrs. Ellicott took me on as a scullery maid out of kindness. I know things about this family they don't even know themselves."

"And how long has it been since Peter came back?"

"More than a month since he got back to Thrush's Green, though

210

he was in London well before that. Lord Summerfield's known all about it too, but he was against Peter coming home too quickly. Peter made enemies during the war and afterward—a few officers on the front, and people in France, some of them in law enforcement. It was messy, and awful for him, and he came back dragging not just his memories of going through living hell, but with a lot of baseless, brutal rumors snapping at his heels. There was unpleasantness between Lady Summerfield and Peter before he went to the front too. She wasn't on good terms with him and might be liable to believe anything that painted him in a bad light. His Lordship asked Peter to wait to come home, until everything was properly managed. I've been looking after Peter all along at Lord Summerfield's request—seeing to it that the mill cottage is comfortable, getting his meals, and bringing him books or whatever else he wants from the house."

Abigail said the last with a pleased and proprietary air, and inwardly Wil flinched.

"And the two of you?" Wil asked. "How long have you been . . . close to one another?"

"It happened only a few days after Peter got back," Abigail answered with a soft smile. "It wasn't anything I ever expected—how could I? But there was this pull between the two of us. A rightness. We understand each other, and why shouldn't we? We're not so very different. We've known the same place and the same people all our lives. Home means the same thing to us. I'd do anything for him, and he would for me."

Wil knotted her hands together on her lap as doubt ate away at her insides. "Abigail, are you absolutely *certain* of him? Because there have been other girls, and he's risking nothing by being with you. You're the one risking everything. Not just your reputation—maybe even your life. My mother, Jenny Bright, Kitty—none of us truly knows what's going on here, and until we do—"

211

Abigail cut her off, her expression stern and her eyes sparking. "And until we do, Peter will keep me safe. I just told you, Wil; we look after each other. I'd have thought you'd understand, given the way things are with you and Edison."

Wil's stomach soured.

"*I* don't even know how things are with me and Edison," she protested. "We've been friends for years, since long before I came to the Grange. And things have changed between us, but I don't know what I hope for or where I think we're headed. Sometimes I think nowhere. That it's all impossible, and we'll wake up one morning and realize this is too difficult, that there's too much against us, and go our separate ways. We won't say anything; we'll just stop speaking to each other, because silence is easier than acknowledging the world was too much for us. That we weren't enough, even side by side, to stand against it."

"That would never happen with me and Peter," Abigail said adamantly. "I'm sure of him, and I've never met anyone stronger. If he wants me, there's nothing and no one that will change his mind."

For a minute Abigail and Wil sat and regarded each other, one of them fierce and full of confidence, the other weighed down with uncertainty and cares.

"May I ask you something else?" Wil said. An awful grief welled up within her for Abigail, who was gambling all she had on someone Wil suspected was a very poor bet. "You've been here so long, I expect there isn't much you don't know. It would have been before your time, but have you ever heard anything—rumors or gossip, even—about why a nursemaid called Margaret Willis left the Grange?"

Abigail frowned. "Margaret Willis?"

"They'd have called her Maggie," Wil offered. "Does it ring a bell?"

"I don't know anything specific," Abigail said. "Only that she went away under some sort of cloud. She'd been negligent with the children, they said, and possibly worse than that. There were marks found on them, and Master Edison especially was growing sensitive about all manner of ordinary-seeming things. As if he was always afraid. And then there was some sort of illness or accident that was mishandled and led to her being sent away. That's all I know."

"How awful," Wil said fervently.

"Yes. Well, you'd better leave. I need to dress and get downstairs."

Wil did as she was told, wandering back down the attic corridor past its silent and open rooms. And she couldn't say why, but their very emptiness felt like a reproach.

*   *   *

"We'll bury her tomorrow," Peter Summerfield said authoritatively as Wil stood, a quiet and waiting presence beside the conservatory door.

Whatever initial shock or joy had washed over the Summerfields during the morning as Peter's presence in the house became known, Wil hadn't seen it. By the time they'd arrived in the conservatory for afternoon tea, it was all over. Every one of them looked as calm and unruffled as if Peter had never been gone. Their serene acceptance of the unthinkable made her skin crawl. It was as if they'd exchanged Peter for Kitty and never noticed the difference.

Or so Wil thought, until Peter brought up the funeral.

"We can't just keep her sitting there," Peter went on, helping himself to three scones and a fresh cup of tea. "It isn't fair to her, or to any of us, or to the staff. If you ask me, it's gruesome. You've got to let her go, Mama."

Lady Summerfield fixed her eyes on him and smiled. She seemed clearer than usual—less distant from the world and its goings-on. "Of course, Peter. I'm sure I can bear it, now that you've come home."

If there had ever been any unpleasantness or tension between them as Abigail claimed, it seemed to have vanished, dissipated entirely by the family's acceptance of Peter's return.

"It'll be a small funeral," Peter went on. "I know she'd have preferred a show, but I don't think anyone will blame us, under the circumstances, if we keep it a quieter family affair. Papa and I can be pallbearers, along with Ed and Uncle Jamison—Ed, are you listening?"

"Yes," Edison said, from where he'd been sitting hunched over and staring into the dregs of his cup of tea. It was the first time he'd spoken since the family had filed in and took their places, like a set of clockwork figures. "A pallbearer."

"Can you manage?" Peter pressed, and his voice had a cutting edge.

"Of course I can manage," Ed shot back, but Wil could see his hand straying every minute or so to his pocket, where he kept his notebook and pencil. "Everyone will be at the service, I suppose? We'll invite all the staff?"

Without answering Edison's questions, Peter turned back to their parents. "About the staff. I've been thinking that with Kitty gone and life at the Grange so much quieter than it once was, we ought to economize a little more. Half the rooms are shut up, and it's only the four of us for meals—it seems ridiculous to keep so many servants. We ought to let some of them go."

"Peter," Lord Summerfield said, a warning in the words. "Matters like that are best discussed privately."

But Peter turned and fixed his gaze directly on Wil. She stayed motionless, letting his careless eyes rake over her. Though she strove for calm, she could not help noticing how the porcelain teacup he held was dwarfed by his hand, or how even Lord and Lady Summerfield seemed to bend to him as master of any situation.

"You mean Shepherd's granddaughter?" Peter said. "I don't think we need to worry about her. God knows Shepherd's been a loyal foot soldier. I was thinking we should let Daphne go, and Jack Hoult. There's no sense having a footman any longer; Shepherd can manage on his own. Oh, and we don't need two housemaids—Abigail should go as well."

Wil didn't know what she expected. For someone to stand up on behalf of the people Peter wanted, so casually, to deprive of their living, perhaps. But no one spoke. A palpable tension built in the air until Lady Summerfield smiled again and set down her cup.

"If you think it's best. We'll wait till after Kitty . . ." Her voice trailed off.

"No," Peter said firmly. "Don't wait. Better to do it now, so it's not hanging over us. I can speak to Shepherd and Mrs. Forster myself—no sense any of you being put out. In fact, there's no time like the present."

Wil could do nothing but stand at her post as he brushed by her. Everything in her burned at the news that was coming to those downstairs, and when she thought of Abigail, she was forced to set her jaw to check her rising temper.

It wasn't only anger at Peter or the Summerfields either—Wil was furious with herself. She ought to have been more forceful with the girl. Ought to have conveyed her objections to what Abigail had confided more sternly. If only she could have made Abigail see the foolishness in what she'd said.

But there had been Edison, putting the lie to any argument Wil might have made. Edison, who now sat, white-faced and voiceless, staring into the bottom of his cup as if he'd heard nothing of what went on around him. He hadn't spoken a word in any of the staff's defense. Just let Peter have his way. His inaction hurt all the more, because Wil knew he could be brave and had seen him rise to the occasion. He'd been brilliant when he'd faced down Lord Summerfield in front of a whole tableful of guests, but that had been for her. He had an interest in her—Abigail, it seemed, was no one special to Ed. No one deserving of his protection.

When Edison glanced over at Wil, his eyes finding hers as if she was a lifeline, she couldn't hold his gaze.

CHAPTER TWENTY

EDISON

Abigail was already gone, and her absence felt as if it was eating holes in Edison's brain.

By the time Wil left the house that night, it was done—Daphne and Jack and Abigail had all left the property, life at the Grange continuing flawlessly without them. It was tolerable with Daphne and Jack, even if guilt over them rested like a cold, hard stone in Ed's stomach. He knew them well enough to believe they'd find places for themselves with little trouble. They weren't alone, either—Jack had a family in the village, and Daphne had her parents, still safe in the Summerfields' employ. But Abigail was different. For as long as Edison could remember, her entire existence had been the Grange. She'd roomed in the attics, which housed a dozen people before the war and later held only her. During Ed's midnight wanderings, she'd been one of the things he counted on. Now he didn't know where she'd gone, or if she was looked after. Her absence and Peter being home felt terribly jarring to him. It wasn't a good routine that held him together—Ed had no illusions that his new habit was the sort of thing a healthy person would do, or that it was ultimately sustainable—but it had been working up until now.

The attic's stark emptiness haunted him. It was a lifeless row of room after hollow room, a ghost floor at the top of the house that had once been filled with busy, laughing servants. They'd all gone, either dismissed or dead, and the two circumstances had begun to get tangled up in Edison's mind. It was why he needed to know with certainty the whereabouts and well-being of everyone Wither Grange's shadow had fallen upon.

Peter's presence haunted him too. His brother's room, which had stood empty for so long, was occupied now, light shining from under the door when Ed passed by. If there was an explanation for Peter's miraculous return, Edison certainly hadn't heard it, though he supposed his parents had. As for his other ghost—well. Whether it was due to some inscrutable motivation of the restless dead or Edison's own jangling nerves, the nursery wing's dark inhabitant was in rare form. The constant, eerie refrain of "Green Grow the Rushes, O" was enough in itself to rattle him, but the bathtub had filled with fetid, weed-thick water once more and would not drain. Every splinter of glass still left in the place was fogged over, shadowy figures moving in some hinterland beyond the mist. And when Ed finally slept, exhausted, past two in the morning, he fell immediately into the same dream that had crawled through his mind before.

The bricked-up fireplace. The falling mortar, the shattering bricks. The gruesome, decaying body that crawled out and laid hands on him, begging wordlessly for some sort of help.

But this time it carried on differently. Before, Ed had ended up in a cold sweat, with the creature's bloated hands gripping him as he stood entirely alone. This time he turned and saw Wil in the doorway, watching with something like disgust written across her perfect, relentless face.

"Wil," Ed's dream-self pleaded. "I can't bear it. *Help me.*"

She only looked at him, unmoved.

"If you can't bear it," Wil said slowly, "what makes you think I can?"

And then, in the way of dreams, everything changed. It was no longer

Edison standing rooted to the spot, the dead thing grasping at him for solace and support—Wil was in his place, and *he* was the loathsome creature pawing at her skirts. She was stronger than he'd been, though. She cast off his ruined hands and strode away, out through the nursery wing's open door and down the hall, until she'd faded from view and Ed was left behind, entirely bereft.

He woke under no illusion that sleep would come again. Nor would he have wanted it to—in only a matter of hours, they'd be burying Kitty. In his secret heart, Ed had been relieved by Lady Summerfield's refusal to have it over and done with. So long as her death hadn't been marked in any way, he could pretend she'd gone off to visit friends, as she'd often done during summer, flitting from house party to house party like a glad butterfly. The coffin was only an empty box, so long as it sat in the Grange's grand entrance rather than resting in the cold earth.

But today that would change. Today Kitty would go into the ground, and Ed would have to face up to the fact that her absence wasn't temporary but a thing that would last forever.

Instinctively he felt a need to reconcile her passing, knowing that if he could not find a way to come to terms with it, she'd become yet another thing out of joint within him. Another ghost of the mind and soul. If he ever hoped to heal over the void at his center, rather than patching it with endless wandering and meticulous record-keeping, he needed to make sense of Kitty not being missing but gone for good.

Edison dressed quietly as the nursery wing light fixtures rattled against the walls and its ghost sang down the chimney. He put on his best black suit, not seeing the point in needing to change later for the funeral. He smoothed down his hair as well as he could without the use of a mirror and slid on his cleanest pair of shoes—Kitty, like all the rest of the family, had chided him often for not taking more care with his appearance. It calmed something inside him to dress with the express

218

intent of honoring and mourning his star-bright sister. It was a sort of ritual, like wandering the Grange and keeping records, and the sense of repetition and inevitability that rituals carried with them was holding Edison together for the time being.

When he'd finished dressing, Ed went down to the grand foyer. It was cast into shadow, though the sun had risen fully. The Summerfields still held to the traditions so many were casting off, and in commemoration of Kitty, every shade in the house had been drawn—save for the nursery wing, where there were no drapes or shades, and where no one but Ed would mind their absence.

Something in Edison drew him to the flower-strewn coffin at the foyer's center. He set his hands on it, but that wasn't enough. He wanted to see her—needed to see her, if he was to fully grasp the truth of her absence.

Gripping the lid of the coffin, Edison pushed to raise it, only to feel resistance and hear the sound of metal on metal. Glancing at the lid's center, he saw something entirely incongruous.

A latch, joining the coffin's lid to its base. And through it, a padlock, which prevented anyone from viewing the casket's contents.

"Edison," Lady Summerfield's voice said sternly from the shadows. "What are you doing?"

She got up from where she'd sat, unseen by Ed, keeping a silent vigil in her black mourning clothes. As she drew closer, her face was harsh and unyielding, and Ed could already feel himself beginning to quail, even as a rush of sick, groundless suspicion flooded through him.

"I want to see her."

"You can't," Lady Summerfield said. "It's been days. She's not the way you remember her."

"Why is the coffin locked?" Edison pressed. He wasn't sure what he thought—all he knew was that it seemed terribly unnatural, to lock Kitty in or him out. Either way, he wanted to see her, needed to see her, and the lock only honed that necessity to a keen and consuming requirement. "I have to see her."

"No." Lady Summerfield placed a hand on his arm, her voice soothing now, her face kind and reasonable as it hadn't been for years. She was almost fully present—only the faintest sweet scent of sherry lingered on her breath, mingling with the heady, overpowering aroma of jasmine, and her eyes were clear. "Your sister died a week ago. You can't look at her—it's not what she'd want, and it would be . . . damaging . . . for you."

"Why is the coffin locked?" Ed repeated, angry insistence undercutting the words. "There's no reason for it."

"Kitty's being buried with some of the family jewels," his mother said. "It's Summerfield tradition. And we lock the coffin to deter any light-fingered staff or grave robbers. It's only a precaution, you know."

Edison put his head in his hands. Everything felt foggy—as if he couldn't think clearly. As if whatever shadowy creatures roamed the glass within the nursery wing had gotten into him, muddling his senses and his reason. Dimly he could recall a funeral from when he was a very small child. His grandfather's, perhaps. With his mind's eye, he could see the coffin laid out in an unfamiliar room. It had been a plain pine box, and there were no drifts of flowers. But there had not been a lock, either. He was sure of it.

"I remember a funeral from when I was younger," Edison said adamantly, looking up once more. "There was no lock then. Why would you lie to me, Mother?"

Lady Summerfield's reasonable, empathetic look never faltered. "It isn't a lie. You're not remembering rightly."

"Let me see her."

Ed was nearly shouting now. Something was wrong, but he couldn't tell what—all he knew was that he needed to see Kitty, more than he'd ever needed to see anything else.

220

"Edison." Lady Summerfield's voice was a reproach. "You're being foolish. Understand what I'm trying to tell you—*I* couldn't bear seeing your sister now. She'll be a ruin. Death is kind to none of us. The smell alone—"

"I need. To see her." He bit off the words, as commanding and imperious as even Peter could be at his most lordly.

But Lady Summerfield was a match for him.

"You can't," she said unbendingly. "And if you must know, the things Kitty's being buried with are only half the reason for the lock. I asked for it myself, not because I don't trust the staff, but because of you. Do you think we haven't noticed how erratic your behavior's become since she died? Do you think we aren't all holding our breath, waiting to see whether you fall apart again like you did after Peter? It's enough of a blow to lose a child. But having another who can't cope? Who's too fragile to bear up and be a comfort and a support to his family as he ought to? That's a twist of the knife, Edison. Your father and I had one hope for all our children—that they'd learn to stand on their own two feet and be a credit to the family, rather than a burden and a source of shame."

The words cut deep, but Ed was past caring. What he owed his parents didn't matter any longer—Kitty had lost her life in some way because of him. It was the only debt he could focus on now, and with the fog clouding his mind, he could do no more than follow his conviction that the lock was wrong, that Kitty's death was wrong, that he needed to see her.

Everything would end in disaster if he didn't see her.

"Either you let me look at my sister," Edison said, with a violence and a warning in his voice that it had never carried before, "or I will fetch a crowbar and tear her coffin open myself. And what will people say about the mad Summerfield boy if she's taken to the church like that?"

A look of irritation and disdain flashed across Lady Summerfield's face.

"Very well," she said, removing a key from her watch chain. "Have it your way. But don't come to me for comfort when you've seen something you can't cope with."

She swept away down the crimson-carpeted hall that had once been bright and sun-soaked, but which Kitty's death had cast into darkness. Without hesitation, certain he was in the right, Edison turned the key in the padlock, pulled it from the latch, and swung the coffin lid open.

A single breath was all he needed to realize his own folly. A wave of stomach-turning rot billowed from the casket, and Edison choked, forced to turn away until he could compose himself.

You could go, his better angels said silently from within. *You could stop all this.*

But he couldn't. Not really. The need to see Kitty, to know he'd been told the truth about her, was too strong. He'd brave anything for his sister, as she'd done for him.

So Edison turned and looked.

Lady Summerfield had been right. The thing in the coffin was not Kitty any longer. Oh, there were bits and pieces that still spoke of her— the shade of her auburn hair, the outline of her nose, the little sunburst ring she wore on the index finger of her right hand. But she'd become something else. Bloated, discolored, transformed by monstrous decay. Edison recognized her not as his sister, as Kitty with her lightness of being and her glad, hollow laughter, but as the pitiful, ruined creature from his dreams.

With steady hands, Edison set the key to the padlock down in the interior of the coffin, beside what was left of Kitty. He closed the casket lid and snapped the padlock shut. Then he walked past the coffin and its masses of flowers. Down the length of the Grange's gunshot corridor. Past the conservatory, where he could hear his mother and father and Peter in hushed, conspiratorial conversation.

"He insisted. . . ."

"Keep a watch on him, he was bound to go to pieces again. . . ."

"Maybe it's for the best, after all. . . ."

But Edison didn't stop. He carried on, out through the Grange's far door and into the blaze of a midsummer morning. The sun, for all its brightness, had no power to warm him. Not that it was the sun he wanted—he wanted, more than anything, to go home. To get to the one place where he'd always felt safe, and well, and whole.

So Edison walked on, into the mill wood and along its winding trails, until he came to the clearing among the beeches where he and Wil had made it their habit to meet since childhood. There he stopped and threw himself down amid the green and fragrant undergrowth. He lay with his face buried in his arms, letting the forest and the breeze and the earth leech away the poison that had gotten into him, until all that was left was a crystal shard of grief.

When he sat up, Wil was there.

Of course she was—no place was home without her. She sat a few feet away in her faded uniform, a dustrag still clutched in one hand and a worried frown on her face.

"I saw you leaving," she said. "And I knew you needed me. So here I am."

Ed wiped bitter tears from his face with the back of one hand.

"Where's Abigail?" he asked, because it was the first thing that surfaced from the turmoil of his thoughts. "Did she have a place to go?"

Wil let out a small breath, and for the first time in what felt like days, her eyes fixed on Edison's, seeing him fully with no walls between them. "She said she has a cousin out on the far side of the village. That she could stay with them until she's able to find another position."

"And she made it there all right?" Ed's hand strayed to his pocket, reaching for the notebook hidden there.

"I don't know," Wil said. "I should think so? But I can't say for certain."

"I'll have to go and make sure of it," Ed told her. "I need to mark it down."

"I know you do," Wil said. "But you've got a lot to keep you busy today. It's going to be miserable. I'll be halfway to Abigail when I go home tonight—I can walk out first thing tomorrow and look in on her for you."

"No. No, I should do it," Edison said, mindful of his dream. It had been from Kitty somehow, and whatever she'd become, he ought to listen. "I lean on you too often. I've always thought you were a marvel, Wil, but you're still only human. This summer's been terrible for both of us, and I'd rather die than be the reason you drown."

"I've been meaning to say something about that." Wil shifted forward on her knees, drawing closer to him, and it blunted the edge of grief inside Ed, that she still wanted closeness between them. "It's true you've been leaning on me a great deal. But haven't I done the same to you in the past? We were friends before anything else, and this is what friends do—they bear each other up. They stand by each other, even when everything's falling apart. Even when the whole world's going wrong. I lost sight of it for a little while, but there's no one else I'd rather be needed by than you, and no one else I'd rather need when life seems impossible. I love you, Ed, and it would be a shallow kind of love that turns aside when trouble comes."

Edison's eyes closed of their own accord as she reached out and brushed his cheek with the ball of one thumb. His throat was hot with fresh tears, but they weren't the grieving kind anymore. They were only the manifestation of his overwhelming relief, because Wil loved him and he loved her back, body and soul, and as long as the two of them were all right, he could weather any storm.

Ed didn't know what he expected next—a kiss, perhaps. A repeat of the clandestine, hungry passion that had escaped from them both the night Wil unearthed the nursery-wing ghost, or the morning he'd freed her from the stable shed.

Instead he felt Wil's arms go around him, and his own mirrored the gesture without any thought required on his part. Hadn't they held each other so a thousand times before? It was easy as breathing to be with Wil Price. He ducked his head, pressing his face to the sweet curve of her neck and shoulder, and she whispered words for only him to hear.

"Darling boy. You lean on me all you need—I know you'll be there for me too, when the time comes."

*　*　*

The funeral was every bit as terrible as Wil had predicted. Ed felt as if he was watching it from outside himself. Surely it was someone else walking down the church aisle, burdened by the weight of Kitty's coffin and the thing death had turned her body into. It could not be him standing in the cemetery afterward, looking at the freshly mounded grave earth, shaking hands and making polite remarks when required. It was a different Edison—an automaton who could move and act without thought or feeling, while the real Edison Summerfield cowered within its mechanical depths.

Then it was done, and they were home. Lady Summerfield let out a sigh as they walked through the front door, starting immediately for the music room and the sherry bottle it contained. Peter and Lord Summerfield carried on into the study and shut the door firmly in their wake. Ed was left standing alone at the center of the foyer, in the place where Kitty and her coffin had been.

The air still smelled of jasmine, undercut by a lingering trace of rot. And all at once Edison couldn't stand it any longer. He hurried up the stairs and away from the nursery wing. He didn't want a haunting—he wanted to remember Kitty as she'd been in life. So he went to her rooms, only to stop on the threshold as he swung the door open.

Nothing looked as if it had changed. But a smell of fresh mortar hung on the air, and the fireplace seemed different somehow. Ed walked around the bed and found a drop cloth and trowel still sitting out.

The fog he'd felt surrounded by when opening Kitty's coffin had returned with a vengeance. Dimly Edison heard heavy footsteps on the stairs. He'd know them anywhere, and he couldn't help but flinch as Peter walked into the room.

Like Lord Summerfield, Ed's brother was a commanding presence. He made Edison feel small, not just physically, but in some indefinable manner of the spirit.

"There you are," Peter said brusquely. "You just disappeared after we walked in. Papa wants to know if you'll come into the study for a drink."

"What happened in here?" Ed asked, gesturing to the drop cloth and the fireplace. "Why has something been changed?"

It was difficult to speak with the fog pressing in on him, but he forced the words out.

Peter waved a dismissive hand. "Mama couldn't sleep last night. Which is understandable, given the circumstances. She kept saying that Kitty had complained this spring about the fireplace causing a draft, and that she'd been putting off the repair because it didn't seem important with summer on the way. She said she wished she'd just done it—it was weighing on her. Little things like that do when you're faced with death and loss. I saw it often enough at the front. So I did the work myself."

"When?" Ed asked in bewilderment. "I never knew any of this was going on."

"You were in bed," Peter said. "It was an absurd time for it, but I don't like seeing Mama that way. Are you coming down for a drink?"

But the idea that something could take place at the Grange without his noticing had set panic closing in on Edison's chest like a vice.

"I couldn't have been asleep for more than two hours at once last night," he said. "I should've seen you—"

"Ed," Peter interrupted. He set one heavy hand on his brother's shoulder, and Edison fought the urge to pull away. "What are you going on about? It's a *good* thing you got some sleep. Papa says you've been restless. None of this matters, and you can't keep an eye on everything at once. Not at a place the size of the Grange. It takes a whole family to run a house like this one, and we've all got to pull together, especially now Kitty's gone. If you're worried about something, just come to me, but you don't have to try to keep tabs on everything all alone."

If such a reassurance had come from any other member of his family, Edison would have found it a relief. But not Peter. There had been too many instances, when he was younger, where Peter had pried some confidence from him only to casually use it at a later point to wound.

"I don't want a drink," Edison said flatly.

Peter shrugged. "Suit yourself. Only I thought it was kind of Papa to offer. But you've always liked to be the odd man out."

Edison waited until Peter had left Kitty's room and made it out to the corridor. Then he walked over to the doorway and called after his brother.

"Where exactly have you been all this time?"

"In hell, to begin with, and thanks for the reminder," Peter said grimly. "Then afterward I had some trouble in France before I could get home."

"What sort of trouble?"

"None of your business."

"Why didn't you wire us after the war, at least?" Edison pressed. "You know Father would have sent you anything you asked for and done anything to get you home sooner."

"Where I go and when I do isn't your concern," Peter shot over his shoulder as he made his way down the stairs.

CHAPTER TWENTY-ONE

WIL

Wil stood uncertainly on the doorstep at the address Abigail had left with Mrs. Forster. She'd seldom been to the far end of Thrush's Green, and the line of rowhouses she'd come to was decidedly seedy. They lacked the pretty front gardens of the homes near Wil's—instead there was only packed earth and scattered rubbish and wash lines hung with threadbare undergarments.

The woman who opened the door at Wil's knock was tired-looking but couldn't have been more than ten years Wil's elder. She balanced a chubby-fisted baby on one hip while a slightly older child peeked out from behind her skirts.

"I'm looking for Abigail Phelps," Wil said, with a smile she hoped held a little brightness. "Is she at home?"

"Abby?" the woman said blankly. "You mean my mam's cousin's girl? Why on earth does everyone seem to think she'd end up here?"

Wil's pulse quickened. "She's been working at Wither Grange, and they let her go. She said she'd be coming to you. That was early yesterday."

The woman in the doorway shrugged. "Haven't seen her. But I

wouldn't worry about Abby—from what I know of her, she always manages to look after herself. Is that all?"

"No. Has someone else been out looking for her?" Wil asked.

"Mm." A nod of assent. "Elderly gentleman came by yesterday. Nice black suit, white hair. Had a way about him. Looked like he was *somebody*, if you know what I mean."

Wil did know. She knew exactly how John Shepherd looked.

"Will that be all?" the woman in the door asked impatiently as the baby in her arms began to whine.

"Yes," Wil said. "Yes, that's all. Thank you for your time."

The door shut. Wil stood for a moment on the front step, staring down at her shoes. A terrible suspicion had begun to creep over her—what Edison seemed to have felt all along. But for Wil, there was somewhere else to search for a lost soul besides the land of the living.

Before entering the halfway realm, though, she needed to be sure of one thing, even if it would require all her courage to do it. Steeling her nerves, Wil walked back through Thrush's Green. Past the post office, which would be closed for hours yet, though Mrs. Grey was already up and peering narrowly out the window at her. Past her own rowhouse, which Wil's grandfather had undoubtedly left behind already, heading for the Grange. Wil herself cut through the mill wood, drawn inexorably to its dark heart. To the pond with its placid surface, which had known so much of death.

Hesitating at the edge of the clearing that housed the pond, Wil pressed both hands to her face. She did not want to go forward. She did not know what else to do besides that, though. So she took a step and began to walk along the outskirts of the millpond, looking closely at the water, at the reeds and the banks, and praying all the while that she would not find anything.

At last she'd circumnavigated the pond in its entirety. And there was nothing. No sign of Abigail. Slowly Wil's pulse began to calm. Perhaps all this worry was foolish. Perhaps Abigail had simply wanted a fresh start, away from the people and the place that had been her life until they cast her aside.

But Wil was careful and thorough, and she would search everywhere before returning to Edison. She walked a little higher up the pond's banks to where the earth was dry and sat herself down.

It seemed to her that the doorway between the world of the living and the halfway realm was widening. Where once it required concerted effort on her part to slip into that shadowy hinterland, now she was forced to stay on guard against it. Any distraction could lead to an incursion by the dead or a sudden fall into their plane. Slipping into the halfway realm felt like letting go of tension—as if she'd been hunching her shoulders for days and then suddenly let them rest.

Around Wil, the mill wood shimmered and lost its color. The leaves vanished from the trees. The surface of the pond went from dimpled blue and green to an oily slick. Near her something hunched in the reeds, formless and vague and singing darkly to itself.

One is one and all alone, and evermore shall be so.

But despite the spirit's bleak words, it was not alone. Twin souls hovered on either side of Wil—the air of concern emanating from one and rage radiating from the other identified them immediately.

Her mother and Jenny Bright.

"I'm looking for a girl called Abigail," Wil said to her mother. "Is she here?"

In answer, Mabel's ghost and Jenny's each stretched out phantom limbs. Reaching back to them, Wil took their insubstantial hands, fingers closing cold and long and spiderlike around her own, and let herself be led like a child.

They brought her around the shore of the millpond to where the old miller's cottage stood. The door lay on the ground, fallen from its hinges. The windows had, as was common in the halfway realm, been shattered long ago. Wil hesitated on the threshold as Jenny took up a position outside the door, but Mabel led her on, into the cottage's interior.

A creature unlike anything Wil had seen in the land of the dead before crouched by the cottage hearth. Its shape was more physical than that of Wil's mother and Jenny—whereas they were recognizably beings of spirit, this one had somehow managed to cling to the semblance of a body. Decaying and bloated, it wore the tattered remains of a silver gown, which gleamed in the unlit cottage like a fallen star.

"Kitty," Wil breathed.

The dead soul's head snapped up, and Kitty fixed a pair of milky, preternaturally wide eyes on her. As she shifted, Wil saw what she'd been doing. Long gouges had been scratched in the bricks of the mill cottage hearth, and Kitty's fingers were torn to stumps, a blackish ooze seeping sluggishly from them.

"There's always a draft," Kitty said petulantly, and it was her own musical, living voice that emanated from the corpse's twisted mouth. "Always a draft in winter. Can't you feel it?"

Wil fought for calm as Kitty reached up and pulled her down by the wrist, pressing Wil's palm flat against the damaged bricks at the back of the hearth. She could feel nothing—no cold air, no stir of wind. Or at least not at first. When she tried to pull away, the dead thing that had been Kitty Summerfield wrenched her hand back to its place, holding it insistently to the bricks. Wil took in a sharp breath, and tears pricked at the backs of her eyes as pain shot through her wrist, but Kitty was insistent.

So Wil waited. And then a vibration. A moment of contact as something struck the bricks from the opposite side. She glanced up in surprise, looking Kitty full in the face.

But as soon as Wil had felt the brickwork shake, Kitty seemed to lose her prior focus. She got up and began to wander through the cottage, feebly turning over bits of charred paper and damaged furniture.

"Always a draft," she repeated faintly. "Always a draft in winter."

Once again Mabel took Wil by the hand. The dull, throbbing pain in Wil's wrist had settled in, growing in persistence. There'd be bruises if she was lucky, though she suspected a sprain. And none of what she'd seen made sense—that was the worst of it. No sign of Abigail. No message to help her.

A frustrated sigh, halfway to a snarl, escaped Wil as Mabel led her back out of the cottage.

"Why can't you just *tell* me things?" she said desperately to Mabel and Jenny. Her voice sounded overly loud in the dead land, echoing back from the bare earth and the gray sky above. "What is it you want from me? Is everything really as it seems? Was it my grandfather who's done all this?"

No answer was forthcoming. All Wil could hear was a cold, sorrowing wind and the presence at the millpond's fringe singing.

A fifth for the ferryman in his boat;
in a place between, her soul still floats.
I'll sing you one, O.
One is one and all alone, and evermore shall be so.

*　　*　　*

The Grange seemed no less haunted than the mill wood. Mrs. Forster was nowhere to be found, and Mrs. Ellicott stood dourly at the stove, stirring a vast pot without her daughter to keep her company. Wil could see John Shepherd through the open door to his study, but he sat motionless behind the desk, only his eyes shifting as he scanned the pages of a household ledger. She could not avoid the thought that there was no one else left between her and him now. She was the last housemaid standing.

How long before his ire fell on her, as it had fallen upon her predecessors?

Tying on her apron, Wil resigned herself to a long and lonely day of drifting through the immense old house, the only one remaining to try and keep its warren of rooms in order. Upstairs she went methodically from conservatory to music room, picking up two glasses that smelled of sherry as she went. There was mud tracked through the foyer too—someone had gone out either awfully late or dreadfully early. Wil swept it up and left the grand entryway gleaming. The foyer was the one part of the house's ground floor that still seemed lived-in. She could hear the low drone of male voices and an occasional outburst of jovial laughter from Lord Summerfield's study, where he and Peter were obviously making up for lost time.

After her perfunctory tidying, Wil went back downstairs to fetch the things she needed to lay a fire for Lady Summerfield, who never woke before ten. A stab of pity lanced through her as she let herself silently into Edison's mother's room. An indistinct form in the bed was all she could make out of the Grange's mistress, and the room smelled overpoweringly of spirits. On the dressing table a clutter of powders and lotions had been pushed to one side, replaced by an assortment of medicines, at the head of which stood a single, near-empty bottle of laudanum.

As quietly as she could, Wil cleared the hearth and laid the fire. Lady Summerfield's retreat into a realm of her own struck a chord with Wil—she could understand the temptation. Wil, too, often wished for the opportunity to retreat from the realities of her own life. But her unrelenting determination would not allow Wil to shrink away or turn aside. There was a hardness and a grim sort of resolve in her that gave no quarter, even when persistence came at a cost. Even when seeing a thing through was a detriment to her or those around her. Wil could not bear retreat—she was a creature of forward momentum only, even when a strategic withdrawal might serve in her favor.

So she finished setting Lady Summerfield's room to rights and carried on to the nursery wing. Wil had expected to find everything peaceful—Ed either still asleep or sequestered in the hidden library, perhaps. Instead strange noises were ringing out from behind the nursery wing's shut door.

Without bothering to knock, Wil let herself in. Closing the door behind her, she turned and stopped abruptly.

Edison knelt before the hearth, just as Wil had in Lady Summerfield's room. But he was not creating order, as Wil had done. He had a crowbar in his hands and was fixedly prying away chunks of mortar and sections of brick. There was an indistinctness about him Wil had never seen before—it wasn't the fog of Ed's own soul beginning to depart. It was something else entirely, and she couldn't place the look of it until she spoke Edison's name and he turned his head.

His eyes were aglow with an eerie blue-white light, which Wil recognized immediately. It was no longer Edison staring at her, or not Edison alone. Who he was had been replaced by a ghost's flickering, gas-lamp gaze. And that indistinctness Wil saw wasn't Edison's own soul leaving him—it was something alien. An already dead soul lying over him like a shroud.

For the first time Wil knew why the people of Thrush's Green seemed to view her connection to the dead as a curse, and her capacity to channel them as frightful and unnatural. Because everything in her flooded with a sense of wrongness at seeing Edison overshadowed by one of the restless dead.

"What are you doing?" Wil asked carefully.

When Ed spoke, his voice was both his and not his. There were echoes of the boy she knew and loved, and ringing notes of something entirely other.

"Looking for something."

"What are you looking for?" Wil pressed.

Ed turned back to the fireplace, wrenching a section of three bricks free with a frustrated, preternaturally strong movement. "Something lost."

He peered into the darkness behind the hearth wall and reached through the new hole to scrabble about with both hands. A dissatisfied hiss sounded as he withdrew his arms again, fingers smeared with soot and tangled with cobwebs.

"Empty, empty, empty. Still gone. Still in the halfway place."

Ed picked up the crowbar once more and tossed it aside in frustration. As it clattered across the floor, he rocked back on his haunches and buried his head in his filthy hands as if it ached.

"Edison," Wil said. "Come with me."

She kept her voice firm, the words not a suggestion but an order, and Ed got to his feet at once, wandering over to her in the dispirited way of a bewildered child.

"Let's take a walk," Wil suggested, tucking one of his hands through her arm.

She knew the nursery wing had long held some dark sway over him, and that place and history were tied up with the capacity of the dead to breach the living world. All Wil wanted was to get Edison away—to take him somewhere bright and alive and unfamiliar so that he could reclaim control of his own body. Whatever possessed him did not fight or argue. It seemed content enough to allow itself to be led through the Grange and into the sunny garden, then on through the outskirts of the mill wood, until they reached the wildflower-strewn meadow surrounding the Brights' cottage. There, in the shadow of the trees, Wil sat Edison and the thing inhabiting him down among the cornflowers and took their hands in her own.

"I need you to go," she said, not to Ed but to the trespassing spirit. "I know it's hard. I know you're trying to help and that I've been terribly slow. But I'm doing my best, I promise you. And I need to speak with Edison now."

For a long moment, he only stared back at her with those haunted balefire eyes. Then tension seemed to drain from Ed. The light bled from his gaze, leaving it ordinary and human once more. He blinked, confusion washing over him. While Wil could recall every moment of a temporary possession by the dead, there was no such comprehension from Edison, and she realized that her uncanny sense for death must be the thing that kept her aware and herself when another soul took over.

"Wil, what are we—" Edison began, but Wil stopped him with a finger to his lips.

"Why would you be tearing out the back of the fireplace in the nursery wing?" she asked. "Is there anything that would drive you to do that? Does your ghost take a special interest in that sort of thing? Because they've shown me a hearth too, with something caught behind it."

"I've had dreams like that," Ed told her with a shudder. "A hearth and a body crawling out from it. And Peter said something about the hearth in Kitty's room, but it's getting so hard to *think* at the Grange. Everything's a muddle—it feels like I'm hardly myself sometimes."

"That spirit in the nursery wing," Wil said. "It's been tampering with you. You pried out half the bricks behind the hearth, and I brought you here so it would have to let go. They're so bound to places, the dead I see—they can't stay long in a spot that's unfamiliar. It's like they can only come back to things they knew well. What did Peter say about Kitty's fireplace?"

Her mind was racing. Though she kept calm and unflappable on the outside, inwardly she'd begun to spark. Wil always knew when she was close to pulling together the disparate pieces of an equation or a translated verse or a new idea—she could feel that everything was about to fall into place and that she'd come out on the other side of confusion into understanding.

"There was a draft," Ed muttered, running a hand across his face as if his head still ached, and then scowling at how dirty his own palm was. He wiped both hands on the clean grass as he continued speaking. "Mama told Peter that Kitty always complained of a draft from her fireplace, and that she couldn't sleep for guilt over never having tended to it. So Peter repaired it himself."

"That's it," Wil said decisively, scrambling to her feet. "That's where we're meant to be looking. That's the answer to the question we've been asking."

Ed got up too, shaking his head at Wil. "You've gotten too far ahead of me as usual. I'm afraid you're going to have to spell all this out—what are we looking for? What have we been asking?"

Once more Wil took his hands, cleaner now, and pressed a kiss to the back of one of them. "Right now, more than anything else, we want to know where Abigail's gone. Because I went to her cousin's house this morning, and you were right to worry—she hasn't been back. She's missing, Ed, but I can't find her in the halfway realm. And your nursery-wing ghost told me it's looking for something lost and trapped between places. It can't leave those rooms, though, or force you to act outside them, so it keeps showing you its own hearth, over and over. . . ."

"When we ought to look behind Kitty's," Edison finished for her. "But Wil, I've been dreaming about a spirit climbing out from behind that fireplace since well before Abigail vanished."

"*L'âme a ses raisons que l'esprit ne connaît point*, to misquote Pascal,"

Wil told him. "Somehow a person's soul always knows when death is on the way. I've foreseen at least a dozen deaths before they happened. And those same souls that I've seen departing are what's left in the halfway realm. Why shouldn't they be able to anticipate mortal peril for someone else as well as for themselves? They're barely a shred of who they were in life, but they're hanging on. And *our* ghosts—my mother and Jenny and your sister and that creature in the nursery wing—they're all trying with everything they've got to explain or help in some way. They can hardly think, but they're working so hard, and I love them for it."

The last came out triumphantly, and Wil was shocked by her own words. She'd always viewed her deathsense as an inconvenience at best and a curse at worst. She'd begun searching for answers on behalf of her mother and Jenny Bright because she felt obligated to—because there was no one else to advocate for them, and it seemed like her duty. But now a blaze of affection seared through her. She wanted to help her lost souls. Wanted a safe harbor and a right ending for them. They deserved to rest, and Wil no longer felt it her duty to provide that; she *wanted* to do it. Because they were not some force pitted against her, trying to obfuscate. They, more so than anyone in the world of the living, were doing everything possible to drag the truth to light.

It took only an instant for Wil's epiphany to settle into her bones. Edison was already on his way back through the woods, striding toward the Grange with renewed purpose, and Wil gathered up her skirts to hurry after him.

All the way up the Grange's main staircase and down the hallway to the nursery wing, Wil kept hold of Edison's hand. She could *feel* the presence of whatever spirit haunted him pressing in, like a blanket of cold fog. But it didn't settle on Ed—it only surrounded the two of them as Edison retrieved the crowbar, a chisel, and a hammer from the nursery wing. Then they were in Kitty's room, both kneeling on the wide hearth side by side, Wil working with the hammer and chisel and Ed prying the larger pieces of brickwork loose.

Mortar cracked. Gaps appeared. Wil hurried to the dressing table and lit a lamp, holding it at the angle she thought best as Edison was finally able to force his head and one arm through the hole they'd made.

"Wil, it's her," he said, a frantic note behind the words, which were muffled by the splintering brickwork. "It's Abigail. And I think she's still alive."

CHAPTER TWENTY-TWO

EDISON

There was a gurney in the foyer where Kitty's coffin had been.

Abigail was laid upon it while the village doctor and the constable fussed about, and they didn't seem to be doing things nearly fast enough, not for Edison's taste. There was mortar dust in Abigail's hair, and her skin was deathly white, with hints of blue around her mouth and at her fingertips. She hadn't regained consciousness—not when Ed and Wil tore down the rest of the new bricks in a panic, not when they got her onto Kitty's bed, not when John Shepherd went for help.

"Excuse me, shouldn't you be taking her to hospital?"

Both the constable and the doctor glanced up, their hushed conversation brought to an abrupt halt by Ed's frustration.

"Edison," Lord Summerfield snapped from where he and Peter stood near the office door. "That's enough. You speak civilly to your elders."

The constable frowned at Edison, gnawing at the end of his stub of pencil. "Where was it again that you said you found her? In the back of a fireplace?"

He sounded skeptical, and Ed involuntarily scanned the room, searching for reinforcement. Both his father's and brother's faces were hard and closed off. Several of the servants hovered worriedly in open doorways, including Wil, who'd knit her hands together and was staring fixedly at Abigail.

It was on the tip of Ed's tongue to call her forward. To say she could confirm his account of things, and that she'd been there too when he pulled Abigail from the space meant for her tomb.

But as he began to speak, Ed's eyes drifted to Peter. And his brother was not watching the constable, nor Edison himself. He was watching Wil with a look of interest written across his mobile, intelligent face.

"Yes, I found her with—behind the fireplace, as you say," Ed answered the constable.

"And what was it that made you think to look back there?" the constable pressed.

Peter's eyes were on Edison now, his gaze so focused that it felt as if something was searing the boy's skin. But Ed didn't care anymore. He was tired of being quiet and afraid.

"Peter bricked up the back of the hearth," he said. "It seemed strange to me. I didn't know what reason he'd have to do it."

The constable gaped slightly. "Is that an accusation?"

"Of course not," Lord Summerfield cut in, disdain dripping from his words. "Look, Fawkes, you know the boy's unstable history as well as I do. He's spent time under care for delusions and wild fantasies. If he thinks there's been some sort of foul play here, it's only because his mind has him always on the watch for that sort of thing. The truth is, the girl on that gurney roomed in our attics. There's a passage into the chimney up there for sweeps to use. I assume she was cleaning it out and lost her balance. Accidents happen—there's no reason to look for anything reprehensible."

"Why would she be cleaning out the chimney passage after being sacked?" Ed had grown mulish. He squared his shoulders and set his jaw, the same obstinate spirit that had led him to stand against his father at Kitty's house party taking hold of him again. "You'd dismissed her from service. There was no reason for her to be in the attics, much less working up there."

There was thunder in Lord Summerfield's face. "How the hell should I know? That's a question for Mrs. Forster, not for me. Have you finished speaking, or do you mean to continue making your brother out to be some sort of brute?"

"I suppose it would be more to your taste if I made him out to be mad instead?" Ed answered sharply before turning and striding away.

He went to the hidden library and rifled through a book there, scanning its pages for something particular. After a moment Wil's voice sounded from the door, which he'd left ajar.

"What are you doing?"

"Looking up the address of the police station in Wynkirk," Ed told her without glancing up. "If anything's mad in this house, it's that we haven't made proper police reports or had a real inspector down before now. I'm going to see it done."

"Do you think Peter did that to Abigail? Because that's what seems most likely," Wil said.

Ed tensed. "I don't know. I hope not, but he's always had a tendency toward cruelty. I can't make it all fit in my head, though. The dates won't come out right."

Wil frowned, stepping forward and shutting the door so that they were enclosed in a small, private space together. With Abigail alive and Wil nearby, Ed knew he ought to feel better. But he didn't. He was miserable.

"What do you mean, the dates?" Wil said.

"If it was Peter who did this to Abigail, I would assume he had a hand in all the deaths here at the Grange. But I don't think he'd have touched Kitty—that's the one thing Papa always insists on, that blood's thicker than water and that family loyalty comes before anything else. Besides that, Peter wasn't back yet when Jenny died. I saw bills from a London hotel Peter was staying at before coming back here, and he was burning through money at gaming tables too—a habit he seems to have picked up on the Continent. So he couldn't have been involved in what happened to Jenny."

"What if Jenny really was an accident?" Wil offered. "Couldn't everything else have been Peter then?"

Edison shook his head. "Do you think that's possible? Jenny's the most violent of all our ghosts. She tried to strangle me, Wil. I don't know much about the afterlife—you're the expert. But it seems unlikely someone would harbor that sort of fury over an accidental drowning."

"No, you're right," Wil said, looking defeated. "But it would have made things easier. Who else could it have been?"

"It couldn't have been my father, not even with him paying off Abigail to look after Peter," Edison said at last, unable to meet Wil's eyes as he did so. "To start with, he'd never have touched Kitty. But there's also this—he was in London when your mother died. I remember him coming back. I remember being so angry because neither he nor Mama seemed to care very much when they found out about Mabel, and I knew it would be awful for you."

Now it was Wil who could not look at Ed as he glanced over to her.

"Who fits the dates?" she asked.

"Wil, I—"

"It's my grandfather, isn't it?"

Ed nodded. "I don't want it to be him. But he's always here, he's impossible to read, and he had some feud with your mother and Jenny and Abigail."

"Jack Hoult and Henry Ellicott have been here just as long. So have the groom, and the chauffeur, and Mrs. Ellicott and Mrs. Forster, if it comes to that," Wil said stubbornly.

"None of them had an axe to grind with the housemaids."

"No. But I saw them, or at least some of them, meeting with your brother in the mill cottage not long before he came home. Grandfather, Mrs. Forster, Jack, Sam Jenkins from the stable. They were all there. There's more going on than we've sorted out yet. It's too soon for accusations, Ed. And what about Kitty?" Wil went on. "Or that spirit in the nursery wing? How do either of them fit with Grandfather?"

"I don't know," Ed told her. "At least not yet. But I did see Shepherd arguing with Kitty—the fact is, he fits best."

"Abigail's cousin says Grandfather was asking after her. Why would he be looking for Abigail if he thought he'd already pushed her to her death?"

"Again, I don't know," Edison said. "To cover his tracks? Or perhaps he hadn't found out where she'd really gone yet—maybe what happened was the result of him finding her."

"If that's what you believe, then why on earth would you all but accuse Peter to the constable just now? What are you playing at?" Wil was radiating frustration with him, as she so often did since her arrival at Wither Grange. Ed felt his own temper sparking in response and did his best to force it down.

"Because there's a wickedness in Peter I've always hated. Because he deserves to know not every member of our family is on his side. He sees people as expendable or as game pieces he can move about to his advantage and their disadvantage. I want him to know I won't be treated like that any longer or let him do the same to anyone. I want him to know I'm different than I was before he left home. That he can't use me to his own ends, and that he'd better steer clear of you too."

Wil turned away from him, running a finger over the spines of the books nearest to her. "But none of that is what you mean to tell this inspector you're bringing in from Wynkirk? Instead you plan to say that you believe my grandfather is behind everything that's happened here?"

"I'm trying to do what I think is right. I would have thought you of all people would appreciate that."

When Wil faced him, suppressed anger was evident in every line of her. "I understand. But I don't think you do. If you bandy Peter's name about without sufficient proof that he's done wrong, it means nothing. It won't harm him in any way. You cannot, with your words, rob him of his position or reputation or lifestyle. But you could destroy my grandfather. Do you really think your parents would keep him on overseeing their household while he's under suspicion of murder? Of murdering *their own child*? Do you think he would ever find employment again, at his age, with that cloud hanging over him?

"I'm not afraid for myself. If he's truly done something monstrous, I hope justice is served. I can make my own way in the world if need be. But I can't live with an innocent man's downfall on my conscience if we're mistaken. Why do you think I haven't sought out help in all this? Because I'm prideful? Because I believe myself capable of resolving a string of murders all on my own? I feel like I am failing at every turn. I would ask for help if I could. But I trust no one, except the dead, to be above the influence of money and class and prejudice. They are the only unimpeachable witnesses here, so until I can make sense of what they're trying to say—until I can find a way to give them back their voices in the world of the living—I refuse to point a finger at anyone."

For the first time that he could remember, Edison found himself truly furious at Wil. She stood there, straight-backed and high-minded and unfaltering in her ideals, and he realized he would never be able to hit the mark she'd set out for him. Could never live up to her standards of perfection. But if she claimed to be doing her best, he was doing the same with her safety in mind, and he'd continue to do so, whether his efforts met with Wil's approval or not.

"Yes, well," Edison said, biting off the words, "we don't all have the luxury of speaking with the dead. Some of us have to make sense of things with no more than what the mortal world provides us."

Pushing past Wil, he left the hidden library and did not look back as he strode away down the Grange's crimson hall.

* * *

Wynkirk was nothing like the serene, well-ordered environs of Wither Grange, nor the sleepy village of Thrush's Green that sat on its doorstep. A prosperous and bustling market town with a warren of busy central streets, it was full of people whose lives had nothing whatsoever to do with the Summerfields—an odd sensation for Edison, who was, if he owned it to himself, nearly a recluse. With the exception of Wil, his life had been spent at home or in school. He seldom ventured to London when his family traveled there, and on the few occasions he'd joined them, he'd stayed holed up in his bedroom with a stack of books.

Wynkirk was exactly what Ed wanted, yet it gave him an uncomfortable sense of his own unimportance in the grand scheme of things. Ignorance forced him to stop and ask for directions to the police station not once, but twice, and each time the instructions were given to him impatiently, without any of the deference he was used to at home or any of the affection he was offered by Wil.

It's good for you, you entitled fool, he reminded himself sternly. *You aren't important at the end of the day. You're just another boy on a bicycle, albeit one who happens to be embroiled in something that could cause a monumental scandal.*

At last the police station appeared before him. Leaning his bicycle against the wall beside the door, Edison stepped inside. The air was thick with cigarette smoke and the drone of subdued voices, cut through by occasional raucous laughter and the shrill jangle of a telephone. Tentatively Ed made his way to what seemed to be the front desk.

"Good afternoon," he said to the brassy-looking young woman behind the counter. "I'd like to make a report."

She grinned and gave him a quick once-over—a perfunctory look from head to toe that seemed to sum him up entirely and put him in a neat file. *Edison Summerfield: less than he ought to be, all things considered.*

"What kind of report, love?"

Ed faltered. He wasn't sure. He didn't even have definitive proof that the deaths at the Grange were anything but accidents, beyond the word of an old woman and Wil's certainty based on her connection to the restless dead. But ghosts and the elderly parents of housemaids hardly made credible witnesses.

"I'm not sure?" he began, and fell back on a habit he always found insufferable when used by his family. "I'm Edison Summerfield—Lord Summerfield's son, from Wither Grange. We've had some deaths among the household, and the village coroner ruled them all accidents, but I'm concerned something may have been overlooked."

The girl behind the counter seemed entirely unmoved, both by his name and the mention of deaths among the staff. Before the war she might have been, but a great deal had changed since then, and for the better, in Edison's opinion. The Summerfield name carried less weight than it once did, and rightly so, though it was an inconvenience at present.

"I can sit you down with an inspector," she said, reaching forward and patting one of Ed's hands, which he'd set nervously atop the counter. "But I don't expect anything will come of it. They don't like to overturn

247

a coroner's inquest, and people just die sometimes, love. There's no use seeing anything untoward when death's a part of living. Don't suppose you've got a liking for detective stories?"

"Well, yes," Edison admitted, though it pained him to do so. He knew it would only make her think him less reliable, but he didn't think it wise to lie.

The girl nodded sagely. "I thought so. But let me see who's free, and you can get whatever you want to say off your chest."

"Thank you," Edison said, without much hope that his trip to Wynkirk was going to make any difference. "We've only just had my sister's funeral, and I couldn't sit idly by anymore. I had to do something."

The girl behind the counter glanced up sharply, concern showing in her eyes for the first time. "Your *sister*? Do you mean Kitty Summerfield—the one who's always in the society column?"

"I suppose," Ed answered, a little at a loss. "I don't think there's another Kitty Summerfield. And she was always going from one party to another."

The secretary was on her feet now, a hand on a bell switch behind the counter.

"People *adore* Kitty," she said. "At least young people do. She's always doing something mad or getting into some sort of scrape that proves how ridiculous all that stuffiness from before the war was. She's like . . . a crusader, only better dressed."

"Was she?" Ed asked numbly. "I didn't know."

"Kitty Summerfield, dead." The girl looked genuinely crestfallen. "And there was nothing about it in the papers at all. Not a word."

"No, I think my family wanted to keep it quiet. Though they ought to have had *something* put in—it's expected."

From somewhere behind the desk, a buzzer rang as the receptionist pressed the bell switch.

"I'm not supposed to pry, but what happened to her?" the girl asked.

And Edison couldn't withhold the answer when it clearly meant something.

"A riding accident," he said. "At least that's what they say. That she was thrown from her horse in our village churchyard and hit her head against a gravestone."

The receptionist's already troubled face clouded over. "I think you were right to come in. Do you know, it was only last year she rode the Grand National? Not the race itself, of course, but they'd just announced the National would be run at Aintree again, after it was moved to the racetrack at Gatwick during the war. Kitty was seeing Nick Donahue then—he owns a horse called Empress Lea, who was the odds-on favorite for the National. Apparently she told Nick that a male jockey could never really understand a mare, and that she'd be able to get a better time out of Lea than any National jockey ever could. Nick let her run Aintree on Lea, and if it had been anything official, she'd have set a record. Then when the National actually came around, Lea foundered—refused two jumps outright and finished with an abysmal time. Meanwhile, with your sister in the saddle, she'd sailed over everything, clean and clear."

Edison blinked. "I never heard any of that. I always knew Kitty was headstrong, but I'd no idea she was so reckless."

"Fearless, is what I'd call it," the girl said fervently. "Lord love me, what a loss."

As she spoke, a pair of suited men appeared behind her.

"Now then, Millie, what is it you need?" the older one asked. He was short and grizzled, with black hair just beginning to go gray and a florid white face seamed with a scattering of premature wrinkles. The man beside him stood in stark contrast—taller, with an easier manner and ready smile, and unlined terra-cotta skin.

"Edison Summerfield, these are Inspectors Dawes and Singh," the girl said, suddenly businesslike. "Inspectors, I think the boy has something you'll want to hear."

The interview was both better and worse than Ed had expected. He was taken seriously, at least. Asked to surrender his notebook, full of the dates and times of each household member's location, along with a number of additional notes and receipts as to where everyone had been when Mabel died, and Jenny Bright. And he was promised that the inspectors would be paying a visit to Wither Grange, a thought that filled him with simultaneous relief and dread.

Relief because the pursuit of truth would no longer rest solely with himself and Wil. Dread because if his father had been outraged by Ed mentioning his suspicions about Peter to the village constable, he would surely be livid over having police inspectors nosing about. And there was the inevitable moment too of Lord Summerfield bringing up Edison's prior stay at a hospital for those of unsound mind, at which point the inspectors might simply chalk Ed's concerns up to delusion and leave.

But. He'd taken a step in what felt like the right direction. And, mindful of Wil's reproach, he'd said nothing about John Shepherd—only laid out his concerns and the records he'd collected. It would be for the inspectors to draw their own conclusions. Ed had done his part. For the first time since Kitty's death and Wil's brief disappearance, the anxious piece inside him that demanded he keep track of everyone, and shoulder the burden of their safety himself, felt a little calmer.

Or at least he felt calmer until he walked out of the station and found his bicycle missing. With a sigh, Ed stuffed his hands into his pockets and resigned himself to a long walk home.

*   *   *

The Grange loomed ahead of Edison. All was dark and quiet within—he'd taken advantage of the resignation and calm that had settled over him, pushing it to its furthest ends by wandering the byroads between home and Wynkirk. The need to know where everyone was rested sharp and urgent in him now, but he'd gone hours without writing anything down—maybe in time he could shed the compulsion altogether.

As Ed drew closer to home, he made out a single dim light shining from the ground floor. The fire in his father's study. He could just make out the silhouettes of Lord Summerfield and Peter sitting in their arm-chairs, each of them with a glass in hand. A sudden longing for that sort of comfortable companionship shot through Ed—he'd never felt so with anyone besides Wil. He wanted her all at once, even though they'd parted on a sour note and things were more complicated with them than ever before. He wanted to tell her he was sorry for not always understanding the world as she did; for being an ignorant fool; for not living up to her expectations, impossible though they may be.

Truth was, even if Wil's standards were impossible, Ed would rather spend his life falling short of her mark than exceeding anyone else's.

Slipping through the front door, Ed took care to be soundless so his father and brother wouldn't notice him and ask where he'd been. He took his shoes off before going in because they were all over mud, and while he might have been careless about cleanliness before, he'd become acutely aware of anything that might cause more work for Wil.

But his caution failed to produce the desired effect. The study door was open, ruddy firelight spilling across the foyer floor, and Lord Summerfield's voice called out to him as he reached the bottom of the stairs.

"Edison. Come in here a minute."

Reluctantly Ed went. He knew what would come next. A lecture over the state of his shoes and his mud-streaked trousers. An interrogation about where he'd been.

But Lord Summerfield surprised him. Though he looked at Ed and could hardly fail to notice his general dishevelment, he chose to say nothing about it.

"I think we need to clear the air," Lord Summerfield offered instead, and Edison's surprise was so great, he swayed where he stood. "The truth is, I owe you an apology. I've been holding your past against you, Ed, when you've weathered a difficult summer awfully well. I know we haven't always been good friends, but we're family, and it's time to mend fences."

"We're stronger together," Peter added. "What Papa means is that it's time we all turned over a new leaf. Stood side by side instead of taking shots at each other. Then perhaps something good will come out of losing Kitty. She'd have liked that, I think. Seeing all of us united at the end."

Edison felt entirely at sea. He wasn't sure that was something Kitty had ever badly wanted, but then it seemed he hadn't known her very well.

"Will you accept my apology in the spirit it's offered and try to view your brother in a more charitable light from now on?" Lord Summerfield pressed. "You know, we only kept the news that Peter had come home secret from you and your mama because he was in some trouble. I wanted to ensure it was dealt with first and that it wouldn't cast a shadow over the rest of us. But Kitty was eager to have Peter back and chafed at the delay. She wanted to have him brought home during her party—a triumphant return for the Summerfields' prodigal son. Just think how glad she'd be to know the whole family had reconciled."

As he spoke, Lord Summerfield poured a shot of whiskey into an extra glass and handed it to Ed. Edison took the proffered glass and looked down at it blankly. He *wanted* to see the best in his family—to think they could grow together and get past the darkness and difficulties that had plagued them over the years. It was unspeakably lonely to feel out of step with them, trapped as a creature who existed in their world while not truly being *of* it. Surely he could make them see reason now that they were all striving for understanding. He could explain away the appearance of the police inspectors he'd enlisted as an attempt to clear the family's name. He could—

Ed had begun reaching for the glass but was interrupted by a thunderous crash emanating from the nursery wing. It was so loud, it made him start, and though his father did not react, Peter's gaze, which rested on Edison, seemed to intensify.

One is one and all alone, and evermore shall be so, Ed thought involuntarily.

"Of course I accept your apology," he said, ignoring the sound and fury from upstairs. "And I've always striven to judge our family impartially, a practice which I hope to continue. It's gratifying to hear we plan to turn over a new leaf, though I wish we could've done it without losing Kitty."

He took the glass which Lord Summerfield offered but did not raise it to his lips.

"I've been thinking that perhaps you'd like to move back out of the nursery wing," Lord Summerfield said after a moment. "It was bad luck, that being the only place to put you while the house was full. But you could take your pick of the empty rooms now. Find a place and make it your own."

Ed considered the offer. He could see his father meant it as an olive branch and guessed, by the way Lord Summerfield's gaze cut to Peter, that it had been his brother's idea. It was highly likely Peter had looked in, seen the state of the rooms, and known that the thing that had haunted Edison previously had returned with a vengeance. Odd then, that Peter would use that knowledge not to wound or disadvantage Ed in some way but to push for his comfort.

Perhaps they *were* all on the verge of a fresh start.

And yet. It was the nursery wing's violent resident who'd managed, through its chaotic force of will, to alert Ed and Wil to Abigail's plight. Ed had been as much an instrument in its wild and fumbling attempts at communication as Wil, and he disliked the idea of missing some intended message. Disliked it so much that he reluctantly turned down his father's offer.

"No, thank you," he said politely. "I appreciate it, but I've quite settled in. I'm happy as I am now."

Peter's curious attention became a narrow, searching look, but Lord Summerfield only shrugged. "Suit yourself. I only thought I'd offer."

"It was kind of you," Edison said, hating to seem ungrateful, or as though he hadn't received the peace offering in the spirit with which it was intended. "And I hope we can all become better friends, as you said."

Lord Summerfield nodded, waving a dismissive hand. And then there was nothing left for Ed to do but climb the stairs and carry on down the hall, letting himself into the haunting he'd chosen, as a blue ghost-fire roared on the nursery-wing hearth and shadows moved across all the fogged-over windows. The source of the crash he'd heard was obvious—the heavy electric light fixture overhead, which had hung from the ceiling on a chain, lay on the floor, boards splintered beneath it and a gaping hole in the plaster above.

"I hope you heard all that," Ed said testily as the ghost's customary singing began and the stink of rotting pond weeds drifted over from the bathroom. "I hope you heard me choose you, and that you'll be less of a nightmare as a result."

The only answer was a scrape of wrought iron on wood as the ponderous light fixture came clattering across the floor toward Ed. It moved like some enormous and otherworldly insect, picking up speed as it went. He had just enough time to step aside before it collided with the wall where he'd stood, embedding itself in the plaster and sending up a cloud of dust.

"No," Edison said. "I should have known better than to expect gratitude from you."

CHAPTER TWENTY-THREE

WIL

The arrival of a pair of police inspectors on the doorstep of the Grange the following morning caused a general upheaval. Brusque and businesslike, they immediately sequestered themselves in the study with Lord Summerfield and Peter, though word of their coming burned through the remaining staff like wildfire. Wil, burdened with the monumental task of keeping the entire house clean and in good order, was one of the last to hear they'd come. But it made little difference to her—there was still the work of trudging upstairs to ensure Lord Summerfield's and Peter's rooms looked fresh and untouched, as if they'd never been slept in.

On her way back down, Wil couldn't keep her gaze from cutting anxiously to Edison's shut door. He was asleep still, she expected—he stayed in bed far later now that his nights were broken up by anxious wandering and ghostly disturbances. Guilt gnawed at her as she thought of how they'd parted ways the day before. She'd been hard on him—too hard, perhaps. Much as it irked Wil when Ed couldn't intuit the realities of her life, it was foolish of her to expect him to do so. Nothing about his upbringing had cultivated empathy or an openness of mind in him, and yet, against the odds, he'd managed to foster both qualities in himself.

Particularly now, when he was still stumbling under the loss of his sister and the troubles of the Grange, she ought to be patient.

Yet Wil had her own troubles and worries, and they left her short-fused and exhausted, with little energy to spare for explanations or understanding.

For the briefest moment she stood on the landing and contemplated going to mend fences. But if Ed was asleep, she hated to wake him. Instead she shifted her grip on the broom and dustpan and wastebasket she carried, and continued on.

Downstairs a buzz of low conversation echoed through the corridors of the servants' domain. Wil emptied her dustpan and basket into a larger bin in the housemaid's closet and frowned as she straightened.

The door to her grandfather's study was ajar. John Shepherd *never* left doors so—nearly a lifetime at the Grange had instilled an unbreakable habit in him of ensuring they were shut fast. Leaving her things, Wil slipped across the hallway and knocked gently on the doorframe. There was a sound of someone moving about within the room, though no one answered her knock.

"Grandfather?" she ventured after a moment. "It's Wil. May I come in?"

"Yes. And shut the door behind you," he said in a strangely agitated tone.

With worry already twisting in her stomach, Wil did as she was told. Inside she found the butler's study in uncharacteristic disorder. Drawers yawned half-open, ledgers sat scattered about, and the sampler Wil had made years back was missing from the wall.

"Is everything all right?" Wil asked as John stuffed books and papers into a satchel.

"No," he said tersely. "There are police inspectors upstairs."

Wil's heart felt as if it would beat out of her chest. "Is that . . . a problem for you?"

256

"It is a problem for all of us," John said. "And so you and I are leaving."

Drawing in a deep breath, Wil summoned all her courage. She planted her feet and looked at her grandfather levelly.

"Did you kill my mother?" she asked, her voice flat and toneless. "Or Jenny Bright, or Kitty Summerfield, or Abigail? You've never been a gentle man, but I can't recall ever having been lied to by you. So I'm asking right out. Did you kill your daughter, or any of the others?"

John's face had gone dead-white and strained, and his hands trembled as he clasped the satchel.

"No," he said, his voice a match for Wil's dispassionate question, regardless of his appearance. "I never laid a finger on any of them. But that doesn't make me guiltless. It doesn't make any of us guiltless. I have another chance with you, though, so we're leaving. I ought to have done it sooner. I've been a fool to stay so long, no matter what I gained by it."

Wil remained as she was, stock-still and immovable. "I'm not going anywhere."

John straightened up, the satchel held in one hand, and while he'd always been stately and patrician, suddenly he looked terribly old.

"Would you come with me if I tell you the truth of what happened to your mother?"

Everything in Wil felt frozen in amber. The truth was all she'd been striving after, but truth without justice was a hollow and purposeless thing. Yet until she learned the truth, she had no way to see justice brought about.

"Yes," Wil lied, and her conscience did not so much as twinge. "I'll go with you if you tell me what happened. But I want to hear it now."

John nodded. "Not here, though. We'll go out to the mill wood, then home for our things and away."

* * *

257

At the heart of Wither Grange's beech wood, the millpond lay dark and dreaming beneath overhanging boughs. Its surface was all browns and golds and reflected hints of green. As if he'd already forgotten his word, John made to walk past it and homeward, but Wil stopped stonily on its gentle, sloping banks.

"Here," she said. "This is as good a place as any."

And she sat just where she was on that damp, ill-fated ground.

With a sigh, John joined her, settling himself down with the same rigid grace he employed when serving in the Grange's elegant dining room.

"What is it you wish to know?" he asked.

"Who killed Mabel Price?" Wil said bluntly. Her nerves were jangling, and the rift between worlds lay so close and so open, she could feel it tugging at her.

"I don't know," John answered, and she could see it was the truth. "Not for certain."

"Who do you *think* killed Mabel Price?" Wil tried again.

Her grandfather ran a hand across his face, a weary and more human gesture than she'd ever seen from him before.

"I want you to understand," he began slowly, "that this is something I've never spoken of before. None of us have. And knowing who you are, Wilhelmina, I'm sure you'll see that silence as cowardice. Maybe that's true in part, but everything I've done, every secret I've kept, was for your sake."

"Don't drag me into this," Wil said, stern and unyielding. "I never asked to be kept in the dark. Just tell me what happened."

"What do you know about Peter Summerfield?" John asked.

"Edison doesn't like him. Says he's cruel. And I trust Ed more than anyone."

John winced at that last statement, and though Wil had intended it

258

to sting, remorse twisted inside her. But she hardened her heart—until she had the truth from John Shepherd, she would not allow herself to soften.

"As a young man," John began, "Peter had a habit of taking advantage of the Grange's youngest housemaids. Anyone who stayed belowstairs was all right—the family doesn't see them. But your mother was not just my daughter and expected to go into service; she was also by far the prettiest girl in the county. I'm sure you can imagine where this is all leading."

"Yes. Of course I can." There was a viciousness in Wil's voice that somehow seemed to meet with John's approval. He nodded to her.

"I felt the same. Could see the same thing coming. By the time your mother was fourteen, the Summerfields had begun to ask when she'd enter service. I was in their employ, so it was understood that she'd do the same. Most of the girls we took on came to us when they were younger than her—eleven or twelve, so they could be trained properly. It wasn't that the family said straight-out that Mabel had to follow after me, but it was implied. And I was a fool—I ignored my better judgment and convinced myself that because I was always at the Grange and always looking after things, I could look after her if she came to the house too. It was easier to give in, and I have regretted choosing the path of least resistance ever since."

John glanced uncertainly at Wil as if he were searching for some form of encouragement or absolution. But she met him only with the unreadable blankness he'd taught her so well.

"For two years your mother and I served at the Grange together," John went on. "And I saw nothing untoward. No signs of any special attention paid to her or ill-treatment. She never seemed unhappy either, until one day she came to me and said she intended to give her notice. That she was no longer interested in service and wanted other things from life. Furthermore she intended to go north, to live with some of her mother's people. Of course I fought her on it—she had a respectable job in a well-known household where I could look after her. But she was adamant. We could both of us be unyielding, and we had some dreadful fights until at last she did as she'd said. Gave her resignation to Mrs. Forster and left.

"A fortnight later, she sent word that she'd become engaged to a tenant farmer's son. A boy called William Price. She claimed she'd met him the day of her arrival and that it had been love at first sight—that they were made for each other. Only a few weeks later they were married. I was both unable and unwilling to attend the wedding, thinking she'd thrown herself away. That she could have done better if she hadn't taken a sudden turn toward willfulness. But when word came that you'd been born early, only seven months after the wedding, I began to wonder. You weren't small. You weren't sickly. And I began to realize perhaps it wasn't Mabel who'd ruined her own chances—perhaps I was the one who'd done it by allowing her to come to the Grange."

Wil could feel herself blanching. Her hands began to tremble as she thought of Edison. Of the way she loved him, body and soul. And it wasn't only that—she felt as if part of the bedrock of her life had suddenly split open to reveal a fault line. The memory of Mabel and William had always been perfect to her—the one untainted aspect of a shadowed family and a bleak childhood. To learn they might have been less than she believed was an awful blow.

"Do you mean to say I may be a Summerfield?" she asked bluntly, the words coming out hoarse and unnatural. "That in all likelihood Peter and not William Price was my father? That my mother only used William as a way of covering up someone else's crime, because she had to bear the consequences? Because I *am* the consequences?"

"I honestly don't know," John said. "I could never bring myself to ask your mother, and she never told me the truth of it all. Once she came back, we never spoke of why she left. Because it didn't matter to either of us—you were hers, and she and I would look after you, come what may."

"It matters to me!" Wil scrambled to her feet, everything in her screaming that she should *go*, somewhere, anywhere, so long as she was moving. "It matters more than anything."

"I would tell you if I could," John said, regret behind the words. "But I can't. Only your mother knew the whole of this story, and she's gone."

Focus, Wil told herself. With implacable resolve, she forced herself to calm. To sit once more on the grass beside her grandfather. To school her face into serenity and put aside any thought of what John Shepherd had just told her, and what it might mean for herself and Edison.

"What happened when Mama came home?" Wil asked, once again glacial in her composure.

"Nothing, to begin with," John said. "She resumed her position, and life carried on. Your father's death had been a blow, but she bore it well. And Peter had moved on—there were other staff who'd caught his eye. I thought perhaps the worst was behind us, until your mother came to me and said she knew something about the Summerfields. Something she said could cause a scandal and be the ruin of them, if it got out. I assumed I knew what it was, of course, and begged her not to breathe a word of it. But she said it wasn't what I thought—that she'd learned of some secret from years back after a chance meeting in London with a woman called Margaret Willis, who'd been a nursemaid here. I'd no idea what it could be about, the nursery being entirely outside my purview. Maggie Willis was the sort of person who'd kept to herself, and she had been busy with Master Edison, who was a nervous and sickly child. Little Kitty we saw often enough, but months could pass without me catching more than a glimpse of the nurse and Edison day to day. I did warn

261

Mabel that Margaret had been sent away in disgrace and that her word couldn't be trusted, but Mabel wouldn't hear it. She was determined to use what she'd found out to some advantage for you. You were already a precocious child, and she wanted you to have some money set aside, to provide an opportunity for an education."

Wil's stomach turned over. She'd seen the way Edison looked when he'd learned of the reason behind Kitty's death—that his sister had been watching out for him and died while trying to keep him safe. Now she could see the same sort of revelation coming for her and was powerless to stop the truth from hitting its mark.

"I couldn't dissuade her," John said, and his face, normally an emotionless mask, was twisted with remorse. "We fought again, just as we had before she left the first time. But she was stubborn, like you. She told me she'd made an appointment with one of the family to secure your future. The next morning I found her here, washed up among the reeds."

"Who did she speak to?" Wil's voice was vibrating with her need to know, her desire to find out regardless of the cost. Futile rage lanced through her as John raised a pair of hands helplessly.

"I don't know. To this day I don't. She didn't tell me—we were too much in the habit of keeping secrets from each other at that point. After her funeral, Lord Summerfield spoke to me and to Jenny Bright, for we were both discontented in the wake of your mother's death. His Lordship said Mabel's passing was a sad accident, and that if either of us claimed otherwise and tried to falsely malign the family, he'd see us cut off from everyone we loved and sent to the workhouse. I had you to look after, and Jenny had her parents, so we kept quiet. After a few months, His Lordship made overtures to keep the peace. He began to pay Jenny and me twice what we'd earned previously, and he has to this day. Later there were others—Mrs. Forster, Sam Jenkins, Jack Hoult. I don't know what they'd learned that required bribery for their silence, but they all received the same payments. Peter handled anything clandestine while he was still alive—His Lordship didn't have a taste for it, and Peter was happy enough to keep his father's hands clean. As soon as he returned he took that up again, even before he'd come back to the Grange. We were sent to the mill cottage for our thirty pieces of silver, every one of us too ashamed to speak to another about it afterward or to try to set things to rights. But now Jenny's dead and you've come to Wither Grange, and it's time for us to take our leave. I have savings set by—I put every extra penny paid to me aside in your name. So, in a way, Mabel accomplished what she intended to. She did secure an advantage for you. We'll go and make a fresh start somewhere. I won't let history repeat itself, Wil. I only ever meant to look after you, even if I failed your mother."

Once again Wil rose to her feet. There was something in her that pleaded for kindness—that said, wasn't her grandfather family? Didn't he deserve a second chance?

But the greater part of her was struggling with the intolerable weight she'd borne since Mabel's death, and the new revelation that her parents might not have been charmed and fated lovers, as she'd always believed. That it was possible she wasn't the product of some sweet fairy-tale union, or even William Price's daughter at all, but the result of her mother's violation. A Summerfield. Tied by blood to Edison, when what she wanted was to be bound to him by heart.

Every passing day, every new twist of fate unearthed, only added to her growing despair, and a sharp instinct in her longed to settle some of it on John's shoulders. Perhaps it would not lighten her own load, but it would satisfy the root of bitterness within her to know that he felt the same exhausting pull of guilt and responsibility that she did.

"If you meant to prevent history from repeating itself," Wil said, clear and unrelenting, "you're three deaths too late. You didn't just fail my mother. You aren't just failing me. You failed Jenny and Kitty—and

Abigail too, if she doesn't recover—but I don't intend to do the same. I will *never* let cowardice or money stand in the way of my own efforts to do what's right. To speak for those who can no longer speak for themselves."

"Where are you going?" John called after her despairingly as she started away from him.

"Back to the Grange," Wil said. "I won't leave until I'm dead myself or see justice done, or until that cursed house lies in rubble at my feet."

CHAPTER TWENTY-FOUR

EDISON

O ne is one and all alone.
One is one,
One is one,
And evermore shall be so.

The words ran sluggishly around Edison's mind, both a product of his own overwrought brain and of the nursery-wing ghost, which had been singing adamantly throughout the night. Ed had tried to get up twice to do his rounds, only to give in halfway through and stumble back to the wing for another failed attempt at sleep. Exhaustion weighed so heavily on him that it felt as if his limbs were lead, and the whole world seemed at a distance somehow.

But at last the sun rose, spilling its implacable light through the bare windows and empty doorways of the nursery wing. With a ragged sigh, Ed dragged himself out of bed and dressed hastily, raking a hand through his hair and not bothering to attempt a look in the shattered and fogged-over bathroom mirror. At the door he stopped and stood for an instant with his hand outstretched.

He knew exactly what waited for him out in the soulless clockwork corridors of the Grange. Peter and his father in the breakfast room together, somehow always earlier than Ed, no matter when he woke. They'd be halfway through their breakfasts already, and though neither of them had chided him about the police inspectors coming the day before, it hung over Edison like a cloud. His family disapproved. His family thought he had behaved badly and betrayed their trust. They did not have to say anything for him to understand, or to feel the sting of it. Neither Lord Summerfield nor Peter would speak a word to him— they'd speak only to each other and leave him behind when they were finished, alone with his guilt and confusion and lifelong sense of being out of place. As for Lady Summerfield, she never emerged from her rooms until nearly noon and had no particular desire for Ed's company after she'd done so.

Abruptly Edison changed his mind. He turned away from the door leading out to the Grange and went instead to the opposite side of the nursery wing and the narrower door, behind which lay the servants' stairs. Clattering down them, he made his way to the kitchen, where Mrs. Ellicott stood alone at the broad range stove.

"Good morning," he ventured hesitantly.

"Good morning, Master Edison," Mrs. Ellicott said with a thin smile. "I trust you slept well."

"Not especially," Ed answered, sitting down at the broad kitchen counter. "Is Daphne all right, Mrs. E.? Is my family going to give her a reference if she goes looking for other work?"

Mrs. Ellicott took a kettle of freshly boiled water off the stove and turned to face Edison fully for the first time.

"She's all right. Already found herself a position doing the baking and cooking for a tearoom in Wynkirk, as a matter of fact. Pays better than here, so I suppose the only downside is that we won't see as much of each other."

"I'm sorry for that. Really I am."

Mrs. Ellicott softened. "I know you are, Master Edison. You look worn out this morning. Cup of tea?"

"I'm not sure that will cut it today, if I'm honest. Maybe a pot of strong coffee?"

With a nod, Mrs. Ellicott reached for an upper cabinet. "I'll need a minute for that."

"Wait." Ed got to his feet and went around the counter to join her by the range. "If you show me where the percolator and the coffee are, I could do it myself."

"I don't mind at all," Mrs. Ellicott said, giving him an odd look, but Ed felt suddenly that it was important. That here at least was something he could do.

"Why don't *you* sit?" he said. "And I'll fix the coffee."

The cook's eyebrows shot up. "Master Edison, I'm not sure—"

"I want to," he told her. "I know how to do it; I learned from a friend who taught me out in the mill wood. When we were younger, we'd play at being shipwrecked on a desert island. She'd smuggle the percolator and grounds out of her house, and we thought we were terribly daring, lighting our own fire and drinking coffee on the sly."

"Well, all right then." Mrs. Ellicott laughed and sat, pointing to the cupboard on Edison's upper left as she did so. "Everything you need's in there. Pot, coffee, cups, sugar. Use the water that's already hot, and it won't take nearly so long to brew."

Ed went hunting through the cupboard, rather pleased with himself as he fumbled about. He wasn't efficient, and it took him a few moments to sort out the percolator, but Mrs. Ellicott sat with an amused smile on her face and let him muddle through on his own. When he set down a steaming cup of coffee in front of her and went to sit with his own, it occurred to Ed that he couldn't remember the last time he'd felt as if he'd

267

accomplished something at home. At school, yes. In the forest with Wil, often. But never at home. At the Grange he was superfluous at best, and a burden at worst.

"That hits the spot," Mrs. Ellicott said as she nursed her cup. "I don't suppose you're looking for a post as a kitchen maid? It's only me down here for most of the day now, and I don't like the quiet."

Ed glanced over at her solemnly. "I'm afraid kitchen maid is the *one* position school hasn't prepared me for. I'm reasonably good with the classics and mathematics, but you've just seen the extent of my domestic skills."

"Don't run yourself down like that, Master Edison," Mrs. Ellicott said. "If you can manage coffee, I'm sure you could stretch to a cup of tea."

"In that case, I hope you'll consider me for the job."

"Hired." Mrs. Ellicott held out a hand, and Ed shook it.

They were still grinning at each other when a bleak voice sounded from behind them. "Good morning."

Wil stood in the kitchen doorway, looking more like her aloof and unreadable grandfather than ever.

"Coffee?" Ed asked, and Wil shook her head.

"No, thank you. I can't stop for long—I only came to see if Mrs. E. has any clean rags. I've run out."

"Let me take a look." Mrs. Ellicott got to her feet, and the moment was over. Once more, Edison felt at odds in his own skin and out of place in his own home. Wil seemed not to notice, or if she did, she gave no sign of it. Mrs. Ellicott returned with a pile of neatly folded rags, and Wil vanished into the whitewashed corridor.

"Do you want me to do the washing-up?" Ed offered, a note of forlorn hope in his voice, but he knew what the answer would be.

"No," Mrs. Ellicott said firmly. "It's kind of you to offer, Master Edison, but I'll leave it to do along with the breakfast dishes, once

268

Mrs. Forster brings those down. It's time for you to be getting back upstairs."

Ed knew she was right. He wandered out of the kitchen but couldn't help stopping at the housemaid's closet, where Wil was emptying a pail of ashes into the larger waste bin.

"Can I come in?" Ed asked.

"It's your house," Wil answered without looking up.

Edison stepped inside and shut the door behind him. "I didn't say anything about your grandfather when I spoke to the police inspectors. I remembered what you told me, and I didn't say a thing."

"How benevolent you are."

Once again, there was some tension and unspoken frustration singing through Wil, and Ed had no idea of its origins, though he thought he could guess.

"Is something wrong?" he asked. "If there is, I want to help. I'm sorry I was an ass about your grandfather and that I fought with you about it. You were right, and I—"

"He's gone," Wil said. "Grandfather gave his notice yesterday afternoon and took a train to Lincolnshire. There's only me at home now."

Ed felt as if the wind had been knocked out of him. "Shepherd's gone? So it was him after all."

"No." Wil was adamant. "No, it wasn't. I don't have anything besides his word to assure me of that, but we spoke before he left, and I believe everything he told me. I realize it looks terribly suspicious, him leaving like that, but he said he couldn't stay at the Grange if I did, because in all likelihood I'll end up like my mother."

"You will *not*." Ed took a step forward and reached for her, but Wil shrank back, dropping the empty ash pail, which sent up a small puff of leftover dust.

"Please don't touch me."

Ed shot Wil an anguished look and saw for the first time that there were tears shining in her eyes.

"The things my grandfather told me," she said. "They make a difference for you and me. Just . . . just listen while I tell you."

Ed did. By the end it felt as if everything inside him was a spreading network of bruises. The knowledge that it must be a member of his family who'd been behind the deaths at the Grange hurt, but knowing that he and Wil could never be what they'd hoped was worse. As he looked at her steadily, though, he realized that he could not show how deeply he felt it. Because loneliness had written itself across his beloved friend's face, and despair showed in her very posture.

"It doesn't matter," Edison said, his gaze unwavering. "If it's true, it changes things for us; there's no getting around that. But we were friends before anything else. I love you, Wil. Always. I'll never lose that, but I can alter the shape of it if I have to. I can find a way for us to be . . . family."

"It's not what I wanted," Wil whispered. "Ed, I—"

"Of course it isn't. But either your grandfather lied, or what he said is true, and we have to live with it. I can see you're convinced, and I trust you, so here we are. There's no getting around it."

"I don't *want* this," Wil repeated, fiercely now, as if she couldn't get past that one thought. "I don't want to be connected to someone who killed my mother, no matter who it turns out to have been. I loved her, Ed. I didn't see as much of her as I would have liked because she was here at the Grange so often, but I loved her. And I don't remember much about him, but I loved William Price too. He was as much a father to me as anyone could be. I want *that*. I want the story I was told as a child—that I am the daughter of a farmer and his wife, who were so taken with each other, they married within days of meeting. It is pretty and sweet and simple and a comfort. But to think I might be Peter's instead? And the result of his brutishness? After which, there is every chance that he killed my mother? I don't know how to carry that through life with me. Even if I never know for sure, everything's spoiled now. Who I thought my parents were. What I wanted us to be."

Wil's voice caught on her last words, and Edison didn't know what to say. He didn't know how to console her, because he could see from the skittish way Wil held herself and how her eyes cut furtively to him that he must not touch her. Woodenly she gathered up fresh rags and a duster, and yet another waste bin.

"The last thing in the world I want to be," she said as she passed him and slipped out through the door, "is a Summerfield."

Edison stayed where he was, Wil's words ringing in his ears. All his life he'd been out of tune with his family, and he'd longed to find a way to better fit the place they'd laid out for him. But lately he'd begun to feel as Wil did. And if Wil herself was a Summerfield?

Ed, too, would rather be anything else.

*　　*　　*

"I need answers about all this," Ed said desperately, sitting across a desk from the two police inspectors. He'd cycled into Wynkirk a second time on Kitty's seldom-used and rusty bicycle. Ed needed, more than anything else, a way to feel useful, and as if he were moving toward some resolution of the troubles that plagued Wither Grange. "Surely you've come up with something."

The inspectors glanced at each other, and Ed's stomach sank.

"We did come up with something," the older of them, Dawes, said gruffly. "Your father and brother told us you've been . . . unsettled before. That you spent some time at a hospital, run by a Dr. Winstead."

"I did." Ed tried to channel Wil—her flawless calm and composure. But he couldn't help himself. His throat dried, and his palms began to sweat. "It was years ago, though, and I've never had to go back. We

271

were having a difficult time as a family, but I promise you I'm of sound mind now."

"It's understandable that you'd be disturbed by everything that's happened in your home," the younger inspector, Singh, said reassuringly. "You've had an awful run of bad luck. But sometimes hardship is just that—bad luck from beginning to end."

"What about Abigail?" Edison said. "How is that bad luck? She was bricked up behind a fireplace. Thinking that could be an accident makes your judgment questionable, not mine."

"We saw the attic hatch," Inspector Dawes answered. "There were scuff marks around it, and a bit of her apron had torn off on one of the hinges. She'd been cleaning up there and had a fall, like your father said."

Fighting for calm, Ed stuffed his hands into his pockets and balled them into fists once they were out of sight.

"Surely," he said with aggressive restraint, "if she'd fallen three stories down a chimney, she'd have broken bones and bruises from head to toe. I can't see how a person would even survive that. But she looked untouched in that way when I found her. Nearly suffocated, yes. And she's apparently still unconscious, though I can't understand why. Has the doctor at our village hospital even looked into that? Shouldn't someone offer a second opinion?"

"I assure you, we'll leave no stone unturned," Inspector Singh offered diplomatically. "But you should prepare yourself for all this to come to nothing, so that it doesn't provide the sort of shock you had after your brother's death."

"Only, my brother didn't die," Ed said, getting to his feet. "My sister did. Two housemaids did. Abigail very well might. I should prefer to resolve this before that number is added to."

With Wil, most likely, he thought silently, and even the idea of it set his heart pounding.

"Of course," Dawes said. "Leave it in our hands."

But as Edison cycled back home, he could not escape the understanding that this particular effort had been in vain. There would be no outside help for him and Wil. They had only themselves to depend on.

Caught up in the mire of his own thoughts, Ed did not at first realize that he was humming under his breath. Eventually, he became aware of it. That wretched tune, over and over. "Green Grow the Rushes, O."

And it occurred to him that he and Wil were not entirely on their own, after all. As she'd said before, they did have help in their pursuit of truth and justice. The only trouble was, their allies resided in Wil's halfway realm and numbered among the dead. But they had a voice in the form of Wil Price. As their numbers grew, they'd become stronger and clearer and more vocal. They'd used their combined wits to forestall Abigail's death. What else could they manage if properly channeled?

With startling clarity, an idea presented itself to Edison. A potential solution to their problems that could be brought about at any time. Picking up speed, he flew down the country lanes between Wynkirk and Wither Grange, dropped his bicycle on the gravel drive before the house, and tore inside.

"Edison, what the devil—" Ed heard his father call out, but he did not stop. He let himself through the door that led to the nearest set of servants' stairs and went down them two at a time.

The house's lowest floor seemed nearly deserted in the absence of the gregarious footmen and chattering maids and omnipresent Shepherd, whom Ed had grown up with and always known. But he needed only one person now, and he found Wil in her grandfather's empty office, sitting blankly at his desk.

"What would you do to put an end to all this now?" Ed said breathlessly, shutting the door to Shepherd's office behind him. "If we could dredge up the truth and finish everything tonight, would you be willing to take a risk? I'll look out for you, Wil, I promise."

She blinked, her golden curls a halo around her despairing face. "I don't know what you're talking about."

"My family—*our* family—has one cardinal rule." Wil winced as Ed spoke of their family, but he carried on undaunted. "It is to look after your own. To close ranks in the face of any trouble and never betray our own blood. It's why I never said a word to you about how awful Peter was to Kitty and me, or about being sent away to hospital. But someone here has already turned Judas. Kitty was as Summerfield as they come, and she's gone. So we're going to let her name her murderer in front of everyone. If no one outside Wither Grange can bring a Summerfield to justice, then we'll see it done by the Summerfields themselves."

"But the dead aren't like that," Wil argued. "They can't just tell their stories the way you or I can."

"They can't *alone*," Edison said. "But they've managed to communicate more each time someone's added to their number. I think they strengthen each other. Your mother's pity and sorrow. Jenny Bright's anger. Kitty's force of will. And whatever determination has kept that thing in the nursery wing clinging to the edges of life all these years. Together they're becoming more than they were at first. Wil, do you think you could channel all of them at once?"

Wil swallowed, visibly discomfited by the suggestion. But Ed knew her better than anyone, and she'd never backed down from a challenge.

"I can try," she said at last.

Ed nodded. "Good. If the living can't bring an end to all this, we'll see if the dead can. Tonight we hold a séance."

CHAPTER TWENTY-FIVE

WIL

Wil chose the conservatory for what she darkly thought of as her spiritualist debut. Ed had wanted the empty laboratory because it seemed the only room of the house he really felt at ease in, but Wil couldn't picture the flawless and tightly laced Summerfields seating themselves on the floor to listen to their housemaid as she summoned the dead.

Of course, they weren't being told that was the purpose of the family conference. Edison was bringing them together under the pretext of having some important decision about his future to announce. Why they believed him, Wil couldn't imagine—she'd felt a thousand ways about Edison Summerfield in her lifetime but had always known he was a little aimless. Still, he assured her that everyone would assemble at ten o'clock in the evening once they'd had a chance to eat their dinner and refresh themselves afterward.

Wil had just time enough to clear the dinner things, tidy herself a little, and set out glasses along with the whiskey and sherry the Summerfields preferred for their respective nightcaps. The wide bank of windows that wrapped around two sides of the conservatory showed a warm and velvety summer night—the sky a glistening swath of stars, the lawns and garden peaceful and dreaming, the mill wood beyond a brooding shadow. It suited Wil to have the night looking in on them. She craved its quiet solace, and it felt like the first of her allies—the foundation on which she would stand as she attempted to do what she'd never managed before, and draw truth from the bewildering dead.

Ed came in first, and whatever he and Wil were to each other now, his reassuring nod still lent her courage, even while her heart twisted at the sight of him. Within a moment Lord and Lady Summerfield and Peter had filed in as well. Wil kept her back to the wall, a silent presence until called upon, but she could not escape awareness of Peter's occasional glances in her direction. Ed noticed too, and a muscle in his jaw twitched as he got to his feet, transparently nervous to be addressing his family as a body.

"Ah, Mrs. Forster," Ed said at once, seeing the housekeeper lingering in the doorway Wil had ensured remained open. "Won't you come in?"

Mrs. Forster did as she was bidden, a look of confusion on her face.

"Edison, what is this?" Lord Summerfield asked with an impatient sigh. "What on earth can you possibly have decided about your future that requires the housekeeper to be a party to?"

"I have something to ask her about that you might not be aware of," Edison said stalwartly, though Wil, at least, could see anxiety in his eyes. "Mrs. Forster, who is that standing next to the door?"

Mrs. Forster glanced over at Wil, her confusion growing. "Why, that's Wilhelmina Price, Master Edison. John Shepherd's granddaughter."

"And is there anything . . . unusual . . . that the girl is known for, down in the village?"

"Well, yes," Mrs. Forster answered reluctantly. "If I'm honest, there is."

Peter rolled his eyes. "Dear Lord, I think I know where this is going. I've heard a few things about the girl since coming back."

Wil watched him closely as he spoke. If Peter knew of a connection between them, he certainly hid it well outside of a spark of hungry interest, which was no more than he seemed to demonstrate for every serving girl.

"Mrs. Forster," Ed said sternly, cutting Peter off with a sudden flare of the brazen courage he'd shown when defending Wil at the dinner party, which seemed to have taken place a lifetime ago. "What is it you know about Wilhelmina Price?"

"She has a reputation," Mrs. Forster began reluctantly.

"Well, we can't keep her on if she's loose in her morals," Lady Summerfield said, looking offended at the very thought. Ed ran a hand across his face in frustration.

"Can you all just *listen*?" he said. "You're making an already difficult job even harder than it needs to be."

Lady Summerfield subsided, and Ed turned to Mrs. Forster with an encouraging gesture. "Go on."

"Wil Price has a reputation for being able to speak with the dead."

Lord Summerfield let out a sharp bark of laughter, and Peter made a disparaging noise.

"Mrs. Forster," Lord Summerfield said sternly, "you may go."

Wil watched as the housekeeper left. She'd known what she and Ed were planning to do was a risk and a long shot, but it seemed their chance at forcing the family to reckon with its own sins would be over before it had begun.

"Edison Clive Summerfield," His Lordship said. "We've had enough of your nonsense. First those police inspectors, now—"

But he stopped speaking midsentence. The door, which Mrs. Forster had shut behind her, was slowly drifting open. Even inured as she was to the presence of the dead, Wil couldn't help sidling a few steps away, farther down the conservatory wall. As the door swung and stopped, a breath of cold, damp air billowed in from the corridor, along with an eerie, childish voice.

Come and I will sing you.
What will you sing me?
I will sing you one, O.
What will the one be?
One is one and all alone,
And evermore shall be so.

"What the hell are you playing at?" Peter snarled. The question was addressed not to Ed but to Wil herself, and she felt suddenly trapped between the voice of the nursery wing's nameless ghost and Peter's disdain.

But Lady Summerfield was on the edge of her seat, leaning hungrily forward, her eyes fixed on Edison.

"Do you hear that?" she asked. "Tell me I'm not the only one who can."

"Of course I hear it, Mother," Ed answered. "I've been hearing it for years. Only I thought it was Peter at first. It isn't, though—it's someone else."

"Tricks," Lord Summerfield scoffed as Peter rolled his eyes in disgust. "This village charlatan you've brought among us is taking advantage of your naïveté, Edison. Turn her out, and we'll hear no more of this."

Lady Summerfield seemed unconvinced, though, and when Ed's eyes found Wil's from across the room, an electric shock passed between them.

It's now or never, Ed's gaze told her. *Time to do or die, Wil Price. Time to see what that gift of yours is really worth.*

So Wil loosened her hold on the world of the living. Like a stone tossed into still waters, she fell backward into the land of the dead.

And found them waiting.

The mirror image of the conservatory, as with everywhere Wil visited in the halfway realm, was in woeful disrepair. The floor glinted hazard-ously with a snowfall of broken glass; the night air and darkness yawned in; and beside the fireless hearth, Wil's dead souls had gathered. They stood clustered together as if afraid to drift too far apart. Mabel and Jenny, twin pillars of spirit and emotion, one grief, the other fury. Kitty Summerfield in her awful, decaying body, hunched over like a beast of the fields. And clinging to her hand, a shadowy, formless thing Wil instinctively recognized as the nursery wing's resident. It streamed duck-weed and foul pondwater, leaving a puddle beneath it, though it seemed to have no tangible shape.

But they were not the only things present in that corner of the halfway realm. Completing the tableau were Lord and Lady and Peter Summerfield, seated just where they had been in life, the colors of their hair and faces and clothing so fiercely bright, Wil had to squint to look at them. They carried on speaking in an agitated fashion as if they could not see or hear Wil and the dead, nor the ruinous plane they partially inhabited. Only Edison was absent, still fully grounded in life.

Wil was not sure she would have had the courage for what came next, were it not for the way the Summerfields sat, enthroned among the half-way realm's inhabitants. She was struck by a sudden and ferocious urge to sully them somehow—to drag them down from the pedestal of their own making and force them to face the trials and darkness she and Ed had both endured. They would no longer shine when she had finished. They would be as overshadowed as everything else in that wretched place, which had haunted Wil for nearly half her life.

So she stepped forward to where the dead waited by the hearth. In a gesture of welcome, Wil Price held out both hands.

"Little lambs," she said, the words ringing out like a clarion cry in that lifeless place, an echo of the tender care Mabel had once shown her. "I've come to lend you my voice."

*　　*　　*

Afterward Wil could never remember much about the first moment of possession besides blinding pain. She was not made to contain so much, and the dead, she was certain, would tear her apart. But the pieces of Wil that felt the agonies wracking her mind and body were forced into the furthest corners of her being. It was no longer her in control—all she could do was retreat and suffer and watch as others pushed her back toward the rift between realms.

With a sickening jolt, she felt herself returning to the living world. A dizzy, nauseating pull dragged forever back toward the halfway realm, and Wil knew suddenly what she could do. It was not her the pull worked on—it was the restless dead, and she could keep them in the world of the living for as long as need be. With all the force of her stubborn nature, she anchored herself, and she felt the pull lessen to a degree.

Even as she did so, some other force was animating her. She moved to Ed's side with jerky, half-human movements. Wil could feel the way the consciousnesses within her were struggling—one coming to the fore, another dropping away, each striving to find their place, their wit, their story. All she could do was bear down on the backward pull that the halfway realm exerted, keeping them in place until they were able to speak. Dimly she knew the Summerfields were watching her with something akin to horror—if it was clear that something unnatural was occurring within Wil when she harbored a single dead soul, how must it look now that she housed four?

A hand reached out and grasped her own, warm and solid and living. Edison.

With a sudden, triumphant surge, the dead found an accord.

"Well," Kitty Summerfield's unmistakable voice said, dropping from Wil's lips like music. "Here we all are again. And isn't this *cozy*?"

Every living soul in the room froze, and within Wil, Kitty Summerfield all but purred. Even now, it gratified her to be the center of attention.

280

"Oh, darlings," she said, her lightness and carelessness carrying a razor edge as they never had in life. "You can't have expected I wouldn't be back? Not after the way I left? Or should I say, not after the way I was forced to go?"

"Kitty," Ed said evenly from beside her. Kitty tossed her head, glad to be back in a living body. It was such a *thrill* to feel the blood in her veins once more, the beat of her heart, the filling and emptying of her lungs. "What do you mean by that?"

For a moment the question puzzled Kitty. It was so hard to think clearly—her wits kept fragmenting in the most unaccountable way, only to be pushed back together as if by some outside force.

"I don't . . . Edison?" She turned to him, bewilderment welling up within her. "What are you doing here? Where's Captain? I was in the churchyard."

"Yes," Ed answered, his eyes fixed intently on hers. Kitty glanced over to her family, but at the sight of her parents and Peter, the confusion she felt only grew. Gently Ed turned her face back to his with one hand. "You were in the churchyard. Do you remember why?"

"Just look at me, Wil," he added under his breath. "Not at them. Just me."

Kitty's disorientation was becoming a torment. Didn't he know who she was? Didn't he know his own sister, who *belonged* here?

"I was meeting someone." Irritation crept into Kitty's voice, placed there by the frustrating sense that something was wrong, that they ought to recognize her and be glad she'd come home. Hadn't she been away somewhere? A country house, perhaps, or on a trip to London. "It was . . . it was Peter. I was meeting him in the churchyard. He was spoiling my birthday, but that had been spoiled ages ago by so many things, and I needed to speak to him."

"Do you remember what you wanted to speak to him about?"

Ed's eyes were the only thing that seemed to make sense. He'd always been good to her—better than anyone else, which she'd thought odd, given what the family had finally told her about him. And there was something unfamiliar in her now—some foreign piece that felt as if Edison was the one person she most wanted to see, and who alone could steady her in a maddening world.

"About a lot of things, but mostly that I didn't want him coming home," Kitty said, the answer coming back to her in a sudden rush. "He'd been planning to show up the night of my birthday to spite me—you know he was always like that, loving to steal anyone else's spotlight. I only found out because I overheard him telling Abigail about it in the mill wood. And I didn't want him, not just because of the party and the attention, but because I knew we'd be worse off with him home. I'd meant to take you with me when I spoke to him that last time—strength in numbers and all that, but something happened. I can't recall what; it's all a muddle. There was something, though. Some warning that I couldn't have you by my side when I spoke to Peter. That if I did, it wouldn't end well. We both knew a secret about you, Peter and I, and I wanted to tell him as I forced him off that it didn't matter. That you're a Summerfield through and through, and that he ought to leave you be. He ought to leave all of us be. He'd done enough harm already."

"How did you know Peter was back?" Ed asked. "Mama and I had no idea."

"Jenny told me," Kitty said. "She was always loyal to me first, rather than to the family. She said Peter was living in that mill cottage like some vagrant, because Papa thought it was for the best. I expect it was Papa's way of punishing Peter for staying away so long and getting himself into trouble in France, when it was meant to be his path to redemption. Peter told Abigail some ridiculous story, of course, which she repeated to Jenny, all about how he was a heroic and wronged party, and that nothing that had happened on the Continent was his fault. All those gambling debts weren't his, and the girl he'd landed in hospital had been a mistake.

"But you and I know Peter better than that. If there was one girl, I'm sure there'd been more. And I was so sick of it—living under the shadow of lies and possible scandal, and the constant work of covering up Summerfield transgressions. I went to the cottage to see Peter several times. Said it would be best for everyone if he never came home. Papa could give him a more-than-generous allowance, and we'd all be free of one another. He didn't like that idea, especially not of you becoming heir to the title and the house. He said you didn't belong with us, but I told him no, of course you do, we're family. Summerfields look after their family."

"Do they?"

The way Ed spoke the question twisted within Kitty, her confusion growing unbearable. She glanced away from him and caught Peter's eye, and his cold gray gaze was a mirror of what it had been that night.

The churchyard. Captain. The final row they'd had over Edison and Jenny and Mabel and Peter's homecoming.

She'd told him to leave in no uncertain terms. Said if her elder brother didn't turn around and shake the dust of Wither Grange from his boots, she'd see him brought to ruin, even if it meant taking everyone else down with him.

And then.

Kitty's hand went involuntarily to the back of her head. She'd felt every second of it. The explosion of light and agony as her skull had shattered; the few desperate, paralyzed moments as Peter had stood over her and life had drained from her body, dragging her into the twisted realm of the dead.

"Peter," she whispered. "My head. My heart. How *could* you?"

Her eyes went to him involuntarily, but Peter gave nothing away. He sat stone-faced, unresponsive.

When Kitty lowered her hand once more, it was not her own. And yet it came back from the memory of that killing blow unaccountably slick with blood, which dripped from unfamiliar fingertips onto the cream-colored conservatory rug.

"You'd have expected it, if you knew everything I knew." A harsher, rougher voice cut in, as Kitty stepped back into herself, giving way to Jenny Bright. The older woman seized control with relish, flexing the fingers she'd been given and shaking tension from her arms. She wiped the blood from her palm, leaving a crimson smear across the white apron of the demure maid's uniform that felt so familiar. "I only told you pieces of it, because you never know with a Summerfield. Could be you'd have seen me as a threat. So I confided some of what I found out once Peter had come back, but not everything. Didn't say what I knew from before. Not like I did to His Lordship."

Jenny's attention riveted on Lord Summerfield. She was aware of Edison at her side, her hand still clasped in his, but he didn't matter to her. He never had. What mattered was the bitterness she'd been swallowing back for years, forced to make a living serving a family she despised. Her grip on Ed tightened until she heard him take in a pained breath, but Jenny's eyes never fell from Lord Summerfield's. Not until he faltered, and his gaze dropped to the floor.

There. For once, she was master. For once, he would bend to *her* will.

"I tried." Each word was a drop of poison as it fell from Jenny's lips. "I tried to save you from yourselves. Told you I knew what Peter had done, and that history would only repeat itself if he came home. Said I wouldn't be bought off or cowed into silence this time. We were afraid the first time—all the staff—after Mabel died. We knew how things had gone between her and Peter, and so none of us believed she'd slipped into that pond. It seemed like justice when Peter Summerfield was killed at the front. *No more crimes at Wither Grange,* I thought to myself when that news came. I couldn't have been more wrong."

Lord Summerfield was putting on a good show of carelessness. He cradled his drink in one hand and sipped at it nonchalantly, but Jenny knew. He was no Peter. What he'd done rested uneasy in him, whereas his son bore all transgressions lightly.

"I thought it was the sins of the father that became the sins of the son, not the other way around." Jenny stalked forward, bending at the waist, her face bare inches from Lord Summerfield's own. The gesture wasn't quite right, she knew. Wasn't quite human, for she'd lost the knack of embodiment. But it didn't matter. A half-suppressed shudder ran through His Lordship, and Jenny's borrowed face split into a ghastly smile.

"Do you think I don't remember it all?" she hissed. "The way you pretended you'd give way, when I found out Peter was still living and told you he mustn't come home? How you came up behind me, the feel of your hand on the back of my neck, the drop when I fell into those reeds, the way that pondwater filled my lungs? I wanted to stop some-one from ending up like Mabel Price did, not follow after her myself. Poor Mabel. Poor Mabel. Poor—"

Jenny choked, unable to stop the overwhelming recollection of drowning from rising up and stealing her voice.

Mabel herself slipped into the silence. It felt wrong to her, to wear her own child's body, and yet there was a rightness about it too. A sense of coming home. In an old, self-conscious gesture, she smoothed the front of her apron with both hands.

"Blood is thicker than water," Mabel murmured, and her voice was softer than either Kitty's or Jenny's had been. The room fell utterly silent as everyone strained to hear her speak. "If I'd had a pound for every time I heard a Summerfield say something similar, my Wil would have had her future bought and paid for. That's all I wanted—for the obligations of blood to be honored. I said *nothing* about the way I'd been used by

285

you, Peter. I just wanted surety for my girl. And what I got for bringing up blood was water, in the end. I grew up in the shadow of the Grange. I chose the millpond for a meeting place because I wanted the family to know that I share *all* your secrets.

"It was a relief, in a way, when you weren't the one who came to that meeting, Peter. I hadn't relished the idea of a confrontation between the two of us. And while I wasn't sure you'd care about Wil, or care if I spoke about her publicly, I thought you *would* care that I knew about what had happened at the millpond.

"What I hadn't expected was that someone else cared more."

Slowly Mabel drew away from Lord Summerfield. Slowly she crossed the conservatory to where Lady Summerfield sat, and she knelt at her mistress's feet.

"What wouldn't a mother do for her child?" Mabel asked in her soft voice. "What wouldn't I have done for my Wil? And what haven't you done for your Peter? But if blood will out, then a piece of my Wilhelmina is yours, too. Just as little Edison was yours as well. You oughtn't to have laid a finger on me—first the tea with laudanum, then the walk by the pond with my head spinning, and the fall where you held me down. I'd have kept the Summerfield secrets, if you only promised to look after Wil. I'd never have breathed a word about what Peter did to me, or to other girls, or to Edison. I'd never have said who and what your youngest boy truly is."

Deep within herself, Wil was working furiously, trying to patch together all the disparate pieces of information her ghosts were laying out. As yet, she was unable to think of what might happen after the spirits left her. She was consumed by the occupation of the moment—by trying to make sense of the voices she'd spent so long yearning to hear.

"They say the sins of the father are the sins of the son." Mabel's voice was so soft now that everyone besides Lady Summerfield reflexively leaned forward to hear her. But Her Ladyship was tense, pushing back into the chair she sat upon as if she could escape Mabel's reproach in some way. "Not here, though. Here, the sins of the son have become an inheritance for the entire family. I'm not sure I could have done the same in your place. Not sure that I could have betrayed one lost son so thoroughly in order to protect the one that remained. And then to have him repeat his sin a second time, with Kitty—my heart broke on its way into death, but I marvel that yours still beats at all."

With that last indictment, Mabel rose to her feet. Unlike the other spirits, who had been overcome by confusion or memory, she seemed to have said everything she intended to. Wil felt it when her mother withdrew. When she ceded her place to the last and least comprehensible of the Grange's troubled ghosts.

But nothing of sense came from the nursery wing's chaotic inhabitant. It stood, in possession of Wil's body, and did no more than stare while muttering the same words over and over under its breath. *"I'll sing you one, O. One is one and all alone, and evermore shall be so."*

Dimly Wil was aware of frustration rising among the room's living inhabitants.

"She's taken leave of her senses," Lord Summerfield said. "All these scandalous lies spouted in an attempt to blackmail us, and then the girl goes and has a fit. It's disgraceful. Shame on you for enabling this, Edison."

I'm here, Wil thought to the nursery wing ghost, moving forward just a little. *Can I help you?*

There was a shift within her, a sudden retreat during which she realized, for the first time, how small and frightened and isolated the spirit who haunted Edison truly was. It had no real voice beyond the foolish words it so often sang. No way of putting its experiences into words. But it had memory, and had once had sight. With a final effort,

Wil opened not just her body but her consciousness to this wandering soul. She allowed a sort of possession she'd never permitted before—one not physical, but spiritual. And while her own voice rang through the conservatory next, what she saw in her mind's eye were the final recollections of the nursery's lost spirit.

"I am . . . small," Wil said, the words coming out distant and detached, as she struggled to adequately express what she could see. "Everything seems unaccountably large and looks new. Not as if I haven't seen it before—I know this place—but as if I don't entirely understand it. There are trees everywhere, and someone with me, holding my hand as we walk down the forest path. I understand them, at least. I know them—they're familiar, but I'm afraid of them."

Wil could not see with her own eyes. All she saw was the ghost's recollections. Had she been able to see with her body, she would have noticed that for the first time, the air of reserve and uncaringness that the Summerfields had maintained slipped away from them entirely as she spoke. They were all white-faced, wide-eyed, distressed.

"There's something ahead of us," Wil went on, fighting to make sense of what she saw, and to put it into the words the nursery wing ghost lacked. "A lake. No, it's the millpond. It only seems like a lake because I've grown so small. I'm not happy to see it, though. It feels threatening to me in some way. I've just been told to go play by the reeds, and I'm obeying, because I know things might go badly if I don't, but I'm still afraid. I want to cry, but I won't, because if I do, they tell me, 'Shame on you, Edison, a great boy like you. You should be braver.'"

There was barely enough of Wil left to register shock at the words proceeding from her own mouth. But it went snapping through her nevertheless, like the nasty jolt that comes with an unexpected fall.

"I've gone over to the reeds, just like I was told. Someone's calling for me, wondering where I am. But they know where I've gone—it's only a game, and one I can't fully understand. I'm meant to hide, I know that much. So I do. I pull back into the reeds, but it's not enough. I can't really hide from them, not ever, even though I try. And I *am* crying now, though I want to keep quiet. Something's coming through the reeds, and I—"

A sob choked Wil. She'd never felt such fear, animal and untempered by any sort of reasoning or self-restraint. It belonged to the spirit she was sharing her entire self with, but so fully had she intertwined her being with that of the dead soul that her usual reserve and composure utterly failed. Wil's breath began to come hard and fast, her heart to beat like desperate moth wings in her chest.

I can't, I can't, the sole fragments of her undiluted self thought frantically.

But then she felt something. A lightening of the fear. It was not so much that it had gone; rather, it had been spread thinner. Within the bounds of her fathomless soul, the rest of the dead had each taken their share of it.

And Wil, who had taught herself time after time, under a thousand different circumstances, to bear up and carry on, rose to the occasion.

"Surgite," she breathed, and with a supreme effort, channeled her own fortitude toward the small lost spirit she harbored.

A sense of palpable relief flooded her, as if for a dozen years or more, the creature that led its hollow existence within the bounds of the nursery wing had never been shed of that fear. Now it experienced the first brief taste of freedom from it, as well as a glimmer of recognition at the word Wil spoke.

Together they bore up. Together they carried on.

The images continued, reeds choking Wil's field of view. Her voice droned on once more, dispassionately chronicling the last moments of this small, helpless boy.

"I'm crying," Wil said, the words once again even and distant. "And

I try to push farther into the reeds, but they're too thick. There's water up to my waist now, soaking my clothes, and I know Nurse will be cross when we get home. It doesn't matter, though, because someone's coming for me; they always do. I know what it means when they catch me. Water. Always water. I go under, and I can't breathe, and they keep me there until I stop fighting. 'Just stop fighting,' is what they always say. 'If you'd give in, I'd make it easier on you.'

"But I can't help it. When they push me under, I have to fight. They're coming now. They're getting closer. And I—"

Once more, despite all her reserve, emotion broke Wil's voice. But she and the little ghost had collected themselves in a moment.

"I remember everything," Wil said, and it was her voice, her words, but the little ghost's memories. "The reeds. The pond. All the times this had happened before, each one inching us closer to what would come. I remember who it was when the water rushed in and never rushed back out. And I remember what they said."

With a sudden wrench, the nursery-wing ghost seized total control. If Jenny and Kitty's possession of Wil's body had been unnatural, this one was grotesque. The body that was Wil's surged forward, toward Peter, until its borrowed face was mere inches from his own.

"Got you," the high, eerie voice of a very young child said. "Got you, Eddie. And I won't let go."

And then, in a wild rush, Wil's dead souls flooded from her body, flowing back through the gap between realms like an unnatural tide. She was left empty and aching, little more than pain and fragmented pieces. Every one of the Summerfields had their eyes fixed on her, but beyond them, Wil could see her own reflection in the darkened glass of the conservatory windows.

Or rather, she saw what would have been her reflection, were it not obscured by swirling mist as her soul began its departure.

CHAPTER TWENTY-SIX

EDISON

Ed had listened to the accounts of the spirits that plagued Wither Grange with a dread that gradually resolved into sickening fear. It had never occurred to him that every member of his family might be equally involved in the Grange's tragedies—he'd always assumed it must be one of them acting alone. A single bitter fruit, rather than the roots of the whole tree rotted and decayed.

Now that he'd heard it all, there was only one thought consuming him. For the moment his feelings about the vicious things his own kin had done did not matter. The insinuations and confusion over who he might be were of no consequence. All that did matter was what might happen next. Because Ed had expected his family to mete out justice upon their own, only to learn they were all equally guilty and there would be no justice here.

In his foolishness, he'd dragged Wil into a den of wolves.

Ed saw the moment she reclaimed her own body, and the flash of horror that ran through her as she caught sight of something beyond his field of view. It was gone in an instant, though, replaced by a vacant, disoriented look.

"What happened? Why's everyone staring at me so?" Wil said in a lost voice. "Did I say something that's upset you all? I'm awfully sorry."

She lied with perfect guilelessness, taking to it as quickly as she did to any other endeavor. Ed knew at once what she was doing—only he had any knowledge of her talent for the dead and how it functioned. Her sole chance at leaving the house alive was for the Summerfields to believe she was unaware of the things she'd said. That only the dead spoke, and that Wil channeled their voices without awareness of their words. Quick-witted as ever, she'd immediately divined her single hope for escape and grasped for it.

Silence stretched out, thin and threatening as a garotte. Not one of the Summerfields spoke, and Ed kept quiet, knowing Wil was her own best defense just now.

"Oh," she said at last, her confusion fading into flawless humiliation. "I never should have agreed to this when Master Edison asked if I'd help him. It's . . . it's never ended well for me. But he insisted—said I might give some comfort to the family, and you've all been struggling so, I thought perhaps I could. If there was anything offensive in what I said, understand I'm not of the same mind. It's easy enough to say don't shoot the messenger when you're the one who's delivered unpleasant words, but whatever they were, they weren't what I'd have said. Please . . . don't make me give up my place; it's all I've got now that my grandfather's gone."

She was so desperate, so beseeching, that even Edison half believed her. Perhaps housing so many souls at once really had rendered Wil oblivious to the sense of all they'd revealed. Then he glanced down at her hands, twined together behind her back. Even white-knuckled and clasped tight as they were, she could not still their shaking.

The silence carried on, a weapon for the Summerfields to wield against her. Tears pooled in Wil's eyes, and as they began to track down her face, she gave a small, resigned nod.

"Very well," she said. "I can see I've ruined my chance. And I'll go. But I swear on my mother's grave, I only meant to help."

At her final words, a sharp, calculating look passed between Lord and Lady Summerfield. Edison's heart jackknifed in his chest, but it was Peter who broke the family's silence.

"Let her leave," he said lazily. "She's obviously hardly more than half-witted. And who wouldn't be, with a curse like that riding them?"

As they always did, the family gave way to him.

"Agreed," Lord Summerfield said. "Girl, you're dismissed. Don't bother asking for any pay owed you—we want you out at once."

Wil gave a last tearful nod and was gone.

As the door shut between her and the Summerfields, Ed's relief was so great that his knees all but gave way beneath him. But no sooner had she gone than the prodigious weight of their joined attention settled on him.

"Someone will have to go after her," Lady Summerfield said coolly. "But you were right, Peter—better she be dealt with away from the house. We're under too much of a shadow as it is."

"A shadow that would be significantly lighter if Edison had just left well enough alone," Lord Summerfield answered, disdain lacing his words. Though they spoke to each other, their eyes were fixed on Ed, who stood just as he was—still and silent, a creature caught in a snare. He did not have Wil's quick facility for solving problems, even when his own fate hung in the balance. All he could do was stand and listen with that dull, agonizing fear gnawing away at him.

"The boy is a problem," Peter said. "I've never seen anything in him to indicate he has the fortitude to truly stand with us."

"Kitty liked him." Lady Summerfield spoke her daughter's name like a reproach. "She thought he was one of us. That if we only told him how he came to be here, he'd have kept his counsel just as well as you or I."

Peter let out a mocking sound of disbelief. "Kitty was planning to go to the police herself and accuse *me* of everything—Mabel and Jenny, and of intending for that first accident with Edison to happen. Of course one turncoat would think highly of another."

"That's enough." Lady Summerfield was imperious in her anger, rousing herself from her usual detached lassitude and fixing Peter with the piercing look of an offended queen. "Kitty understood loyalty to family, unlike you. She spoke up for the boy because she saw him as our own. She did not have the jealous streak or the taste for dominance that taints your nature."

"For the last time, Mama," Peter said, his voice low and impassioned, "it wasn't jealousy, what happened with Eddie. It was a *mistake*."

"Then explain your sister," Lady Summerfield shot back furiously. "That was no accident."

"Enough." Lord Summerfield's voice silenced all of them, his raised hand a stay against argument of any kind. "What happened with Kitty was regrettable but unavoidable. You know what she was like once she set herself upon something. Just as stubborn as the rest of us. And it wasn't only Peter on the line if she'd spoken. It was everyone and everything. The family, the Grange. We agreed to protect Peter and each other, regardless of the cost. Kitty herself promised she'd do so. When she stepped out of line, she forfeited her right to that protection."

Slowly the family's attention had shifted from Edison as they spoke among themselves. He'd just begun to contemplate attempting to edge out of the room when it fell upon him again, Lord Summerfield's gaze swiveling to him with sudden intensity.

"Ed, you've always been eager to prove your worth. Well, here and now you can cement your position among us. I want you to go after that girl. Shepherd's granddaughter. There's obviously some rapport between the two of you. Take her to the White Hind in Wynkirk, and pay for her to stay the night. It doesn't matter what you have to say or do to get her there, and you needn't do anything beyond that. Tell her you'll come for her in the morning, then leave. You've offered time and again to be the sort of support the rest of us can rely on—here's your chance. When you get back home, we'll take you into the family confidence, as I should have done years ago."

It did not even seem to occur to Lord Summerfield that Edison might refuse. But Peter let out a short, dry laugh.

"He doesn't have the nerve to be one of us. He's already fallen to pieces once; I'm amazed this evening hasn't driven him into another breakdown already."

Ed's voice cut across Peter's. "Yes, Father."

"Good." Lord Summerfield nodded approvingly. "Be as quick about it as you can, and come let us know when it's done."

Without a backward glance, Edison strode from the room. He would do as he'd been told and find Wil. Because when it came down to it, it didn't matter who he was. Sooner or later he'd learn the truth, and for now he knew where his loyalty lay.

*   *   *

If Wil was foolish, Ed thought as he cut through the shadowy labyrinth of the mill wood, she'd have gone home to collect herself and her belongings. But Wil was no fool. She was blisteringly clever—clever enough to know her best chance for survival upon exiting the Grange was to stay hidden. The late train had already come and gone, and with it all hope of a swift exit from the environs of Thrush's Green. She'd have to walk out, and there were any number of country lanes or ripe fields she might be arrowing across by now.

There was more to Wil Price than cleverness, though. Ed knew her heart and soul, and beneath that formidable wit lay something else.

295

Determination and loyalty and a rigid set of personal standards, which she would live up to come hell or high water. If Wil had been merely clever, Ed would have had no hope of divining her whereabouts. It was loyalty that led him straight to her.

When Ed stepped out from the darkness and into the moonlight silvering the clearing where they'd always met, Wil sprang to her feet and flew to him. She'd been sitting among the roots of an oak tree with damp earth on her hands and a jar cradled on her lap, just as she had been the first time they had met. When she pressed herself to him, he could feel her trembling, the force of her panic causing his own fear to pale in comparison.

"Ed, thank God," she breathed, voice shaking like the rest of her. "Are you all right? I've just been waiting for you, wondering if I ought to go back. Everything's so—"

Words failed, and she buried her face against his shoulder. It was only the second time Edison had ever seen Wil brought so low, and a dizzying sensation of power rose up in him as he realized that *he* was the one person who could leave her undone. First when she'd foreseen his death, and now when she'd believed him in danger.

"Wil," he said earnestly, taking her hand in his. "I'm going to look after things, but you need to come with me. We can't stay in Thrush's Green."

"Of course we can't," she said, a little of her customary spark returning. "Why do you think I came *here*? Not just because I knew you'd find me, but because I've got money. Everything I've hidden since we were children, and that I've earned from your schoolmates. But where will we go? What will we do?"

"Come with me," Ed repeated.

Mutely Wil nodded and followed after him. In a few minutes the glitter of moonlight on the millpond cut through the trees, and then they were out on its banks, the wind whispering ghostly things among the reeds. Only when Ed brought Wil to the dark mill cottage did she stop and fix him with an uncertain look.

"I don't think . . . ," she began.

"Trust me," Edison said, and Wil did.

Inside she stood with both arms wrapped around her waist as he rifled through drawers, searching for something. At last memory did its work. Ed pulled a worn copy of *Middlemarch* down from one of the cobweb-strewn shelves and drew an envelope from between its pages. Inside was a sheaf of banknotes—six years' worth of Christmas gifts from Aunt Porter.

"You're not the only one who's been saving up for a rainy day," Edison said triumphantly. "I used to use this place a personal hideaway—I never expected Peter would someday do the same. Between the two of us, we should have enough to get well away and make a fresh start. I'm afraid this won't be much use to us right at the beginning, though. Every train for miles connects at Wynkirk, and that's where the family wants you, so we'll have to skirt around it entirely. I don't dare pay to put us up anywhere either—not for a few days, at least. I'm sure Mother and Father will come up with some story and have constables on the lookout. We'll be lodging in hedgerows and copses for a little while."

"I don't mind," Wil said. "We always wanted to camp out for a whole night when we were small. Not that I ever envisioned doing it under circumstances like these."

"Do you know," a voice drawled from the doorway, "I had a suspicion you might decide to play the dashing hero, rescuing his damsel in distress. You always had a vulgar taste for fairy stories and romance."

Though Ed could not make out Peter's features, silhouetted as he was by the backdrop of the moonlit clearing, his voice, his posture, and the fear that crawled down Ed's own spine identified him at once. Hadn't

297

Peter stood in Ed's doorway in just that manner a thousand times before, ready to impart some nasty insult or barbed comment or frightening story that would rob him of sleep?

"Why everyone's always been so certain of you is beyond me," Peter said, stepping into the room. His looming presence was like an entirely different sort of ghost, for while he haunted them just as doggedly, Peter in the flesh was far more immediate and menacing than the dead. Ed wondered how he'd ever mistaken the nursery-wing spirit for his elder brother—while it could be chaotic and violent, it had never possessed Peter's knack for targeting one's specific fears and weaknesses.

"Kitty was forever defending you," Peter went on, "and even Mama and Papa act like you're one of us, or could be, when the truth is, you've never been the least bit like a Summerfield. Though I suppose there are some similarities between you and Eddie. He was a quiet, spineless little coward too. But he was also a child—if you were ever really going to live up to our name, you'd have outgrown any sort of meekness by now."

Behind Edison, Wil shifted. As he stood between her and Peter, anger flared up in him, hot and clear enough to burn away most of his fear. But he kept it hidden, locked away as tightly as any emotion Wil herself chose not to reveal. Instead Ed made a show of faltering. He took a hesitant step away from Peter, farther into the lightless depths of the mill cottage, and farther from Wil.

"You ought to have realized from the beginning that something was wrong. That there's always been something lacking in you that the rest of us possess," Peter said spitefully, following Ed without hesitation, drawn to perceived weakness like a moth to flame.

"I could hardly have failed to notice," Ed answered. "Not when you took every opportunity to point out my differences and shortcomings. Though of course I've never known the root of them."

"The root," Peter said, taking another step forward as Ed fell back, "is that you are the inadequate solution to a stupid childhood accident, which Father and Mother view as my first and worst mistake."

"Why not stop hinting and tell me all of it?" There was a hint of steel in Ed's voice now, though Peter seemed not to notice. "God knows you've spent long enough attempting to make me feel like an outsider. If I truly am, come out and say it."

A step forward from Peter. A step back from Edison. The path to the door was clear for Wil now, but damn her, Ed knew she wouldn't go. He could see her casting about herself for some weapon or method of defense and coming up with nothing.

"Look at me when I'm speaking to you," Peter barked, and Ed instantly shifted his attention back. "You're a *replacement* for a real Summerfield. A filthy, vermin-riddled little foundling who was brought in because you bore a passing resemblance to the cowardly invalid who was my brother. Edison Summerfield drowned in the millpond just outside, because he was so afraid of me that he wouldn't take my hand and let himself be brought to safety. And my parents, convinced that his death would cast some indelible stain on my character, chose to bring you into the house— an imposter—rather than simply claim that what happened with Ed had been an accident. They changed over his nurse, claimed he was dangerously ill, and no one questioned it when a sallow, skin-and-bones child who looked passably like the boy who'd gone into confinement finally emerged from sickbed. But you're no true Summerfield—you've got less of a claim to the Grange than even *that* one."

Peter nodded in Wil's direction, and Ed's restrained anger burned hotter.

"Keep your eyes off her," he said, each word a threat he had no way of making good on. In answer, Peter laughed.

"Or what, little orphan? The police inspectors you brought in have

299

been convinced you're unreliable, not that it took much effort. Kitty is no longer here to defend you. If you go bearing tales about anything you've heard tonight, not a single soul will believe you. From this point on, you're in my power and will obey me, because so long as you're a good boy and do as you're bid, I'll see to it that no harm comes to your friend." Peter pivoted, fixing the full force of his gaze on Wil. "As for you, you'll remain at the house and in our service, where we can keep a close watch on you. Don't think I haven't noticed the way you two oddments look at each other. I know you want the boy safe just as badly as he wants it for you.

"Here is what will happen," Peter went on with perfect confidence. "We will all go back to the Grange together. We will carry on in the roles life has laid out for us—Ed as the family's lesser brother, the girl as a devoted servant who may someday be elevated to housekeeper. We will not speak of the dead. We will go about the business of living. The alternative is this."

Peter produced a pistol from his jacket pocket, which he set down meaningfully on a chipped and splay-legged end table next to him. "I shoot the girl and swear to the authorities I saw Edison do it. That he'd been fixated on Mabel's death, and our younger housemaids uncovered evidence that in his obsession, he had reenacted the very thing with Jenny Bright. First the maids confided in Kitty, who Ed killed to cover up his earlier crime. Upon my return, the girls confessed to me, but I was regrettably too late to prevent my brother from dealing violently first with Abigail, then with Wil Price."

"One of you dead and one of you hanged, *or* my secrets and indiscretions all kept with the same diligence Mama and Papa have exercised. It's for you to choose."

Peter, of course, knew next to nothing about Wil. He could not recognize the fleeting, blank look on her face that meant she'd retreated beyond the world of the living to call upon the only allies she had. But Edison could. And a chill ran through him as she spoke in a voice that seemed to contain both herself and all her manifold ghosts.

"I choose justice," said Wil and Mabel and Jenny and Kitty and the small boy who had been Edison Summerfield first.

"A myth," Peter scoffed, as he leveled the pistol at her. "A saccharine idea for infants still tied to their nurses' apron strings. What you're choosing is a refusal to live in the world as it is and to look out for your own interests. Pity. You might have been an asset to the family."

"I am the family," said Wil and Kitty and the other Edison. Wil took a step toward Peter, then another, and he did not falter. He was all courage and bravado, standing there with his broad shoulders, pistol securely in hand. But there was a light in Wil's eyes Ed had seen there before—a ghost light, a bale light, and it froze him to the marrow even as Peter failed to notice.

"Then you'll come back to the house quietly and keep silent about everything you've heard tonight. The family looks after its own," Peter said dismissively as Wil stopped short just before him.

"We know," she answered.

With serpentine speed and precision, Wil's hands snaked out, even as her head tilted to one side and her eyes widened into an inhuman stare. A pall settled over her—a supernatural semblance of creatures who were no longer properly embodied, but only soul and a twisted memory of flesh. She grasped Peter by the neck and wrist, the pistol he held clattering to the ground as the powers that inhabited her lent preternatural strength to her grip. Ed watched in dumbfounded horror as Peter's face began to redden, then turn white, which quickly ceded to deathly gray. An audible snap cracked through the air as his brother's wrist broke, but though Peter's expression twisted in pain and his mouth worked, no sound came. It could not have lasted more than moments, but to Ed, it seemed an intolerably long time as he stood in an agony of indecision, entirely at a loss as to what he should do. At last Wil cast Peter from her, and he landed in a pathetic heap against the mill cottage wall.

Peter choked and retched where he lay, filthy pondwater streaming from his mouth and nose. Only once he'd caught his breath with a sobbing gasp and cast a petrified look at Wil, eyes glazed with fear, did she surge forward and pull him to his feet.

"Again," the spirits rasped, and there was nothing of Wil Price in their joined voices any longer. "You will suffer as we suffered and more."

The same desperate, drowning look swept over Peter's face as the spirits in Wil's body held him up. He seized and struggled futilely, unable to escape their joint strength and fury. Ed was sick with watching—he could not bear to see someone tormented before his eyes. Whatever wrongs the Summerfields had done, whatever crimes they'd committed, it was intolerable to him to see another living soul suffer. Hardly knowing what he was doing, Ed scrabbled about the cottage's uneven floor, coming up with Peter's abandoned pistol.

"Wil," he begged, leveling it at her just as Peter had done, though Ed's hands shook where Peter's had been steady. "Please, you have to stop this. We wanted justice, not cruelty. This isn't right."

Without loosening her grip, Wil turned to him, rendered all but unrecognizable by the creatures in possession of her body. She was a half-dead thing herself, her features barely recognizable.

"Wil's not here," a chorus of voices said spitefully. "There's only us now."

Her grasp on Peter tightened, and then she cast him aside once more. Coughing and strangling on fetid water, Peter Summerfield gathered his prodigious strength and force of will and struggled upright.

"It's that *thing* or me, Ed," he managed to get out, the words hoarse and raw, the whites of his eyes gone crimson with burst blood vessels. "She made her choice. It's time for you to make yours."

"I know she's still there somewhere," Edison breathed, fixing his eyes on Wil's, changed as they were. "She'd never leave me behind."

But in the moment the spirits' attention shifted to Ed, Peter rallied. With a ragged curse, he launched himself at Wil, who spun to face him with all the force of her inherited and unholy rage.

A pistol shot rang out, earsplittingly loud in the close confines of the cottage.

"Let. Her. Go," Ed demanded as Peter reeled and fell, scarlet spreading across the pure white of his shirtfront. Edison spared only a single glance for his fallen brother—a quick look, which revealed Peter on his back, eyes gone sightless and his body limp. "It's done. He's gone. Drag away whatever of his soul you want, but give Wil back. She doesn't belong to you; she belongs with me."

The spirits were relentless. Closing the distance between themselves and Ed, they raised one of Wil's hands, tracing the line of Ed's jaw. Their voices jangled together, discordant and unnatural. "Who's to say we won't see an end to you next? And then finish off the rest of our wrongdoers after?"

"I had nothing to do with any of your deaths," Ed said evenly. He was out beyond fear now—too suffused with shock to even feel it anymore. "And Wil believed you eager to protect the innocent, rather than harm them in precisely the same way you yourselves were harmed. So I ask you again to let her go."

Nothing. The gaunt, hollowed-out appearance that had settled over Wil did not fade. Her staring, gas-lamp eyes did not regain their usual light or proportions.

"Very well," Edison said, frustration ringing through the words. "I won't ask *you* then. I'll ask her. Wil Price, where the hell have you gone? Wherever it is, you've got to come back. I want you here with me. Everything's fallen apart, and I need you."

303

His voice broke at last, and maybe it was that rather than the command that summoned her back. Whatever it was, Ed watched as in a moment, Wil's face rounded out, her eyes cleared, and without hesitation his own beloved friend stepped into his arms.

"Edison?" Wil said after a long time, though she stayed just as she was, the two of them holding on to one another as if it was all that kept them from going to pieces.

"Wilhelmina?"

"This isn't over. There's still Lord and Lady Summerfield, and—"

"No, I know. We'll get to them. We'll see everything made right, sooner or later. But not like this, Wil. Promise me not like this."

"Never again," she said vehemently, burying her face against his shoulder for a moment. "I couldn't bear to lose myself that way again."

"We're all right, though." Ed reached down and tilted Wil's chin up with one finger, infinitely relieved to see her soft gray eyes restored to what they'd always been, and her crown of golden curls gone silver in the moonlight. "You came back in the end."

"Foolish boy," she sniffed. "I came back for you. Don't you know I always will?"

WIL

Wil Price knelt alone in the mill wood. A cold, misting autumn rain beaded on her hair and the thick plaid wrapper she'd pulled over her shoulders. But the mackintosh square beneath her was still relatively dry, and it was good to have earth on her hands.

After a moment she set aside her trowel and wiped her hands on the voluminous gardening apron she wore. There was no maid's uniform beneath it, but her preferred checked skirt and blouse. Though the rain deadened the sound of footsteps, Wil could feel when someone came up behind her.

"I'll never get used to that," Edison said, and Wil nodded.

Before her stood a small, unassuming headstone, flanked by two white crosses. The crosses bore the names of Mabel Price and Jenny Bright, while the stone was etched with the name Edison Summerfield, and the dates were a scant three years apart.

"They've had enough of green rushes, especially Eddie." Wil shifted as she spoke, making room for Ed on her mackintosh square, though it was hardly big enough for two, and they were forced to sit shoulder to shoulder. "I wanted to plant some spring flowers for them instead. They'll bloom after the winter."

"Of course you did."

Wil stole a glance at Edison. He looked pale and worn out, but more resolute than he ever had in the time before her tenure at the Grange.

"Was today awful?" she asked quietly.

Ed glanced down at his hands. "Yes. They sentenced Mother and Father. Life in prison for both, though there was talk that they might hang Father to make an example of him. I think Mother confessing to everything and helping the prosecution may have been what saved him, though she said she was doing it for Kitty's sake, not his."

"A loyal Summerfield to the last," Wil said, and couldn't help the trace of bitterness that crept into her voice.

"She asked if you'd visit." Ed did not meet Wil's eyes as he brought up the request. "Said you're all she has left of her children, and that she'd like to see you."

"Never." Wil's bitterness shifted to a vicious edge. "They don't deserve another moment of my time."

Ed nodded. "I thought you'd say so. And I told her as much."

"I can't think why you're still going to see them," Wil said, toying with the handle of the trowel to hide her frustration. "They shouldn't be anything to you after all that's happened."

This time Ed looked at her. He fixed her with his solemn gaze, half obscured by raindrops on his spectacles, and smiled sadly. "I know. But I can't help thinking of them as family, even after all this. They're where they should be, they're getting what they deserve, but they're also all I've ever had."

"Do they *want* to see you?" Wil asked, at which Edison shrugged.

"Father says no. Mother says yes. But I suppose they'll both be glad of me in time. None of the more distant relations want anything to do with them now. And I've been sent some rather nasty letters by the more far-flung family, though Aunt Porter in London said I'm welcome to go to her. She's always been the black sheep of the flock—married someone who made his fortune in trades, then she got involved in women's suffrage. You'd like her, I think, if you came to visit."

"As if anything could keep me away," Wil answered, resting her head briefly on his shoulder. "Is that where you'll go for certain then?"

"I suppose," Edison said, though he sounded unconvinced. "God knows there's no place else for me. You know, I don't even have a name beyond the one the family gave me? The court proceedings found the workhouse Father took me from, but I'd been left there without a scrap of information. And I've only ever lived at the Grange and school since then. The bank's already tried to sell the house to pay off outstanding debts—the family's efforts to keep our skeletons locked firmly in the closet ensured there were a lot of those—but no one will touch the Grange, so they're boarding everything up."

"You could choose a new name. Try for a fresh start, like Grandfather and I mean to make in Lincolnshire. He's hired a tutor for me, if you can believe it, and insists that I'll be off to college in a year or two. Which is all right, because Abigail's going to come to us, now that she's on the mend, and help with the shop Grandfather plans to open," Wil said. "She can't remember much of what happened, which is a mercy, between your mother dosing her with laudanum and Peter bricking her up behind that fireplace while she was helpless. All she can recall is that Peter was going to cast her off, so she meant to leverage what she knew about the family. Meant to get some sort of payoff. I suppose they were tired of paying to keep things quiet."

"The thing is," Edison said hesitantly, "it's so easy to forget the dead and the past. I thought if I kept this name, there'd be no fear of me ever doing so. Do you suppose he—the first Edison—would mind?"

Wil looked over at the little headstone. "I don't think he would. I should think anyone would be proud to have someone like you to remember them and carry on for them. But I can't ask him—they're all gone now. I went to the halfway realm this morning to look."

"Even your mother? Wil, I'm sorry."

"No, it's what I've always wanted for her," Wil said with forced brightness as she scrambled to her feet and gathered up her gardening things. "That she'd be able to move on and find some measure of peace. I wonder, though. Ed, why do you think little Edison only started to reach out to you after Peter was considered dead? He hadn't really been killed—it isn't as if they met in the halfway realm and that precipitated it. What could it have been?"

"That's the thing," Ed told her, squinting as he glanced up. "I don't think, looking back, that it did all start then. With Peter the way he was, I always assumed while he was alive that any sort of disturbance in the nursery wing was due to him. But now I'm not sure it was. Some of it, maybe. But I think that the other Edison might have been trying to tell me what happened from the very first. He just . . . didn't know how to do it in a way I'd understand."

"Poor lamb," Wil murmured. "Well, he's resting easy now, wherever's he's gone. Come on. I want a last look at the house."

Ed shivered as he gathered up the mackintosh square and folded it neatly. "I don't know why."

"So that everything feels finished," Wil said. "You of all people know that I like things done thoroughly."

On the narrow trail through the woods, a single lonely figure made its way toward them, resolving into the form of Mrs. Bright. As they met, the older woman reached for Wil, who took her hands with a sympathetic look.

"Mrs. Bright. I'm so glad to see you."

"I thought I'd bring them all something," Mrs. Bright said, gesturing to the market bag stuffed with asters that she'd slung over one arm. "It's a dreary day. Perhaps they'd like a bit of color."

"Great minds think alike," Wil said warmly. "I've just been doing the same, though the bulbs I put in won't bloom till spring."

"I'll look after them until then," Mrs. Bright promised. "I know you're leaving us, love, and I think that's only right. Thrush's Green hasn't been kind to you or your family, nor your young lad, either."

"You have, though," Wil told her. "You've been kind and more. Everything that's come to light might be still be secret if you hadn't trusted me."

With a sad little nod, Mrs. Bright carried on. Wil turned to watch her go until she was hidden by the mist and let out a faint sigh.

"It breaks my heart," she said. But it took the edge off her melancholy when Edison's arm went around her shoulder immediately, and he pressed a kiss to the top of her head.

"Don't break your heart. I want it in one piece."

Wil couldn't recall why she'd ever had an aversion to Ed growing maudlin before. Maudlin, she thought, was lovely. It made a nice change from morbid.

Wither Grange appeared from between the curtains of rain like a wraith, gray and weathered and forbidding. A small crew of workers were busy boarding up the windows, as if the house had resolved to shut its eyes and dream until such a time as someone came to wake it. Wil hoped, fiercely, that it would be left to its own devices for a long, long time. That eventually it would fall into nothing more than a harmless ruin.

Her wish redoubled as she glanced up to the second floor, where a workman on a precarious construct of scaffolding was nailing up boards. Near him was the bank of open, blank-eyed windows that led to the nursery wing. Wil's heart began to beat faster as lamplight flared beyond the windows, illuminating the half-solid form of a broad-shouldered young man with an imperious posture and calculating face. He looked down at Wil with a knowing smile, then raised a finger to his lips, as within her, the familiar tug toward the halfway realm grew slightly stronger.

But Wil braced herself against the pull, and it dissipated altogether as a train whistle sang out through the fog and rain—a call from the world of the living to come away and leave the dead, at last, to their own devices.

"It's only a ghost," Wil said, turning her back on Wither Grange and reaching for Edison. He lifted her hand to his lips and pressed a kiss to the back of it, his eyes saying everything they did not put into words. That they were meant for each other, as they'd always known, even through the storm that had raged around them. "And we've had enough of those for one lifetime."

"I couldn't agree more," Edison said fervently.

Still, before they vanished into the mill wood, Wil couldn't help glancing over her shoulder one last time, to where she knew the empty house and its restless occupant would always be waiting, beneath rain and snow and sun, as time wore them down into no more than shadows and old stone. Someday, when even she and Edison lay dead, nothing would likely be remembered of them. People would remember this, though—that wickedness had been done among the foundations of Wither Grange, and ghosts had once walked its halls.

ACKNOWLEDGMENTS

Though the act of writing is solitary, the construction of a book is a team effort. Many thanks to the wonderful Nicole Fiorica, with whom I've been lucky enough to create three captivating novels now. Nicole, I'm indebted to you for helping to give this story its final form and reminding me of its value when my confidence flagged. Thanks to Lauren Spieller, the first and fiercest champion of this book, who loved the concept from the very first. I am also grateful to the incredibly talented Marcela Bolívar, whose beautiful art has brought Wil and the haunted interior of Wither Grange to life. I've been incredibly lucky to have the brilliant Debra Sfetsios-Conover create the final design for two book covers now and am always thrilled with her thoughtful work and attention to detail. Thanks to Steve Scott for the interior design—people may judge a book by its cover, but at least for me, the unsung work of artfully laying out a page can make or break the reading experience! Thanks also to managing editor Eugene Lee, copyeditor Nicole Tai, proofreader Jasmine Ye, and production manager Elizabeth Blake-Linn. So many people are involved in the creation of a book besides just the one who gets her name on the cover, and I'm grateful to the entire team that works to take my stories from raw ideas to beautiful, physical volumes readers are able to hold in their hands.

While the act of writing is undertaken alone, no author is an island, and my work is brought into the world with the indispensable help of many literary midwives. Mom, thank you for being my first and only alpha reader. No one else gets to see my words the way you do. Jen, Joanna, Steph, Hannah, and Anna, I would be lost without all of you in my life. You keep me in one piece. Lauren and Maleeha, I'm so fortunate to have your love and support. Can't wait for our next virtual girls' night in! Wendy, this book would still be a squishy, confusing, rambling mess without your plotting assistance and expertise. I hope we see each other for real again soon.

Lastly, thank you to my family. To my dad and my sisters, who've put up with a lifetime of me being eccentric at best. To my houseful of silly, loyal, and endlessly entertaining animal friends. To my person, Tyler, and my wild girls—life with the three of you makes me not just a better writer, but a better human.